A.D. Mill ton. His
first novel set in
modern Russia – was shortlisted for the Man Booker Prize, the
James Tait Black Prize, the *Los Angeles Times* Book Awards. the

...her is
...y the magazine's ...
Editor. He lives in London with his

'Powerful and moving. I loved *The Faithful C...

'Compelling, elegant and deeply insightful. Yo...
forget it' Claire Messud

'*The Faithful Couple* is a gripping work of unsettling power a...
grace' Emily St John Mandel author of *Station Eleven*

'This could be the *One Day* of male friendship ... A book of
deep insight from a writer emerging as one of our leading nov-
elists' Jonathan Freedland

'Couldn't stop reading – intense morality tale' Martha Kearney
(@MarthaKearney)

'Blown away by #TheFaithfulCouple next novel by
@ADMiller18. You won't find a better more taut exploration of
male friendship' Tim Samuels (@TimDSamuels)

'I was mesmerized by its versatility ... I adored the story of Neil
and Adam ... towards the end, it felt as if I knew them both,
and the moral questions raised throughout are so universal ...
[A] beautiful story' Elif Shafak

'Miller is an energetic, muscular writer with a talent for story-telling and a fine ear for dialogue ... unlikely to disappoint' *Independent on Sunday*

'The book *The Faithful Couple* most brings to mind is the best-selling *One Day* by David Nicholls ... but Miller has the edge on Nicholls as a writer, and is skilled at the economical turn of phrase. Friendship, he writes, is "a luxury in any utilitarian calculus" "no money, no sex, no tangible pay-off of any kind". Except for readers of *The Faithful Couple*, who reap dividends' *Sunday Telegraph*

'Lucid and engaging ... *The Faithful Couple* is a thoughtful, frequently witty and insightful book' *Guardian*

'It's easy to imagine A.D. Miller as a literary David Attenborough ... Miller reveals a zoologist's eye for the rituals and dynamics of mateship ... A portrait of a male friendship, free from the whiff of trenchfoot or "Iron John" silliness or new man self-consciousness, is a rare thing' *The Times*

'Two things make Miller's writing dazzle. One is his glorious perspicacity about people and relationships of all sorts: friendships stained with betrayal and competitiveness, work acquaintanceships and love relationships alike. He's witty as well as insightful ... Miller's other great strength is the aptness and originality of his metaphors and similes ... It was a challenge for Miller to impress as much with his second novel as he did with his first, but it is one to which he has risen with assurance' *Spectator*

'Gripping, affecting and memorable' *Financial Times*

The Faithful Couple

A.D. MILLER

ABACUS

First published in Great Britain in 2015 by Little, Brown
This paperback edition published in 2016 by Abacus

1 3 5 7 9 10 8 6 4 2

Lyrics reproduced from 'Roll With It' by Oasis (Sony/ATV Music Publishing LLC),
'Nobody's Perfect' by Brisset/Cornish/Kelly/Mentore (Hal Leonard Corporation),
'1999' by Prince (Universal/MCA Music Ltd) and 'Take It Easy'
by The Eagles (Kobalt Music Group Ltd).

A CIP catalogue record for this book
is available from the British Library.

ISBN 978-0-349-14058-2

Typeset in Caslon by M Rules
Printed and bound in Great Britain by
Clays Ltd, St Ives plc

Papers used by Abacus are from well-managed forests
and other responsible sources.

MIX
Paper from
responsible sources
FSC® C104740

Abacus
An imprint of
Little, Brown Book Group
Carmelite House
50 Victoria Embankment
London EC4Y 0DZ

An Hachette UK Company
www.hachette.co.uk

www.littlebrown.co.uk

Just for Emma

Contents

1993

HE WANTED to concentrate on the girl, but he found himself glancing at the young man in the corner of the yard. She was telling him about her course at USC, and the details, when he caught them, were reasonably interesting, but there was something about the man that was distracting. Perhaps they had met before, Neil thought, though he couldn't place him.

'... and after that I'm hoping for an internship in the Valley. Anyways, what do you do, Neil?'

The baseball cap. It was the baseball cap.

'Soap,' Neil said. 'Soap and shampoo.'

Not just the cap: it was the cap and the shoes together. The guy was wearing suede Timberland boots, notionally designed for walking but not looking as if they had done much. The cap was from San Diego Wild Animal Park and featured several animal silhouettes roaming around the zoo's logo. The boots belonged to a fashionable adult, well-off and image-conscious; the hat suggested a goofy adolescent.

'Uh-huh?'

'I mean, I used to be in soap. I worked for a pharmaceutical company before I came out here. In London. Or, you know, nearby.'

'You're in research?'

The man appeared to nod at him.

'Salesman. I mean, it was a graduate scheme,' Neil lied, realising that he should try to impress her. His heart had gone out of it. 'I'm going to look for something else when I get back to London. Or I might, you know, start my own business.'

'Okay, so you're an entrepreneur?'

The hat, the boots and the eavesdropping. The man was sitting at a table in the shade. As well as the cap he was wearing green swimming shorts and a beige T-shirt. Sand matted the blondish hairs on his legs, darkening and thickening them. He was pretending to read *Time*, but Neil could tell that he was listening and observing from behind his sunglasses.

'Yup. Entrepreneur. Well, you know, that's the idea. That's the plan.'

'What kind of business?'

'You know, I'm not sure yet. I haven't really thought it through, to be honest.'

Neil laughed self-deprecatingly, aiming for a raffish nonchalance, but he could tell she wasn't charmed. He couldn't see the guy's eyes but he was definitely watching them. Ordinarily, in Neil's experience, when two young, unacquainted males appraised each other like this, there was something gladiatorial and menacing in the gaze, and they quickly looked away. On this occasion neither of them did. The man smiled. Neil smiled back.

2

'That's too bad.'

He had seen this girl on the beach the night before, had wanted to try his luck, had tried and failed to engage her around the illicit bonfire some surfers had lit after dark. She wasn't interested, he had concluded, probably she hadn't even noticed him. He was pleased to have manoeuvred her into this almost-private conversation, after the barbecue that the hostel had laid on for lunch. She was from Phoenix, but studying in LA, a Masters in Business Development, Neil thought she said; she had come down to San Diego for the beaches, went to Italy last summer, wanted to see more of Europe. She mentioned something about Scotch-Irish ancestry. She was staying elsewhere but had a friend who was working at the hostel (Cary, or possibly Cory, he hadn't taken in the name). She had an arresting sharp manner and oddly unkempt eyebrows, which contrasted appealingly with her otherwise disciplined appearance. Those ideal teeth.

Now Neil had screwed it up. He and the man in the baseball cap between them.

'Well,' the girl said, sensing his distraction and rising, 'good luck with it all.'

She re-tied her sarong, tilted her sunglasses from the crown of her head to her eyes and walked to the gate that led from the yard to the beach. She moved at a relaxed pace that, Neil figured, was meant to dispel any suggestion of retreat or defeat. The man in the cap watched her go, too. There was no one else in the yard; the two of them followed the girl's departing curves in what felt to Neil like collusive appreciation.

'Know what I think?'

He was English, too.

'Do I want to?'

'It's your socks. Definitely the socks.'

Neil instinctively processed the man's accent for class and geography, as the true-born English must. Received Pronunciation, southern but not London. Posh (those giveaway vowels): not so posh as to be alien, but unmistakably a few rungs above Neil, at the upper, genteel end of the expansive and nuanced middle. They hadn't met before: that wasn't what the connection had been.

'They're my best pair.'

'No socks.' The man removed his sunglasses and put down his magazine. He was handsome in a straightforward, symmetrical way, and slim, with a medium-rare English tan. He was roughly the same age as Neil. 'Uncool. Not even with your trainers. Trust me, really. They make you look like a kid.'

Neil glanced down at his off-white, tennis-style socks, and at the man's boots, into which his slender legs slid naked, then felt gulled and foolish for looking.

'Thanks for the advice,' he said. 'Who should I make the cheque out to?'

'Don't mention it,' the man said. 'This one's on the house.' He laughed, loud and confidently, rocking his head back.

Neither of them found a way to graduate from one-upmanship to conversation. The man picked up his magazine, smiled and followed the girl out through the gate, watched by Neil alone.

THERE was a keg party in the yard that night, with all-you-can-drink beer for the guests and anyone else who wandered in from the beach. Neil came down from his shower just as the biker who supervised the entertainment was hauling in the barrel and pumping apparatus. The sandy breeze blowing in from the ocean civilised the heat. Neil already preferred the evenings in California: he could legitimately cover up the pale, unmuscular body that embarrassed him on the beach in the afternoons. His features suited the half-light: wide-set, almost-black eyes, long, feminine eyelashes, lipstick-pink lips that sometimes appeared theatrical against his luminous skin. He had a large beauty-spot mole on his left cheek, with a matching blemish on his neck. When he swivelled his eyes downwards the mole on his cheek seemed to him to loom blurrily at the edge of his vision.

He stationed himself at the side of the yard and leaned against the wall, his back to the hostel's door. A voice behind him said, 'Buy you a drink?'

Neil didn't turn. 'It's your round, Casanova.'

The man approached the barrel and filled two plastic cups with watery American beer. He had ditched the baseball cap; he had shaggy, dirty-blond hair, in the low-rent Romantic poet style that, Neil knew, was fashionable among a certain breed of public schoolboy. They stood side by side against the wall, swigging in unison. The biker produced a microphone and a pair of thigh-high speakers, which he set up on the landward side of the yard, outside some unfortunate guests' window.

'Adam.'

'Neil.'

'I know.'

They shook hands.

Adam proved to be franker than the types of people Neil was used to, and the casual manner of his openness suggested he would have been the same if they had met at

5

home. This wasn't intimacy, exactly. No dark secrets were disclosed: Adam didn't give the impression that he would have many of those, rather a clear run of frictionless and unblemished accomplishments. He was transparent in the manner of someone who doesn't expect to lose anything by it. He had graduated from university in June – history at Durham, he said – and come out to California before starting work. I wonder who's paying, Neil thought.

Actually he was supposed to travel with his girlfriend, Adam continued. It had been her idea, Chloe's, she had always wanted to visit Los Angeles, see Venice Beach and the Hollywood sign. They both had. They split up just after their finals – it was mutual – but Adam had thought, fuck it, I'll go anyway. No, he didn't have a job waiting for him in England, but he planned to get into television: ever since he saw the footage of the Ethiopian famine, he had wanted to make documentaries and a difference. Before he flew out he sent off a load of applications and begging letters; he was hoping something would have come of them by the time he got home. His mother was keeping an eye out for any encouraging envelopes. He had landed in LA but come straight down to San Diego on the Greyhound, intending to meander back up the coast.

'When did you go to the zoo?'

Adam took a few seconds to work it out, half-lifting a hand towards the phantom cap.

'Yesterday. I saw it on the telly when I was a kid. Always wanted to go there.'

After that it was Neil's turn. He wasn't accustomed to talking about himself, he feared his biography wouldn't captivate, so he kept it short: economics at Sheffield, then the pharmaceutical sales job, which, in reality, had involved driving around the south-east for almost two years with a sinister-looking case of hand cream and tampon samples, 'until I got totally sick of it. They offered me a marketing thing at head office, up in Birmingham, but I turned it down. Last month, that was. Yeah, crazy, I know, but I'd saved up enough to come out here, so. I'll find something else when I get back. Or, you know, I hope I will.'

No, Neil had never been to America before. He had only been abroad a handful of times: 'We went to Spain, once or twice, when Mum was ... with Mum. Costa Brava.' He took a swig of beer. 'And, you know, booze cruises to Calais.'

Adam nodded unconvincingly.

'I'm heading up to LA next week,' Neil continued, 'then San Francisco.'

'Me too,' Adam said. 'Maybe Yosemite after that. Are you on your own?'

'Yeah,' Neil replied. 'On my own. I'm on my own.'

They were quiet. Neil said, 'Another round?'

The yard was filling up. The girl in the sarong was back, now wearing a strappy white mini-dress and chatting to another woman over by the gate. She and Neil seemed to have made an unspoken pact not to acknowledge one another, curiosity flipping into surliness through some binary logic of unconsummated flirtation. When Neil finished pumping the beer he saw that Adam was talking to two other men. He felt irrationally jealous.

'This is Neil,' Adam said.

'Spilled a bit,' Neil said. 'Shit.'

'Ben,' one of the men offered in a southern American accent. Neil was tallish – my six-footer, his mother had called him, albeit before he quite got there – but this man was taller and well-built with it. 'What are you two doing in California?'

'We're hairdressers,' Neil said.

Adam turned towards him, too sharply. Don't, Neil thought. Don't look at me or I'll have to laugh.

'Cool,' the other, shorter American said.

Look at them and we can keep it going.

Neil had played this game before, mostly in clubs, on nights when he and his friends decided it was the most fun they were likely to have with the girls they were pursuing. The aim was to see how far they could push the lie before losing either the girls or their straight faces. The funny thing was, in California, the lies they told felt almost true. Or, if not true, at least possible, as if Neil might plausibly be someone new if he and his new friend willed it.

'Yeah,' said Adam. 'We finished hairdressing college in Cardiff, then we came out to work with a stylist in LA.' He gets it, Neil thought jubilantly; he's perfect at it. 'When it comes to fringes,' Adam went on, 'England is light years behind.'

Neil bit his lip: Don't overdo it. 'We're going to drive across America,' he put in, composing himself. 'You know, cutting hair along the way. Campsites, motel car parks, that kind of thing. We figure five bucks a pop will get us to New York. How about you guys?'

'Graduate school,' the shorter man said. 'We're engineers. On our way down to Ensenada. You two detouring to Mexico?'

'Not this time,' Adam replied. 'We're heading north.'

Afterwards Neil thought the men must have seen through it, with that courteous American acuity that Britons often miss. But the strangers played along, helping to make him and Adam feel bonded and separate, until they left to join the queue for the buffet set out on a table in the corner.

Adam and Neil low-fived and had another beer. 'Bottoms up,' Adam said, raising his cup.

The waves rolling onto the beach were just audible above the chatter in the yard. Before the pause could turn awkward he pressed Neil about the job he had resigned. To Neil's surprise he seemed genuinely interested, and, though nobody else ever had been, he was: for Adam, employment was still a land of myth, populated by fabled creatures – the Secretary, the Boss – that he was yet to encounter in the flesh. Neil explained how the company had delivered crates of free samples to his father's house in Harrow in the middle of the night; how he would shop them round to wholesalers and retailers and the occasional department store. The idea was to distribute the samples and gather orders in exchange. Half the time the orders were cancelled by the pharmacists afterwards, but that didn't matter to the salesmen, Neil explained, because they counted towards your monthly sales figures anyway.

'Got it,' Adam said. 'Of course. Any, you know, action?' he asked, retreating from the world of kickbacks and sharp practices to more familiar territory. 'You know, secretaries or whatever.'

'Not really. I never went to the office much. Unless,' Neil deadpanned, 'you count this old woman with a beard who ran a chemist's up in Bishop's Stortford. She pinned me to my car once, said she wouldn't let me go unless I gave her another crate of free shampoo. Coconut, I think it was.'

'What did you do?'

'I gave her the shampoo and she gave me an order. I think that was the time I won salesman of the month. I got a weekend in a hotel in Brighton.'

'Did you take the old woman?'

'I took my dad. Sort of had to, you know.'

They drank, the repartee checked by the mention of Neil's father, its opaque dutifulness, but only temporarily.

'What's he like as a wing man?'

'Better than you,' Neil said.

After a few seconds they both laughed, Adam aloud, Neil almost silently, his lips drawn across his teeth in the semblance of a grimace.

THEY had another drink in the queue for food – almost nothing was left by the time they reached the table, a few rectangles of overcooked pizza and some token celery that no one else had fancied – and then another as they ate. The beer was cold and light and stronger than it tasted.

The biker had hooked up a karaoke machine to the speakers, and he checked that the microphone was working with the ritual taps and *Testing, testing.* He perched the screen on the edge of the buffet table and, without preamble, began to sing – 'You Shook Me All Night Long', followed by 'Sweet Child of Mine' – in one of those affected growly voices that substitute attitude for intonation. People applauded. Next two German women did a Whitney Houston medley, and a bare-chested Australian man mutilated 'Need You Tonight'. There were a few sarcastic whoops, and someone threw a not-quite-empty cup at him. The cup hit the man on the shin, the beer splashing his leg.

'I will if you will,' Adam said.

Neil looked at Adam and at the humiliated Australian. His stomach knotted, then relaxed. He knew he had to do it.

'Together, right?'

'Of course,' Adam said.

They flicked through the tracks on the karaoke machine.

Although neither of them especially liked the Eagles, they settled on 'Take it Easy' (short, and an easy tune). Somehow the music came on quicker than Neil was expecting: he almost cried out 'Wait!' but managed to contain the panic. He never went in for this kind of exhibitionism, always envying the unselfconsciousness of people who did. He sensed his skin warmly colouring and didn't join in until the second line: *I've got seven women on my mind.* His voice was lower and flatter than Adam's, his eyes locked on the miniature screen even though he knew the words, the lyrics of half the Eagles' songs being etched in his memory, along with those of the other seventies classics he had been obliged to appreciate at school.

But the two of them grew stronger and louder, like people singing 'Happy Birthday' in a restaurant. By the second verse they were clasping the microphone together; by the end of the third their spare arms were around each other in tipsy communion.

No one threw anything. When they finished, the Mexico-bound Americans high-fived them. The girl from that afternoon in the yard came over and said 'Good job' to Neil. He half-expected her to solicit an introduction to Adam, but instead she swayed suggestively, as if she were willing to forgive his earlier obtuseness and dance. He ignored the hint, curtly said 'Thanks', and turned to Adam to discuss what they should sing next.

Somebody had given them both another beer. They were halfway through them when Adam said, 'Let's go for a swim.' He repeated the proposal when Neil didn't respond, louder, shouting into his ear to be heard above 'Mr Tambourine Man'.

They went out through the gate, across the running and

rollerblading path and onto the beach. Some kids were shouting somewhere along the shore, playing soccer in the dark. In the other direction, couples were giggling invisibly on the sand. Neil and Adam had the stretch of beach behind the hostel more or less to themselves. They pressed their beers into the sand, one by each of the volleyball poles, and stripped to their underwear. Adam saw that Neil had taken his advice and foresworn socks that evening, and Neil saw him notice, but neither of them commented. Adam undressed first and won the race to the surf.

The moon had clouded over and they didn't gauge the height of the waves until they were waist deep. The water was warm. As they were jumping backwards into the crests, a few metres apart, a piece of seaweed wrapped itself around Adam's shoulders; he caught it, raised it above his head like a banner, and let himself fall backwards into the ocean. He had a beginner's hairy chest, a wiry knot between his pectoral muscles that heralded the full Chewbacca his genes were promising. Neil's chest was narrower and baby-bald.

They splashed around and shouted into the Pacific until Neil dragged Adam out in a mock rescue. Adam resisted, but submitted before the wrestling became too fierce, allowing himself to be dumped where the wet and dry sand met. The two of them scrambled up the beach and sat against the volleyball poles, finishing their beers and watching the breathing, black-and-white ocean as they dried. The karaoke was over.

'Listen,' Adam said, 'don't take this the wrong way, but I suppose we could, you know, go together.'

'What do you ... Go where?'

'Up the coast. On the Greyhound, maybe. Or we could, you know, get one of those cars you deliver for someone else.

12

Driveaways, I think they're called, I read about them in the *Lonely Planet*. We could take it up to San Francisco. What do you reckon?'

Neil was sober enough to catch and question his own response. He couldn't account for the sense that he was being flattered, wonderfully flattered, and he resented Adam for this rush of gratitude. Adam wasn't older than Neil, or more experienced (so far as he could tell), or cleverer or funnier; he outscored him mainly in the unearned virtues of luck and class and those Athena-poster looks. At the same time he had his openness, and his poise, and there was a fit or alignment between them, something unfinished and possible, that it would be a shame to waste.

'Okay,' Neil said. 'Why not?'

All this – California, the sea, the adult, sovereign choices – was the kind of escapade that, as suburban teenagers, Neil and his brother had once fantasised about. He held out his cup for Adam to clink with his own, and he did, though the cups were plastic and noiseless and already empty.

A PAIR of surfboards were draining in the shower when Adam went for a piss at dawn. A woman was in bed with the Norwegian in the bunk opposite his, both of them asleep and naked. Adam climbed up again to his mattress, lay on his back and mapped the stains and cracks on the ceiling. The sand in his bed was as dark as dirt, the sheets damp with seawater; he could hear the waves. His wasn't a serious hangover, just dry mouth and sour breath, plus a dull ache, a sort of manifest unease, at the back of his head. Sleep was gone.

Adam wasn't regretful or embarrassed that he had sung and swum and persuaded this stranger to join in. Unlike

Neil he was a practised exhibitionist, especially when he had been drinking: jokily synchronised dancing in clubs and at the odd countryside rave, acceptably risqué sixth-form revues, charades around the pool of the chateau that his father sometimes borrowed for a fortnight from some shipping millionaire. He was likewise used to getting people to do what he wanted them to – a dividend of being an eldest child, who had honed his will on indulgent parents before redirecting it at his idolatrous younger sister, and afterwards at what so far seemed a gratifyingly pliant universe.

His queasiness was neither shame nor simply alcohol. He remembered how he had propositioned Neil, and in the morning's clarity could see that he had rushed into this, on the basis of half a day's acquaintance, some one-liners and an out-of-tune duet. Adam saw the impetuousness, but that wasn't what unsettled him. His fear was that Neil might have changed his mind: that he might have forgotten his pledge to drive up the coast together, or might pretend that he had forgotten.

Adam wouldn't think the worse of him for that. The previous night had been a kind of hallucination, probably impossible to reconstitute and best consigned to pleasant memory. But he hoped otherwise. Neil was uncool, but he didn't seem to mind, which was itself a kind of coolness; his indifference had a negative power of its own. There was something intriguing in the way he faced the world, wary and not entitled, with low expectations set to be exceeded, rather than, as with most of Adam's aequaintances, inflated hopes that were destined to be thwarted. He was similar as well as different (they got each other's jokes), open yet unknown: for all their mutual frankness there was a part of himself that Neil seemed to be protecting, as he shielded his moon-white skin from the sun. He had done things that Adam hadn't. Neil was the kind of coiled person who, when you met him, you had a hunch that something interesting could happen to, and you wanted to know him long enough to find out what it might be. A person you could measure yourself by.

Adam got out of bed. The interloping woman was lying on her front, her face in the Norwegian's armpit, her arse a bikini triangle of white encircled by chocolate tan: a road sign made flesh. He brushed his teeth, thought about shaving but decided not to, put on his shorts and shades and went out to buy a coffee at Burger King.

Neil was eating his breakfast in the hostel yard when Adam returned. He was sitting in a strange position, on a bench facing the wall, so that anyone who might want to speak to him would have to make a decision and an effort to disturb him.

'Morning, Neil.'

He turned around and smiled. 'Morning.'

Adam sat down next to him, astride the bench. They discussed their hangovers, as was customary, the sandiness of their sheets and the naked woman in Adam's dormitory. They talked about the volleyball game that the blackboard announced for later that morning. They heard themselves talk about the weather. Adam saw that he would have to be the one who raised and risked it.

'So are we still on? I mean, the car. You know, San Francisco. Los Angeles. Do you remember?'

'Yeah, I remember,' Neil said. 'We're on.'

THEY picked up a freesheet that listed the driveaways available in San Diego and assessed the offers in the yard that evening. They circled three that seemed promising: one

15

vehicle to be delivered to Portland, one to Seattle, one to somewhere in Montana. They called the relevant agencies; Adam did the talking, specifying their ages, nationality, the particulars of their driving licences. Neil tried to decipher the notes his friend was scribbling in the margins, his insides inexplicably fluttering. They decided that Portland would be far enough, especially since the owner would allow them several more days than the trip strictly required. On the following morning they were to go out to the suburbs, towards the Mexican border, to collect the car.

They packed, settled their hostel bills and rode the trolleybus in the direction of the address Adam had been given. It was a warm blue day. They walked the last few, rundown blocks, sweating and joking that they might never find their destination, might search endlessly for a house that didn't exist. But, eventually, it did: a decaying clapboard bungalow with a bleached porch and a high-volume argument in progress inside. At first they weren't sure whether to intrude, or to give up and leave, go back to the beach, forget the whole plan. Neil pushed the buzzer, curtly, once; a young woman with tattooed biceps opened the door and called for her father, who came out, tanned, tall and overweight in serviceman-gone-to-seed style. He made them sign two copies of the paperwork, grumblingly inspected their foreign driving licences and led them to a brown pick-up truck with a covered bed. He handed over the keys and an address in Oregon and watched from the pavement, hands on hips, until they rounded a corner and headed north.

The pick-up was a bigger vehicle than either of them was used to. It had an extra set of headlights above the windscreen, like something out of *The Dukes of Hazzard*, a scratched leather interior and a mysterious tarpaulin in the back, tied and chained up, under which squatted a heavy, ominous lump. ('Gun-running,' Adam speculated. 'Body parts,' Neil countered.) Parking was hairy, and on the north-bound highway they were flanked by an endless sequence of outsized lorries, streaming up to Los Angeles at impossible speeds. But at other times and on smaller roads they were almost on their own. And they were in California and free.

To save money Neil preferred to sleep in a hostel in Los Angeles, or in the back of the truck; Adam agitated for a motel. In the end they compromised on a shared room in the cheapest motel in Hollywood – Neil waiting at a phone booth, pretending to make a call, while Adam checked in alone to avoid the double occupancy charge. Neil knocked twice on the bedroom door, their needless, prearranged signal. Adam pulled him inside and stuck his head into the forecourt, scanning left and right in mock anxiety at being rumbled.

'Don't flatter yourself,' he said, as Neil eyed the lone double bed, keeping hold of his rucksack as if he might reconsider. 'You're not my type.'

They undressed and got into bed, at first keeping to the edges. They talked about *L.A. Law* and *Moonlighting*. They argued about how to make the bedside fan work, but neither of them managed it. They skirted politics, Adam evincing the soft-left bias prevalent in their generation, bolstered, in his case, by an undergraduate interest in the history of protest (suffragism, Gandhi, Martin Luther King), Neil grunting along diplomatically. They heard the murmur of televisions in neighbouring rooms, a flush from a stranger's bathroom. They talked about Chloe.

'I've never had a, you know, a relationship,' Neil said. 'Not like that. Couple of months, max. I just didn't ... To be honest, I don't think I know how to.'

'It's pretty easy,' Adam said. 'You get on top—'

'No, you dickhead, I mean the ... you know, the commitment' – this last, advice-column phrase spoken by Neil in a defensively ironic falsetto.

Whereupon they made a deliciously juvenile exchange of their sexual histories, including where and with whom they had lost their virginities: Neil when he was sixteen, with a girl he never saw again, underneath the dining table at somebody's party, Adam in a copse with a sixth-form girlfriend from the sister school near his own.

'Pitch black,' Adam said. 'We could hardly see each other.'

'Figures,' Neil said. Adam hit him with a pillow.

After that came their general histories. Neil was two years further into adulthood, but, at twenty-three, only a year older, having gone straight from school to university, whereas Adam had spent a year desultorily teaching in India before he went to Durham. Each summarised his family, which, though they wished it otherwise, was still most of who they were. Adam's father had done well in shipping insurance and moved them to the country, dispatching the children, he and his sister Harriet, to boarding schools in Sussex. His mother, Adam said, busied herself with local causes and campaigns (unwanted bypasses, charity fêtes, imperilled hospitals). Neil explained that his father, Brian, ran an office supplies and stationery shop in Wembley, but it was clear, Neil said, that he wasn't naturally suited to retail. He spent too long in consoling chats with polite ladies who ultimately bought nothing, neglecting less civil but more lucrative customers. Neil's brother, Dan, was two years older than him. Dan was living in Southampton, there was work down there, apparently; he had a baby on the way, though Neil and Brian hadn't met the girlfriend.

'Mum,' Neil concluded. 'She ... Nine years ago, nine and a half ... She's dead.'

'Sorry to hear that,' Adam said, straight away realising his response was inadequate and ridiculous. It was so long ago, he didn't know her or the circumstances, he barely knew Neil.

'It's okay,' Neil said. 'Don't worry.'

The percussion of the drink and ice machines kept Neil up half the night, along with the voices and footsteps in the forecourt, the revving and subsiding of engines, the sirens out there in America. When he awoke in the morning he was alone, and, for a minute, had no idea where he was, until Adam came in with two complimentary coffees in Styrofoam cups. Adam had a camera with a time-delay function, and he insisted that they put it on the bedside table and take a picture of themselves sitting on the coverlet, the forecourt and the pick-up visible through the window behind them. They were gesticulating, their arms spread and palms open in a what-am-I-doing-here pose: here in this hired room, with this strange man, in a foreign country. In truth, they both knew. At the same time they knew – Neil with a sharp pre-emptive melancholy, Adam more serenely – that this moment was irreducible, could be felt only as it was experienced, and would not afterwards be understood through photographs, shaggy anecdotes or snapshot memories, including by their own later selves.

Adam was determined to do the sights – the Chinese Theatre, Sunset Boulevard, Rodeo Drive, all the kitsch Americana that colonised the imaginations of star-struck British kids in the seventies and eighties – which gave Neil permission to put aside his pretended indifference and go too. It was all precisely like itself, just as they expected it to be, the palm trees and convertibles, as if they were extras in a film about America that everyone all over the world had seen. Adam wanted to drive through South Central and Watts, where the riots had happened; Neil was reluctant, nervous of the invisible urban boundaries between safety and danger, but they did, and it was all fine. They calculated that they could fit in Las Vegas if they only stayed a night; driving in from the desert they saw the sails of windsurfers in the dunes, the surfers themselves out of sight, before the steamboats, pyramids, palaces and volcanoes reared up psychedelically from the dust. They blew a hundred dollars playing blackjack at the Mirage: they agreed never to mention the loss to each other again. They won the money back on a single red-black bet at a roulette wheel, followed by another hundred in profit – enough to cover a double room in one of the dowdier casinos on the old Vegas strip, with a few dollars left for a steak dinner and some drinks.

'We're masseurs,' Adam told the robotic, peroxide croupier. 'On our way to North Dakota. They're having a massage festival next week.'

'Uh-huh,' she said, sweeping the chips from her baize. 'You boys stay out of trouble up there.'

Walking along the Strip, they talked about the future. In Neil's mind, he said, the future was always an escape, somewhere pristine, inhabited by a revamped him.

'It's not like that for me,' Adam said. 'It's more like, keeping what we've got, I mean Mum and Dad, but doing something else on top, something big. You know, people talking about you, your face in the paper. It's like when you were young and you sort of commentated on your exploits in your head, you know, climbing a tree or whatever, scoring a try. The spotlight.'

'I don't remember doing that,' Neil said. 'In our house it was always Dan who was going to do it, the big thing, whatever it was. He was going to work on a ranch in Argentina, or once, after he dropped out of college, he had this plan to go to Australia, something about being a policeman in the Outback. When I picture it – the future – I'm trailing along, you know, watching.'

'Watching who? Your brother?'

'I'm not sure any more,' Neil said. 'You, maybe.'

Adam laughed.

NEIL had never considered himself underprivileged. Compared with most of his peers at school, his family had been comfortable, and resenting everyone who had retained both parents would have been too exhausting. Adam's better fortune grated mostly when he strained to be sensitive about it: his tact constituted an extra layer of superiority that was one too many for Neil.

As it proved when, in a bar at the Riviera, they talked about his father's shop. Neil had worked there as a teenager, and was resigned to helping out again when he flew home, just for a few weeks, while he looked for something better and while, as would be unavoidable, he was still living with his dad. Adam planned to move in with two friends from university, Chaz and Archie, somewhere in west London, they hoped.

'It should be useful, shouldn't it?' Adam offered, out of his depth but meaning to be considerate. 'You know, dealing with the customers and all that. I mean, for whatever you do afterwards. Your business career.'

'Not really,' Neil said, thinking of the zoned-out, insincere retail patience that he would have to recultivate, and of his teenage runs to the bank with the takings, convinced every villain in Wembley knew by his gait that he was couriering an inch of tenners. 'It's a dead end, that shop. He should have closed it years ago.'

'I'm sure it can't be all that hopeless,' Adam said. 'In any case it's a kind of anthropology, isn't it, that sort of work?'

The waiter brought their drinks. A few seconds later, Neil felt provoked. Behind Adam's questions and in his tone he sensed another enquiry: what do you *really* want to do? The tyranny of vocation among well-bred graduates. It was a form of arrogance, Neil thought, this notion that everyone ought to be a nun or a sculptor, have some urgent calling, as if they all mattered so much that there must be something in it for them beyond money. The idealism that someone else was always paying for.

Teaching in India. Anthropology!

'You know what, yes, it is useful, in a way. Because, whatever you do, everyone's selling something to someone in the end. Even you.'

'Am I?'

'Yeah, Adam, you are. You will be.'

'I'm not so sure,' Adam said, laughing, his awkwardness emerging as condescension. To him the actual making of money was something someone else took care of, out of sight, like butchery or coal-mining.

Beyond the bar the slot machines kept up their perky jingles and machine-gun payouts; the ignored piano player went on playing. An illusionless discomfort, rather than plain silence, descended on them. Neil fingered the mole on his neck, a nervous tic that Adam began to notice that evening.

'Let's do a bunk,' Adam said.

'What do you—'

'You know, leg it.' He mouthed 'without paying', returning to normal volume for, 'Haven't you ever done that before?'

'Sure,' Neil said. In Sheffield, when they were skint students, he and two friends had run away from an all-you-can-eat pizza restaurant. Once, when they were teenagers, he and Dan had bolted from a snooker club in Cricklewood without paying for their Cokes. Even by his parsimonious standards, the Californian road trip had been cheap: free refills, supersized fries, the bounteous quantity of America. Their shared rooms. He could afford the beer. But he saw how Adam's ruse would reposition the two of them against the world, like their lying game, only more so, as if they were daredevil children.

'You get up to go to the loo,' Adam instructed, 'but instead of coming back you wait for me by the slot machines. Got it?'

'Roger that.'

'Synchronise watches.'

They drained their beers and clinked their empty glasses.

It didn't go smoothly. The toilets were in the wrong direction and to reach the entrance to the bar Neil had to double back past the low table at which Adam was sitting, which might have looked suspicious had anyone been watching. Adam stood up after a couple of minutes, pretending to yawn and stretch, then followed, eyes fixed on the floor. He picked up pace as he marched past Neil and was running before he reached the main doors, with Neil in pursuit. They ran for much longer than they needed to, racing each other as much as fleeing anyone who in theory might have been chasing them. The race was the point. To begin with Adam was faster, as he had been on the beach, and Neil experienced a fleeting, weird panic that he might have lost him, lost him for ever, an anxiety that was more acute than his receding fear of being caught. But Neil had better stamina, more grit, and overtook outside a Venetian palazzo. They came to a halt when Adam got a stitch, sat on a wall and panted, taking in the meaningless neon spectacle, the warm Vegas atmosphere that was both childish and corrupt.

They left the city early the next morning. Obeying their preconceptions, the road in Death Valley dissolved limpidly in front of them. Adam took a photo of the two of them sitting on the sizzling bonnet of the pick-up. As they drove through Fresno, resolving to do better, he asked about Neil's mother.

'You were – how old were you?' He kept his eyes on the road.

'Fourteen,' Neil said. 'Just fourteen. They only told us at the end, or almost, me and Dan, that was just before my birthday.'

'I'm sorry,' Adam said. 'That must have been ... I can't really imagine how that must have been.'

'We were in the lounge,' Neil said. 'She told us and then she went straight into the kitchen to chop something. Chop chop chop, you know. Like she was beheading someone. Dad went up into the loft. Me and Dan went up to the park, and he threw me down this slope – I remember, it was a wet day, I got covered in mud, but I didn't mind, because it was Dan, you know, and in those days anything to do with Dan ...'

Adam said, 'I don't know what ... I'm really sorry.'

'It's funny,' Neil said. 'I've never, before today, I've hardly ever ... I don't talk about it much, to be honest.'

At an outlet mall on the way into San Francisco Neil

24

bought suede boots that were similar to Adam's, somehow manly and fey at the same time. In the evening he experimented with wearing a sweater slung over his shoulders, as Adam sometimes wore his. At Adam's urging they drove over and back across the Golden Gate Bridge three times. When they arrived at the hostel they had booked in San Francisco, they looked almost like brothers.

ROSE introduced herself as they were milling around the parking lot, waiting for the minibus that would take them out to Yosemite. Adam had nudged Neil with his elbow when she arrived with her father. She was wearing tight velour shorts; her dark hair was in a ponytail; she had long, elastic legs and high breasts, and, for them, was unquestionably the group's main attraction. Otherwise it was an eclectic yet disappointing bunch: a meek, greying couple from Yorkshire, a haughtily athletic American who always wore singlets, three sober Germans, two sixty-something hippies from New Mexico and a middle-aged gay couple from Reno, both 'in landscape gardening'. Plus their guide, a bearded treehugger named Trey, who strove to project an air of primitive wisdom and harangued them all about litter. Trey would do the cooking and put up the tents they were to sleep in for three nights. Adam and Neil would arrive a day or two late in Portland because of the tour, but they figured the driveaway client was unlikely to sue. They parked the pick-up in the tour operator's lot.

She mooched over to speak to them, distractingly bending one leg behind her as the three of them talked, leaning on their car for balance, heel pulled into her buttock as if she were limbering up for a run. Rose; from Colorado; she had come up to San Francisco with her father. She asked where

else they had been in America and how long they were staying, looking them in the eyes and grinning. Her T-shirt said
'Colorado State'. She was pleased they were there, she said,
rolling her eyes in the direction of the others in a hammily
exasperated gesture.

Her father came over and offered his hand. He was a large
man – not tall, and not fat, exactly, but with a rectangular,
troglodytic torso and powerful, tree-trunk legs. Forty to forty-
five, Adam guessed, youngish for a man with a grown
daughter, and with the ingratiating manner and untucked,
sophomoric dress sense of a person who was keen to seem so.
He had a crushing handshake but a surprisingly high voice,
and a hair-trigger giggle that he tried endearingly if vainly to
suppress. His name was Eric and he was a real-estate salesman. He and Rose had left his wife and son in Boulder to
take this California trip together. The two of them, father
and daughter, seemed gracefully at ease with each other,
mutually respectful and natural in front of outsiders.

Trey rattled them out to the park in the minibus, then
gave them an introductory ride around Yosemite Valley (the
ground was dry as dust in the summer heat, the plants and
trees magically lush); in the early evening the group
meandered through a grove of sequoia trees. Neil gazed
upwards, knowing that the trees were supposed to make him
feel something, some ecstasy or epiphany that the others
seemed to be experiencing, and sensing approximately what
the feeling was – awed, inconsequential, humbly serene –
but not quite managing it. When he lowered his eyes he
found Rose standing next to him, holding up a hand to shield
her eyes from the setting sun. Down the sleeve of her bent
arm Neil made out the stubble in her armpit. She said,
'Wow', smiled and walked away, towards her father.

Adam's favourites trees were two monster sequoias, the deep-grooved trunks of which were fused together at the bottom: only by craning your neck could you see that, a long way up, they divided. They had been competing for space and sunlight for ever, Trey said, yet depended on each other's succour to survive. They only existed together, in their rivalrous embrace. The plaque at their joint base said *Faithful Couple*.

'Shall we have one of us lads?' Adam asked Neil, holding up his camera.

They roped in the greying Yorkshireman to take the photo, arranging themselves beside the Faithful Couple sign. For the picture they pretended to bicker like old spouses, Neil making a fist and Adam turning up a palm as if he were remonstrating. But their other arms were around each other's shoulders. They and the Faithful Couple were chequered in shadow from the other trees.

Adam retrieved the camera and thanked the Yorkshireman. 'It probably won't come out,' the Yorkshireman said. 'Rotten light.' But it did.

THEY were in the high meadows when Rose snatched Adam's hat. The campsite was just outside the entrance to the park; in the morning they left their tents standing and Trey drove them up a steep trail, putting them out to walk the final stretch when the path became impassable for the minibus. Adam and Neil amused the others with bravado about tracking and wrestling bears, irking the hippies and the gay couple when they kept up their wisecracks for too long. The meadows at the top were surrounded by grey-white granite hills, the horizon finished by a postcard blue sky and a few stranded clouds.

There was a meltwater lake, ringed by pine trees, which looked inviting after their uphill hike. At first only Neil and Adam braved the water, stripping down to their underwear and sprinting in, yelling, swimming in circles for warmth and ribbing each other about their retreating genitals. Once they had acclimatised to the temperature they began to harry and dunk each other, out in the middle of the lake.

Something made a splash, and a body made its way towards them in a determined front crawl, the face alternately buried in water and obscured by spray as it breathed, so that they couldn't make out who was approaching, except, from the shape and the swimming costume, that it was a woman. For the last few metres before she reached them the swimmer submerged entirely, popping up to splash Adam from close range.

It was Rose. She was wearing a discreet but flattering purple one-piece that she must have carried in her day bag. She coughed out some water and grinned.

Adam splashed her back; Rose splashed Neil; he and Adam went for her together, pincer-style and mercilessly. 'You guys,' she protested, her eyes screwed closed as they converged to point-blank distance. She screamed cartoonishly as Adam dunked her – in the circumstances, reaching out to pressure the top of her head felt uncontroversial. He was alarmed when she didn't resurface after he lifted his hand, but she came up a few seconds later and a couple of metres away, rubbing her eyes, spluttering, and sweeping back her long hair with an attention-seeking jerk of the neck and slick of her palm.

'You guys,' she said again, laughing. 'You're such bullies.' She pushed away a final, mock-petulant splash and back-stroked to the shallows. On the shore Eric extended a towel to wrap her in.

Adam had a two-tone trucker's tan, his face and forearms browning but the rest of him less bronzed. Neil was white all over and beginning to worry about the sun. They swam back to their clothes and their matching, lined-up boots. With his back turned Adam didn't see Rose darting across the rock to grab the baseball cap he had replaced after their swim, racing away with the trophy in her wet bathing suit and bare feet. She squealed and dropped the cap when Adam almost had her, then jogged back to her father.

'She's up for it,' Adam said to Neil, panting.

'That hat is ridiculous.'

'She is, I'm telling you.'

'Ad,' Neil said. 'We ... do we need her?'

'What are you talking about? We're in. One of us is, anyway.'

They examined her, not very covertly, as she dried her back with the towel. Her nipples were conspicuous inside her swimsuit; a sprig of pubic hair had escaped from the crotch. She was womanly from the thigh up, and she walked like an adult, confident and unexaggerated. But there was something vulnerable and admonishing about the pigeonish angle of her standing feet, and the way her knees knocked together with the rhythm of her towelling. Adam's gaze met Eric's; the older man raised his chin and gave a corners-of-the-mouth smile.

'Bit young, maybe,' Neil said. 'Don't you think?'

'If there's grass on the pitch ... ' Adam joked, a second-hand vulgarity that he had heard but never himself uttered before.

'In any case,' Neil said, 'what about her old man?'

'Aw, he's a sweetie,' Adam said. 'Look at them – not now, you idiot, he's watching us – they're a right-on family. Stop making excuses.'

29

'Okay, Ads, okay,' Neil said, capitulating as he had over the singing and the dip in the Pacific. 'Let's play.'

Eric held up the towel to shield Rose, averting his eyes as she slipped back into her clothes.

HE LET her have a beer that evening. At least, Rose appeared to be drinking a beer – Neil saw her gulp from the bottle and wipe her mouth with the back of her hand – though it was possible, he later realised, that she had taken one swig and passed it back to Eric. Father and daughter were sitting next to each other by the campfire that Trey had built after he served dinner. It was a warm dry night and they didn't need the heat, but a fire was expected, and they used the flames to toast marshmallows. They could see each other sporadically in the flickering light.

Next to Rose sat one of the Germans, a woman in her late thirties with short blond hair and ropy English. Next to her were the couple from Yorkshire, and beside them were Adam and Neil. Those two were drinking – they and some of the others had bought beer in San Francisco – but they weren't drunk that night, not really. The other Germans and the gay couple were on the far side of the fire; the elderly hippies and the solitary athlete had already retired. No one had done anything difficult or brave, no perilous climbs or punishing hikes, but there was nevertheless an air of outdoor cama-raderie, a communal will to make this be or seem the frontier trip of their imaginings.

They talked about what they had seen in the meadows that day and what they were hoping to see on the next, flora and fauna and soaring rock, peering meditatively into the flames when there seemed to be nothing left to say. Rose pulled her baggy sweater down over her legs and hugged them to her body. Eric and the Yorkshireman began to discuss computers. Eric put his faith in them; the Yorkshireman used an old-fashioned word processor.

'You wait,' Eric said. 'In ten years, I'm telling you, there'll be a computer in every village in Africa. One hundred per cent easier – everything. School, business – you wait. And be sure and remember me when it happens!'

'They can't eat computers,' a German man said from the other side of the fire.

'Guess not,' said Eric, laughing and taking no offence.

He stirred the cinders. Neil used Adam's penknife to open two more beers.

'Hey,' Eric said, rallying. 'You guys ski?' He was looking at them.

'Of course,' said Adam.

''Fraid not,' said Neil.

'Too uncoordinated,' Adam said. 'He'd be laughed off the slopes.'

'You two should come see us in Boulder,' Eric went on. 'We'll teach you. Shouldn't they, Rose?'

'I guess so,' Rose said, sweeping away a hair with a hand mittened in sleeve.

'Any time. Love to have you. Wouldn't we, sweetie? November to April, best skiing in America. Twenty minutes and you're on the slopes. And, no kidding, a hot tub in the yard!' He giggled.

'Be careful what you wish for,' Adam said.

'I mean it,' Eric said. 'It's great to meet you guys. From England. I don't think Rose has met someone from England before, have you, honey?'

'Sure I have,' Rose said, poking the ground with a marshmallow stick.

'How did you two meet?'

'Playing rugby,' said Neil.

'Yes,' said Adam. 'We were playing against each other. I was playing for Cambridge and Neil was playing for Birmingham. We had a drink in the bar afterwards. That was three or four years ago.'

'Who won?' Rose asked.

'We did,' Adam said.

The English couple whispered to each other. The Germans and the gay couple retreated to their tents. Trey went to wash up the dinner plates in a plastic tub. Eric stood, clutched his back, and wandered into the trees to pee.

'So, Rose,' Adam said. 'What's your story?'

The woman from Yorkshire turned sharply towards him, as if she were about to say something, but instead she looked away. Neil laughed at his friend's insouciance, tried to disguise the laugh as a cough and only just kept in his beer. Rose blushed. She blushed in two stages, each discernible by the orange light of the campfire. Her face coloured, and a few seconds later darkened again, the blotch spreading down her neck as her self-consciousness kicked in, the embarrassment self-perpetuating, like a quarrel that lives on its own momentum after the original insult has been forgotten.

There was something new and grating about Adam that night, Neil thought. He had interrupted him twice; he needn't have made that crack about Neil being too clumsy for skiing; he had hijacked their lying game, which they were supposed to play against outsiders, not versus each other. Or, there was something different about the two of them together. Up till then their rivalry had been playful and polite, like a tennis knock-up with no score, kept in check by joint enterprises, curiosity and affection. This evening it was overt and raw. Rose was the contest more than she was the prize. Somewhere else, on another night, the discipline would have been arm-wrestling or Trivial Pursuit.

'Well,' Rose said, recovering herself, 'it's pretty short.'

Neil stood, padded past Adam and the English couple and sat next to Rose in the spot that had been Eric's. He leaned back on his elbows, and straight away began talking to her in a voice too quiet for anyone else to hear, and almost too quiet for Rose, so that, to follow him, she had to lean back too, extending her legs in front of her and crossing them at the ankles.

Eric returned from the trees, humming. He glanced at Neil and Rose and sat next to Adam, the weight of his torso rocking him back on his haunches before he righted himself.

'When you heading home?' he asked.

'We've got these flexible tickets,' Adam said, peering around the circle, beyond the English couple, to where Neil was reclining with Rose. He was impressed, even faintly pleased, with his friend's ruthlessness, as well as aggrieved. 'A week or two, probably. You?'

'Right after Yosemite,' Eric said. 'Rose has to get ready for school.'

School, Adam thought. They called everything school, didn't they? That Colorado State T-shirt. 'Yes,' he said absently, 'I suppose so.'

'Sophomore year already,' Eric continued, shaking his head in the standard parental amazement. 'My girl. You believe it?'

'What's her major?' Adam asked, speaking American.

'Major?' Eric said, giggling. 'High school sophomore's

what I mean.' He stopped laughing and turned towards his daughter.

'Of course,' Adam reassured him. 'My mistake.'

The Yorkshire couple cut in to quiz him about Cambridge – they had a nephew who had studied there, maybe Adam knew him, etcetera – and he was obliged to keep up the pretence, even though it was no fun on his own and he sensed that his act wasn't convincing. He was telling them how he had read philosophy and been on *University Challenge*, how he had given up rugby after breaking his leg on tour in South Africa, all the while monitoring Neil and Rose. Neil was making her laugh, he could see that; she was making patterns in the dust with her outstretched feet. Tough luck, pal, Adam thought. Technical disqualification.

Eric stood up and announced that he was turning in. 'Don't stay up late, honey,' he called to his daughter. 'Half an hour, deal?' He ruffled her hair as he passed her.

'Night, Daddy,' Rose said, smoothing it back. He waddled to their tent, looking back once over his shoulder.

Adam was about to interrupt them, but the Yorkshireman insisted on telling him about his haulage business, and then Neil was wiping a bug from Rose's shoulder, or pretending to, the deviously tactile bastard. Now the woman was on to the Prime Minister, how he seemed a decent enough bloke but the rest of them were chancers, and Neil was laughing along with her, and, Adam asked himself, how serious was it likely to be, anyway?

Eventually the woman said good night and went to their tent, but the man hung on. Beyond his chatter (the virtues of corporal punishment), Adam caught Rose asking whether Neil had a girlfriend and Neil saying he wasn't sure, he would know later that evening, a corny line that made her grin. Neil had beaten him, his clever little tricks had beaten him, and after all, Adam thought, this was what he wanted. He had done this to himself.

Adam finished his beer. The fire had nearly burned out, but when he stood and brushed the dust from his shorts he thought he could see that, though she wasn't drinking anything, Rose was swallowing nervously, as daunted girls did when they had made their decision. Neil's hand was on her knee.

The Yorkshireman was dozing off, his chin making futile anti-gravitational jerks from his chest. Adam saw the smile on his friend's face. High-school sophomore ... This wasn't his business. When he opened his mouth, all that emerged was 'Good night'. Rose reciprocated in a voice that tried to sound composed but came out too high. Neil lifted his hand from her leg and waved. Adam walked slowly to their tent.

FOR Adam that night would always be associated with itching, a fierce sensation he could almost feel if he inadvertently thought back to Yosemite. He was in the tent, in the no man's land between waking and sleep, when he felt Neil's hand on his shoulder.

'Adam,' Neil whispered. Then, louder, shaking him harder: 'Mate, I need the tent.'

'What?'

'I need the tent.'

Adam tried to focus on the ghostly features before panning towards the tent flaps. Through the opening he distinguished the girl's legs, standing in the moonlight, one of them rotating on a pointed sneaker.

He hesitated. The tent smelled of beer.

'Neil,' he began, 'have you ... '

'Don't worry,' Neil told him. 'Boy scout.' He tightened his grip on his friend's shoulder. 'Adam, come on.'

Adam kneeled, bunched up his sleeping bag and crawled outside in his boxer shorts and T-shirt. Rose's face as he passed her was open and eager, as if she had won her own dare. He saw her bend and enter the tent, and Neil following her in.

He should have taken himself further off, beneath the trees at the edge of the campsite or beside the expiring fire. Instead he dropped his sleeping bag a few metres from the tent, blearily considering that to be his assigned place in the world.

He was nearly close enough to touch them and thought he heard almost everything. They were whispering, and now and again he lost them, but even then he caught the rhythm and the gist. They bumped into and tripped over each other as they settled themselves inside. There was some stranger-ish apologising, followed by silence, from which Adam inferred that Neil had used the entanglement to kiss her.

Outside the night was cooler than the tent had been, but it was warm enough for Adam to spread out his sleeping bag and recline on top rather than zipping himself in. When he lay down, uncovered, he hadn't reckoned on the midges, or what-ever the insects were, some unsquashably tiny and incessant creatures that tormented his forearms and legs. When he moved to scratch or wave them away, the lining of his sleep-ing bag crackled, interfering with his eavesdropping and potentially alerting Neil and Rose. He lay as still and stoically as he could for as long as it lasted.

The tent was small (standard issue from the tour operator), and two or three times an elbow or other extremity stretched the fabric in a slapstick bulge. She was giggling, and Neil was shushing her, then he was giggling too. There was quiet, punctuated by rustling as clothes were shed. Neil whispered something that Adam couldn't decipher and Rose replied inaudibly. A minute later he heard her say, 'Sure'.

The itching was overwhelming but he didn't move. He could hear Neil going through his bag, taking things out, putting them back. Neil swore. That's it, Adam thought. But there was more whispering, and some panting, and it was on again.

'That much?' he heard Neil asking her. 'How much?'

'Sorry,' Rose said.

'Okay?'

'Okay.'

Adam knew when it was over. He swatted helplessly at the midges and zipped up his sleeping bag. He felt a fuzzy, insomniac dread, like a person who suspects he has left the oven on (*High school sophomore's what I mean*). Even so, his alarm was subordinate to another feeling: a new, disconcerting jealousy. He hadn't expected to be beaten, he wasn't accustomed to losing, but it wasn't mainly that.

Adam was jealous of Rose. She had come between them. She had taken away his friend. The two of them were still in the tent together, whispering, when – just as he was sure he would never manage to – Adam fell into a brief, uncomfortable sleep.

ERIC'S first instinct, his instant threat, was to call the police. They had been careless and unlucky. Rose stayed longer than she should have; she, then Neil, fell asleep. Her father woke as it started to get light, saw that she wasn't with him and shuffled out to look for her. They heard him rummaging around the camp and she panicked, scrambled into her

37

clothes and outside, and he caught her leaving the tent. His shouting roused Adam, along with most of the others.

'Fifteen,' Adam heard Eric yelling. 'Did you know that, you asshole? Fifteen! I told you guys!'

'Nearly sixteen,' Rose said quietly.

'No, you're not,' he snapped. 'You just had your birthday. Jesus . . . And your mother!'

Neil was saying 'I'm sorry' over and over. He was standing next to Rose in his boxer shorts, his legs pasty and thin, holding up his hands in a *Don't shoot!* pose. At one point, apparently thinking of Eric's friendliness and invitation, he added something about there having been a 'misunderstanding', but he quickly saw that straight apology was wiser. The hippies, two of the Germans and the gay couple were already there, hovering a few yards away, as if there were an invisible cordon holding them back.

'Damn right you're sorry,' Eric said. 'Don't go anywhere, you asshole.' He surveyed the other campers, as if to enlist them as sentries. 'Where's that fucking guide?' He peered around for Trey. 'Where's the nearest phone? Jesus Christ, come here, honey.'

Eric seized Rose by a wrist and marched her away to the other side of the campsite. 'What's the matter with you, you asshole?' he growled at Adam as they passed him. Adam heard Rose say 'no' repeatedly, her volume rising each time, the voice between a shriek and a plea, though he couldn't make out what it was that she was rejecting – an imputation of duress, maybe, or a threat of disownment, or the call to the police.

The English couple arrived, the woman in an incongruous dressing gown, and they and the others spontaneously formed a loose, citizens' semicircle around Neil, the tent hemming him in behind. Neil's shoulders were slumped, his face bone white. He kept his eyes on the ground until, timidly, he looked up at Adam. After a few seconds Adam pushed between the Germans and joined him.

'Morning,' he said.

Neil nodded, smiling with his eyes.

Trey approached the tent as they were struggling into their clothes. In a hard, unfamiliar tone, he said, 'He wants me to get the police. I mean, what the fuck, you guys? I don't know about England, but in California you're looking at two years in San Quentin. Jesus, this is the last thing ...'

'Is this what they teach you at Cambridge?' the English woman said, as Trey stomped away. What? Adam thought. To her husband she said, loudly, 'We thought they were such nice boys.' The Yorkshireman tutted. I am a nice boy, Adam thought. I am.

The female hippy covered her eyes with a hand. The gay couple were staring, mouths open, intermittently shaking their heads. After a few, long minutes Neil said, 'Look, I'm just stretching my legs, okay? Just over there, okay?' Nobody stopped him. The athletic American crossed his arms imposingly on his chest but stood aside.

Adam found him leaning against a skinny tree. They were wearing their lookalike boots. Neil said, 'Suppose I should have known.'

'How should you?'

'I don't know. I just should have, to be honest. You know – her knickers.'

'What's wrong with her knickers?'

'Nothing, they were just ... I should have known.'

'You know, I tried to ...'

'What?'

'Nothing.'

They were quiet for a moment. It was getting properly light. Adam scratched his leg.

'You used something, right?'

Neil didn't answer. He broke a twig from a low branch and bent it in his fist; it was too supple to snap and he threw it aside.

After a minute Adam said, 'I guess the skiing's off.'

'Ad, don't. Didn't you hear what he said? About San wherever it was.' Adam said nothing. 'Who am I going to call?'

'What?'

'You get one call, don't you? Or is that only on television?'

'I don't know,' Adam said. 'I'm sorry. I'm sorry.'

Neil pinched the bridge of his nose, closed his eyes, and in a different voice, quieter but firmer, as if he had been rehearsing in his head, said, 'It was what you wanted, wasn't it? I mean, you wanted it too. You started it.'

Adam knew what he meant. The harmless competition, the innocent collusion, the rapt exclusion of other people's feelings from their thoughts: all the ordinary elements of friendship that had brought them here. The words he had spoken about the girl, as well as the crucial ones he hadn't. 'What are you talking about?' he replied.

They trudged back together. Flight would have been impractical, but, in any case, the idea never occurred to them – some ingrained deference to the law, and the paralysing numbness of their predicament. They stood in silence, anticipating the police, the handcuffs, Neil's right to remain silent, Adam privately wondering whether he might be fingered as an accessory. Those two years in San Quentin.

Presently they heard raised voices at the edge of the campsite. They saw Eric gesturing at the two of them with a

40

thumb. They saw Trey pat him on the shoulder and Eric brush off his hand. Trey walked over to them in what seemed like slow motion.

'There's a shuttle you can catch,' he said. 'I'm on my way, he tells me to hold it, now they ... Just take the shuttle, there's a bus to the city.'

'But ...' Neil began.

'He's changed his mind. She must have persuaded him, how the hell should I know? Could be she told him nothing happened. Or he doesn't want to put her through it. But he wants you out of here.'

'Thanks,' Adam said. 'Really.'

Trey spat in the dirt. 'Just get the fuck out of here, will you?'

Neil ducked into the tent to pack up his kit. Adam jogged over to the extinguished campfire, where Trey had half-arranged the breakfast things, to get some water for the journey. Three of the previous evening's beer bottles sprawled in the ashes. He was dizzy with relief: no police, nothing to be an accessory to, the surreal peril lifting, nightmare-like, as suddenly as it had struck.

As he turned from the water cooler, Eric intercepted him. Adam looked over the broad shoulder for Neil, or for anyone. He shuffled sideways, but Eric blocked him off. 'You,' he said, 'you little ... It's not for your sake, believe me ... What kind of people are you?'

Not knowing what to say, Adam offered a tense smile.

'You think this is funny?' Eric said. 'Big joke for you guys, isn't it? My little girl ... What did you do, make a bet or something?'

'He said he was sorry,' Adam managed. 'We're both very sorry.'

'I want you to remember this,' Eric said. 'One day, you'll have your own ... You do your best, you think you're doing right. I hope for your sake you never know how this feels.'

Eric half-turned to go, and Adam thought it was over, but he reconsidered and turned back. Briefly Adam feared Eric might punch or throttle him. 'You know what,' he said instead, 'scratch that. I hope you find out exactly how this feels. I told you, you asshole. I fucking told you. I should never have let her stay up ... I hope you do, and when that day comes you better remember me.'

At last he walked off, which at the time felt to Adam like a mercy, Eric's *one day* being too remote and hypothetical to seem troubling.

Adam stuffed his kit into his rucksack, silently and fast, and they were almost out. At the very end, as they were heaving their bags onto their backs, Rose marched up to Neil, holding out a torn piece of paper on which she had scribbled her name and her parents' address and phone number. She had changed into a T-shirt with a Charlie Brown motif; she inclined her face for him to kiss, her eyes red but no longer crying, chest heaving despite her visible efforts to pacify it.

Eric watched, now squatting on a tree trunk with his palms on his temples. He seemed somehow shrunken, like a terracotta statue of himself. He balled his hands into fists and let them hang beside his calves. Much later, Adam wondered whether, along with all the other emotions he must have experienced, Eric might have been proud of his daughter at that moment, as she strode across the campsite. Adam saw him avert his eyes as Neil raised a finger to Rose's chin, gently tilted her face forward and kissed the crown of her head, like a blessing.

She controlled herself until he and Adam hurried away. As they left the campsite they heard a single sob, deeper and longer than her rollercoaster squeals at the lake. Turning back, inadvisably, as they went, Adam saw Rose sitting on her father's knee, her face buried in his chest, his in her hair.

THE odd thing was, or so it came to seem, that for all the blame they were to apportion, all the secrecy and forgiveness and revenge, they didn't feel so very much at the time. Or perhaps it wasn't odd, given how remorse can sometimes accumulate, the intimate sort especially; how events can take on a different complexion or valency the further they recede, or the more they seem to have happened to someone else; the more entangled they become, as Rose would, with other memories and resentments. They talked about the drama as they took that shuttle, they talked about her on the bus to San Francisco, Neil briefly studying her note in his lap, but scarcely at all as they delivered the pick-up to Portland (a long straight drive with no detours), where the grateful recipient, the man from San Diego's older and calmer brother, took them out for a burger to thank them. This glossing-over was partly tact, and involved at least some shame, but also, that summer, a giddy, distracted sense of scale. They didn't register the pivot in their lives, as you might notice a scratch without anticipating the infection.

They were both due to fly home from Los Angeles, and both with the same airline, but on different dates, so Neil called and changed his ticket. On the Greyhound to LA they made unwisely loud jokes about the consequences they might suffer if they ventured into the badlands at the rear of the bus. On the plane Neil fell asleep in the aisle seat with his head on Adam's shoulder. Adam leaned across, reached into the luggage compartment for a blanket, and draped it over him.

Adam's family was meeting him at the airport. He and Neil patted each other on the shoulder, and, after a moment, embraced. Even the hug felt easier and less compromising than what they wanted to say.

'I'm sad,' Adam finally managed.

'So am I.'

Walking away through the terminal, Neil turned to see Adam being enfolded by a man with greying hair and posh-pink trousers, and a girl he presumed was Adam's sister. He watched them for a few seconds before heading down into the Tube.

1995

'THEY should be in this afternoon.' Neil leaned across the scratched countertop. 'Can you come back for them? I don't know – four-ish?'

'Sorry,' the young woman said. 'Afternoon off today. Monday any good?'

'Hope you're doing something nice with it.'

The telephone rang in the back office. One rotary double-shriek, a second, and Brian's muffled voice answered.

'Such a lovely day,' the woman said. 'I might go up the reservoir.'

She leaned against the cash register, crossing her left leg over the standing right. Her cotton jacket rumpled open, disclosing a flash of shoulder and smooth armpit between the fabric and her sleeveless dress.

'Neil!' Brian called from the office.

'All right for some,' Neil said. 'I won't be here Monday, I'm afraid. Last day tomorrow.'

'Sorry to hear that.'

'I could run them up to you, if you like. Might be heavy.'

The woman was a secretary at the chartered surveyors' practice above the hi-fi shop, a business that in the past two years had been among Collins & Sons' best customers.

'Would you?' She twisted a lock of hair around a finger.

'Neil!' Brian shouted. 'For you!'

'Sorry,' Neil said. 'Just a second, okay?' He offered her a rueful, raised-eyebrow smile. 'Who is it?' he asked Brian as they crossed at the internal doorway.

'No idea,' Brian said, shaking his head. 'Like a bunch of teenagers.'

Neil sat at the back office desk. A stationery supplier's marketing calendar, illustrated with photos of envelopes in bundles and in-trays, or half-tucked into pockets, hung on the wall in front of him. Wrong month, wrong year.

'Hello?'

'This is the Metropolitan Police,' the familiar voice said. 'We've had a report of disorderly conduct at a pub in the Waterloo area. We would like to speak to you and an extremely handsome blond man.'

Leave the police out of it, Neil thought. But quickly he felt the reliable surge of adrenalin, the instant recharge: something to do with laughter – the muscle memory of old jokes and the anticipation of new ones – and an inchoate appreciation that this friendship was itself a kind of joke, a random jackpot.

'Oh, hi,' he said. 'You almost had me.'

'Don't take that tone with me, young man,' Adam said. 'This is serious.'

Jokes and beaches and freedom, beamed instantaneously into the back office.

'I'm sorry, sir, it's just, you know, the only blond man I

know doesn't really fit your description. He's sort of a runt, to be honest, posh as hell, you know, thinks he's Lord Byron or something . . .'

'That'll do, Philly. I'm just checking, still on for Sunday, aren't we?'

'Yeah, great. I mean, if that's still okay with you.'

'Of course. I'm all yours, Claire's finishing her dissertation.'

Towers of old catalogues sagged under and on top of the desk. The musty odour of decomposing paper mingled with the whiff of imperfect drainage from the water closet (chain-pull flush, grime-grooved soap). The desk, the filing cabinets and the museum-piece safe were smothered in luxuriant, Rembrandtesque dust; the entire room seemed not to have been cleaned since Neil revised for his exams there.

'Great. After lunch?'

'About three?'

'Done. And, you know, thanks.'

'I haven't done anything yet.'

'No, I mean, you know, the cheque.'

'Forget it, Philly. It's nothing.'

'I've got most of it already, it's just, I need to get a few things, and if I use the whole lot on the deposit I'll—'

'Listen, I've got a team meeting in a minute. I'll see you Sunday, I've got the address.'

'Roger that.'

Jokes and beaches and discretionary kindness. And trust. Neil hurried back into the shop, smiling privately.

Brian was sitting behind the counter, shoulders hunched, hands in his lap, thumbs twiddling. Alone.

'She's gone,' he said, without looking up.

'But she—'

'They're sending someone up before closing. Not her, not the woman. Office junior, she said.'

'Right, but I was going—'

'Neil,' Brian said, still facing away. 'Neil. I know you're slinging your hook, but – don't shit on your own doorstep.'

No one was watching him but Neil blushed anyway, cross and embarrassed at once. Sitting down at the other end of the counter he remembered how, when he was fifteen, he and an almost-forgotten friend had been chased off a bus by a posse of troublemakers, making it back to Neil's house breathless and scared. 'You should have smashed a bottle, you two should,' Brian told them as they fumbled with the door chain. 'You should have smashed it, held it up and said, "Who's first?"' The friend made screw-loose signs behind Brian's back.

Don't shit on your own doorstep: another glimpse of his father's foreign prehistory, an obscure past that Neil knew he would never reconnoitre. He had certainly had his chance, two long years' worth of chances, but the moment had never seemed right, he hadn't known how to begin, and he had wasted them. They both had.

A customer came in, a man in an unseasonal mackintosh and old-timer's Trilby. He scanned the printer inks, wrote something on a notepad and left without uttering a word, the bell on the door tinkling him in and out.

'Time-waster,' Brian said. 'Price-checking, that's all.'

Two years, give or take the few, scattered months of the short-term contracts Neil had managed to land elsewhere: telesales (insurance), market-research questionnaires (refrigerators). After a year he had written to the pharmaceutical company to ask for his pre-California job back, but his former boss had moved on and his successor said there were no

48

vacancies. Finally Neil was leaving, to a media company near Tower Bridge and, with Adam's help, to a rented bedsit in Burnt Oak.

'And the parking charges,' Brian added. 'What the hell do they think they're playing at?'

Neil and Dan had spent their school holidays stacking these shelves, taking apart and reconstructing stationery displays, their private, outsized Rubik's cubes. They scribbled rude jokes about the customers; they slunk out to play the slot machine in the café two doors away. There was painful hilarity with bulldog clips. Their mother would make jam sandwiches for their lunch; afterwards they went up to the Wimpy for cardboard chips and synthetic milkshakes. One blissful morning they found a stash of pornographic magazines in a second-hand filing cabinet.

Neither Brian nor Neil ever expected him to be back. *Collins & Sons*, the shopfront read, but Brian hadn't fathered any sons when the glass was etched, and, after they were born, he never anticipated that either of them would join him behind the counter when they grew up. He had been paying Neil fifty quid a week, which Neil knew he hadn't earned, and moreover knew they couldn't really afford on what the shop was taking.

They sat. Brian's chair was caught in the rhombus of sunlight refracted by the shopfront. He dozed off in the warmth, chin on chest. He was fifty-nine, and in reasonable physical condition, apart from some routine spreading, some greying and thinning on top, and a neglectful attitude to ear and nasal hair. But he napped like an older man: a worn-out man, deep-down finished, obliterating his afternoons in miniature, reversible suicides.

The bell startled him awake. A man in shiny grey trousers

and a blue shirt asked, 'Fax paper?' Neil began to rise, but Brian sat him down with an air-pat of his hand, creaking to his feet to show the customer to the shelf.

Almost two years – his two flatlining years since California – and, if Neil were honest with himself, nothing at all to show for them, not counting his friendship with Adam. Say what you like about Dan, down in Southampton with his child, its errant mother and his booze, at least he had escaped Collins & Sons. He hadn't made it to Argentina or Australia but he had at least managed that.

'Thanking you,' Brian said, handing the customer his change. The man counted the coins and left.

In the beginning Neil had tried to persuade his father to rejig their displays. He wanted to put the biggest sellers near the door, with impulse buys, such as they were (staplers, hole punches, Sellotape dispensers), beside the cash till. Sell the customer what he wants to buy; don't waste the customer's time: he knew that much from the pharmaceuticals job. He would move the stock and the fittings himself, Neil had offered, he would see to it one evening after closing. All he needed was his father's say-so. Brian didn't see the point. The megastores had taken over, was his mantra, the high streets were just as screwed as manufacturing, but retail lacked the grandeur and the romance of industry, it missed the angry unions and the picturesque strikes, so you never saw it on the news.

A day and a half to go, Neil's final shifts before his real life began, and still he glanced at the door every half a minute: in hope (of a break in the boredom, the joint loneliness), and pre-emptive distaste (the self-effacement that some customers expected, the impression of his own invisibility, and of his father's, which they conveyed), and, since the robbery the previous autumn (the knife held to Brian's ribs before he could reach the panic button), a cold undertow of fear. An hour before closing Brian took the cash and the cheques from the safe and totted them up on his antique calculator. He strangled the bills into hundred-pound bundles with grubby rubber bands, put the bundles and a deposit slip into a brown envelope and gave it to Neil to run up to the bank for the last time. Neil crammed the envelope into a trouser pocket and bolted for the door, the pavement, the sunshine.

AT HALF-PAST five that afternoon Neil turned the sign on the door to *Closed*, stepped outside and pulled the grille halfway down the shopfront. The slot in the tessellated metal for their mail was temporarily suspended at eye level, looking to Neil like the peephole of a prison cell.

'Just going to say hello to Bimal,' he called out.

'Right,' Brian replied from the back office.

'See you at home.'

'Righto.'

Neil paused for a few seconds, Brian's last ever chance to object. Nothing. The bell on the door rung him out.

Bimal was one of the very few local boys Neil had kept up with: hellos in the street when they were back from university, since then a few brisk drinks, at the most recent of which Bimal tried to recruit him to his pie-in-the-sky merchandising start-up. A plausible engagement, but in fact they weren't meeting that evening. Instead Neil went to the video store, where he shuffled the cases in the *New Releases* rack and tried not to eye the *Adult* section too conspicuously. Next, the travel agent, where he flicked through brochures for cruises and Caribbean resorts that he confidently expected never to visit (*Time-waster!* the shopkeeper in his

51

head reproached). Finally, after dawdling for long enough to evade his father, he crossed the road to the bus stop.

He couldn't face the car journey. Somehow those fifteen extra minutes at the end of the day had become too much, obeying an alternative, decelerated timescale. In the shop they had designated roles, they were functional and blessedly interrupted. The silence in the car was heavier. Two or three times a week Neil would make his excuses and either walk or catch a bus. *Nipping out to see Bimal. This needs to go in the last post. Got to see a man about a dog.* If Brian saw through them, Neil hoped he would likewise see the whiteness of the lies.

Two years.

The bus from Wembley to Harrow was almost full. He found a place in the middle of the upstairs deck, next to a statuesque woman in a sari. She rotated her knees to usher him into the window seat. As the bus pulled away Neil bet himself that he could close his eyes for a minute and know precisely where he was on this overfamiliar route. He tried and failed.

Five schoolgirls clattered up the stairs, one of them shrieking when she was thrown against the plastic stairwell as the bus moved off, laughing as she recovered. The girls stood in the aisle, holding onto the upright railings and the backs of seats, a few rows in front of Neil's.

Two black, two white, one Asian. Three of them had bunched and knotted their shirts around their midriffs, exposing the skin above their short skirts. They were taking turns to listen to a slug of pop on somebody's Walkman, two at a time, a headphone apiece.

Sixteen, Neil estimated. They probably didn't see him at all. He felt rebuked by their uniforms and looked out of the window, into the upper floors of the pebbledash suburban houses, at the branches and defaced trunks of the city trees. Blossom ran past his window in intermittent blizzards. Something about the girls had jarred, or chimed, one of them in particular, the nearest, standing with her back towards him. Her ponytail, or – no – the way she had raised a hand to balance on her friend's shoulder, the other hand reaching behind her to bend her heel into a buttock. She jiggled on her standing leg, the unselfconscious gestures undermining her studiedly grown-up imprecations. The shape of her as she executed that stretch unsettled Neil. His eyes closed again.

He had scarcely been able to see her in the tent, and the visual impressions he retained from inside it were static and disordered, chiaroscuro snapshots of poles and canvas folds and unerotic body parts: her knitted brow, a shoulder, her elevated knees as she pedalled back into her giveaway knickers. His strongest tactile memory of that evening was from earlier, around the campfire. After he moved to sit beside her, when Adam and some of the others were still up, he had slipped his index finger underneath her sweater, surreptitiously touching her skin above the elastic of her shorts. She bridled, just for a second, as if he had administered a mild electric shock, then tried to relax, letting his hand stay where it was. That was when Neil knew: that she had chosen him, he had won, that she might be his.

He opened his eyes. The legs in the aisle began to recede; the girls swung themselves around the railing at the top of the stairs, practised and orderly as firemen, thudded down them and skipped off the bus. The doors emitted their steam-train hiss as they closed and the driver pulled away.

Neil rarely thought about the American girl. There was no particular reason to think about her, let alone the morning-after tears, his ten-minute dread of the thunderbolt disaster. Speaking to Adam today, and the prospect of seeing him at the weekend, must have prompted this association, Neil figured, though in fact they had never talked about her in London. Not once. As an anecdote she lacked a useful classification: the episode was neither salacious nor amusing, neither wittily self-deprecating nor aggrandising. Neil had slept with three other women since, and while those English liaisons were transient and awkward in their own ways (two of them had wanted more, the other time he had), none involved any taint or shame. There was nothing to say about that night, and after all California was their golden time, their creation story. A misunderstanding. Regrettable, but accidental. No one had done anything wrong.

Neil's stop was approaching; he leaned across the woman in the sari and pressed the buzzer. But her voice, her pure middle-American accent, was still almost audible to him, as if she were talking to him as he disembarked the bus and turned the corner of his father's street, only through a wall or from under water.

WHEN the doorbell rang that Sunday Neil was standing on a chair in his bedroom, retrieving a photo album from the swamp of old comics and decomposing sticker collections on the top shelf.

'Dad,' he shouted, 'the door!'

The bell sounded again, an effortful rusty wheeze. Neil heard indistinct voices in the hallway. He dropped off the chair and jogged down the stairs.

'How do you do?' Adam was saying.

'Come in,' Brian said. 'Come through.' He ushered Adam inside, flourishing his whole arm, almost bowing.

Neil caught up with them in the lounge, made to embrace his friend, but checked himself. Too intimate, somehow, in front of his father. 'Hello,' he said, more coldly than he meant to.

'Hi, Neil,' Adam said. He smiled. It's okay, the smile seemed to Neil to say. Show me all of it. Adam had never been out to Harrow before; Neil had invited him once or twice, but half-heartedly. On Adam's mental map this whole suburban ring, with its low-rise shopping arcades and identikit semis – the doughnut of London between the green belt and the costume-drama core – was still marked *There Be Monsters*.

'This is Adam,' Neil told Brian. 'He's—'

'Yes, I know, I know, the chap from America,' Brian said. Neil had never heard his father use the word 'chap' before.

They stood in the middle of the room. 'Very nice house you have,' Adam offered.

'Have a seat,' Brian said, indicating the armchair that faced the television. He retreated to the mantelpiece, resting his elbow in front of the urn.

'Well, then,' Brian said, looking out between the net curtains and into the driveway. 'Come far?'

'Maida Vale.'

'Very nice,' Brian said.

Twenty seconds, then Adam asked, 'I've got the car, shall we ...?'

'Yeah,' Neil said. 'Come on. Come upstairs.'

'I'll put the kettle on,' Brian said.

They escaped to Neil's room. 'Let's do the big one first,' Adam suggested. He bent to pick up the box.

'I'll take that end,' Neil said. 'I know where we're going.' The base bulged and threatened to split. 'Put your hands underneath. No, both of them.'

'Okay,' Adam said. 'Fuck, Philly, okay.'

Neil backed out of his room and reverse-pivoted to the stairs. 'Watch it here, it's slippery.'

The carpet was frayed almost to nothing on the lip of the top step, a few tenacious strands of fabric stretched across the rounded edge like a bald man's comb-over. Theirs was a womanless house: cleanish but neglected, the decor untouched since before Mrs Thatcher got in, a place of prepackaged meals rather than ingredients, brown processed food that Neil and Brian heated in the microwave and ate in front of the television, all the talking in the room done on the screen.

'Careful,' Brian said from the bottom of the stairs, almost too softly for them to hear. He stood by the front door, a one-man honour guard, as they edged through and deposited the box on the crazy paving in the driveway. Adam opened the boot of the car, rearranged his parents' wellies and his father's golf umbrella, and they loaded the box in.

'Tea?'

'Very kind of you, Mr Collins ...'

'Dad, we've got to get on with it.'

In the bedroom Adam lifted a stereo speaker. 'Load me up, will you?' he said to Neil, rolling his eyes towards the speaker's twin.

'I'll take that one, you'll never manage both.'

'How much do you want to bet? Million quid?'

Neil watched his friend descend the stairs, the solid physicality of him and the bone-deep confidence. He made it.

'I had a lady friend down there once,' Brian said as Adam negotiated the front door, catching his knuckles on the frame. 'Maida Vale, you know. Not far from the canal, Harrow Road side. Long time ago now, that was.'

Brian had never mentioned this woman to Neil before. 'Dad,' he said, 'we've got to get on, okay? It's two trips anyway.'

'Righto,' Brian said, flapping his hand in a surrendering farewell.

THEY laid the speakers, a suitcase and a cork pinboard across the seats and got in. Adam nudged the car out of the driveway and into the road. 'You'll have to direct me,' he said.

'Right,' Neil said. 'No, I mean left – left here, then left again. That's it, up to the roundabout.' They passed a launderette, a bookie, a chippy, an Indian takeaway. A hairdresser's and an optician's. 'When are you off?'

'Wednesday. We're all flying out together, with the cameramen and the sound guys. I've got to help them lug the kit.' This would be Adam's first location shoot: holidaymakers in Tenerife.

'So how are they? The reps and what have you. Your contacts. All lined up?'

'They're sorted, I think. There's this one guy, Gavin, he runs a bar, he's been very helpful. It's kind of popular sociology, you know, the country seeing itself in the mirror. That's what Jim says.'

'Jim? Right at the lights.'

Adam spoke about his television career with a confidence that, to Neil, hinted at some plan or agreement for his advancement that he was sadly not at liberty to disclose. A confidence that was apparently justified: after a few purgatorial months at his first job, at an unglamorous firm that made training videos, he had moved to a cutting-edge production company. Adam seemed to Neil to be carried aloft by invisible hands, like a stage-diver conveyed to safety by a well-wishing crowd.

'Jim the executive producer. Anyway – did I tell you? –

Claire might come out for a few days, if the production manager lets us. Bit of a witch.'

'Jesus, and you're supposed to be her boyfriend.'

'No, I meant the production man— Fuck off.'

'Pull up on the right. I haven't even met her yet.'

'When I get back. You can be my character witness.'

'Yeah, here, that's fine. What's my commission?'

'You can have her sister.'

'Does she have a sister?'

'No.'

They drew in alongside a brown, grimly functional modern building. There was a convenience shop on the ground floor and cage-like fortifications on the upper windows, as if the inhabitants were expecting a siege. Neil's immediate neighbours were a pawnbroker and a Bengali women's association. He descended a set of switchback metal steps beneath the shopfront; Adam followed, at the bottom stepping over the newspapers, chip wrappers and Fanta cans that Neil had kicked into the well of the basement. Inside he had a single room, with a cupboard kitchen and a bathless bathroom. There was an acrid smell of damp. The furnishings comprised a penitentially narrow bed, a single plastic chair and a washing-up tub in the sink.

'It's great, Philly,' Adam said.

'It's a shit-hole,' Neil said. 'And you know it.'

'Come on, I think it's terrific,' Adam insisted. 'You'll never have to say "Your place or my dad's?" to another girl.'

'Oh fuck off,' Neil said, gently punching his shoulder. He opened the only window. 'Thanks again. I mean it.'

'No problem,' Adam said. 'Really. I've got the car for a fortnight, they're out in Perpignan.'

'No, I mean the deposit. I'll pay you back. With interest.'

'Don't be ridiculous.'

There was no escape from money in London, they were discovering, from its double magnetism, which drew the well-off together and drove them and the struggling apart. In the flat Adam shared with Chaz and Archie there were double beds all round, a whirlpool bath and a sun-trap roof terrace; two of them, Adam and Archie, had moved in before their first pay-check. Neil had been out with them all, once, but the graft hadn't taken.

'I mean it, Ad. Few months and I'll have it.'

'Pay me back when you make your first million.' They both laughed. 'You start next week, right? Break a leg.'

They carried the cargo down the stairs. Neil stood the pinboard, an improvised photo display, against the wall opposite the stair-obstructed window, in the basement's lone oblong of natural light. Neil and Dan when they were teenagers, wearing shades and gurning. The two of them, younger, with their mother on a pebbly beach, Neil turning his face from the camera and up towards hers. A picture of Neil and Adam at the motel in Los Angeles, another of them fooling around beneath the Faithful Couple, the lip of a path running in front of the double trunk, a backdrop of lush foliage, their two conjoined figures at the base, someone else's bare arm intruding at the frame's left edge. Adam had made copies for Neil after they came home.

For a moment they stood in the basement, looking at the photos together in silence. Then they bounded up the stairs, instinctively racing.

'Well,' Neil said on the pavement, 'I'll miss you while you're over there.'

'Stay alive,' Adam said hammily. 'I will find you.'

*

THERE wasn't much more to fetch: the fat body of the stereo and its black tendrils; half a dozen hangers' worth of shirts; the tubular segments and disc-shaped base of a floor lamp; some linen; a box of plastic ornaments that Neil had collected as a child, his boyhood's special things, some of them, Adam noticed, old promotional freebies from cereal packets.

Adam loitered in the lounge while Neil gathered his kit. A couple of china figurines sat on the mantelpiece, above them a framed floral print that his mother would without question have described as 'ghastly'. The urn. He tiptoed across to examine it.

The previous autumn, after they had been to a film at Marble Arch, Adam had reminisced about going to the cinema with his mother when he was very young. About how, in the intermissions between the features, she would give him and Harriet money for popcorn or a lolly (never both), sending them up to the usherette to buy their treats, the two of them waving back at her from the queue, considering this the most thrillingly grown-up privilege in the world. Adam had begun an edited account of his mother's life: her grandfather the judge, the much-mythologised spell in Tangiers before she married, her kooky taste in jewellery, how much he loved her cooking. Standing in front of the mantelpiece in Harrow, he remembered how he had stopped himself that afternoon, and clumsily apologised.

Neil came back down the stairs. Adam said, 'Don't you want to . . . ?'

'He's asleep. I'll call him later.'

'You sure?'

'Yes.'

Neil closed the front door, depressing the latch with his

finger to minimise the click, leaving almost silently, as if from a dormitory, or a wake.

At the second set of traffic lights a hunched old woman crossed the road in front of them, dragging a rectangular shopping trolley. Adam said, 'At your house ... at your dad's place. You know, on your mantelpiece ... ?'

'Yeah,' Neil said. 'I don't know what it is really. He can't decide what to do with her, or can't bring himself to, maybe. Wouldn't happen if Mum was here!'

He gave a short choke of a laugh, louder and fiercer than his silent, grimacing, true laugh. He told Adam about the night, after his A-levels, when he freaked out some friends by tipping ash from their spliff into the urn, stoned homage disguised as bravado. Even then they hadn't asked about her, Neil said, just averted their eyes in silence.

'Do you cry when you think about it?'

'You mean, did I cry then?'

'No, I mean do you cry when you think about it now?'

Neil paused. 'To be honest, I don't. Cry, I mean.'

'Never?'

'I can't remember the last time I cried. When I nearly do, you know, when I feel like it, the ducts or whatever gearing up, it's always for some silly reason, over nothing, that bloke who fell over at the Olympics or something. Why, do you?'

'Cry? Sometimes. Not that I've ... I've been lucky, you know.'

They were quiet for a minute, but comfortably. The silence had a new timbre that they both heard, an ease that felt like an accomplishment.

'Your father,' Adam finally said. 'Your dad. He isn't ... He wasn't how I expected. You're always so, I don't know, down on him. He was really try—'

'It was different,' Neil said. 'He was. You being there, it was easier.'

'It's just, the way you talk about them – your brother, too.' Adam reflexively compared Neil's father with his own, Jeremy, a man who always let him feel that all manner of things would be well – not just that they would be, in fact, but that they were *already* well, could never be otherwise, and that Adam's role was simply to perpetuate and ramify the wellness he inherited. 'It's not what I'm used to, that's all.'

'You don't have to live with him.'

'Neither do you.'

'No!' Neil exclaimed. 'Fuck.'

'Take it easy, you can always move back.'

'No, you idiot, we've gone the wrong way.'

Adam turned into a driveway and began to reverse out again, but stopped. The shirts were hanging from a strap above the rear passenger-side window, blocking his view of the traffic. Neil leaned between the seats and tried to pin them behind the stereo, but they escaped. He thrust himself backwards, clasping a headrest with one hand and reaching for the shirts with the other.

'How's that?'

'Don't be ridiculous.'

'No, go on,' Neil said. 'I'll call you out.'

Looking sideways Adam saw the pale, hairy calf below the hem of Neil's jeans, an obscurely improper glimpse of skin that was ordinarily concealed. He gently tugged the trousers towards his friend's ankles. Little by little, Neil was uncovering: his father (Adam picked up a dim genetic echo between their gummy Collins smiles), his brother and his mother. Those photos of them on the pinboard, alongside Los Angeles, the Faithful Couple.

'Adam?'

He put the car into reverse.

'GAVIN?'

'*Que?*'

'Señor Gavin?'

'*Non.*'

Adam flew to Tenerife three days after he helped Neil move. He found the place on his second afternoon. The grille was down, the pavement outside less carpeted by broken glass than were the stretches on either side. Eventually he roused a defeated-looking Spanish caretaker, who trudged round from the back of the bar carrying a mop.

'Look, just let me ...' Adam tried to edge past the caretaker to find the rear entrance. The man blocked him off.

'Close. No Gavin.'

'There is, I've spoken ... I know there is.' He tried to steer the man out of his way, hands on shoulders, gently, he intended.

'You fuck!' the caretaker shouted.

'Take it—'

'Fuck!'

The caretaker's spittle landed on Adam's cheek, followed by the damp strings of his mop. Adam's sunglasses flew into the gutter.

The main drag felt like the aftermath of a festive war, with a left-over stench of sun cream, cheap rum, deep-fat fryers and vomit. He asked at six or seven other nightspots, but the only person who admitted to knowing Gavin tried to hit him up for a debt. 'These kids,' the Mancunian who called himself Gavin had said to Adam, 'they show up for work drunk, or they don't show up at all, you give 'em the push and they expect you to hire them back the next day. And you do. You fucking do!'

On the phone this person had promised Adam unfettered access to his customers, dancefloor and erratic seasonal staff. Adam had promised all these things to Natasha, the producer.

'Fuck's sake,' Natasha said at the villa when he told her what had happened.

'It's not my—'

'No filming, Adam. No fucking filming until you bring me a story.'

The other researcher, Will, pushed his black-rimmed glasses up his nose and smiled. This wasn't what Adam had expected.

Adam was afraid of Natasha, because everybody seemed to be. The origins of this general fear were obscure to him, lost in the company's sedimented prehistory, a dark chronicle of shaggings and sackings and atavistic rivalries. In London she was one of the aloof, spiky-haired women who rode their chairs around the office like chariots, to gossip, but not with him. The real, make-or-break action always seemed to Adam to be elsewhere: in the smoking room, in the lift he had just missed, at the drinks he found out about afterwards, now on the shoots from which he was disbarred.

He chased up the other holiday reps and nightclub entrepreneurs he had contacted in London. He stalked new subjects around their pools and on the fag-ash beaches during the afternoons. He had anticipated some fly-on-the-wall gravitas amid the levity: broken dreams or relationships, working-class poetics, hypocritical euroscepticism. But when he mentioned these ideas to Natasha she called him a 'pointy head' and pinched his cheek, slightly too hard. She, Will and the others seemed to Adam to be cultivating a coercive unseriousness, as if there were nothing left in the world for anyone to be serious about. They all went up at the end of their sentences, like characters in an Australian soap opera; in Will's case the unenquiring interrogatory was complemented by a meaningless arch irony, ersatz rather than genuine, since it concealed and implied nothing.

The worst night came when Adam forgot to ask two podium dancers from Huddersfield to sign the release form while they were sober, an oversight he could not adequately explain to Natasha or to himself.

'Unfuckingbelievable,' Natasha said.

Will said, 'I'm sure you'll crack it next time, sport?'

All Will's remarks came enclosed in invisible quotation marks, intoned like jokes without punchlines. He pushed his glasses up his nose and smiled.

In the end Adam found a rhythm, working most of the night, knocking off for a drink at five in the morning, sleeping until the dry heat woke him at lunchtime. He never honed Will's knack of enlisting and coaxing the super-exhibitionists – he suspected Will might be paying them – but he had a good eye for montages and a fine ear for the voiceover script. He puffed the communal hash that the sound man had smuggled inside a pot of Marmite, but was agape at the flagrant adulteries of the production manager and one of the cameramen, with each other and later with assorted tourists. With his hard-wired manners and bedrock obedience, Adam was too well brought-up for all that. He began to worry that he was *too* well brought-up.

The work was titillating at first, of course it was. Still, after a few weeks the dancefloor flashers, copulators in DJs' booths, mega-binge drinkers and doggy-style simulators became routine, then nauseating, as depredations tend to.

'Amazing, isn't it?' Adam said to Will by the pool. 'They never come and find us the next day and ask to be cut out. The puking or fighting or whatever.'

'That's why they do it?' Will said. 'It's for the cameras, isn't it? It's not in spite of them?'

'Audiences,' Neil had said to Adam on their return trip to the bedsit. 'That's your product, isn't it? Got to give them what they want.'

They were both right, Adam saw. Televised scrutiny of ordinary people revealed that what ordinary people wanted was to be on television. The feeling was mutual, he was realising: anyone would do, in the new, cut-price, live-and-watch-die economy of scandal, so long as they were shameless or outrageous enough, and so long as it was someone else.

The main trouble with Will was that only one of him and Adam was sure to be kept on when their training contracts expired. 'It's a pyramid,' Natasha explained to him one morning at dawn. 'Lots of grunts at the bottom, a few fuckers at the top. Lots of dying along the way.' Adam hoped he had done enough – and anyway it was all worth it, they said to each other afterwards, for the four days of Claire's visit. She came out on one of the cheapo flights, among the early-doors drinkers and aghast middle-aged holidaymakers rapidly realising their mistake. She and Adam sniffed amyl nitrate in a bar near the one that wasn't Gavin's; they had well-acquainted but still urgent sex, the carnal heyday between courtesy and habit, hoping that no one in the villa overheard. She let him feel like a prince, the dauphin he had grown up believing himself to be, with a skill and alacrity that almost troubled him.

On her last morning her head was on his chest, her hair obscuring her face, when he heard it say, 'I love you. I love you, Adam Tayler.'

He heard himself say, 'I love you, too.'

NEIL left his glass on the table and crossed the room to the payphone outside the gents. The twin aromas of piss and lemony urinal cubes leached under the door, mingling with the fug of cigarette smoke. He lifted the receiver and dialled: the call to the no-show that was the only, futile remedy of the stood-up. You could be lost for an evening, or, almost as easily, you could be lost for ever. Your friendship, your past, could be finished if you chose – as most of Neil's prior friendships were, thinning back to mere acquaintance en route to total severance. His and Adam's could have ended at the airport, if one of them had wanted it to.

The ten-pence piece hovered over the slot; Neil put a finger in his free ear to block the music. Just as the impatient beeps cut in, they arrived.

'Sorry, Philly,' Adam said. He had flown back from Tenerife at the weekend. 'Tube's buggered.'

'Pleased to meet you.'

'How do you do?' She had thick Iberian hair, English-rose skin, full breasts inside her angora turtleneck.

'I've heard a lot about you,' they both said. 'What can I get you?' Neil added. He went to the bar for drinks: pints of lager for Adam and him, some syrupy alcopop confection for her that he pincered between the taller glasses.

'Sixteenth-century engravings,' Claire explained, when he asked about her dissertation. 'Mostly German and Dutch. You know, Dürer and that lot. It was fifteen thousand words, agony. I'm waiting to hear.'

Adam kept his eyes on her, Neil noticed, grinning vapidly, like a figure-skater or a game-show host. This was more than he had anticipated, Neil saw. He felt belatedly nervous.

'Right,' he said. 'That lot.'

'I think it's such a fascinating moment,' Claire persisted. 'You know, when art becomes commodified. They're so beautiful, but, you know, capitalism is taking over.'

I think, sang the stereo, *I'm gonna take me away and hide*

Adam was beaming.

I'm thinking of things that I just can't abide

Neil pictured Claire growing up on one of London's plusher edges (Surrey, possibly Berkshire), a father in a blazer, a mother in a twinset, a sailing boat moored at a marina on the south coast, someone's chalet in the Alps. He pegged her as the sort of girl he and his former friends had encountered on sorties to the West End, posh girls from private schools whom they had coveted in vain. He invented her, in the usual way, the misconceptions persisting in his brain, like libels in the ether, even after he knew them to be untrue. At the same time he saw himself through her invented gaze. He was ashamed of his jumper, his shoes, the two years with his father. He was ashamed of his new job, which, he knew, would seem grubby and meaningless to her. He was ashamed of his shame, the whole exhausting rigmarole of failure.

'That's capitalism for you,' Neil said. 'Can't mind its own business, can it?'

Straight away he wanted to take it back. At the same time he wanted to scream, *I voted Conservative, I voted for Major. What are you really going to do?*

Claire laughed nervously. Adam did a thing with his jaw, a kind of foodless, one-side-of-the-face grinding, which Neil had learned to recognise as a sign of irritation. The worst thing was that he was entirely himself with her.

Neil made an effort. 'So how was the island?'

'There were some lovely parts,' Claire said. 'Fishing villages, you know, mountains, volcanoes, when you got away from Playa. Have you ever been?'

'No.'

She had a way of smiling – eyes widened, head slightly projected – that to Neil suggested some unmet expectation, a graceful disappointment, as if she had offered him a hint or cue that he had failed to take.

'I didn't see much of them myself,' Adam said. 'I was up all night most of the time – you know, filming in nightclubs, sometimes the hospital, you wouldn't believe—'

'All that sociology, I remember,' Neil interrupted. 'The country in the mirror and all that.' Again the instant regret.

'The next project should be more serious,' Adam said. 'They're talking about Yugoslavia.'

Neil saw her squeeze Adam's knee under the table. He wondered how his friend would have briefed her about him. He wondered what they would say about him later. *He isn't normally like that ... No, he was sweet.* The private lights-out communion. She would be in his life now, too.

He tried again, and for a while he kept it up. He talked to her about auction houses, the prospect of her working in one. Remote, Claire said. Near their table a group of patently underage boys were playing a quiz machine, one double the others' size, like a bullock reared on superstrength hormones.

When she went to the ladies, Neil asked, 'So what's she like?'

'What do you mean?' Adam said. 'You can see what she's like.'

'No, I mean . . . You know what I mean, Ads.'

'Come on, Neil. Not here.'

'Out of ten?'

'Don't. She's coming back. She'll be back any minute. I said, don't.'

'Fine, but we've always—'

'Don't.'

Adam felt betrayed. He wanted his friend to endorse his choice of Claire, but he also needed Neil to vindicate her choice of him. Neil was supposed to make him seem popular and dependable, and he was flunking. At the same time he had a vague sense that Neil was entitled to his sabotage, that he should submit himself to it.

Claire tussled Adam's hair as she slid in next to him. 'So how's it going?' Adam asked. 'The job.'

'Okay,' Neil said. 'Better than the shop, anyway.'

'Claire, it's – how would you describe it again?'

'Media sales. Magazine publisher near Tower Bridge. Ad sales, you know. It's a pretty cut-throat industry – the pay's almost all commission, and the management keep raising the thresholds, you know, for the incentive scheme.'

Politely Claire asked, 'What are your colleagues like?'

'Well,' Neil said, 'to give you an idea, they've got this thing called the animal – it's an ugly old cuddly toy, like a Muppet or something, totally filthy – and if you sell more space than anyone else that week you keep it on your desk till the Friday after. Everyone has to make gorilla noises when they pass you.'

Adam laughed. 'What happened with that business thing, Philly? What was his name? Your friend.'

'Bimal.'

'Philly?'

'Collins,' Neil said, though it was a shame, almost, to let her in on it, the nickname bond, the quiddity of him and them, a pledge masquerading as humour.

'Of course, Bimal. Have you decided?'

'Turned him down,' Neil said. 'It's a nice idea but I can't see it working.'

Adam went to the bar. Just for a moment Neil thought there was a silent, eye-contact flicker between Claire and him, a fleeting sense of a bifurcating possibility, like those he thought he shared now and again with strangers coming down the escalators on the Tube as he rode up them. He noticed her belt, a wide leather strap with a fat metal buckle, an accessory that to him implied both chastity and availability. Valuable, locked – but look, here's a way to open me. Probably he had imagined it, or it was a tease, part of some game with Adam or with herself in which he was only symbolically involved. They swapped mildly embarrassing anecdotes about Adam to fill the time – his lucklessness at the dog track in Walthamstow, his fondness for *Dallas* reruns – demonstrating their closeness to him by their licence to belittle him.

Adam distributed the drinks. 'Did I tell you we're going down for the weekend?'

'What are we doing?'

'What? No, not . . . I mean, Claire and me. To my parents'. I'm, you know, introducing them. *Da na na naahhh*' – the cliffhanger opening of Beethoven's fifth.

'Congratulations,' Neil said, turning towards the bar.

He had been to the house in Somerset, once, the previous summer. It was most of what he expected, a converted farmhouse with a dry stone wall, but the rest of the family had been away. The revered father in pink trousers whom he had glimpsed at the airport, the doting mother, the blond sister . . . Adam's inaccessible past. Whenever Adam mentioned his childhood, his pets, his sister falling into fish ponds, their ice-cream calamities, sacrilegious outbursts at Midnight Mass – memories that, for him, seemed too abundant to cherish – Neil had an urge to tamper the records, doctor the photos, insert himself, somehow, into the Tayler mythology, a sort of reverse Stalinism, adding rather than subtracting.

'Separate bedrooms,' Claire said.

'Naturally,' Adam said. 'Very proper.'

She had a slow, precious way of drinking, Neil noticed, tiny sips like a monarch wary of poisoning.

'Harriet's going to be down,' Adam went on. 'She'll probably do her possessive act, you know, sitting on my lap, making me sing our special song from *Lady and the Tramp*.' Neil had slept in Harriet's room, under a quilt with her name stitched into it, her adolescent pin-ups still fixed to the pastel walls.

'Don't be such a bully,' Claire said, slapping Adam's forearm.

Their basic imbalance wasn't money or jobs but people. Chaz and Archie and Claire and his eternal happy family: Adam had back-up. Neil had Brian, and Dan, who had visited only a handful of times since California. Once he came alone, went out for the evening with some mates who hadn't left the neighbourhood, and rolled home late and drunk, rattling around the kitchen and slurping water straight from the tap as if he were seventeen again. Twice he brought his child with him (never its mother); on the first occasion Neil had cradled it, feeling more than he anticipated, the baby somehow seeming a time-travel charm through which they could all go back and try again. Then the child had shat, the force of the excretion blasting the helpless body off his lap, and he passed it back.

'Another?' Adam said.

'School night,' Neil said.

A number for Dan was scribbled on a Post-it note on the fridge, but the brothers hardly ever spoke – no ill-will or diagnosable bad blood, a drift more than a rupture, but nearing the point at which awkwardness and pride would turn one into the other. In Dan, mighty Dan, Neil saw an image of what he could have become, with some bad luck and worse decisions, and could still. The fragility of life without a safety net.

Claire rescued them at the end: 'Adam showed me your photos. You know, from America. Pretty wild by the look of things. That one of you two on the bed. Where was that again, San Francisco?'

'Las Vegas,' Adam said.

Not Las Vegas . . . Neil caught his eye and Adam turned away. *Look at her and we can keep it going.*

'Didn't I tell you?' Adam continued. 'There was this croupier, Neil got talking to her. What was her name again? Daisy? She took that photo in our room.'

'Or was it her friend?' Neil said.

'No, I've got it now, it was that bounty-hunter guy, you remember?'

'You boys,' Claire said. 'You boys.'

ADAM didn't tell Neil about Gavin's disappearance or his mishap with the consent form. That wasn't his role in their double act, he reflected in bed that night, Claire flushed and clammy beside him, gangsta rap and sporadic laughter emanating from the sitting room. He couldn't. Nor had he mentioned another event in Tenerife that, in a way, had distressed him more. It was a small thing, and he couldn't explain quite why it was so preoccupying. No one else in the team was likely to remember it, Adam suspected, or not for long. These things happened, they would think, you had a laugh and a joke about them and then you forgot them. No big deal. No harm done.

He and a cameraman had gone to the beach to film some *general views*, pictures that would be spread across the series, helping to segue between storylines. The cameraman had panned across the black, volcanic sand, scouting for volleyball games and cavorting beauties, and doubletaked back again. He locked onto something in the middle distance that Adam couldn't decipher without magnification, under or near a clump of yellow sun umbrellas.

'Take a look,' the cameraman said to him, grinning. When Adam bent his eye to the viewfinder he saw a couple locked together beneath a beach towel, unmistakably fucking.

They carried on filming, even though they knew the footage would never be used. At least, it couldn't be broadcast. It could be used, and it was used that evening, before they went out for their night's work, to entertain the team at the villa. You could see the two bodies much more clearly on the villa's television; everyone gathered round to score the performances for style, stamina, physique. The producer of the week, a Scot named Alex, supplied a deadpan commentary, as if this were a horse race or a boxing match ('... and they're into the final furlong ...'). The girl was mostly covered by the man's torso and the towel, apart from her legs, which stuck up and out like a crab's. Every thirty seconds or so she seemed to have a dim access of shame, trying with one hand to wrap the towel around her legs, the palm of her other

74

hand flat on the man's back, but the material wouldn't stretch. On the screen her face was well-defined, but still it was hard to tell whether her slack-jawed expression implied pleasure, pain or simply far-gone inebriation.

What you could see for certain was that she was young, most likely in her late teens. After a while Adam couldn't watch. He looked down at the terracotta tiles on the villa's floor. He scratched his left forearm with the nails of his right hand.

Adam wanted to discuss that girl with Neil, but somehow he never found the right moment. Claire had been there that evening and he didn't want his girlfriend to know about her, not yet, and after all there was no harm done, and probably he had left it too long. Neil might not want to be reminded of her, and anyway they were never going to see her again. Adam considered that to be important, then, actions and their invisible consequences not altogether counting, he assumed, nor liable to rebound, if the counterparties were out of sight, finished and lost for ever.

It was less than a lie, he told himself. It was an omission, a nothing about nothing, the square root of nothing.

Major? High school's what I mean.

1999

LATER Neil liked to think he had sensed Farid would be a force in his life, as he was sure he knew in the hostel yard that Adam was to be. In truth his first reaction to the man was disappointment. He came out of the sarcophagal lift – cramped, slow and clad in distressingly frank mirrors, which emphasised his vampiric hairline – expecting to find a twitchy entourage, a wall of blinking data screens, the electric aura of redemptive wealth. Balding, diminutive, only modestly overweight, Farid was sitting alone at a fake-mahogany dining table, bare besides his coffee. No water, no biscuits. The venue was a rented apartment: Neil spotted a kitchen counter through one of the internal doors before Strahan quietly closed it. Farid gestured for the three of them to sit opposite him, the glare from the window at his back and in their eyes. Strahan watched from an armchair set back against the wall.

Bimal introduced Neil as an award-winning salesman (that weekend in Brighton with his dad), Jess as a designer who had worked on projects across the country (her A-levels in

Hull). The executive team was supported, he said, by a panel of advisers boasting decades of experience in retail (Neil's father) and utilities (Bimal's).

In his head Neil ran through the pitching guidelines he had refined during his eight months with HappyFamilies. Sit, don't stand. Keep your hands together so they don't shake, or under the table and out of sight. Address the investor only, never speak to your colleagues, which would imply that you need back-up, and so are either weak or lying.

Look at him and we can keep it going.

After Bimal handed over, Neil raced through the requisite jargon (digital disruption, value chains), the plucked-from-thin-air projections (conversion rates, average spends), before framing the main proposal:

'We're a small company right now. We know that. You know that. But we are confident that we will soon be an extremely profitable company. And you – at this exciting pre-revenue stage, you can acquire thirty per cent of our company for less than a million pounds.'

Neil tried to convey urgency without desperation. Happy-Families was seeking only the right kind of investor; they wanted Farid as much for his experience as for his money, though in fact they had no idea where Farid's experience lay and preferred not to. When Neil finished, after a sod's-law struggle to power up her laptop, Jess displayed a dummy version of their homepage and their hypothetical products, the families emblazoned on them immortally healthy and beautiful.

Ecstatic young mothers and their pukeless infants. A beaming middle-aged father with his teenaged daughter.

Farid sipped his coffee and regarded the table top. He wrote something down on a very small notepad, afterwards appearing to cross the jotting out. He gazed out of the window. For an infinite minute there was silence, except for the lawnmower buzz of traffic on the Edgware Road.

Bimal was about to speak but Neil cast out an arm to stop him. Submission was part of the exchange, he knew. You had to let the customer inconvenience or insult you if they felt like it. That much he had learned during his involuntary years in the shop.

In the pause Neil noticed a trio of family photos on an otherwise empty bookshelf. Wife, he presumed, though perhaps he shouldn't; a younger and (surprisingly) fatter Farid crowded with children, two pretty girls and a younger boy; a pair of impeccably kempt toddlers who might be grandchildren.

Farid looked up. 'Don't sell me your company,' he said. 'Not one customer is buying your company, Happy whatever it is. Sell me your products. Why should I buy these trinkets?'

The accent seemed not to belong in nature, Arabic with a trace of Levantine French, coarsened by what sounded like a Slavic rasp. Beneath the paunch and his distraction Farid gave out the occasional hint of what must have made him rich in the first place, a fecund compound of rashness and caution, enthusiasm and cynicism. You glimpsed it for a second before the mask came down again.

Sell the customer what he wants to buy. Neil harvested saliva from his cheeks to lubricate his tongue. He swallowed. 'We are selling,' he gambled, 'new ways to tell your family that you love them. And to tell yourself that you love them. Everybody wants to think that about themselves, don't they? That they love their family as much as they can.'

Farid looked away.

Bimal handled the other questions, of which there were few. Farid smiled thinly, rose and walked out, not saying goodbye or shaking hands. The kitchen door swung shut behind him. Strahan ushered the three of them into the lift.

'He gets it,' Jess said as the coffin descended.

'Don't think so, to be honest,' Neil said. 'He didn't give us much.'

'That's it,' Bimal said. 'Guys, I'm sorry.'

They were melancholically drinking cheap wine in a chain bar on Oxford Street, the Something & Something, when Bimal took the call. It wasn't Farid, it was Strahan. His first words, Bimal told them afterwards, mimicking the pukka drawl, were, 'I'll need your bank details.'

Jess was at the bar, blowing some of Farid's investment on champagne, before Bimal could recount the rest. 'I'll need your bank details!' Bimal said by way of a toast.

'HappyFamilies!' Neil said.

'To HappyFamilies!' Jess repeated.

That night, when Bimal left, she taught him how to drink flaming sambucas, the expert way, a procedure she had learned in Prague, apparently, which involved two glasses, a lighter, a napkin and a straw. Other people in the bar watched them, men especially, covetous attention that Neil, to his surprise, found he enjoyed. They were shimmering that evening, radiating luck and strength, like the aura he and Adam had projected during the karaoke in San Diego. Neil inhaled the liquoricey gas and laughed his grimacing laugh.

On the pavement outside Jess fell behind, as if considering, then strode wordlessly towards him, inclined her face and, finally, kissed his mouth. He was momentarily thrown by her approach, that determined, déjà-vu stride, so that his lips took a few seconds to respond to hers.

It's happening, Neil thought as Jess opened the door to her flat. My real life is happening.

He was catching up with Adam. He called Adam in the morning.

SOMEWHERE outside, in the garden of the basement flat or in the street, foxes were mating or killing each other in a coloratura frenzy. Adam opened his eyes and rolled onto his back; a strand of Claire's hair adhered to his lips. She had slept through the yowling. Clean conscience, that was what people said, wasn't it?

The bedside clock said six forty-four. He caressed her shoulder, her upper arm. She might be awake, Adam told himself, or almost. From her arm to her hip and then her thigh, one finger tracing an expanding arc that soon took in a buttock. She straightened her legs. He reached across her torso and gently squeezed both breasts in his palm, an encompassment that she had once told him she enjoyed. In Adam's mental diagram of his wife this consoling micro-fetish was linked, via a dotted line, to the timing and violence of her parents' divorce.

They were awake now, anyway. His penis grazed her thigh – accidentally, the first time. Claire curled up and pulled the coverlet over her.

The fox sounds were disconcertingly human, long hyper-ventilating shrieks, like a passer-by stumbling upon a corpse.

Six fifty-two.

Adam got out of bed and slouched to the bathroom. He met himself in the mirror and breathed in. His was a nice little gut, nothing vulgar or conspicuous when clothed, but flabby enough, on exposure, to undercut his once-automatic confidence in his metabolism and physique, a faith as blithe as his ingrained assumption that he would one day inherit the Earth. The hairs encamped on his chest had dispatched reconnaissance agents to his shoulders. He was twenty-eight.

Shit shower shave aftershave deodorant teeth blast of hairdryer that woke Claire up.

Eleven minutes past seven. Adam went into the kitchen. There was a mouse in there somewhere; he had heard its scuttle, the eccentric rhythm of something alive. He should tell the landlady. He listened to the answerphone message while the kettle boiled – an invitation from Chaz, boozing with him and Archie and two or three others, always strength in numbers these days, body count replacing intimacy, a group absconsion from adulthood. Together they had passed some unmarked inflection point, Adam sensed, at which longevity began to diminish closeness rather than enhance it. They were evanescing, his student cronies, without ill-will or grudges, as old friends evidently could when there was nothing left to say.

Claire came into the kitchen in her towelling dressing gown.

'Anything special today?'

'Lessons Learned at three, God knows how long this one'll go on for. You?'

'Catalogue day.'

'There's a mouse in here somewhere.'

'Risotto for dinner?'

'I'm out tonight, remember.'

'Where are you meeting him again?'

'That new place by the river, you know, with the bowling.'

Not a word about the penis. Perhaps she hadn't noticed; or possibly, for her, all that male insistence had long since become unremarkable, a familiarity Adam preferred not to contemplate. He could make out a breast inside the towelling, its convex perfection.

His coffee, her tea. Two pieces of toast. Just the one penis: a necessary quota, obviously, but also a chasm and, in a way, a sadness, that she would never get it, the urgency and then the shame.

'Did you take out the recycling?'

Seven thirty-seven. She sipped.

Adam had observed this social attrition in older men, men of his father's generation, how they wound up glumly fraternising at their wives' engagements, as if the chromosomal match with other husbands were a sufficient bond. He knew his recent, second-hand male acquaintances as single traits, like supporting characters in a bad film: James, Libby's boyfriend, always toting his dry cleaning; Paul, comes with Cherry, asks for his steak to be 'cremated'. Poppy from the gallery and John the effete cinéaste.

'Did you finish the mortgage form?'

'Tomorrow night,' he said.

'You prom—'

'I know, I'll do it. I said I'll do it.'

Neil was the exception in this cast of has-beens and monochrome newcomers. Neil gave more and demanded more, and Adam owed him more.

He swept the crumbs into his palm and brushed them into the sink. The rubbish truck was in the street, someone was shouting.

'What is it this time?'

'What?'

'Your Lessons.'

'Knife crime. The spike in the summer, you remember, that silly moral panic, lasted a fortnight.'

They would miss that evening's chronicle of the day's granular irks and half-imagined insults – his from the jittery open floors of the department, hers at the subterranean print gallery just off Piccadilly, the coveted art job that had turned out to involve more hard-selling than Claire had reckoned on, and many more hours standing in a basement showroom, rocking on her heels and watching dust motes spiral in the half-light from the pavement-level windows. The Dinky duet: a reciprocal compassion, like oral sex but more frequent.

D-I-N-K-Y: Dual Income, No Kids Yet. Even now, though, Adam didn't share and show her everything. During their honeymoon, on their bed in the cabana, he had asked, 'Is there anything I could do, or, you know, that I might have done in the past, that would make you not love me?'

Claire said, 'Of course there is, don't be silly. What are you trying to tell me?'

'Nothing,' Adam had backtracked. Even murderers told in the end, he had reflected – on their deathbeds, sometimes earlier, you read about them showing up at police stations, a decade on, turning themselves in. The next day, in the morning, the man – the father – could have given him away, easily, and that would have been the end of them, him and Neil, right there at the campsite.

We thought they were such nice boys.

Seven forty-three. The leaves on the tree outside their front window were still thick and green. It was the tallest tree in the street, its trunk reaching to the eaves of the subdivided house, the shade cast into their kitchen. Adam had imagined its strong branches saving him as he leaped from the window to escape a fire or when cornered by a burglar. He had dreamed of a burglar climbing up it, too, his face obscured by the foliage. Someone was screaming, not Adam, someone else, a woman. A woman or a girl.

'What about the life insurance?'

He had dreamed that dream three or four times, here in the rented flat in Shepherd's Bush, with their spider plant, and the yucca plant, and the ugly, square dining table that they had bought in an auction house instead of one from Ikea, and the sofa that was from Ikea, Harriet's sofa, sometimes, and, in the gaps between his bedsits, Neil's. The Greeks ought to have a complex for this syndrome, Adam thought – the impulse not to usurp his parents, or to fuck them, but to *be* them. The headlong fast-forward to the age of dinner parties and being someone, practised little bickerings and wordless attunement, his too-real too-fast life.

He put his plate in the dishwasher. He put his book in his bag. He hung his security tag around his neck, a pre-emptive adornment that he had regarded as defeatedly gauche when he first observed it on his departmental colleagues, but had fairly soon adopted.

'Love you,' Claire called from the sink, not turning round.

At ten to eight Adam trotted down the stairs, past two other Dinky abodes, three piles of unclaimed post. The front door boasted geometric, stained-glass panels, relics of an Edwardian household wholeness. He stepped out onto the begrimed pavement.

FARID, Bimal, Jess: later they came to be bound up together in Neil's internal accounting, memory shaping one of its false contiguities for his convenience. In fact he had known Bimal for ever, in the ordinary way of knowing, and in the end he concluded that he never knew Farid, not really. Of the three he was only close to Jess, and yet, looked at in a practical way, she left the shallowest indentation on his life, her mark on him swiftly filling out and disappearing, like a fingerprint on rubber.

For all Bimal's pursuit of Neil, the two of them hadn't been especially tight at school. Both had been marooned in the unsatisfactory netherworld between the tough, cool kids and the bullyable pariahs, an intermediate caste whose members ought to have formed mutual-defence alliances, but didn't. Bimal's family lived a couple of streets from Neil's in a near-identical semi; as a child, whenever Neil ran into Bimal's father, he was invariably wearing a suit, because of which Neil had assumed he must be an accountant or a doctor. He learned only as an adult that the man had worked for the gas board for thirty years. Neil's default image of Bimal was glimpsed from behind his own mother's back, when they had both been twelve, or thereabouts: Bimal standing on the doorstep, smiling goofily as he tried to sell some tomato plants he had grown in his father's greenhouse, his father standing in the driveway in his suit. His mother had bought one of the plants, Neil remembered, and kept it on the kitchen windowsill. Bimal had grown up tall and plausible, and wore contact lenses instead of his thick-rimmed spectacles, though he retained his throwback bowl haircut as if it were a mascot.

It was less affection that had kept them in touch than some half-acknowledged intuition that they might prove useful to each other one day – as now, at HappyFamilies, they were. The idea had come to him, Bimal confided, while he was working at a computer-software firm. A colleague had returned from a long weekend in St Petersburg with a bespoke set of *matrioshka* dolls, each figurine hand-painted with the image of one of his own relatives. The likenesses were creditable, and the dolls had been absurdly cheap, knocked up overnight, the colleague said, by an artist he met in a street market. People would pay proper money for these, Bimal had reflected. He had begun to think of other ways in which punters might be helped to celebrate themselves, to feel immortal and resplendent, which was how everybody wanted to feel these days. Tea towels silk-screened with family photos, snow-shakers that used the photos as a backdrop, classic film posters – *Vertigo*, *The Italian Job* – with a loved-one's visage substituted for Jimmy Stewart's or Michael Caine's.

After a long courtship Neil was persuaded by the World Wide Web. In Bimal's revised business plan, the customers would browse the products online, order online, upload their photos online, pay online. Virtually no overheads. No gravity: magic.

'That's less than I'm earning now,' Neil told Bimal when they discussed terms. 'And that's saying something.'

'Plus your four per cent,' Bimal said. Bimal wanted him, Neil suspected, as much to redeem his own teenage loneliness as for his putative sales acumen.

'Seven.'

'Five and a half.'

'Six.'

'Done.'

Neil's business card said Marketing Director, but his most valuable skill lay in what quickly became their main preoccupation. Angel investors, small-time venture capitalists, the directors of greeting-card and novelty firms: Neil proved to be good at soliciting money. Where Bimal was rambly, over-enthusiastic, Neil was more focused (*Don't waste the customer's time*), less sentimental. He was learning to read the rich, their vanities and contradictions; how they tended to resist that label, referring chippily to other, slightly wealthier people whom they instead placed in that bracket, yet at the same time seemed dimly baffled that you were not already rich yourself. Six per cent of HappyFamilies was Neil's forward-dated ticket out of subterranean bedsits; his chance to one day do something for his nephew – a tutor, maybe the odd holiday – since, heaven knew, the boy's father never would.

He met Jess when she and her boss pitched for a contract to design their logo. At first sight he would have guessed New York rather than Hull. She was working for one of the voodoo marketing agencies that were infesting London, developing their minutely nuanced offerings in a warp-speed, boom-time corporate evolution – 'brand' and 'image' combined with 'management', 'strategist' and 'consultancy' in increasingly exotic combinations. She had interestingly short hair, a fancy, clingy suit, a dirty laugh and a twenty-a-day smoking habit.

When their eyes locked during that meeting Neil thought the ocular come-on was a negotiating technique. You'll have to try harder than that, he thought. In his self-image he remained the pasty and narrow-shouldered also-ran of his adolescence, his perception fixed at the harshest moment, like a clock stopped during an earthquake, the moles on his cheek and neck still the visual magnets they had been in the bathroom in Harrow. His hair had begun to recede at the temples, giving him (he thought) an unwholesome widow's peak, like something out of *The Munsters*. By his own reckoning he was still a proposition that no grown woman was likely to prefer to, say, Adam.

On the pavement afterwards Jess held onto him for longer than their handshake required.

'You'll hear from us.'

'Will I?' She laughed aloud at the pregnancy of their farewell, nervous and brassy at the same time. He like the unapologetic, male way she smoked, and, later, the taste of smoke in her mouth.

'Fuck it, let's hire her,' Bimal said. 'We need a designer anyway.' Bimal frequently wanted to hire people, and almost as frequently to fire them, which for a time resulted in a gruesome attrition rate.

'I'm not sure,' Neil said. 'Not sure we can afford her.'

Don't shit on your own doorstep.

Bimal insisted, and Jess – on the lookout, like half of London, for her jackpot move, her dotcom apotheosis – accepted. She moved into their ramshackle single room above a shop in Camden, where there were more phone lines than employees, and more employees (six, including her) than desks. She and Neil sat opposite one another, separated by a metre and a half of table top and two fat, humming computers, emailing each other in suggestive exchanges that he found deliriously flattering, and which were much less covert than they imagined.

'MORE than four thousand,' Adam said, three hours after he closed the stained-glass front door in Shepherd's Bush. 'Probably. No, definitely.'

'How many more?'

'Hard to say. Depends on the Youth Justice Boards. I suppose you could say "at least four thousand".'

'Okay, "at least". Christ.'

The spin doctor made the change on screen and printed out the speech again. He sighed and mumbled inaudibly as he headed for the photocopier, honing the offhand charmlessness that was evidently considered essential in his trade.

He returned with three copies of the speech in the sacrosanct double-spaced, single-sided, non-stapled format.

'Chuck that one away,' Adam said.

'I have,' the spin doctor said. 'I will.' This man was only a couple of years older than Adam, but he spoke to the minister every day, the Home Secretary every week.

'Don't mix them up.'

'Okay. Christ.'

'Tea, coffee?' Colin asked. He was making the rounds in his office slippers, two empty mugs castaneting between his fingers, both of them his. Colin drew the line at washing up: the previous week he had fixed a hand-scrawled sign above the cluttered sink that said *What did your last slave die of?* 'Adam, anything?'

'No thanks. I'll page you with anything else,' he said to the spin doctor. 'Page and line number, all right?'

Version control was an infamous nightmare. Adam had heard horror stories of career-ending oversights in which officials sent their minister to a podium with the wrong iteration of a speech: mangled statistics, unmeetable promises that ought to have been excised.

'Four o'clock kick-off,' the spin doctor said. 'Some further education place in Bermondsey. Principal is onto me about her capital budget!'

He gave a mean little chuckle. You could already see in his mottled cheeks and tinted nose that he drank too much.

A-S-B-O: Anti-Social Behaviour Order. Or rather, son of ASBO, that was the crime directorate's current focus, and therefore Adam's. Quicker and harsher sentencing for the degenerates, community punishment for entry-level villains, plus some extra cash for after-school clubs and mentoring schemes: the standard carrot and stick one-two. These days wayward kids were the government's main enemy, Rat Boy, Blip Boy and Spider Boy the new, pre-pubescent Most Wanted.

They were fourteen and fifteen, these kids. Thirteen, some of them. Returning to his desk Adam remembered how, when he was fifteen, he had drunk two-thirds of a bottle of cider in the cadets' hut and thrown up outside the fives courts. One of the housemasters was investigating the mess, interviewing the boys one-on-one in his study, promises of immunity for informers, the works. Half-resolved to confess, Adam had phoned home for his father's endorsement.

'Little white lie,' Jeremy said.

'But—'

'Just this once.' That had been his introduction to the prime genteel commandment: *First, get yourself off.*

When Harriet was fifteen their mother had found, in the pocket of her coat, a note she had written about a boy (not *to* the boy, even, but *about* him), and had kept her in for half the Christmas holidays, enlisting Adam to disturb her weepy internal exile for meal deliveries and health checks.

Fifteen: sometimes, in the past few years, that number, that age, had seemed to Adam to be stalking him.

At twenty to one he went out to his preferred Italian deli in the narrow lane opposite the crenellated ministry. Standing in front of the glass display, watching the disembodied hands make his lunch, Adam thought they were short-changing him on chicken. He ground his jaw in disapproval; one of his fingers twitched towards the glass. The sandwich-maker (Indian or Pakistani, he guessed, tired-looking, striped apron) glanced up with an expression of abhorred pity. Adam turned sharply away from the man's eyes and the sandwich and towards the streaked parquet beneath his feet.

Three years in the Civil Service, eighteen months in the Home Office, two or three of these cherished sandwiches a week. Adam ought to be grateful to Jim, he supposed: Jim the executive producer, with his balding crew cut and mockney accent, the man who had inadvertently landed him in Whitehall. Three and a half years before, Jim had sent his secretary to extract Adam from the open-plan grid and deliver him to the corner office. He had offered Adam a pursed, funereal smile, like the smile of the examiner who failed him at his first driving test, virtually Adam's only other substantial failure until this one. When Jim looked out of the window as he began to speak, towards the sky-scrapers across the river in the City, Adam immediately understood.

'First of all I want to thank you for everything you've done for us.' *Us* and *you*. There was an ornamental chilli plant on the windowsill.

Jim was mercifully brief, but throughout the few, tor-menting minutes Adam worried that he might be sick. Everyone outside the goldfish-bowl cubicle would soon know why he was sitting there, he had realised. Or perhaps everyone knew already, Will already knew, and he was the last to find out. He half-turned his head to see if Will was watching.

'I would keep you if I could, you know that, we could keep everyone ... '

Adam's mind flew back to Tenerife, to Gavin the chimeri-cal bar manager – fucking Gavin! – and slid from him to the girl on the beach.

That poor girl. And the two of them. Amazing, the things you caught yourself thinking about, and when. That was the moment it struck: afterwards he thought he could trace his fifteen-o-phobia to Jim's cubicle, one crisis summoning and eliding with another.

No, Adam told Jim, there was nothing he wanted to ask. He heard himself say 'Thank you' as he rose to leave, like a condemned aristocrat tipping his executioner, the indiscriminate euphoria of something happening.

The following evening, in Soho, he had indeed been sick, Neil holding his hair back from his face as if they were teenage girls. Adam pinballed between the tables on his dash to the toilets, spilling several drinks. Two of the spillees stood up – rugby types, play-acting toughs – and Neil interposed himself, his hands raised in his *Don't shoot!* pose. 'Just leave it, mate,' Neil said to the larger man, his voice descending the social register to imply an acquaintance with violence.

Sitting on the kerb, toeing the broken glass in the gutter, Adam had tried to explain how he felt. How, for him, life was like one of those childhood line-ups in which everyone stands against a wall to be measured and ranked, except for Adam the comparison wasn't biannual but always, and the comparators were everyone, the rankings vertical as well as horizontal, featuring all the people he had ever been to school or worked with, and his father and his grandfathers and his great-grandfather the judge, all of them eternally jostling in the eyes of some super-arbiter, his stature suddenly the lowliest.

'I know,' Neil said. 'I understand. But it isn't like that, Ants. It's just a job. You'll get another job, I know you will. It's not, you know, all of you. It's not a vital organ or something. It's what you do for money, that's all.'

His other, evanescing friends were useless, as if there were an asterisk in their contracts that excused them at unhilarious moments. And this was the least of it, Adam knew, the divorces and nervous breakdowns and dying parents and heartbreaking children were still to come. For the first time he could remember, his father let him down. 'Every life needs a twist and a turn,' Jeremy said on the phone, mysteriously affecting a Scottish brogue, as if he were quoting a song from some old Highlands musical that didn't actually exist. Adam had expected more from him: sharper anger, sturdier protection. Claire kept her distance, treating him like a ticking bomb in an action movie, wary of pulling the wrong wire.

That night he had almost told Neil the truth about California. Adam was incontinently grateful for his sympathy, and the secret felt like a burden too many. Neil seemed so close, there was nothing they couldn't share, Adam would tell him and be forgiven in an instant, and then that episode would open up to them. He managed not to, cowardice or tact that afterwards he half-regretted.

'SERIOUSLY, Neil, I don't know what you see in him. I mean, what did you do in America, rob a bank together?'

Neil flinched. They were in her bed, two months after they met Farid, Sunday morning fornication. Jess was exploiting the post-coital amnesty, the very temporary truce.

'The way he took the mike and walked around like that. All that "my wife" crap. And making his father his best man . . . What a tosser.'

Jess had lived in London for five or six years, more than enough to count as a local, but Yorkshire hung on in her vowels, an accent that to Neil's southern ear made her jokes sound funnier and her judgements harsher. She was immune to Adam's charm, their personalities somehow failing to intersect. On the three occasions they had met, the latest being Adam's wedding, she had laughed when he wasn't making a joke and missed the punchlines he intended.

'Don't,' Neil said, rearranging his leg so that his thigh was no longer touching hers. 'It's complicated.'

'You know what, Philly old boy, in my experience, when people say things are complicated, they never are.'

He knew Jess was onto something. For all Adam's seigneurial confidence he thought in straight, obedient lines, was content to be defined by the government's consoling acronyms. The wedding had obeyed its type: the adequately pretty English church, the vicar keeping the hypocritical God content to a harmless minimum, the lawn parade of tepid canapés and novelty cummerbunds, the inevitable marquee. But that wasn't him ... That was all irrelevant ... The money Adam had lent him for his first deposit, the nights Neil had spent on their sofa, when he was between bedsits and couldn't face his father's – he and Adam staying up, giggling like imbeciles, until Claire came to shush them, hands on hips, some primitive affinity of gender trumping his friend's allegiance to her. A week, then five days ... Those favours weren't what mattered either, they were the currency and not the feeling. The way he had felt, six years earlier, when they met on the concourse at Paddington Station, beamed back together in London, or felt when, a week before that, he took Adam's first phone call:

It's me, Neil. It's Adam.

Adam? Hi – Adam! I've got it, Dad, I said I've got it ...

'What is it, a class thing?' Jess went on. 'Sort of, you know, a yeoman and master type arrangement? Does he get to fuck me, too?'

'Knock it off, Jess,' Neil said, turning away from her. 'Me and him – you don't understand.'

'Don't sulk,' she said. 'I was just ... I'm sorry.'

After Adam and the wedding came the ritual introductions to their families. The first, Jess's mother, was unplanned. Neil asked where she was going, whether he could go too, and she said, 'Believe me, you don't want to.'

'Don't I?'

'Okay,' she said. 'Your funeral.'

They were halfway to Hull before he clocked it. Contrary to all the self-parodic jokes she had made, her childhood home, a shoebox miner's terrace, had inside plumbing and no coal scuttle. Her mother was immobilised by arthritis and older-looking than Brian, despite being five years younger.

'Very pleased to meet you,' he said as they stepped out of their taxi.

'Likewise,' she said. 'I'm sure.' She carried a cane that she mostly forgot to use. 'You could have warned me, Jessica. Nowt in the house.'

The front room was a 3D album of Jess photos, though none of them was very recent. Jess in school uniform. A teenaged Jess glammed up for a night on the tiles. Jess wearing a mortar board at an ironic angle.

'She's a one,' her mother said to Neil, when Jess went to smoke on the front step. 'Give you much trouble?'

'No. You?'

'Oh yes,' Jess's mother said, rasping out a laugh.

She poured more tea and sat in silence with him until her daughter came back. Jess showed him no mercy, not interpreting or elaborating on the local names and legendary incidents that populated the intermittent conversation.

Harrow was the final milestone, the last museum of their

prior lives. They drove out in Jess's car at the end of the summer.

'Are you Neil's wife?' Sam asked, disobediently opening the front door alone.

'No,' Jess said, keeping her distance. She offered the boy her hand but he ran back into the house.

Brian shuffled up. 'Come inside,' he said, turning away.

Tea and a plate of digestives were pre-arrayed on top of the television. Sam mounted the armchair; as Brian came in he was preparing to hurl himself onto Neil's back.

'Careful,' Brian said, pointlessly.

Sam jumped. He slid down Neil's spine, catching his hand in his uncle's as he landed. Neil looked down at the spiral of hair on top of the child's head, only recently thickened up from babyish thatch. The trace of a birthmark patterned his temple.

Sam wiped his nose with his finger, though it wasn't running. 'Are you *his* wife?' he asked Jess, indicating Brian with his eyes.

'No!' she exclaimed, too loudly for the room.

'Who are you?'

'Tea?' Brian asked.

'My friend, Sammy,' Neil said. 'She's my friend.'

'Okay,' Sam said. 'Now we're playing hide and seek.'

'Are we?' said Jess.

'Milk and sugar?'

'I'll hide, and you count. Ready?' Sam set off for the door. Brian pressed himself against the wall to let the boy pass.

'One,' said Neil.

'Not yet!' Sam shouted, laughing and looking back from the threshold. 'Close your eyes!'

'Just be careful,' Brian repeated, resting a forearm on the

96

corner of the mantelpiece. There was a shy tenderness buried somewhere in his father's voice, Neil thought. Perhaps Sam picked it up more clearly than he was able to, as young ears could reputedly detect certain frequencies that adults miss.

'Two,' Neil said.

Jess ran her hands down her thighs, straightening her skirt. Sam's footsteps skipped across the hallway and echoed up the stairs, the pat of feet alternating with the soft slap of hands and pad of knees, the not-yet-outgrown technique of infancy. Hurry with a hint of dance.

'Careful,' Brian murmured, much too softly for Sam to hear. 'Left him here yesterday. She dumped him on Dan, apparently, he's got something on in Poole, hotel site, he said.'

'This is Jess.'

'Gave me a toy giraffe and a pair of pyjamas and left him. What was I supposed to do?'

Brian had received a health warning from his doctor a few weeks before. He looked slightly awry in scale – all the right and recognisable features, but somehow smaller than life-size. His flannel trousers ballooned clownishly around his thighs.

'Ten!' Sam shouted down.

'Jessica,' Brian said. 'Yes.'

'You go,' Jess said.

'Com ... ing,' Neil sing-songed, creaking up the stairs.

He saw Sam's feet at the bottom of the armchair in Dan's old room, the point of an elbow jutting out horizontally at five-year-old height, the thin arm rotating as Sam picked his nose. Neil mimed an investigation of Dan's wardrobe, empty besides some discarded cowboy-check shirts, and, at the bottom, a pile of hoarded school exercise books defaced with obscene sketches. The giraffe lay on the bed.

'Saa . . . aam, where are you?'

'I'm here,' Sam said, unable to wait any longer. 'Here.'

Neil lifted Sam in the air and turned him upside down, squeezing him against his chest with one hand and tickling him with the other. You didn't have to act with a five-year-old: that was one of Sam's attractions. The mask could come off.

'Stop,' Sam laughed, not meaning it, sighing when the laughter ran out.

'Sam,' Brian called from the foot of the stairs. 'Sam, come down. I'm making you a sandwich.'

Jess was sitting in the kitchen. She had a cup and saucer in front of her, an unbitten digestive biscuit (no chocolate) wedged between them. Brian was at the counter, his back turned, spreading. A tableau came back to Neil: his father frying chips, the only thing he had ever cooked for his sons, and only ever when his wife was away, or hospitalised, or otherwise prevented from dispensing the regulation beans on toast, fish finger sandwiches or pasta with supermarket sauce. The potatoes were always cut string-thin, Neil remembered, and he and Dan would sit at the table, watching, as if their preparation were an alchemic rite.

'There you go,' Brian said, laying the sandwich on the table.

'Yuck,' Sam said.

Later Neil and Jess went up together to check on him. He was splayed on Dan's bed, one arm dangling over the side, another above his head, that hand clutching the giraffe, legs akimbo, as if he had struggled to the end, like those flailing corpses exhumed from the lava of Pompeii.

'They're all cute at that age, aren't they, though?' Jess whispered. 'They peak at three or four, then they turn into fuck-ups and mediocrities like the rest of us.'

'Shhh,' Neil said. 'Don't.'

She invited or instructed him to move in with her while they were downstairs watching television. Brian was washing up; the urn supervised from the mantel. Neil could activate the break clause in his lease later that autumn, she said. Pointless to waste more money on a separate pad.

'Jess,' he said. 'You know I've never . . . I'm not sure I can.'

'Don't worry,' she told him, 'I won't marry you.'

His life was happening.

ADAM was only twenty-five when Jim let him go. His tank was still full. He spanked the Civil Service exams, struck the requisite balance between showmanship and modesty at the final-round assessment centre. When he first arrived in Whitehall the atmosphere had been eerie, millenarian. The old ministers were waiting sullenly to be evicted, the bureaucrats openly anticipating new masters; grimy mesh bomb curtains, relics of the Cold War, still shrouded many of the windows. After the general election the organism of state exhaled, and Adam quickly found he liked the private lingo, the security passes and vetting, the sense of being among an elect. He and some of the other fast-streamers spent long, contented evenings in Whitehall pubs, plotting their routes to Grade 7, a rank that would confer higher pay immediately and, they knew, adumbrate future glory, Adam never seriously doubting that he would soon achieve it.

'If I may?' he interjected at five minutes past three, shortly after the meeting convened. 'Might we consider reviving the amnesty?'

Nick said, 'I'm sure we'll get—'

'The amnesty scheme the previous government operated? The evidence now suggests it was quite effective in reducing knife crime where we rolled it out.'

'Thank you – it's Adam, isn't it? Thanks.'

Five past three: a slight violation of protocol, Adam knew. You were supposed to wait until the senior grades had their say, but he had already learned that particular lesson. Ditch the well-bred reticence in meetings. Sequester your credit from predators. Simulate teamwork but make sure you get noticed. These were the principles that his apprenticeship in television had inculcated, tenets of employment that had been as unannounced as most of adulthood's rules and burdens (taxes, commuting, the many varieties of insurance that, in their household, Adam had somehow become responsible for procuring).

There was a pause before someone from policing, already a 7, said, 'Stop and search ... '

'Absolutely,' Nick said, beginning to scribble on his notepad. Two of the other men were smoking, tapping their cigarettes into shallow metallic ashtrays that appeared to have been lifted from McDonald's.

'Under the new guidelines ... ' the 7 continued.

Actually Adam could use the extra money, the 7 money. The parental subsidies had dried up. 'Short-term cashflow issues,' his father had explained. He and Claire were still okay, financially, they were fine for the time being. He must remember that mortgage form.

They were three-quarters of an hour into stop-and-search, it was almost four o'clock, when the 7 said, ' ... the girl-friends too. The girls. I mean, the young women. They often carry weapons for the men. It's easier for them at clubs and what have you – no pat downs, sometimes they let them bypass the metal detectors. Sixteen, seventeen. Fifteen, some of them.'

Fifteen again. Bad luck. *You're such bullies.*

Adam remembered his father teasingly saying to him (he must have been eight or nine), 'Lollipop, whatever you do, try not to think about pink rabbits digging for treasure at midnight.' Of course the stricture only made the thinking inevitable. His right hand put down his pen and moved of its own accord to scratch his left forearm.

After stop-and-search Nick delineated the 'systemic issues' that had arisen in their external response to the summertime spike in knifings. Nick's office personality consisted in his blue postman shirts and his martyrly hours, a regime he observed despite the moral claims made by the children in the photos pinned to the partition behind his work station. Or presumably they made such claims. Once, when Adam visited his desk late in the evening, he found Nick playing Space Invaders on his computer.

'... roll out best practice,' Nick was saying.

A quarter past four. People were fidgeting and twitching, turning over pages on their notepads and listlessly flicking them back again. They discussed half a dozen policies that no one thought for a microsecond would be implemented. Towards the end someone else, a woman who outranked Adam, revived his knife amnesty idea.

'One to consider,' Nick said, and wrote something down. 'Thanks, Pamela.'

But ... Adam opened his mouth but restrained himself. Two weeks before he had been sent up to Manchester for an event at a community centre. He had checked the backdrop for images or slogans that might be embarrassing if cropped by some unscrupulous photo editor; he was helping to marshal the local worthies, party ringers and bored journalists in the audience. The minister was standing nearby, and Adam, proud of his tradecraft and of his vocation, wished him a collegial 'Good afternoon'. The minister said, 'Good to see you', a formula in which Adam had strained to hear a personal recognition, rather than a bet-hedging, not-sure-if-I'm-supposed-to-know-you fob-off.

It was past five when they left the meeting room, as smoked-through as after a night in a pub. Adam returned to his desk and opened the document he was writing on youth justice. He could sense his less ambitious colleagues eyeing each other across the open-plan expanse, the clockwatchers' stand-off, bags and umbrellas poised for the exit.

'Tea, coffee?' Colin said. 'Last orders. Adam?'

TWO hours later, six weeks after Neil took Jess to Harrow, he and Adam were leaning against the booth at the back of their allotted lane, while the people before them finished their game. They were talking about the serial-killing doctor, talking fast, since there was always more to say than their time together allowed, even when it had just begun.

'Expect he'll top himself,' Neil said.

'You think so?'

'Wouldn't you?' Neil raised his voice against the techno, the fusillades of the shoot-em-ups, the gunned engine of the life-sized sports car. 'I said, if you'd done that – all those people, I mean even if you hadn't been caught – wouldn't you top yourself?'

'I suppose so. Difficult to imagine, isn't it?'

To both of them this subterranean playground felt dimly illicit. Not just the adults wielding children's toys, pint glasses in one hand, air-hockey pucks in the other. The whole place was somehow unBritish in its high-spec levity.

'Haven't you ever thought about it? Suicide, I mean.'

Adam laughed above the music. 'No. Never. It would be, you know, giving up. It would mean you'd lost. Why, have you?'

'Once or twice, maybe,' Neil said. 'Yeah. When I was younger, not seriously or anything. In the end it always seemed to me sort of arrogant. Ostentatious, do you know what I mean? I don't think I'm really worth killing.' The mass-murdering doctor made him think of his mother – the nagging fear that someone had somehow been to blame, that someone could have done something differently, a fear that was also, he knew, a kind of disguised hope, an abashed fantasy of redress or resurrection.

'Of course you're worth it,' Adam said.

'I think that might be the nicest thing anyone's ever said to me.'

'But if anyone's going to kill you,' Adam said, 'I think it should be me.'

The group bowling before them – two men in replica football shirts and a younger, better-dressed woman – came out of the booth, laughing. Someone had spilled a drink; Neil wiped the low, screwed-down table with a serviette and laid his mobile phone on top of it. They took off their jackets.

'Shall I?' Adam said.

'Be my guest.'

Adam selected a purple bowling ball, the heaviest in the chute, and unleashed it in a swift picturesque motion that knocked down all the pins. He raised his fists above his head in celebration, the fluorescent lights illuminating his teeth and the whites of his eyes.

'Beginner's luck,' Neil said.

'Do you play this game for money?'

Neil threw from an ungainly, erect posture. His ball dribbled to the end, knocking out a single pin. Adam whooped.

'I'll give you the early rounds,' Neil said. As the contraption righted itself, he asked, 'So the Millennium bug – is it going to be, you know, a meltdown? I think we should wait till afterwards – the launch, I'm talking about – but Bimal wants to go ahead in December.'

'They're working on it,' Adam said.

'But is it real? Is it, you know, dangerous?'

'I could tell you,' Adam said, 'but you know what I'd have to do next.'

'I'm serious, what do they think?'

'I . . . I suppose I don't know.'

'Right. Okay. I just thought . . . Never mind.'

Adam sat in the booth while Neil bowled again. That mobile phone . . . Sometimes, when he went out for the afternoon, with a minister or on a visit, he borrowed a phone from the depository, a weighty black slab with a government serial number and the phone's own telephone number stencilled on the back. This one was sleek and metallic, and Adam was confident Neil wouldn't have to return it in the morning.

There was still a puddle of beer at the table's lip. It occurred to Adam that he could slide the phone into it. Ridiculous!

With his second go Neil knocked over two more pins. His face shone ghoulishly in the overhead lights.

'He's a ballsy fucker,' Neil said. 'Bimal. You wouldn't have thought it. We haven't earned a penny yet and he's talking about floating. Serious Nasdaq cowboy.'

Adam's friend Archie was loaded, properly loaded, or his

family was, a house in Miami and trust funds all round. Adam remembered another boy, from his boarding school, Philip, whose father had owned and then sold a company that manufactured plastic chairs; the sale price, eighteen million pounds, had been disclosed in a business round-up in *The Times*. Two or three days of jokes and everyone had forgotten about it. Inherited money was relatively harmless, Adam had always felt. You might resent it, but only as you might resent your friend's superior height, or his better looks, or some other accidental advantage that he blamelessly held. Self-made wealth, the kind that Neil seemed poised to come into, might be trickier. Your friend's inheritance was merely an injustice; Neil's earned wealth might feel like a defeat.

Adam retrieved his purple ball from midway along the chute, and hurled it fast and dramatically into the gutter a couple of feet short of the pins.

'Listen,' Neil said as they crossed between the lane and the table, 'you should join us. Seriously. After the launch, we'll be hiring – copywriters, business-development people, I'm sure there's something you could do.'

'I've got a job,' Adam said.

Neil had been dutifully enthusiastic when Adam first mentioned the Civil Service, even though he hadn't known what *Fast Stream* meant. He had envisaged Adam and his leonine hair behind the defensive plastic screen of a benefits office. In his heart he was sceptical about these grass-is-greener switches, these poor-me-I'm-bored lurches from law to teaching, or teaching to law, manoeuvres that, as he saw it, only substituted one whim for another.

'I know, and I know you're doing fine where you are, the government. Brilliantly. I'm just saying, think about it. I could speak to Bimal.'

Instead of answering, Adam held up his hands, palms out, as if he were a celebrity at an awards ceremony, or a politician at a rally, false-modestly shushing applause. He considered for a moment and decided not to say what he was thinking.

Neil's phone beeped. He pushed some buttons and frowned. 'Bimal,' he said. 'Workaholic.'

The memory forced its way out. 'It's like what's-his-name predicted,' Adam said, his tone aiming for guilelessness, though he could perfectly well recall the name he had omitted.

'Who?'

'You know, the American guy.'

'What American guy?'

'Eric. That's right.'

Party like it's 1999 boomed out, an anthem that seemed to be playing on a loop across the Western world.

'Eric who?' Neil asked, instantly knowing who his friend was referring to. The promiscuous giggle and the balled fists. He reached for the mole on his neck.

'You know, Neil. Come on. You remember. Eric from California.'

On the stereo Prince announced that the party was over.

'He wasn't from California,' Neil said. 'They were from Colorado. So what's he got to do with anything?'

'You remember, he went on about how computers were going to take over our lives and none of us believed him. Every village in India would have one, he said. We were around the campfire, it was that evening, you know ... You have to.'

'Sorry,' Neil said, 'I don't remember that.'

'You must, it was the same night, before you—'

'No.'

106

Eric had said, *Remember me when it happens* ... It would be too much to say that she insisted, at that moment when she became serious and resolute and the games had ended. But Neil hadn't needed to press or convince her, either. 'Sure,' she had said. 'I want it to be you.' At first, Adam forced him to recall, Neil had thought she meant, or wanted her to mean, *I want it to be you tonight, Neil: I want it to be you and not Adam.* But a few minutes later he realised that her 'it' had meant something else entirely, an event specific to her and nothing to do with him and Adam.

They were out of time, Prince declared.

Neil stood at the top of the bowling lane, his fingers in the furtive niches but the ball suspended by his side. Somehow, in his head, while he had grown older, advancing from the extreme edge of adolescence to the brink of his thirties, she was frozen in her Yosemite incarnation, so that when he thought about the two of them together now, the age gap yawned even more accusingly than it had done at the time. Once or twice, on the television news, he had seen melodramatic stories about teachers running off with pupils, or teenage girls eloping with Mediterranean waiters, and quickly told himself that they bore no resemblance to him. That wasn't him at all.

Two years in San Quentin. Her Charlie Brown T-shirt. The details had been seared into his memory, saved from the routine auto-erase, by the fuss in the morning.

They bowled again. Neil's balls dawdled to the pins, reliably taking out three or four or six. Adam urged his arm to remember its original technique, but the harder he tried, the more immediately he found the gutter. Neil's face looked leprously white in the spotlights.

They fell back on polite enquiries, the basic mnemonic

responsibility of friendship, the minimum talent that it required. Neil asked about Claire's job, Adam's parents, Harriet. He had danced with Harriet at the wedding, as far as possible leaving the actual movement to her, struggling to hold on to her like a boxer on the ropes; the more she had drunk that evening, the more ingenuous she seemed, and Neil remembered something Adam had told him about their childhood – how their father had wanted another boy, and when Harriet was a toddler had insisted she be dressed in a little boy's sailor suit.

'She's okay,' Adam said. 'She's back at home, job didn't work out. Bit weepy, you know. How's your old man?'

'The same. Not opening the shop on Saturdays any more. Asked after you the other day.'

Neil mentioned Sam, and Adam said, 'You've got this different tone in your voice when you talk about him, did you know that?'

'Do I sound the same for Jess?'

'No.'

They discussed their preliminary plans for millennium eve, the river of fire into which the Thames would supposedly be transfigured at midnight, an object of London's revelrous self-deprecation even before the feat was attempted. They were both trying, paddling away from the edges of the whirlpool. They had two goes left when Neil gave in to it.

'What did you bring him up for?'

'Who?'

'Don't, Adam. I feel like, I don't know, I feel like you're trying ... just when I ... I mean, why did you mention him?'

'Take it easy. You're being ridiculous. It's just, I think it's because, I was at this meeting this afternoon – knife crime – they were talking about the girlfriends, for some reason it—'

'What's that got to do with anything?'

'Take it easy, I'm sorry. You just reminded me of him – the Millennium bug and his computers . . .'

'I mean, I haven't thought about her for years, we've never even talked about it . . . It was just a mistake, you know that.'

'Do I?'

'What's that supposed to mean?'

'Nothing. It's just, like you say, we've never . . . I mean, I've never . . . Nothing.'

A man in a baseball cap from the neighbouring lane pinched Adam's bowling ball. A familiar eighties rock song struck up, but somehow, in their heads, the music had been turned down, screened out.

'Christ,' Neil said. 'You make me think . . .'

'What? What do I make you think?'

'Forget it.'

'Go on, say what I make you think.'

'I said, forget it. Fuck's sake, Adam, why do we have to talk about this?'

'Okay. Jesus.'

Neil picked up a ball but didn't bowl. 'That's enough,' he said.

'But you've got another go.'

He dropped the ball into the gutter.

'But you're winning, Philly . . .'

'It's okay,' Neil said. 'You can have this one.'

Neil raised his chin to indicate to the tourists waiting behind the partition that he and Adam were leaving. They crowded into the booth; he retrieved his phone.

Outside the giant Ferris wheel angled across the water,

halfway to its upright terminus, leaning out towards Parliament as if for a crackpot siege. In the other direction, downstream, was the porcupine Dome. London at the end of history: neophile, frivolous, renovated in splotches, like the make-up on a careless old woman.

'Looks like it might fall,' Adam said. 'It can't, can it?'

Neil didn't reply. He turned his eyes towards the wheel but didn't appear to see it. The project's floodlights blazed along the riverbank.

If this friendship were a proposition that crossed Adam's desk, and he were coldly weighing the costs and benefits, he might deem himself irrational for spending so much time on it. No money, no sex; no tangible pay-off of any kind. Friendship was a luxury in any utilitarian calculus, and yet without it, without Neil, his life would be thin. 'Maybe it can fall,' he muttered. 'Unbelievable.'

They shook hands and then, sensing that the formality was absurd and dangerous, managed a one-armed hug, so that they ended up standing alongside one another, facing out across the water.

2003

AFTER the arraignments he would muster his excuses. He tried to be objective, scrupulous, as if the inside of his head were a court, and he were the prosecutor and the defence attorney, as well as the judge and the accused, or the co-accused. He considered but discounted the weaker extenuations, such as their youth (they hadn't been that young) and the drinking (they weren't all that drunk, not that evening). He admitted the quicksand ambiguity of her appearance and of her demeanour: she had seemed alternately aware and oblivious of her body's power, playfulness eliding with flirtation on a slippery adolescent continuum. He acknowledged the hypnotic momentum of the holiday, for most of which the two of them had scarcely noticed women, being too preoccupied with each other, until finally they had turned their energy outwards, looking for a mediator and a prize, and found her. Found Rose.

In the private hearings he conducted, many each day in the first, hallucinatory week – with several more each night, when he was up and jiggling the baby, or in bed, wasting his chance of sleep – he would leave the obvious argument till last. It had been Neil, he would eventually remind himself, it was Neil, and not him, who had taken the girl into the tent and fucked her. It was Neil who had actually done that, even if Adam had wanted and intended to fuck her himself.

Yet somehow that most material fact felt more like a technicality than a true exoneration. Adam was implicated, he knew that, as a man could be had up for murder though someone else wielded the knife. *You wanted it too. You started it*. He would have been implicated even if he hadn't known about her age, because he was there and because of what he said about her. But he *had* known. *I fucking told you*. If there was room for a beneficial doubt before her father corrected him, there hadn't been afterwards. Every time, always, as in some rerun disaster film that you vainly hope might turn out differently, Adam found himself guilty. He deserved the morning-after curse that at the time he barely heeded:

One day you'll have your own. I hope you find out how this feels.

'She's asleep,' Claire would whisper to him during that week. 'She's asleep already, Adam. Put her in the basket and come to bed. Ad, come on.'

When he tried to recall the reasons he hadn't spoken up, either by the campfire or (his second chance) when Neil evicted him from the tent, the only motives Adam could salvage were sordid and inadequate, pique and revenge that made his conduct seem worse.

My little girl. What kind of people are you?

Or, kneeing him in the coccyx as he lay beside her, four in the morning outrage, Claire would say, 'Adam, she's crying. It's your turn. Fuck's sake, she's going to wake him. What is it, Adam?'

'Nothing. It's nothing, Clezz. Give her to me.'

It was the baby's fault, of course. The baby had aggravated Yosemite from an occasional nag to a disorder. Not just the sleeplessness but the fact of the baby. She recast Adam's memory, as if she were a belated witness who brought vital new information, newly terrifying consequences.

'Is she going to be all right?'

'She's fine, she's just hungry. Go to sleep.'

'No, I mean, when she's older. Will she be all right, Clezz?'

'How the fuck should I know?'

They had passed the girl to him in the operating theatre, a foot of squiddy cord still attached, the limbs slathered in the white birth cream that they all come out in, the elastic mouth emitting a cry at once mechanical and undulating, like the rise and fall of an air-raid siren. The body looked much too big, way too enormous, to have been living inside Claire until a few moments before. 'Adam?' Claire said, because she hadn't seen the child yet, besides a blur when they waved her above the screen. 'Is she ...?' Adam glimpsed the gash in her abdomen when he took the bundle from the midwife, saw the layers of Claire's fat and muscle retracted by the harsh clamps. The wound seemed much too grave for anyone to hope seriously to survive, as if a mid-sized cannonball had punched a hole in her.

'How do you do?' Adam said to the bundle, which was wrinkling its nose and grimacing, as if it were about to sneeze. Because what, really, were you supposed to say? *Oh I see, it's you, I get it, of all the genetic possibilities, you're the one. All the love and worry will be for you.* The grey eyes opened, horrified, closing quickly to shrink the world away.

'Adam? How is she? Is she ...?'

113

Claire was woozy from the anaesthetics they were dripping into her spinal cord. They had rushed her under the knife when the child became distressed, all of it happening with the momentum of an action movie so that Adam barely had time for fear. Put on the gown, put on the mask. Hold her hand. 'She's fine,' Adam told her. 'She's wonderful.' He gave the child to his wife to clasp while they laboriously stitched her up. His eyes met hers, the private, romantic, gulping moment that all just-delivered parents share. *Wow* and *I love you* and *Oh fuck*.

Second time round, he knew the script. Two years before, when Harry was born, he hadn't been sure what to do or say, what or how to feel. They had been to the happy-clappy baby classes but nobody could tell you that part. He had gingerly walked the squawking bundle around the ward, humming 'American Pie', 'The Boxer', 'Take it Easy'. Neil had come immediately that afternoon, he remembered, too soon, really, they had still been disoriented. Neil was pleased to be early, Adam had seen, pleased to get there before their families. A nurse mistook him for the father and showed him how to feed Harry with a pipette. Neil got Harry's neonatal kryptonite shit on his coat.

This time Adam's parents arrived first, performing themselves in an oddly chafing way. 'Out through the sun roof,' Jeremy Tayler joked, the inveterate jollity that was beginning to seem a form of evasion. They and Claire's mother cooed all the necessary compliments and made the standard quips – *She's got a good pair of lungs on her! She's got you wrapped round her little finger already!* – there never seeming to be anything personal to say about a baby, a baby being the most particular yet most generic thing on Earth, just as there was never anything but platitudes to offer at funerals.

Neil came just before chucking-out time. He brought extravagant flowers that the Chinese nurse swiftly confiscated; he held Ruby at arm's length from his bespoke suit, as if she might be booby-trapped.

'She won't bite,' Adam said.

'It isn't biting I'm worried about, Ants.' He handed the bundle back. 'The good news is, she looks like Claire.'

'At least, you know, she doesn't look like you.'

'Boys,' said Claire, tubed-up and aching. 'You boys.' She laid the baby on her chest and closed her eyes.

'Wet the baby's head?' Neil suggested.

But Adam had to go home to Harry. He sent the ritual email, specifying the girl's weight and the satisfactory state of the mother's health, as the mysterious formula required, attaching a photo he downloaded from the camera in which Ruby, purple and wrinkled, looked both a day and a hundred years old. He went to bed, and in bed Yosemite had come back to him. He closed his eyes and they were there: not his own daughter or his sewn-up wife but another father and a different child. It was as if he were watching one of those primitive, flip-through cartoons, jumpy images that nevertheless told a clear story. The jokes, the chase, the conquest. The curse.

The jokes. The whole thing began with the swim, Adam saw on the night Ruby was born, with him reaching out to submerge her head in the lake, her father watching from the shore. The feel of her skull seemed to come back to him, thick with hair (one of his fingers briefly catching in it), but cold from the water like a corpse's. He remembered his sharp momentary panic that she had gone under for ever and he had done something terrible. He remembered the dirty words he heard himself say afterwards, the macho challenge he issued to Neil, as if the girl were a hill to race up or a fence to hurdle. *Stop making excuses.* Then the evening and the campfire, and what he hadn't said, and the scratchy night. He shouldn't have touched her in the water.

Worst of all, almost, he recalled how, the next day, he had trivialised the whole thing, preferring not to see the gravity and the shame, which ought to have been plain as daybreak. He saw how the grubby self-preservation instinct had kicked in, the pukka voice that said, Get yourself off, whatever you have done, deny, abscond, deflect, get away with it. After that, later, regret it if you have to. *Little white lie.*

Adam barely slept that night. He couldn't unremember. Rose and Eric stayed with him as he brought Harry to the hospital the next day; they were with him, the day after that, as he drove Claire and the baby home, at the tortoise speed employed only by new fathers, octogenarians and middle-aged drunks pretending to be sober. He took a week's paternity leave (not that many people would miss him), and they tagged along as he escorted Harry on their chilly we-still-love-you outings. At the aquarium, on Ealing Common, it became urgently important that Adam remember precisely what he had said and done. He derived a masochistic, almost narcotic satisfaction from the details he recovered: the play of light around the campfire, the smile on Rose's face as she entered the tent, the hunch of Eric's shoulders the following morning, as if he might make himself small enough to disappear. He found himself polishing and refining these keepsakes, sharpening their outlines and improving their texture, the better to admonish himself with them. He felt sure he could visualise his own gestures, the leer that Eric must have registered at the lake and Rose seen beside the fire, as if he had borrowed their memories. This, he knew,

was always the most coveted perspective – *What did I do?
Why did I? Who was I?* – and the one that was never truly
available.

He could hear her sob as he and Neil walked away, or
thought he could, the sound long and low like an animal's.
Over and over he saw her father turning back to berate him
beside the burned-out campfire. *One day you'll have your own.*

Now he did. His guilt and the fear fed on each other. The
more he dwelled on Rose, the worse his pre-emptive anxiety
for Ruby; the more he feared for Ruby, the fiercer his guilt
over Rose, what she and her father must have been through.
Worst of all was the hybrid guilt for what might ever happen
to his daughter – because of him, or men like him, at least,
which, morally, amounted to the same thing. The monkey-
grip soles of Ruby's pink feet, the frail, ineluctable clasp of
her fingers on his, those grey eyes. The everything of her.

I hope you find out how this feels.

'DO THAT one more time, Sammy, and we're going back
inside.'

Sam re-reached for the gear stick.

'I'm serious, Sam. It's automatic anyway, I told you.'

The boy laughed. He shifted his skin-and-bone buttocks
in the triangle of leather available to him between Neil's
thighs, brushing irrelevantly against his penis.

'Can we take the roof down?'

'It's raining.'

'No, it isn't.'

'It's going to rain.'

'If it rains we'll put it back. Go on.'

Neil smiled. He was an amateur; he was there for the
taking. He pushed the button on the dash and the canvass

retracted into the compartment behind the jump seat, a feat of puppetry that always seemed to him at once flash and already old-fashioned, retro-decadent.

'Wave at Granddad,' Neil said.

Brian was facing out between the net curtains, leaning forward from his armchair, his head balanced on his walking stick and cushioned by his hands, his medicines out of sight on the nest of tables in the corner. When he saw Sam waving he briefly raised an arm.

'Okay, Sammy, both hands on the wheel. No, higher, like this. Ten and two, remember. Right. Now, don't overdo it. Just the pedals and the steering wheel.'

'Got it. Don't worry.'

'Right. Off we go.'

Neil surrendered the wheel and the pedals and put the car into gear. For want of anything better to do with his right arm he wrapped it around Sam's waist. 'Okay,' he said, and they were off.

'Like that?'

'Bit more ... Just a bit, that's enough. You're a natural.'

The hair on top of Sam's head was a shade or two darker than usual, one slanting patch matted greasily like a mechanic's. It was Saturday afternoon but Sam was wearing his school trousers and a once-white shirt.

'Right,' Neil said, 'I'll help with the corner. Just around the block and then we're going back. No, we agreed. Some-one might see us.'

'Okay, thanks,' Sam said. 'Thank you.'

An eccentric kind of triumphal progress, this ride. Neil had never been very interested in cars (no cars, no football, two key indifferences he shared with Adam). The finish and the colour of the Audi, the upholstery and the stereo, were down to Jess. Sam would have made a better guess at the vehicle's horsepower than Neil was able to. All the same he loved the car for what it represented. It was their first joint splurge, not counting their rent and the holidays and the gym membership at the boutique place in Islington. More than that, it was the first five-figure purchase he had ever made, made with his own money, the serious money, several grand after tax, which was amassing in his bank account with a wondrous monthly regularity – thanks to Farid, the second chance he gave Neil, and the deranged London property market.

If he was ever going to have a pomp to be in, Neil guessed, he was in it now.

'I said both hands. Christ.' He grasped the wheel where Sam had let it go to wipe his nose.

'Okay, sorry. There. Sorry.'

They puttered past Bimal's old house; no lights were on inside. Bimal had two kids of his own now, Neil knew, though he hadn't yet met the second. These days they rarely saw each other, though they were on good terms, no hard feelings, like members of an amicably disbanded rock band.

'How's your dad?'

'Okay I s'pose. Said I'll have to get the bus back, though.'

Brian had shown Neil the contents of an envelope Dan had left with his son the previous evening: a tenner plus change, and a note that said *Bed by 9. Go easy on the TV.* He was trying.

'I could take you if you'd rather.'

'Nah, I'll be fine, honest. Are they – what do you call it again? – quadraphonic? The speakers.'

'Dunno, Sammy. Sorry.'

'What should I do about that bump? That okay?'

Sam relaxed into Neil's torso as he became used to the wheel, warming a patch of his uncle from the belly to the sternum. Almost four years, and Jess had never mentioned children: too proud, too committed to the performance of herself as spikily independent. Neil was allowing himself to believe that her silence meant she had no definite expectations or preferences. Perhaps this car would be their limit.

'Into the chicane,' Sam said. 'He's the youngest driver in the competition.'

'The crowd's gone wild,' Neil said. Sam smiled up at him.

'Sammy, the road.' He gestured at the asphalt with his eyes.

An afternoon at the Tower of London, out on the M1 together to a safari park, soppy admiration for the boy's routine cognitive leaps: Sam had laid claim to what little parental instinct Neil harboured. Sam plus Adam's kids, Harry and the wizened newborn girl, little avatars of his friend he could cradle and spoil.

'I told you it would rain. Bollocks.'

'It isn't.'

'It is.'

'Only spitting,' Sam said. 'Anyway, we're nearly back.'

Neil left the roof down so Brian would be able to see them as they pulled up. 'Let me . . .'

'It's okay,' Sam said. 'I can do it. I can.'

They rounded the final bend. Neil thought he could remember Brian indulging them in this way, he and Dan impatiently taking turns, in the beaten-up red Triumph with its indelible smell of travel-sickness puke and no seatbelts in the back. But he wasn't sure that he trusted the memory, that it truly was one.

'So is he looking after you all right? Granddad.'

'S'pose so. Yeah. He's shit hot on his maths, isn't he? And he's got a roll of old brown paper from his shop, covers all my books with it. School books. Loves it.'

'Does he fry you chips?' Brian had covered his books, too. Neil had forgotten about that. Probably he had never said thank you.

'Pizza,' Sam said. 'We order it, don't we?' Earlier, before lunch, Brian had made Sam wash his hands in the kitchen sink. In the clasping and rubbing of the boy's palms, Neil recognised the motion of his father's hands beneath the tap, and his brother's hands, and, he realised with a jolt, his own.

For his part he didn't want to teach his nephew anything, besides steering: his job, Neil considered, was to help the child know less. There was something gratifyingly discretionary in his feelings for Sam, as if he were poised between the hard duty of family and the free choice of friendship. The stake in HappyFamilies had come to nothing, but Neil was nevertheless becoming a somebody, a man of substance. He would help Sam out, up and out, when the time came.

Sam scuffed the front wheel into the kerb as they arrived. Neil winced, but the tyre was fine. Sam stood up to wave again, arching his body over the steering wheel, but Brian had already turned away from the window. Through the net curtains Neil made out his father's back, hunched over the walking stick.

He closed the roof. He kissed Sam's greasy head.

'Woz that for?' Sam said, ruffling the kiss out of his hair and opening the car door.

At this rate Neil would soon be able to do whatever he chose. He could take one of those Caribbean cruises he used to admire in the brochures at the travel agent in Wembley, though he knew that Jess wouldn't let him. *Naff*, she would say, *I'd rather go to Blackpool*.

He was in his pomp.

ALWAYS a small shock when the train came out of the tunnel (not long to go now), natural light suddenly dispelling the artificial kind, escape from a constriction that Adam almost hadn't noticed. The carriage had filled up. A woman was strap-hanging in the crush in front of him, sixty-five-ish, he estimated, half-moon glasses and duffel coat, old enough to be entitled to his seat and unlikely to be affronted if he relinquished it. His reflexes were dimmed: by the time she had burrowed through his preoccupation, a man with loud headphones and needless shades, who Adam wouldn't have taken for a gentleman, had already stood up for her.

Ordinarily he cherished this commute. One Tube line all the way, from Ealing to St James's, almost always a seat, the beginning of the ride above ground, running alongside the common and then Chiswick Park, the trees letting him feel like a country squire coming up to town. Plus the views through the upper-storey windows, the enticement of which never faded. Once he had seen a woman in a bra slapping a man in the face. The train passed grander and humbler homes the deeper into London it dug, with their richer and poorer occupants, the winners and the clingers-on. Adam's first day back at the department after his paternity leave, and in the sidings he saw sinister wreaths of cables he had never noticed before.

He minded the gap. He bought his cappuccino from the American coffee shop, carefully carrying the scalding cup to the ministry as if it were a votive offering. If he behaved absolutely normally, if he stuck to the agreed routine, perhaps no one would notice that he was now only a shell, a fancy-dress costume of Adam, through the eye holes of which a shrunken, imposter creature now peered out.

He negotiated the revamped security at the entrance to the building (all these scans and metal detectors, the new diurnal indignity that had to be got through, a twenty-first-century equivalent of bygone inconveniences like horse manure or outside plumbing). He made it to the lift, nabbing the prime, safe spot in the corner. He excuse-me-ed his way out when the electric ticker above the doors indicated his floor, keeping his head down as he scurried across the open-plan wilderness, the walk that always felt like a gauntlet. Not in early enough. Not working hard enough.

Not a 7. Still not a 7.

Asshole.

Two or three people called out 'Congratulations'. Adam waved limply in their directions. He made it to his half-concealed cubicle, with the waist-high partition that was his token privilege as Deputy Head of Returns. He logged on, maximised his email, the automated morning ritual. He was too tired.

On that first day back there was another Lessons Learned debrief. Adam, Sheila (the Head of Returns to his Deputy), some officials up from Croydon. This time the lessons were derived from a Kurdish asylum-seeker's much-publicised leap, with his six-year-old son, from the roof of a Glasgow high-rise. Adam saw the disparity in scale, life and death and desperation versus his eccentric self-indulgence. He wanted to concentrate. He tried, but he couldn't help himself. Looking back on the years between now and California – the years between history ending and it shudderingly starting up again – they seemed to him an obtuse, wilfully extended

adolescence. Adam had walked around as if nothing unto-
ward had happened, nothing worth mentioning. He thought
of his recently past self as a patsy in a slapstick film, a clot
who hasn't noticed the piano hurtling towards him from the
sky.

On his second day there was a briefing on the migration
fallout of the coming war. Immigration was an unglamorous
directorate, Adam knew, tarnished by its associations with
xenophobia and failure and with Croydon, the giant appli-
cant clearing-house on the edge of London, a place of mythic
dysfunction, banishment to which was his and his colleagues'
deepest, incessant fear. When he was transferred to immigration from crime, at the end of his initial placement, he had
consoled himself that he was playing against type. Everyone
expected the floppy-haired brigade to gravitate to cushier
berths, in private offices or at the Treasury or the Foreign
Office, not to the sweat and tears of immigration policy. He
could use it as a bridge to somewhere else, Adam reasoned.
In any case, he had the mortgage, and the children, and this
was where he was.

Sheila was a 7. Head of Returns was a 7. Deputy was not.
Neil was called 'Executive Assistant', which to Adam
sounded like a glorified secretary, but in Neil's world connoted 'lieutenant' or 'henchman'. And money. Neil swanked
about in his tailored suits, drove his lurid convertible, and
never gave California a thought. His heedlessness was
another kind of victory.

There was a big-shot spook at the briefing (impeccably
dressed, poshest man in the room), someone from the Ministry of Defence, a Home Office statistician. The big meeting
room on the third floor. This wasn't like him, Adam told himself as, fiddling with his cufflinks, the spook introduced

himself. His immune system wasn't ready for it. He worried that he might be unable to shake off the funk, like some Amazonian tribesman undone by the flu.

In the Tayler household, when Adam was growing up, his family had slept soundly, taken no Prozac and seen no therapists. They had a breezy English pride in their sturdily mechanical brains. An argument or a grief was like a scratch or a broken limb. It was treated; it healed. Only Harriet seemed to have lows – tantrums, their father always called them – but they were as much a source of drollery as of concern. The Taylers touched wood, joshingly tapping each other's crania, but otherwise their native empiricism precluded superstition: no one was the subject of a curse, nor would have credited it if they were. At boarding school, when one of the other pupils was morose or reclusive, some stranded son of a diplomat, say, the boys would hum the theme tune from *Close Encounters* or *The Omen*, joking about how the loner was defecting to the dark side. To moon over a girl was gay. To worry about exams was nerdy. Everyone was supposed permanently to be *on good form*, as if they were all well-conditioned, moodless racehorses. Then and into his adult life, Adam had thought of angst and depression as other people's problems, as acne had been in his teens. Neil, for instance, with his tendency to analyse and mourn a moment when he ought to have been living it. Several times, Adam remembered, when they had shared rooms and tents in America, he had woken during the night to find Neil sitting up, perpendicular, his eyes open, thinking.

They were all or nothing people, Adam realised, his family, his breed. Their only game plan was to get all the way through, right to the end, thinking as little as possible, in the hope that they could outrun it – whatever it was that they were frantically eschewing, the neglect or abuse or adultery. The failure, or the guilt. If it outran you, if it caught you, you were fucked.

'… national security implications in the broadest sense,' the spook concluded. It would have been better if Eric had punched him.

On the third day Sheila's boss, the deputy head of the directorate, declared herself 'surprised' – virtually an expletive in the desiccated language of their trade – at the widening gap between arrivals and returns.

'The minister's alarmed,' she told Sheila in Adam's hearing. 'I'm alarmed, frankly.'

'They happen, these spikes,' Sheila tried. 'There's a cycle to them, the sending—'

'The press are sniffing around this again, Sheila. You might think they had other things to worry about but it seems they don't.' She was a slight woman in ascetic pumps, with a greying helmet of hair, but Adam saw how she cowed Sheila, physically as well as institutionally, despite Sheila's six-inch and fifteen-year advantages, her broad-hipped solidity. 'I don't want to hear about "sending-country factors". We can't have this many FASs running around, we can't justify it.'

'I'll get on to Croydon,' Sheila said.

F-A-S: Failed Asylum Seeker, the hygienic, shrink-wrapped acronym for the human beings they repatriated, or were supposed to. To begin with Adam had felt squeamish about the vocab and the role. But he took solace in the fact that these were never his policies. His job was merely to orchestrate the process as humanely and efficiently as possible, from the immigration tribunals to the detention centres to the planes. Better him than some hang-'em-and-flog-'em

126

hatchet man (*I am a nice boy. I am*). The politicians who did make the policies might be amateurs but they weren't monsters, not in this rainy little democracy. Nor were the uniforms who applied them. Adam had spent three days with an enforcement team from Croydon. Five men in a van, two of them unpleasant, three of them not, three of them lazy, two of them not. One borderline racist, so far as he could tell. The usual loathing for Whitehall toffs, him included.

There was a meeting that afternoon to discuss their response. Adam and Sheila needed to confect some top-notch, bullet-point braggadocio about the money that had left the Home Office and the rejected asylum-seekers who had left the country. By now he knew the form: four points on spending (always up), four on outcomes (up or down, depending).

Deputy Head of Returns. Sitting in his cubicle, Adam's failings bled together in his head. He was scared. He was sorry. Telling would be a penance, and, in any case, if he didn't admit everything, Neil wouldn't understand his dread. He might go berserk – at Adam's silence then, his silence since, or for his breaking the silence now. On the other hand, Adam tried to reassure himself, friends were always disappointing or betraying each other. Forgotten birthdays, unpaid debts, missed appointments, convenient lies, people changing wrongly as they aged, not being who you wanted them to be... Only a friend could betray you. Betrayal, he told himself, was what friends did.

He sent the text before the meeting: *Come round this weekend? Drink? Something I need to say*

A CHALKBOARD menu had ousted the dartboard. A tonne of house-clearance encyclopedias lined the wall where a quiz machine had stood. The puke- and history-saturated carpet had been discarded, the floorboards underneath white-washed: the standard-issue makeover in neighbourhoods like Adam's and Claire's. Pubs were the millennial gentrifiers' first targets, like television stations during a coup. The only relic of the boozer's past was the potman (two wings of hair on a bald crown, the skin between them marbled with liver spots, stains around his flies). He clung on, scavenging empty glasses in exchange for drink, tolerated by the new management out of kindness or indifference.

Four women were at the bar in their high heels and night-out skirts, their twenty-five-ish prime. Neil watched Adam watching them. His friend seemed to have undergone a marginally slower, domestic version of the fast-forward ageing that presidents and prime ministers went through live on television. Cartoon-dog bags beneath his eyes, a smudge of silvery grey in the hair above one ear, the regular hallmarks of parental decrepitude. Yet he was still chiselled and presentable, still emanating a cavalier glamour. Those women might not mind too much if they caught Adam admiring them.

'What shall we be this evening?' Neil joked. 'Firemen? Lion tamers?'

Adam thought he recognised one of the women, but he couldn't work out why. Perhaps it was only from a few minutes before, when he and Neil walked in, an instant memory that to his overloaded mind felt like something deeper. He knew he shouldn't stare. You saw it on the Tube sometimes, this rash scrutiny of strangers, agog middle-aged men tracking svelte legs along the platforms and up the escalators.

They talked. Yes, she was a lovely girl, Adam allowed, utterly lovely, though he hadn't spent all that much time with her, truth be told, his job mostly being to placate Harry while Claire nursed the baby. Also, he said, 'she's had this strange effect on me, I know it's going to sound crazy, maybe it's because she's so wonderful, I look at her and ... I haven't told Claire about this, I can't, but ... This is what I wanted to talk about, in fact ... '

'What is?'

The potman came for their empty bottles, offering them a gappy grin that seemed to Adam both hopeless and defiant. They said 'thanks' and turned away, out of some joint, reflexive consideration for the man's presumed shame.

'Hold that thought,' Neil said, and went to the bar for drinks. He glanced only once at the women while he waited, a rapid, practised up-and-down, but twice at his phone, Adam noticed. The barman crouched to retrieve the bottles from a fridge, dipping comically out of view.

The potman had saved him, if Adam wanted to be saved. Actually the malady seemed to be waning, burning itself out like a spiked fever. The performance of normality might soon evolve into the real thing. Even as he had been itemising his charge sheets Adam had known, some of the time – moments when he saw himself from the outside, like a patient looking down from the operating theatre's ceiling – that Yosemite might not be able to bear the weight of all his masochistic remembrance. She might very well be fine. Almost certainly, they were fine.

Not telling his friend might be more a kindness than a lie. In a practical sense, Adam advised himself, the betrayal would only be actuated if Neil found out. He could live without knowing this; he was living perfectly happily. He was living so happily.

Neil brought the drinks and talked blithely about his

work. 'Net operating income ... loan-to-value ratio ... vacant possession value' – his new, econometric vocabulary, the jagged poetry of money. Increasingly he reminded Adam of the cigar-smoking men he had met when, as a teenager, he had once or twice taken the train to London to have lunch with his father and a few of his associates: restless, distracted, with a pharaonic way of talking about their transactions that seemed at once showy and awesomely casual. These days Neil sometimes said 'two' for two million pounds, or 'three-five' for three and a half, dispensing with the tiresome zeros since millions were the only noteworthy denomination. Adam felt a dim, throwback duty to disapprove of Neil's choices (going in with Farid, putting money first). Or rather, he felt an obligation to project disapproval, a moral conde-scension containing an implicit boast that he, Adam, could do and earn what Neil was doing and earning, if only he dropped his scruples and chose to. What he actually felt was pride – pride in himself, mostly, the gambler's satisfaction at a bet that has come off.

Enough about money. Today Adam surely had the con-versational prerogative, the day-release patient's right to choose their pastime.

'Neil,' he said. 'Philly. Listen, I need to ask you. Do you ever think about it?'

'What?'

'What happened in America. After we had that photo taken, you know, the Faithful Couple. With her. With ... that girl. The girl and her father.'

Neil had raised his bottle to his mouth as Adam began speaking. He kept it there when the question had been for-mulated, his lips locked on the glass but not drinking, buying himself a few seconds. He tilted the bottle upward to finish his swig, closing his eyes as he swallowed. He was doubly surprised: by the out-of-the-blue allusion, and at the same time, he registered, that this had taken so long.

Adam was in some deep, abstruse distress, like a man on the parapet of a bridge. This time it was common charity to respond. In any case, Neil wasn't ashamed. He was as sure as ever – surer – that he had nothing to be ashamed of.

'No,' he lied. He set his bottle on the table. 'Not really, Ants. Do you?'

'Sometimes,' Adam said. He looked down at the reconditioned floorboards. 'I have been. I've been thinking about it a lot. For some reason, I can't stop myself, not since Ruby was born. I know it sounds ridiculous.'

'It is ridiculous,' Neil said quietly. 'It's nuts.'

'Is it?'

The quartet of women clip-clopped past their table to the exit. One must have cracked a joke because two of them were laughing. The potman held the door open, bowing his head as if the women were minor royalty. There are many ways to get fucked up by this world, Neil thought, glancing at the potman and back to Adam, or to fuck yourself, and some of them you only notice after it's too late.

'They're meeting us later,' he tried. 'I spoke to them at the bar. At that place in Waterloo, you know. I told you they were an extra in *Footballers' Wives*.'

'Don't,' Adam said.

'Kit man.'

'I said, don't.' The two-foot diameter of the table was planetary between them.

'Listen,' Neil said after a few seconds, in the tone he used when Sam was being obstreperous, or his father had neglected to take his blood-thinning medicine, 'you've just had a baby. You probably haven't slept for a week.' You had to humour parents, he had learned that from Bimal: you had to ask about the children and commiserate with their exhaustion and tolerate the pious snobbery about their random biological accomplishment. 'I bet you haven't had sex for months' – another gesture towards a joke that he quickly saw was unhelpful. 'What has she got to do with anything?'

'You don't understand,' Adam said, that eternally true and eternally pointless statement of fact. 'It's because of Ruby that I've been going over it. Her father . . .' He sounded both nervous and resolved, as if he had been preparing. 'Or maybe, you know, it's been with us all along, waiting till our resistance was down, but we pretended it wasn't.'

'I haven't pretended anything.'

'Fine, Philly. Of course. But there's something – I'd just like to talk about it. Is that all right?'

Neil's phone rang, the insipid up-and-down-the-scale default tone that he hadn't yet got around to changing. His hand advanced towards the noise. Adam glared at the hand; it froze and remained still until the ringing stopped. That fucking phone. If Yosemite happened now, Adam thought, or if the cellular age had dawned a few years earlier, her father would have called the police immediately, no chance to reconsider.

'You could have a kid out there too, you know.'

'What?'

'You could have a kid. With her. That morning, you said you didn't . . .'

'I doubt it.'

I'll take care of it. Neil could still hear her saying those

132

words, in that indelible American accent. *Are you sure? Yes, I got it.* He hadn't known exactly what she meant by that; probably neither had she. He hadn't let that stop him.

'I asked you, you probably don't remember, but I remember, I asked . . . '

'Fuck's sake, Adam.' Neil sat up straight. He gripped the edge of the table. 'This is it, is it? What you wanted to say to me?'

'No. That isn't what I meant. What I wanted, it's . . . ' He had gone in too hard, made the whole thing sound too much like blame when it was meant to be an appeal. 'What I mean is . . . We didn't think. Why didn't we?'

Neil sighed. He counted to ten in his head. 'Look,' he said, softening. 'Everyone does something they regret.'

'So you regret it?'

'I didn't say that.'

'But you do.'

'Adam,' Neil said, 'it was a long time ago. We were young.'

'We weren't that young. Let's not kid ourselves. If you think about it, that's the point, isn't it? That's why we're still here. I mean, you and me. If we'd been fifteen too we would have lost each other by now. Like with Chaz and Archie and those boys you smoked that spliff with – they're all crazy stories and sepia cricket photos, nostalgia for stuff that never happened in the first place. There's nothing else left.' Adam had hardly seen his older friends since his wedding, which, in retrospect, had been a festive wake for his youth. 'You and me,' he said, 'we were adults.'

'Fine,' Neil said. 'We were adults. So what?'

'So we can't just laugh it off, you know, boys will be boys or whatever. I can't just forget about it, even if I wanted to.

Especially now. Even though, in the last ten years, Claire and Jess, and the children and your, you know, your money, we nearly have.'

'Ad, you keep saying "we" . . . '

'Because it was both of us. I remember what you said about that and you were right. I'm not blaming everything on you, really I'm not, that's what I'm trying to say, that's what this is about. We were both there, and we both wanted her, and that was why it happened. I mean, the things we said – the jokes and the rest – and, you know, later, what I should have said.'

'What do you mean, what you—'

'The other day, I had Harry in the trolley, we're at the supermarket, nappy aisle, and we bang into someone else's trolley, another father, except the daughter is her age, you know, the girl's. And yesterday there was this teenager in the street, she was telling off her boyfriend or something, and she shouted, "No!" Do you remember that?'

'This isn't what you thought then. Come to think of it, on that morning I remember you saying . . . '

I guess the skiing's off.

'That makes it worse,' Adam said, raising his voice and then lowering it again. 'I remember what I said. That makes it worse.'

'Adam,' Neil said, more kindly. 'Ad, you've got this out of proportion.'

'What would you say if Sam did something like that?'

'Sam's nine.'

'But in a few years. What would you say to him?'

'What the fuck has Sammy got to do with it? Leave him out of it, will you? Christ, Adam, it's enough to make me think—'

'Okay, Philly. I'm sorry.' Sam had been another mistake. 'It's just . . . We didn't think, did we? I didn't.'

They were silent for a moment before Neil said, 'Tell you what I think, since you bring it up. I think this is all arrogance. I mean, it's a kind of arrogance. You want to be perfect, you think you can be perfect, it's what you've always thought. I don't blame you, it's how you were brought up, you were probably pretty close to it, once. Maybe you expect it now more than ever, because of the kids and the rest. But you can't be perfect because nobody can. I'm not perfect either,' Neil said, unconsciously reaching for the mole on his neck, 'but I never thought I was. All this guilt is just a way of feeling sorry for yourself. It's, you know, a kind of narcissism or something.'

'Possibly, Neil, but—'

'It was nothing, Adam. Practically nothing, ten years ago. Happens all the time.'

It was thrilling, this honesty, Neil thought. In the end he and Adam were as much about looking as liking: looking down through very deep but translucent water, down and down to the bottom, occasionally feeling vertiginous, sometimes spotting ugly shadows belly-crawling on the floor.

'That's what I'm trying . . . There's something else.'

'What are you talking about?'

'About that night,' Adam said. 'And the morning. There's something else. When we were . . . ' Adam swallowed. 'I knew, Neil. I knew about her.'

'What did you—'

'I knew she was . . . younger. I knew she was too young. I mean before he . . . Not just in the morning, when her father caught you. I knew that night.'

As Adam spoke Neil cast down his eyes at the wooden

table, at the Venn diagram imprinted by glasses and bottles. 'Go on,' he said. 'Tell me the rest of it, then.'

To Adam this felt like a dream, after all this time, surreal and inebriating. 'It was earlier, when we were by the fire, do you remember that? He was sitting next to me, her father was, and he told me she was . . . He told me she was in high school.'

'That's all?'

Adam swallowed again. 'He told me and I meant to tell you, I did, but somehow I . . . You were so . . . determined. Do you remember how we were about it? Later I didn't think you would – that you and she . . . I should have told you. There's nothing else I can say. And then in the morning, he . . . '

Neil held up his palms – *Don't shoot!* – and pinched the bridge of his nose. The epiphany in a film when the hero realises his ally has been a villain all along. Or maybe it wasn't, Neil thought at almost the same instant, perhaps this didn't matter at all, an oversight from a decade ago, heat of the battle, few beers, so much since and closer that counted for more between them. It wasn't as if . . . no one got hurt. He wasn't sure whether to laugh or to stand, let the potman open the door for him and walk out, no goodbyes. He didn't know what the rules were for this. How was he supposed to know?

He stalled. 'Why have you waited . . . Why didn't you tell me this before?'

'Actually, I thought about it. I tried, once or twice, you won't remember, you probably didn't notice. I suppose it never felt . . . urgent. But now, with Ruby . . . You're the only one I can talk to about it, don't you see? I had to talk to someone.'

Neil raised his hand to his brow, covering his eyes. There was some anger, he found. 'You know what could have happened? Her father, in the morning, he was about to ... It looked as if ... '

'I know, Philly. I'm sorry about that. But he didn't, did he?'

Again Neil sighed. 'When you came and stood next to me – do you remember? – in front of the tent, they were all surrounding me, and I was alone, and you – you didn't have to, we'd only known each other a couple of weeks, you could have disowned me, and I thought, it's silly, I know, but I thought it was, you know, the nicest ... But it wasn't, was it? It was just ... '

'I said I was sorry.'

'And afterwards, all these years ... Ten years. I thought we were more than that.'

'We are.'

'Jesus.'

'I had to tell you, let me finish and you'll see. In the morning, the father – Eric – he said to me, it was like a curse or something, he said he hoped ... He said one day, I'd have a daughter, and he hoped ... Well, I do, don't you see? And now I look at Ruby and it's as if – I know it sounds crazy – it's as if it was her. Or that if it was, if it ever was, it would somehow be, I don't know, fair.'

'It isn't like that – life – it's nothing to do with fair.'

'It's as if I wouldn't be able to complain. Like I'd be disqualified.'

Neil's sympathy and patience had run dry. The whole conversation was the wrong way round.

'That's what this is about?'

'What?'

'I could have gone to prison in California, what was it he said I'd get, the guide? Two years. You heard him. Probably I would never have come out. And you expect me to . . . What the fuck do you expect?'

'I said I was sorry.'

'For yourself.'

The ker-ching of the till, the slam of the door, a woman laughing, a glass smashing. Adam said, 'Maybe there always are things like this. I mean things you don't tell each other. Things you've done or said or, you know, thought about each other. Even to you.'

'If you say so, Adam,' Neil said. 'But not things like this.' He snatched a vicious glance at his watch.

'You know,' Adam counterattacked, 'you could have been the one to suffer for this, just as easily.'

'Well, I'm not,' Neil said. 'I'm not suffering. Not about her.'

They sat resentfully, like strangers obliged to share a table. When they finished their beers the potman swooped for their bottles with greater alacrity than he looked capable of. This time Neil looked up at him, momentarily distracted by the effort to determine his age. He could have been anywhere between forty and seventy.

'Have you told Jess?'

'Told her what?'

'Don't, Neil.'

'Okay, no. But I don't see why I should tell her. Tell her what? I haven't told her about the girl I shagged in freshers' week. There are lots of things I haven't told her. I haven't told her about us running away from that bar in Vegas without paying. It was a mistake, Adam. It isn't relevant. An accident.'

'That's what I'm saying, it wasn't an accident.'

'Have you told Claire? What you've just told me.'

'No,' Adam said. 'I can't now, no way. If anything ever happened ... This is between us. You're the only one who could understand. Just us.'

FROM the turn in the stairs, halfway down, Adam could see through the archway to the end of the living room where Neil was sitting with Claire. Neil's hair was swept back from his brow in the manner of a bullfighter or a tango dancer. He was talking too softly for Adam to hear, Claire interjecting the odd 'Really?' and 'That's wonderful'. She was already expert at letting men talk about themselves, allowing them to feel fascinating, a skill she had honed at work-related London dinner parties that, to Adam, always felt like botched auditions. She never expected her interlocutors to reciprocate her interest and, he suspected, experienced only a very mild affront, almost a satisfying vindication, when they didn't.

Her eyes had asked him the question after they came in together. They were back earlier than she expected, Adam looking meaninglessly at the bookshelves like a visitor while Neil asked her how the newborn was sleeping, seconds later distractedly repeating himself. Something had happened. Adam had shaken his head, almost imperceptibly – *Nothing. Don't ask. Not in front of him* – and gone to check on Harry.

'You don't have to,' Adam had said outside the Bear. 'I'll say you were tired.'

'I should,' Neil had insisted, not yet certain what he should do, what he should feel, carrying on while the jury was out. They had walked back to the maisonette in silence.

Adam descended the last few stairs and paused in the doorway. Claire's feet were curled under her buttocks, her skin on the sallow side of pale, one hand over her deflating abdomen, still cradling the foetus that had become the infant asleep on her shoulder. Now she was giggling, the hand holding her Caesarean scar as if she might burst, and Neil was laughing too, his silent laugh that looked like a grimace, his arms out straight and motionless on the armrests.

Neil looked up at him but his expression was blank. Adam had missed the punchline. They could have been talking about anything.

Like a lifer with no possibility of parole and nothing left to lose, Harry burst down the stairs and past him. He seized and tried to ransom Neil's phone, this miniature god that the adults seemed to worship. He launched himself at his mother and sister; Claire deflected him with a forearm and Adam extracted him, Harry cycling his legs in the air in the obligatory show of resistance.

'No, bedtime, lollipop,' Adam said, the endearment and the rhythm of it direct inheritances from his father – *lollipop*, *beetle-bug*, *darling*, they welled up and came out of him involuntarily, as if written into some deep, time-delayed hard drive. In his bedroom Harry denied all wrongdoing, then began to cry, protest followed by contrition, guilt's familiar one-two. He extorted a story from his father, exercising his power to be certain it was real, as tyrants must. His body clock was out, all of theirs were, the family living in that blurry newborn time zone in which night and day elide. Adam kept it short: boy, elephant, ride, squirt. The End.

'One more,' Harry said. His hair and complexion were all Claire, but there was something of Adam in his eyes and mouth.

'Love you.'

'In morning,' Harry said, rolling over. He would be starting at his nursery soon, embarking on his life apart.

Adam hurried down the stairs again, anxious about leaving them alone, past the picture window on the maisonette's half-landing, beyond it the patchwork of skinny, London gardens squeezed between their road and the next, tiny manicured lawns and outsized trees, none belonging to them. In the sitting room Ruby opened her eyes, tried to focus, and saw something she didn't like, a colour or a shape or a shade; she wrenched her gummy mouth into the embouchure of a scream, a silent scream that never came out. She began mouthing the air for milk, like a dog optimistically humping a leg, as if willpower alone might conform the world to her desire.

Adam's eyes asked Claire this time. He might have said, *Do you realise what sort of a man you are married to?* Or, *I thought you might be interested to know …* It was so long ago, before they met, but it might matter to her now, as it did to him. Her eyes were the same.

Ruby hit the roof when the breast came out, always negotiating hardest when she was closing the deal. Claire angled an engorged tit into her mouth; Neil lost his nerve, cast his eyes around the room for something else to scrutinise and settled on his phone.

'I should go,' he said. 'Jess … '

'Of course,' Adam said. 'You go.'

Claire prised the baby from her breast so Neil could kiss the bumfluffed head, smiling her queenly, disappointed smile. No handshake for the men, no shoulder biffs or back-slapping hugs.

'You all right?' she asked Adam. 'You two … okay?'

She was wiser than he sometimes gave her credit for. Remember that, Adam told himself. Don't lose sight of her.

'Yes,' he said. 'Much better.'

NEIL belted up and joined the evening traffic, heading west to east with the others, from the Nappylands of the suburbs to Dinkyville. He turned on the radio – *It's driving me mad, Going out of my* – and snapped it off again.

Neil was furious. He was dazed. He had known. He spat out a laugh. All this time.

He didn't want to think about California, he mustn't, not immediately. Basic rule of business: don't be railroaded into anything. Shake hands, do the sums when you get home. If Farid were there he would have smiled, said *Very interesting* and nothing more, pulverising Adam with his silence.

Neil shouldn't have gone back to the house. That was already a concession. He didn't want to think about it, because if he did, he would have to decide. He was supposed to be in his pomp.

At the end of Adam's road a church was being converted into flats. *Only One Unit Remaining!* – even though the skeletal building was roofless. Churches turning into flats, cinemas transforming into gyms, old boozers mutating into restaurants: the abracadabra of money, magicking everything into something else, a shape-shifting spell that was evidently too strong for megaterrorism or the imminent war to disrupt. Neil Collins from Harrow – Neil Collins of Collins & Sons – metamorphosing into this Neil Collins, the him who was driving his new-model convertible, on his way home to Jess and their chrome and Corian pad.

You could have a kid out there too.

I knew she was too young.

At least, Neil tried to console himself, they had avoided the familiar deaf arguments over Iraq, the argument itself akin to trench warfare, no positions ever altered and no minds changed, Adam against, Neil for, partly, he knew, because Adam was against.

She was too young.

Neil wasn't going to think about them. He didn't want to forgive Adam in a rush, lazily, and he was terrified of not forgiving him. Adam and his preposterous curse.

This car, their flat, his suits: he owed it all to Farid. When HappyFamilies went bust, Bimal and the others had emerged from the rubble as eminently marketable commodities. Old, panicking analogue companies were recruiting digerati in a hurry, and even a belly-up dotcom history was enough to impress them. Bimal had straight away been hired to run the online operation for a luxury goods firm; Jess was snapped up by another design agency, with a grander title and improved salary. They were veterans before they were thirty, like specialists in a new kind of combat. They had learned important lessons while squandering Farid's cash. Don't count on Russian export licences, for one. The Millennium bug, that pantomime Armageddon, didn't strike, but there was a swarm of other bugs, and the website was much too slow, just as customers were coming to appreciate how vital, how urgent, were the extra microseconds it took to log on, boot up and download. Those flickering waits had become an unbearable imposition.

The main lesson had been about wiring, human wiring rather than the electronic kind. Bimal moved them to new offices off Carnaby Street, Neil developed a new product line (key rings, place mats, fridge magnets), Jess organised a slap-up launch in a disused fire station, all on the unexamined presumption that consumers had been rewired: that because they could do something, such as buy a bespoke silk-screened tea towel for £14.99 plus p+p, they would. Of course they would. They must. Program it, and they will point and click. But they wouldn't, not in the numbers needed to keep HappyFamilies afloat when Farid's money ran out. Business was still business, a Stone Age equation of revenue and costs. People were still recalcitrant, inconveniently autonomous people.

If he had told me that night, Neil thought as he drove, I wouldn't have done it. Of course not. If he had told me the following day, while I waited for the police and the handcuffs, I would have repudiated him on the spot. I might have.

He turned into a long, straight, speed-trap street, grand Victorian houses on one side, council estates on the other, the road a no man's land between the two camps. Segments of melon grinned in Technicolor rows beneath the awning of a Levantine grocer's.

Farid had abandoned them. He must have paid the shyster lawyer who negotiated his stake almost as much as he invested – he had sunk over a million all told – but he declined to double down. In the office people were whispering that he had only ever wanted to give his cash a nice dotcom sheen. Bimal filed for insolvency, people were yanking computers, scanners and coffeemakers out of the wall, in a spontaneous and oddly festive bout of auto-looting, when Strahan called Neil. Farid wanted to see him. He found the designated restaurant in Mayfair.

It didn't matter that he knew nothing about property, which, Farid explained, was these days his main concern. No, it was nothing to do with the internet, though they probably ought to have a place-filler website for the sake of appearances. Neil could sell, Farid said, or rather, he could squeeze investors for money, as he himself could testify, which was essentially the same talent. Farid had Strahan, with his picturesque cynicism, for schmoozing and introductions, but he needed a negotiator. Neil was a good fit, he implied, a useful median between the toffs and the cosmopolitan hustlers he dealt with. Farid smiled once, told Neil that Strahan would fix the details, basic plus bonuses, and turned back to his salad.

Fucker wasn't even sorry, Neil thought as he indicated to turn right. Not really. Sorry for her, sure, and for himself, his hocus-pocus evil eye, but not for me. If he had told me after we flew home, that summer ... It was too long ago, he couldn't know what he would have done. He might have laughed about it; he might not have cared.

Carousers huddled outside a pub. Two of them, men in suits but with their shirts hanging out, seemed to Neil to be squaring up. The taller one threw a punch, but stopped his fist short. They laughed, the smaller man laughing hardest, doubling up at the only simulated violence.

Neil rarely saw Farid, even now. He made infrequent appearances at their small but fancily addressed office in Hanover Square, and only brief ones at the parties they threw for investors. Still, he could be intimidatingly present when he chose to be. Neil once saw him eviscerate a straight-guy selling agent who had asked him to document his funds for a project in the City –

Who the fuck you think you are? Ten years I do business with you, you want see my credit card statement? I phone your boss, you fucking cunt, you never my letting agent no more

– and so on, Farid hamming up his broken English in a beautifully menacing cameo. His method was to borrow more than he needed for a purchase, top-skim the loan for his 'personal overheads', and use the change as bait for investors in his next, grander project. The next was always grander. The bankers didn't seem to mind loaning the supernumerary sums: so long as the market kept rising, everyone would get their money back in the end, Farid said.

Neil thought of Farid as a kind of godfather, mostly in the fairy sense, only occasionally in the villainous one. Buying this car with Jess had been the first time he experienced his money as a real, transformative force; felt it to be *his* money, and that he had hurdled the boundary between struggle and success, a frontier that had seemed Himalayan until Farid opened a path across it.

He stopped at a red light. A child was loitering on the pavement in front of a supermarket, out too late. An old man was crossing the road, his spine so curled that his face was parallel with the road. The old man didn't offer the standard wave of acknowledgement, nor even check that the oncoming car had stopped. He was shaking his head at the world.

The light flashed amber. Some imbecile behind Neil hooted.

Adam had been perfect after the stroke, Neil had to give him that. Like a brother, better than a brother, though even Dan had pulled himself together that week. Dan had come to the hospital, flirting with the nurses, depositing Sam to watch football on the television in another patient's room. He was talking about taking a course (plumbing, he said, or roofing). He had some work on; he was straightening himself out.

'Is he going to die?' Sam asked Neil. 'Granddad.'

'I don't know, Sammy. No.'

'Dad got me a Scalextric,' Sam said. 'Did you know that? Second hand, but.'

Sitting with his father on the ward, without the carapace of work that had protected them in the shop, Neil had been ambushed by discordant feelings. Fear (that Brian was about to die). Some fear, at least. Horror (the tubes, the fluids, the caricature of mortality). Awkwardness (the tubes, the fluids). A consciousness of the falsity of the situation: Neil knew, and Brian must have known, that the closeness was a charade. Regret, that it was only a charade, and that it was too late for them to be otherwise, for him to have a better reason to be there, a better way of accounting for his presence to himself than this abstract yet lumpen duty.

Above all, boredom.

On the third day, when Brian was less groggy and tentatively mobile, Neil had tried, for the first and last time, to speak to him about his mother's final weeks, which he remembered as a farce of whispering, increasingly absurd as she dwindled into frailness, followed by a series of over-choreographed hospital and hospice visits that, in his recollection, were always wrecked by vomiting or narcolepsy.

'Dad,' he said, 'I wanted to ask you, why did you only tell us then? Right at the end.'

'Your brother knew,' Brian said, hoarse and unshaven. 'Daniel knew. From the beginning. It was only you.' He paused and closed his eyes, and Neil waited for the explanation. 'Don't forget,' his father said instead, 'to turn around the *Open* sign in the shop window.'

Perhaps there had been a kind of wisdom in that refusal to elaborate, Neil thought, slowing down to pass a cyclist. Water under the bridge.

A pizza delivery moped came the wrong way down a one-way street. Neil hooted. A group of men waited outside a minicab office, laughing at each other's jokes. Adam was a liar, a decade's worth of lies, but he had been kinder and more attentive than Jess, who had calibrated her response to what she knew of his and Brian's relationship. She didn't have much time for charades.

'Anything I can do?' Adam had said. 'I'll come over.'

'You can bump off the guy in the bed opposite him. Stinks, the fucker. Screams all night, apparently.'

'Roger that. Seriously, I hope things are ... bearable.'

'Thanks.'

'I'll come over.'

Adam called every day for a week. Neil suspected he was projecting his feelings for his own parents onto this emptier situation. He had come to admire Adam's automatic love of his family without ever thinking he could emulate or quite understand it, as you might admire the practitioner of some recondite craft or art, a potter or a saxophonist.

That was only a few months ago. They had talked about Brian that week. They often talked about Sam and Harry. These days they didn't talk much about Claire and Jess, out of a combination, Neil supposed, of loyalty and tact. Pretty soon they wouldn't be talking about money, even though having it or not having it, how much you got and how you got it, were becoming the main questions. How much your friends got, and how.

A half-empty bus pulled away from its stop. A homeless man with an overstuffed shopping trolley sat on the narrow bench beneath the shelter, not waiting for anything. The man's eyes met Neil's before he could accelerate.

Envy wasn't quite the right word for Adam's response to his wealth. It would be fairer to describe it as a kind of cognitive dissonance, incomprehension that the chips should have fallen this way. Neil forgave him that much. He had felt

148

something similar about his money, too, as if someone, some pinstriped overseer, might tap him on the shoulder at any moment, explaining that there had been a misunderstanding, he would have to give it back. The previous year he had invited Adam and Claire to join them on a balloon ride, high-altitude champagne over Kent for Jess's birthday, and Adam had accepted. He rang back a couple of days later to say no, sorry, some blather about the babysitter, but Neil was certain the real reason had been the cost. He would happily have paid, but he knew Adam wouldn't countenance that. Whisky and comfort and time were permitted offerings, recognised currency. But money, no. It was different from before, when Adam had loaned him the deposit for his bedsit, because the disparity was permanent, and in Neil's favour.

Under a streetlight, two young men, one fat, one not, were eating chips out of a single paper cone. When he thought about their friendship now, Neil was put in mind of an image he must have seen on the television news a few years before they first met. It was a report about the Channel Tunnel, in which the two teams of diggers, one from England, one French, were breaking through to each other in the middle, beneath the sea. The clip showed two men groping for the other's hand, clasping arms, clawing for each other through a wall of dirt.

Baker Street, Euston, the alluringly illuminated, somehow anarchic avenues of Regent's Park, the pavement operettas of King's Cross. Neil drove back into the up-themselves zone, the laptop and latte territory north of the City that, strange to say, was where he now lived. Sunday-night revelry: always somebody with something to celebrate or a sorrow to drown. Three young women shivered in their miniskirts outside a bar.

Whatever happened now – he didn't know what would happen now – Neil never again wanted to talk to Adam about California. These days he could scarcely picture her face. He would forget her name eventually: he would make sure that he forgot it. He hadn't known her age, even if Adam had, that was a fact and not an extemporised excuse. To begin with, he found himself recalling on the Farringdon Road, she had seemed educated, knowing, ready. *I'll take care of it.* But after they started, or he started, she became still. Still and taut rather than still and relaxed, breathing regularly in his ear as if she were concentrating, or being brave, enduring a minor operation without anaesthetic. Then a deep exhalation when he rolled off, when he should have cradled and kissed her but hadn't.

He pulled over, outside a sushi restaurant, to let a wailing police car pass. Okay, he wasn't proud of it. He certainly wouldn't say that he was proud of it. Better that Adam had stopped it, or that he hadn't started it at all. All the same, she consented; he apologised; it was an honest mistake. These days, in this godlessly promiscuous era, didn't everyone over twenty have some version of this story in their past, some heat-of-the-moment coupling that might be regrettable and sordid, but was also finished and forgivable? In Harrow, when Neil was fifteen or sixteen, Dan let his friend Tezza hide in his wardrobe and watch while Dan had sex with his girl-friend. Tezza had dared him. In the kitchen, after she left, when they generously told him about their exploit, Neil was in awe: of the sex itself, obviously, but also of their gall and the macho priorities. The girlfriend never found out, so far as Neil remembered, though he couldn't have said for certain.

It wasn't only boys or teenagers who accumulated these

stories. Once, when she was drunk, Jess had confided something she had done when she was drunker – in Faliraki, he thought she had said – while she was at university. Her friend, two men they met in a nightclub, a pedalo ... Regret, not a characteristic emotion for Jess, was the reason she brought it up, rather than bravado or some bid to titillate or make him jealous. He hadn't known what to say, hadn't said anything, wasn't sure, in the morning, that she remembered telling him, and they had never talked about it again.

What was the point in dwelling on stuff like this? No harm done. Almost certainly no harm done. It was funny how these incidents came back to you, though, even when they belonged to other people. The nightclub in Faliraki and that pedalo and her friend.

Adam could have stopped him easily. *Quick word, Neil? Jailbait, mate. No, I'm serious. He did.* Some sixty-second exchange along those lines.

Neil found a space in a resident's parking bay; he flipped the car around to reverse in. He was too tight on the driver's side and had to manoeuvre out and back again. Perhaps it wasn't just his money that irked Adam but Jess, the flat, the whole package, so badly that he had resorted to this kamikaze raid on Neil's happiness. That was what their conversation felt like, even if he could never articulate the suspicion. This was one of those things that you both know but you can't say, not because you couldn't prove it – you wouldn't have to prove it – but because once you had said it, it couldn't be unsaid.

He punched in the code and climbed the stairs. There was no particular reason why he shouldn't tell Jess about Yosemite. He would tell her tonight: him, Adam, the girl and her father, all of it. She would probably laugh at his solemnity, call him 'sweet', pinch his cheek, tell him to say a dozen Hail Marys and collect her dry cleaning for a month in penance.

Jess was in bed. He switched on the television – real murder on one channel, imaginary murder on another. The flat was preternaturally tidy, in urgent need of desecration, but Neil didn't feel entitled to disorder the shelves or skew the furniture. Almost a year after they moved in here he still felt like a guest. He performed his efficient evening ablutions (teeth, face scrub, glance at his hairline) and slid in beside her. He would tell her in the morning.

He didn't tell her in the morning. She was in a hurry, so was he, it wasn't the right time. She asked after Adam's brats – did the silver spoon require surgical removal? – kissed him on the forehead and left. Something about a strategy meeting. He would tell her later. Soon.

He checked his phone as he was putting it into his jacket. Two overnight texts: one from Strahan, sent at six o'clock in the morning, which said *Office, 8.15*; the other, from Adam, sent at half-past three, said, *Great to see you. I'm sorry.* Neil envisioned his friend pacing around in the small hours, bearing his infant daughter and the memories she inflicted.

As much as the lies, it was a matter of roles. Adam's was always to be immaculate, intangibly superior. Neil's was to be a kind of scrappy insurgent, amusing and testing but deferring to his friend. They had both seemed to understand that arrangement without it ever being articulated. Adam had been the one to phone the driveaway firms in San Diego; only he could have made the first phone call after they flew home. Yet neither of them were quite the things they had been a decade before. Perhaps Adam had never been what Neil wanted him to be in the first place. The question was whether after they stripped away the made-up stuff, all the mutual invention, after he subtracted these lies, there was anything left, anything true and real, which was worth keeping.

Neil didn't know what had happened that night ten years ago. Adam thought he knew, but he had only a distorted memory of a daze. He wanted to be able to forgive him. Halfway to the front door Neil took out the phone from his pocket and replied to Adam's text.

Ruby is adorable

2005

NEIL wanted a drink, a proper drink, but he wasn't sure if that was allowed. He hadn't seen the menu – Azim had ordered for all of them, shashlik and sturgeon and a delicate Caucasian *calzone* – and he didn't know whether alcohol was included. Finally, halfway through the meal, sweating into his suit and doubting that he could endure the internecine bonhomie without lubrication, Neil meekly asked whether beer was available.

Azim laughed, rocking his head back, mouth open, lips and moustache stretching thin. Elin flicked a finger, once, beckoning an assistant-cum-bodyguard and dispatching him into the courtyard for the drinks.

'This isn't Tora Bora,' Azim said, still laughing.

Standing upright against the wall of the private room, their other flunky didn't move or smile. The world, Neil reflected, was approximately divided into the proprietors of violence – big-shots with assets to protect, hoodlums with nothing to lose, like the muggers who had roughed up Jess at the entrance to their building – and the herds of harmless people in the middle, peering at the carnivores above and below.

'You like the fish?' Elin asked. He had a round, pock-marked, simpleton's face, which seemed designed by nature to appear misleadingly ingenuous.

'Lovely,' Neil lied. They were avoiding business talk, though Neil suspected Azim and Elin were discussing dates and numbers in their private exchanges.

'Super fresh,' Azim said. 'House speciality.'

A muezzin sang out through a loudspeaker, somewhere above the restaurant in the old city. A cat's tail twitched under the empty chair between Azim's and Neil's. He saw Azim notice the tail and for a moment thought the cat might be in jeopardy. Azim pinched some white fish-flesh between his fingers, fed it to the stray and smiled. The cat caressed his legs.

The best analogy Neil could offer himself was with how he felt in that motel room in Los Angeles twelve years before. *I am Neil Collins from Harrow, Neil Collins of Collins & Sons. What the fuck am I doing here?*

To be honest, he knew the answer, which was as straightforward now as it had been in California. There the answer was Adam. In Baku, it was Farid.

Farid had given him a temporary, functional entrée to the plutocracy. Its members, Neil had noticed, observed their own rituals and rules, in traffic jams, at airports, in all their dealings with officialdom. There was a kind of telepathy between them, a family resemblance in manner and sheen that seemed always to be mutually visible beneath the local idiosyncrasies. They were charming sociopaths, for the most part, enraptured by their wealth but able to be ironic about it, to see the joke and the luck of it.

Young women were usually in tow and frequently on offer, like *digestifs*, though Farid had warned Neil, right at the beginning, always to decline, lest he end up featuring in some blackmailable amateur pornography. *Don't shit on your own doorstep.*

Farid was supplying half the funds for a gaudy, multi-purpose tower on the site of a soon-to-be flattened, Soviet-era housing estate. 'Give them nothing,' he had urged as he left the Hilton that morning, condemning Neil to endure their new partners' hospitality alone. By which he had meant, nothing personal, nothing they could use against him later. Farid himself had given Neil nothing all along: those photos of somebody's grandchildren he had glimpsed at their first meeting, with Bimal and Jess in the rented flat near Marble Arch, were as close an approach as Neil ever made to him. Neil felt indebted to Farid, filial almost, but also, sometimes, ashamed.

The beer arrived. Azim became garrulous. Was Blair as strong as Thatcher? Something about a local and much-lamented war that Neil had never heard of. Elin broke in with the personal questions. Did Neil have children? Was he married?

Elin was married. From his inside pocket he produced a laminated, folding set of pictures, a boy and two girls at what might have been Disney World. A pretty woman in lipstick and Western clothes. He watched Neil looking at them. 'My wife,' he said, and smiled. 'My children.' Always the children.

Neil gave them nothing. Not yet. Maybe one day. We'll see.

'Next time you come,' Azim said, putting on the full oriental show, 'you stay in my house. We kill a sheep. You meet my daughter.' Elin said something to Azim and they both laughed.

Neil wasn't sure what the joke was, whether it was on him. 'That would be wonderful,' he ventured.

'Not for the sheep,' Elin said, and they laughed again.

Insincerity wasn't quite the word for these exchanges. They were both false and true at the same time, authentic human contact shot through with cynicism. The blandishments were almost genuine at the moment they were uttered, Neil felt. The same as business everywhere, only more exuberant – the same as life everywhere, come to that, intimacy mixed with exploitation, the mission always to insulate something, some moment or bond, from the contest.

Azim and Elin lapsed into Azeri. Neil had begun wondering whether it would be impolite to look at his phone when, as if obediently, it rang. A twin fire-station shriek, the old rotary theme that was already kitsch history.

For the first two rings he ignored it, smiling inanely as if the noise were emanating from somewhere else. It was unlikely to be Jess: she was in Buenos Aires, seven hours behind him, research for a new Latin American biscuit product, he thought she had said. It might be Sam. Neil had given him a phone for his birthday, with instructions to call should Brian deteriorate, or should Dan. Sam texted him emoticon-studded jokes, mordant synopses of Dan's proliferating benders, occasionally his homework scores; Neil amplified his responses with lavish exclamation marks, as the mobile argot required.

After three rings he took out the phone and looked at the screen. The caller-ID photo told him it was Adam. Handsome bugger.

Azim coughed, then grinned.

Neil's rancour over California had passed, rinsing out of him during the thunderstorm the previous summer, the two of them and those two women. This evening he felt the old warmth – because Adam was in the world, still in Neil's world, in spite of everything, comfortingly persistent – and a more recent, entwined irritation. Of late there often seemed to be something more pressing to do when Adam rang: it wasn't the right time, Neil would call his friend back later, he usually resolved, definitely he would.

'You may answer,' Elin said. 'Please.'

On the sixth ring Neil cupped the screen beneath the table. Pressing the reject button would be too brutal: Neil himself could tell when someone offed him like that, and he always received it as a tiny act of violence. He generally let Adam ring through to voicemail, the lazy medium between the investment of talking and harshness of termination.

Not today. Neil raised and jiggled the phone in his hand, mouthing 'sorry' as he stood. 'Yes,' he said, in a curt tone intended to sound executive. Not just the organ-grinder's monkey.

'I've found her,' Adam said.

'Excuse me,' Neil said to his hosts, putting his hand over the mouthpiece as you were supposed to. 'I have to take this.'

'Of course,' Azim said.

'No problem,' Elin said.

'Just a second,' Neil said to Adam.

He strode into the courtyard but found it crowded with diners, waiters, a half-hearted belly-dancer. He hurried out of the restaurant, bearing the phone like a fizzing hand grenade, and down the steps that led to the seafront. He ignored the carpet salesmen ('Is not shop, is museum!'), crossed the road and found himself on the almost deserted boardwalk that stretched along the shore of the Caspian. No waves, just dead black water.

'Hi, Adam,' he said, rewinding, giving his friend a chance to begin again. To begin differently.

'Philly, I've found her.'

'Who?' Neil asked, although he already knew. A nauseating aroma of oil wafted off the sea. In the distance, beyond the boardwalk and the trees, he made out the silhouette of an offshore platform, a lone orange beacon flashing at its apex in the Caucasian night.

'Rose, of course. I've found her, Neil. I've found Rose.'

Panic surged up Neil's throat. Here they came – the shame, the recrimination, the policemen whom Eric was going to call but, for some blessed reason, hadn't. He fought it down.

'What are you talking about?'

'I said I've—'

'Where?'

'The internet,' Adam said. 'MySpace. I registered and I searched for her and now I've found her. She's . . . hair . . . at least . . .'

The signal cracked up; Neil caught one word in three. He walked up the boardwalk, towards the oil platform. Adam was still there, patchy and scrambled but still with him. Neil raised the handset above his head and waved it in the warm air, hoping to reignite the signal-strength bars in the corner of the miniature screen. Around thirty metres ahead of him, beneath a tree that canopied the boardwalk, another man was brandishing his phone in the air, conjuring the same ethereal magic. To anyone watching it would have looked as if they were semaphoring each other in a strange, short-range code.

Neil turned away from the man and walked back along the boardwalk, towards the restaurant. He regained his signal.

'You still there?'

'Yes,' Adam said. 'Yes, I'm here. Just lost each other for a second.'

'What time is it there? Aren't you at work?' – as if he might disqualify his friend's intelligence on a technicality.

'Yes,' Adam said, 'I'm in the office. I'm looking at her now. I suppose it's her. I'm looking at her picture.'

'What do you mean, you suppose?'

There was a pause at the London end, that air of vacancy and distraction that descends when an interlocutor is doing something else, typically involving a computer, sometimes a television with the sound turned down. The ghostly hiatus of the multi-gadget era, in which everyone is always half-elsewhere.

'She's got a photo on her profile page, it's a funny kind of photo. I was saying – Neil, when I lost you – I was saying that I *think* it's her. Can't be completely sure but it looks like it's her. I'll send you the link.'

'Don't, Ads,' Neil said. 'Anyway, how the hell would you know what she looks like now?'

'You might need to register.'

'Just don't.'

'You don't understand, she might be okay, she might be fine. Maybe she's forgiven us, or, you know, she would forgive us, if . . . '

Neil sensed the panic coursing back. 'Have you contacted her? Sent her a message or whatever?'

160

'No. Not yet.'

'Adam, don't. Don't contact her. Listen to me. Just don't.'

He turned around. The semaphoring man had finished his phone call; two other men, whom Neil hadn't previously noticed, and whose outnumbering presence might have troubled him if he had, rose like ghosts from a bench in the shadows beneath the tree to join him. All three walked away from him and up the boardwalk, towards the oil platform; its orange light pulsed through the tree's upper branches. Neil found himself mindlessly waving farewell with his free hand, though the man could no longer see him and he and Neil were strangers.

Adam said, 'What colour was her hair?'

'What?'

'In Yosemite. Come on! What colour was her hair?'

'Sorry, can't remember,' Neil lied.

'Yes, you can. You can, Neil. She's a brunette in the photo but for some reason I thought she was fairer.'

'What else does it say?'

'What?'

'Nothing,' Neil said, backtracking on his curiosity. 'Look, I've got to go. I'm at a dinner. Local partners, total shysters. You should go too, Adam. Work on whatever it is you're putting into the little box today.'

'I'll send you the link.'

'I'm not interested.'

'It says she lives in Taos. In New Mexico. You know, Georgia O'Keeffe.'

'I said I'm not interested. I'm hanging up now, Adam.'

'It says she has a brother.'

'Adam,' Neil snapped, 'what the fuck is this about? I

thought we were finished with this, I thought you were over this crap. I've tried, I have, but … What are you trying to do to me? It's enough to—'

'She had a brother, didn't she?'

Neil breathed deeply. 'Just don't contact her.'

'Why not?'

'I'm hanging up,' Neil repeated, and he did, pressing the *Disconnect* button hard, hoping that Adam wouldn't send him the link, since if he did, Neil might have to click through and look at the picture. Look at Rose, out there in New Mexico with Georgia Whoeverthefuck.

The traffic on the road between the boardwalk and the old city had picked up, rickety taxis alternating with late-model Mercs. Neil weaved through the vehicles, eager, suddenly, to be back in the private room with Azim and Elin. Since that night in the rain a year ago he had been sure that he and Adam could carry on, just somewhat differently, slightly recalibrated, maybe even for the better. Perhaps, after all, forgiveness could be provisional, a probation rather than an acquittal. He climbed the steps to the restaurant.

The bodyguards stood motionless against the wall. Elin was asleep in his chair, chin on chest. His sheath of family photos had fallen from his lap onto the floor; the laminated face of a small girl, eyes wide, was lying beside her father's Italian shoe. Azim was eating kumquats. He smiled at Neil with his full mouth as he sat down.

Elin woke up when the maître d' came in with the bill. Neil reached for his wallet to contribute. Azim half-wagged, half-pointed a finger at him. 'Your money,' he said, 'is no good in my country.'

He and Elin laughed. Neil saw the joke, and laughed too,

though it was Farid's money, not his, that they were celebrating. Not even Farid's, in fact, though they didn't need to
know that. He gave them nothing.

ADAM wasn't sure that Neil had rung off until he lowered
the phone from his ear and saw the word *Disconnected* on the
screen, below it the call's duration, *7:47*. He wasn't annoyed
by his friend's brusqueness; he wasn't distressed by the
photo. On the contrary, he felt vindicated, almost elated. The
girl was real, and, since she was real, she might be able,
somehow, to release him.

The immigration minister bustled through the office,
accompanied by his condescending adviser, en route to
somewhere more enclosed. Adam scarcely looked up from
Rose's profile. The warmest acknowledgement he could
hope for was another 'Good to see you'.

Heidi appeared at the entrance to his cubicle. He closed
his browser and enlarged the briefing paper he was writing
on the relative efficacy of state and private deportation
squads. These documents were the extent of his discourse
with the powerful. Adam knew that half the time they were
destined to languish, unread, at the bottom of the minister's
overstuffed red box.

'Coffee?' Heidi said. 'Last call.'

'Can't now,' Adam said. 'But later?'

'How much later?'

'Do you mean, what time do I get off?'

'No, I mean, should I just ask someone else?'

Adam frequently coffeed with Heidi, up in the deathly
canteen (his preference) or down in one of the overpriced
chains (hers). Sometimes, in the summer, they would scrim-
mage through the tourists photographing the squirrels to eat

their sandwiches together on the lawn in St James's Park. Occasionally they went for an after-work drink at the ye olde pub in the alley near the ministry. Their boozing male colleagues loosened their ties, stuffed their non-drinking hands into their pockets and thrust out their hips; the women crossed one arm beneath their busts and sipped their gin and tonics; all of them shot prurient glances at Adam and Heidi, who were widely assumed to be having an affair – an impression that arose because they spoke to each other in the office, actual words, physical mouths and ears, and human-to-human contact had come to seem intrusive, *verboten*, a borderline molestation in the high email age.

'Twisted my arm,' Adam said. 'But, look, I've got a meeting with Nick five minutes ago. After that, okay? If I haven't strangled him.'

Nick walked past the cubicle in one of his trademark postman shirts, averting his gaze.

Adam did a rapid overheard-office-insult calculation: insultee's walking pace multiplied by interval between insult and his appearance on the scene, divided by volume of insulter's voice. Nick probably hadn't heard. It was probably just their adultery that he was ignoring.

'Close,' Heidi said. 'Careful.'

'Always,' Adam said, and smiled.

Too much. Heidi blushed, a picturesque Anglo-Chinese burnish. Adam looked meaninglessly at his screensaver: him and Neil at the Faithful Couple, scanned, uploaded and immortal.

Okay, they flirted. They flirted just enough to salve the blow to his ego from the loosenings and sags, the ambushing jowls. But nothing happened, nothing ever had, less even than with those two women on the Strand, and that had been nothing, too. It was mostly jokes, him and Heidi, wisecracks and one-liners, like him and Neil, you could say, plus an implicit mutual acknowledgement, the understanding that he needed to share with at least one person in the ministry: We are still two human beings, even here in the machine.

These days, when he tried to have sex with Claire, she generally kissed him back, kissed him off, the way his grandmother might have done if he had kissed her on the lips by accident – mouth closed and pursed, unyielding, on the appalled side of polite – and Adam rolled away and lay on his back, no part of their bodies touching, offended and ashamed. These days Claire's idea of seduction, when she was sure the children were asleep and felt she ought to, was to reach under the duvet, hitch up her nightie and say, 'We can fuck if you want.'

He couldn't make her want him. When he trimmed the old-man hairs in his nostrils and ears, it was Heidi's notice he was anticipating. She pirouetted and returned to her desk, only her slender top half visible, like some graceful aquatic bird, as she weaved between the serried desks and computer screens.

Adam turned back to his screensaver. Over the years he had wavered about whose arm was interrupting the picture's edge. It might be hers. Very likely it was hers. He had given less attention to the tree itself, the deep grooves in the bark and the hollowed-out crevice that, now he came to focus on it, looked as if it might swallow them.

THE question was straightforward, Nick insisted in the meeting room. Thirty thousand asylum-seekers, give or take, arrived in the country each year. How many of them departed? The minister needed to know. The higher the figure, the better, obviously, but at a minimum they needed a number.

Nick sucked the end of his pen. When he withdrew it from his mouth the lid lingered between his lips; he picked it out with his other hand. Like Adam he had transferred from crime to immigration, but more recently and importantly. Extended acquaintance hadn't made them friends. On the contrary, theirs was one of those office relationships in which longevity instils a firm, empirical assurance that they never would be, a certainty that was itself a kind of comfort. Nick was out of his depth but shrewd enough to realise.

Unfortunately not, Adam explained. The statisticians could rustle up a combined, annual figure for forcible removals and the voluntary departures that were reported to the authorities. But that wouldn't correspond to the number of arrivals for the year and couldn't safely be compared with it.

'Why not? Of course it can.'

Nick bent the pen between his thumbs as if he meant to break it. A noose of pimples ringed his neck above his shirt collar; he had lost much of his hair since their days together in crime and shorn the horseshoe that remained.

They had said something about a brother, one of them had, Adam was sure of it. Taos, New Mexico.

'Adam?'

'Because they aren't processed quickly enough,' Adam said. 'The figures don't tally, you see. The ones we remove this year arrived last year, or the year before, or even the year before that.'

There was a jug of misty water on the table but no glasses.

'Three years ago?'

166

Why shouldn't he contact her? He could do it tactfully, respectfully, enquiring about her welfare. Hers and her father's.

'Yes,' Adam said. 'Have you seen the files in Croydon? It's ridiculous. They're stacked three feet thick. Though some of them, when it takes that long, end up being allowed to stay on compassionate grounds even if their claim has been refused. And of course quite a lot of them sort of vanish in between.'

Sheila, the Head of Returns, was on long-term sick, but Adam was still her deputy for purposes of pay and rank. Adam Tayler, Deputy Head of Returns. He could no longer tell himself that he was playing against type. This was his type.

Nick looked at Adam and then at the far, unoccupied end of the table. 'The permanent secretary would like an answer,' he said in a menacingly calm tone. 'The minister wants to know, presumably so he can tell Parliament. He doesn't want to hear, "We don't know". He doesn't want to say it.'

Nick left it there.

'I'm sorry,' Adam said eventually. 'I'm not sure what we can do.'

Or he could be casual, jaunty: *Hi!!!! Remember me??* As if there were nothing in the world to be ashamed or sensitive about.

Nick blew out his cheeks. 'Okay, take a previous year. Take 2002. Tell me how many asylum-seekers who lodged claims in 2002 have gone. We will extrapolate that into an annual proportion.'

'Sorry,' Adam said. 'Removals aren't tabulated by date of arrival. The stats people are fixing that, in fact – you know,

167

cohort tracking. From this year, I think. But for what you want, somebody would have to go through the paperwork on every decision. Sorry.'

There must have been a time, Adam had concluded, there must have been a moment when he was supposed to have made his move, like a middle-distance runner taking off around a bend. He should have seen a bill through Parliament, owned a crisis, God knew there were enough of them to go round. Half of it – success or stagnation, becoming a 7 or not – was dumb luck, but the other half was taking your chances when they came. There was a slow stream in the Civil Service, less formal but just as tractive as the fast one, and he had stumbled onto it. If he wasn't careful by the end of his thirties he would find himself sitting it out, buckling up for the long, lengthening wait for the pension. Adam saw people doing that, dull behind the eyes after they had given up. That would mean twenty-five years to refine one of the functions available to the bypassed in departmental ecology: to be an avuncular throwback (he would wear braces, hum his school song), or, worse, a 'character' (he would wear odd socks and assault the photocopier). Worst of all, he might be exiled to some acronymous quango, which twice a year would lodge harmless reports on border queues or prison diets in the library of the House of Commons.

Nick scowled, put the pen back in his mouth and bent over his papers. After a minute Adam understood that he was supposed to leave. He stood and returned to his desk.

The evening before he had seen Will – Will from his job in television, Will from Tenerife – being interviewed outside a broadcasting awards ceremony on a reddish carpet. Will from television – on television. He looked slimmer than he had

168

been a decade before, and taller, somehow, though of course he couldn't have been. Cuban heels, possibly. He was controller of one of the BBC's new cable channels; something that he had commissioned had won a gong. Will had smiled and pushed his glasses up his nose as he accepted the interviewer's congratulations.

Adam emailed Heidi: *Survived. Your place or mine?*

He would look again that evening, after the children were in bed. There were only a few hours to get through first.

Who was Neil to say he shouldn't contact her?

HOME for the companionable violence of bath-time, the silent and dependable teamwork with Claire, in the miniature factory the maisonette had become: food in, recycling, excrement, and reasonably clean and well-nourished children out. After the bath came the borderline anarchy of the interlude before bed, Adam poised on the landing outside the kids' bedroom like a referee in a bout of all-in wrestling (*almost* everything is allowed).

'Cartoons tonight,' Harry said, fiddling with his penis. 'One more?'

'Not tonight, lollipop.'

'Me too,' Ruby said. She had Claire's features but hers were finer, almost gaunt. In the bath, with her hair slicked back, and sometimes when she was crying, Adam could just make out the baby in her face, the new-born physiognomy that he knew she would soon lose. She had fallen in the park that day and scraped her little knees.

'Mummy,' Harry shouted down the stairs, 'it's cartoons tonight, isn't it?' – the divide and rule instinct kicking in, as primal, Adam had noticed, as the dancing instinct, the story-telling instinct and the nostalgia instinct.

'No,' Claire shouted up. 'Now get to bed.'

'Bedtime,' Adam said. 'I love you, beetle-bugs.'

'I need a poo,' Harry said.

They'll kill me in the end, Adam thought.

When they were down he closed the front door quietly and got into their key-scratched car, sweeping the accumulated parking vouchers, empty smoothie containers and maps printed off the internet from the dashboard into the well of the passenger seat. Adam had a weekly arrangement with a moped driver from the Bengal Express. The driver, Suleiman, met him at the perimeter of the restaurant's delivery zone, by the side of Ealing Common, to exchange a lamb bhuna and pilau rice for his eight pounds forty-five, a university penchant that Adam had re-embraced in fatherhood. Claire said there were bound to be acceptable takeaways that would deliver to their door and spare him the bother, but the Bengal Express was a dependable pleasure, and Adam relied on it.

Suleiman was standing in the designated spot, near a streetwise London oak, texting with his free hand and smelling of cigarette smoke. If someone had put Suleiman in a police-style line-up, a pageant of wiry men in their twenties all silhouetted or facing away, a plastic bag in one hand and a phone in the other, Adam would have picked him out every time. Something about his posture and demeanour.

'Hi, Suleiman,' Adam said.

'Hi,' Suleiman said, and smiled.

'How you doing?' Adam asked. They weren't well-acquainted but they weren't quite strangers, either. Perhaps it was only ever a question of degree.

'Good,' Suleiman said. 'Good.'

'Look after yourself.'

'See you next week,' Suleiman said. 'Be safe.'

Listening to the Eagles on the drive home, the thought entered Adam's head that he could be one of those men you sometimes read about who nip out on an errand, shouting 'Five minutes, darling', and take off, disappear. He couldn't, of course. Of course not. The children.

He ate his food in the kitchen, mechanically, while Claire munched a salad and watched a vote-me-out-of-here television show, discharging the new civic duty of celebrity democracy: vote for the one you love, or the one you hate, only vote now and often. She shoved her used tissue between the cushion of the sofa and the arm, the umpteenth time, umpteen squared, but he decided not to mention it this evening.

Adam climbed the stairs to their bedroom and plugged in his laptop on the dressing table. He closed the door as the computer booted up, awaiting the insipidly welcoming melody.

HE HADN'T meant to find her, honestly he hadn't. At least, that hadn't been Adam's main or his first intention when he minimised his policy document, opened his browser and began that afternoon's allotted Googling. His own internet footprint was still pathetically shallow: he scored a glancing reference in the write-up of an immigration conference at the University of Nottingham, plus a couple of mentions in online reports of school and university reunions. He searched for Chaz, Archie, Chloe, the university ex who was supposed to come to California, but hadn't, leaving him to Neil, the pick-up, the Faithful Couple. Chloe was married and living in Dubai ... A personalised zombie show, the phantoms parading before him on a whim and a click. The past was back, miraculously navigable like a new-old continent, peopled by the resurrected dead. History was no longer finished, even if you wanted it to be. You could unearth it, and vice versa.

From Chloe, to Neil. He rated several mentions in property magazines, mostly in conjunction with Farid, plus one or two in the business pages of bona fide newspapers, offering mollifying quotes on Farid's behalf. Also the contacts section of the discreet website for Farid's company. There were some internet-ancient mentions in Neil's HappyFamilies capacity, in *schadenfreude*-heavy analyses of the dotcom bust. He was much more prolific than Adam.

From Neil, that afternoon, to Yosemite. He found Trey easily, almost instantly, the distinctive first name making him conspicuous if you knew how to look. Trey was still working as a guide in northern California, but for a different outfit. This new operator's website included a photo of him (filled-out, greyer) dangling a salmon from a fishing rod, an amiable grin in place of the snarl Adam envisaged (*What the fuck, you guys?*). Next he found the gay couple from the camping trip. Their first names, Mike and Patrick, unexpectedly returned to him, along with the excavated details that they lived in Reno, and that one of them (both, he soon established) ran a landscape gardening firm.

It was only after that – after Chaz, Archie, Chloe, Neil; Trey, Mike and Patrick – that Adam came to Rose.

In the past two years, every few weeks, he had tried 'Rose AND Eric AND Boulder', but it was useless without her full name. All he remembered was that she had one of those only-in-America, ethnically oxymoronic portmanteau surnames: O'Malley-Rodriguez, Romario-Johansson, Esquivel-Schlezinger, something like that. He had seen the double-barrel on the slip of paper she gave to Neil when she marched to their tent to say goodbye, trying to be steadfast. The two of them had looked at the name and address, printed carefully in unjoined letters, a wonky xxx appended at the bottom, when they were sitting next to each other on the bus to San Francisco. He remembered that she had drawn a little heart in place of the dot over an i . . . at least one i. He had never seen that scrap of paper again and had no idea what Neil had done with it. Probably he had thrown it away, or left it in his jeans when they went into the wash.

In his cubicle, Adam concentrated. He closed his eyes. Irish-Mexican. Cuban-Swedish. Italian-German. Definitely German, he realised, but it felt like German should come first. German-Balkan. German-Hispanic. German . . . Celtic! Schneider. Koestler. Five minutes later, he thought he had it: Schmidt!

Schmidt-Davies. Schmidt-Evans. Schmidt-McNeil.

He eliminated several dozen other permutations. He had given up and moved on to his father (something about his consultancy work, a letter he had written to a newspaper about the green belt) when, of its own accord, it came to him: Ferguson. Schmidt-Ferguson! Schmidt-Ferguson. Rose Schmidt-Ferguson.

Rose Schmidt-Ferguson.

He was almost sure and giddy and terrified but there wasn't much on her, either. He really ought to get back to his document, prepare for his meeting with Nick. She cropped up in a list of students at a college in Arizona that Adam had never heard of. Class of '00, that sounded about right, they numbered by the year of graduation, didn't they? *High school's what I mean.*

Had to be her. But there was nothing else.

MySpace was his last gambit of the day. He already had a ghost profile though he had hardly ever used it.

She was there. There she was.

He searched for her, her name came up, he clicked through to her profile page, and she was on his screen quicker than he was expecting – too quickly, he wasn't altogether ready for her. He glanced sharply away from the screen and towards the padded partition between his cubicle and the outside world. Be smiling, Adam thought, as he trained his eyes on the list of internal telephone numbers and fire-escape instructions that were pinned to the partition. Please be smiling – untraumatised, unvictimised, too well balanced to be a cause of retribution. At the same time he knew that her smile would prove nothing. Of course she would be smiling. Nobody posted a photo of themself frowning. It was childish superstition to think the image would express her essence and fate, Google-age voodoo.

Smile, Rose. Please.

She wasn't smiling. But neither was she weeping or grimacing or wearing a wimple. The photo was too posed and affected to infer a mood. She sat in profile, a curtain of hair obscuring her cheek, her visible eye wide and staring. Her hair ... She was a brunette in the photo, but Adam had an image of Rose as a fairer girl, almost blond, a blonde wearing a sarong ... He might be mistaken. She might have dyed it. She might have changed beyond his recognition. He had changed. Why expect her to be the same, faithful to his half-invented memory, conveniently imperishable, eternally fifteen years old? (*Fifteen!*) Why should the decay that his mirror averred each morning – the crow's feet around his eyes, the body hair that, having vanquished his shoulders, was mystifyingly colonising his upper arms – be surprising or disappointing in her? Of course it was her.

Adam had scratched his knee. He had called Neil. Probably he would have sent his friend the link he didn't want, if Heidi hadn't materialised in his cubicle. He might have written to her then and there.

FIVE minutes of top-up exegesis at the most, Adam told himself at Claire's dressing table, the computer screen emitting its lunar glow but the bedroom otherwise dark. Or ten. Ten minutes at the outside. There might be something he had missed.

This time he retrieved her profile instantly. Her entry was almost as scant and poorly maintained as his own, as if, like him, she had registered and then lost interest (though for his part Adam wasn't tech-savvy enough for much elaboration). Besides Rose's move to New Mexico, he gleaned the names of two friends, Rio and Todd, and of her brother, George. She had uploaded no further photos, specified no interests and published no blog posts.

Adam wondered how she thought of them now. At first, he speculated at the dressing table, she might have been proud of what had happened, bragged about it, even. She might have become a minor celebrity in her high school on account of her escapade. At first; and that could have been how she depicted that night for a few years. But that, Adam knew, was as much as he could legitimately hope for, and possibly too much. Instead she might have been humiliated by that farewell tableau, too ashamed to forgive her father for witnessing it, her resentment and his incomprehension later curdling into estrangement. (Once, when his parents visited him at university, Adam's mother had stumbled upon the

175

condoms in his bedroom, their eyes had met, and they hadn't spoken for a month.) She might have regretted the liaison instantly, been sobbing for the fact of Neil that morning rather than over his departure. Later, at that college in Arizona, what did she say to people – boyfriends, for example – about the pale Englishman who had seduced her in California, and the overconfident friend who encouraged him and would have seduced her if he could?

He caught his breath as it occurred to him she might be able to see that *Adam Tayler, London, England* had searched for and found her. Unlikely, he reassured himself. In any case, his name wouldn't mean much to her. It wouldn't be his name that she remembered.

In the children's bedroom, Ruby cried out. Adam froze, listening, but the yelp came only once. Bad dream, probably. Rats or bats or witches. He was grateful to the children now, in a way; or, he and they were quits over this. Ruby had induced the fierce remorse, and the fear, both of which Adam knew he might never shake off entirely, might have to live with for ever, dull and tolerable but persistent like a burned-out infatuation. At the same time everything before his children now seemed part of a different innings or account, the two of them forming a human statute of limitations.

He shouldn't have done that to you, Adam might write to her. *We shouldn't have done that to you. We're sorry. I'm sorry.* Some breathless declaration along those lines. Or, *I don't know whether your father told you, but I knew . . . So you see, it was me too, in a way. Me as much as him.* Only after the apology would he write, *The thing is, in the morning, your father . . . I know it's selfish of me but if you could just . . .*

Possibly Neil was right about contacting her. She couldn't have forgotten – nobody forgets that – but she might have relegated them to the back of the closet of her memory, only occasionally uncovering them when she was sifting through the clutter of her childhood. Possibly she thought about it every day. Either way she might not be pleased to hear from him, however urgently he repented. *I just need to know that you're okay. Tell me.*

At the same time, studying Rose's photo in his bedroom, Adam was furious with her. Not for being younger than they first thought (had they thought?), nor for swimming and splashing them. Not for anything at all that she had done, in fact. He blamed her only for existing. Had she not existed, if she hadn't been there, it couldn't have happened. He wouldn't be crouched masochistically over his computer screen; he would worry about his daughter only in the ordinary way, without this superfluous, gnawing superstition. Their friendship, his and Neil's, wouldn't have been contaminated from the start. If she ceased to exist now, there would be no victim, and so, from a certain, twistedly legalistic point of view, no offence to speak of or to pay for. Looking at the screen (*Warning: Battery Low!*), Adam oscillated between an impulse to atone and an urge to obliterate her.

He heard a footfall on the stairs. Or a spontaneous creak. Probably a creak. These old houses.

Or, if not her, could he at least obliterate those few days of his life? If he were allowed to rewind and delete any three of the days he had lived, he would choose the three in Yosemite. His life could be three days shorter: that would be a fair exchange and settlement, surely. Or let him erase that one evening, just those few hours. To be able to go back and cancel a few hours in a whole life – was that really so unreasonable a request? Everybody should be entitled to that, he thought. At least to that.

He looked at the screen; the nails of his right hand scratched his left forearm. His heart sped up. Perhaps without those few hours, Adam considered, there would have been no him and Neil at all. Maybe they had stayed together as might two old lags determined to keep an eye on each other, united by their misdemeanour rather than in spite of it. Turn a betrayal inside out and you found its opposite, a secret and a bond. Perhaps that was what friendship came down to: trusting each other with the very worst things – because you had to, didn't you? You had to trust and tell someone – the shaming weaknesses, the lowest abasements, the flaws and offences that would always be there between you, even if you never spoke of them. A lifelong, affectionate mutual blackmail.

Friendship was keeping an eye on each other. Their bond was Rose.

'WHAT are you doing?' She switched on the light.

'Nothing,' Adam said. He swivelled round to face Claire, reaching behind him to snap the screen as he turned, missing on the first swipe and knocking over a tube of body lotion.

'What is it, Adam?' She was focusing on the flattened computer, or rather on the shallow reflection of the computer in the dressing table mirror. 'Tell me. What are you looking at?'

Curiosity to indignation to rage inside a dozen words. She dipped her head forward expectantly, minus the smile that usually finished the gesture.

'Nothing, Clezzy,' he repeated. 'It's nothing.'

'Oh, Adam,' she said. She gripped her hips as she did when reprimanding their children. 'For God's sake.'

It's funny how trust goes, Adam thought. Part of him

wouldn't have minded, might have quite liked, a chance to say, like a philanderer in a farce, *It isn't what you think*. Some in flagrante gotcha featuring a willing blonde or two and a comically timed entrance by his wife. But not this. This wasn't even the low-risk, high-bandwidth version of that moment that Claire apparently thought it was, in which she would catch him with his dick in one hand and the fingers of the other typing misspelled, all-capitalised instructions to a virtual friend in Latvia or Manila.

This was the opposite of pornography: it was expiation. It really wasn't what she thought. But what was he supposed to say?

'It isn't what you think,' he said.

Claire laughed, caustically and unamused. 'What do I think?' she asked, her voice like a ticking bomb.

He couldn't say to her, *In California, Neil* ... Or, *Me and Neil* ... *Thing is, her father* ... *And then when Ruby was born* ... *Today, at work* ... *Come and take a look*. It wouldn't make sense to her. He confided fears and embarrassments to Claire that no one else could see, not even Neil, vanities and midnight doubts and, recently, his haemorrhoids. His grief at still not being a 7. But not this. It was too late, and Rose was theirs, not hers.

'Ballroom-dancing lessons,' he said. 'For your birthday, there's a place in Bloomsbury. You've spoiled it now, Claire. Christ.'

Adam stretched his legs in front of him and crossed them at the ankles. He folded his arms over his chest. He was fond of his lie. Neil should have been there to appreciate it.

He could see her not believing him. She was staring past him into the mirror – the huddle of cosmetics in the foreground, the computer nestling among them, then the back of

Adam's chair, his neck, the resilient fullness of his hair, and Claire herself, shrunken and open-mouthed in the middle distance. He could see her wanting to rush over, flip up the screen, demand or remember or guess his password and ascertain what or who was in his browser. But she couldn't. The manoeuvre would be too loud an intimation of divorce. And she was too tired.

She said, 'I'm going to bed,' not repudiating his explanation but not accepting it, either.

'Me too,' Adam agreed, not wanting to leave her alone with the computer.

She sat on the edge of the bed to undress, rotating her torso so her breasts were shielded from him when she took off her bra (*Ridiculous!*). She reached under her pillow for the extra-large T-shirt that she liked to sleep in; she went to the bathroom to brush her teeth and anoint her face (the same brand of moisturiser since they met, its aroma part of the smell of her, a scent Adam had thought he would always recognise and love). He hurried out of his clothes, draping them over the chair and the computer, and lay on his back under the duvet, straight and still like a corpse in a coffin on *The Sopranos*. His foot met a stray piece of train set; he kicked it onto the carpet, stubbing a toe.

She turned out the light and joined him, lying on her side, facing away.

'Who did you vote for?'

'You know who I voted for ... Oh, that. No one,' Claire said. 'They're all as bad as each other.'

Nursery-rhyme sing-songs in church halls ... accidental shits in swimming pools ... perpetual laundry. The immurement. If Claire had stayed at the gallery she might have been running the place by now. But the salary/childcare sums had made no sense, even with her mother helping them one day a week, rising to two when she lost the second man, the bloke with the zany cummerbund from the wedding.

'That knee looks sore, doesn't it? Did she fall off her scooter again?'

Claire grunted.

They had got money all wrong, Adam now saw, held it in insufficient respect. He hadn't foreseen how the gap would grow, their line on the money graph rising slightly, then flatlining, while the Neils of the world – while Neil's – shot up faster and for longer, until you would need a squiggly break in the graph's vertical axis to compare their incomes. At the beginning, when it had seemed like a windfall, he had tried to regard Neil's wealth as harmless, amusing, but when it lasted, became a structural fact in their lives, they had experienced money's cleavage, its powerful negative magnetism.

'Nick gave me a going over today. Asylum stats. Imbecile.'

Nothing.

She never said so – you couldn't say it because of the children, the children were supposed to be enough – but he knew Claire had expected more. Not salary or square-footage but a different kind of more. A general rather than a particular, material more. Sometimes, when he contemplated his life, Adam saw himself driving round and round an underground car park with a voucher in his mouth.

She sighed, plumped her pillow, sighed again. Under the duvet she pulled her T-shirt down towards her knees. He raised his head, anticipating a last-ditch conversation – Let's not go to bed on an argument, Claire always said – but she was silent. The Dinky duet was sung out.

In bed, ostracised, Adam remembered how, when they

were very young, he and Harriet had seen his parents dancing together (in his memory they were dressed to the nines: a wedding, maybe) and had thought them as beautiful as a fairy tale, the most beautiful and enamoured couple in the world. It was their fault, all that happiness, or what had felt like happiness to children, leaving him with too little to prove. When he spoke to them now they complained about each other in icy, ominous periphrases (*Please tell your father* ...). He was noticing a new tightness around his mother's mouth, and a new, defensive habit of introducing her remarks with *I'm sorry, but* ... as if the world were perpetually countermanding her (*I'm sorry, but she's beautiful*). At family meals his father constantly refilled Adam's wine glass, and Claire's, to reduce the supply to his wife. Adam had begun to wonder about the bank account and – who knew? – bedroom indiscretions that his parents might be concealing, must always have been.

The known unknowns of other people's marriages, even theirs. Even his: Heidi, and that smooch on the Strand, and Rose.

Claire loved him, he thought. Her anger told him that. He loved her, too. He still loved her, even if, most of the time, the love didn't seem especially helpful or relevant. It wasn't anyone's fault, except maybe the children, adept as they were at finding the cracks and prising them apart.

'Love you,' he said. He rolled onto his side to spoon her, and she let him, though she might already have been asleep.

You see, if you are okay, that would mean ... Could you possibly ask your father to take it back?

THEIR names were Sian and Alida and they were from New Zealand. Alida was Neil's and Sian was Adam's, one of those spontaneous assortments determined instantly by looks, height and ebullience. At least, they said their names were Sian and Alida, who knew what they were really called. Adam had introduced himself as Henry and Neil as Kevin.

'At the opera,' he said, when Sian asked where they had been that evening. 'You know, Covent Garden. *Carmen*. It was a blast.'

'My friend here, Henry, he's a set designer,' Neil put in.

'Papier mâché mostly,' Adam clarified. 'Collages, murals. Castles that they slide out of the wings.'

'Slaves and elephants,' Neil said.

'No kidding,' Sian said.

'Choice,' Alida said.

The two men had been out to dinner at a burger place behind the Strand. It was the summer after Adam told Neil the truth about California, the year before he exhumed Rose. They were ambling in the direction of Trafalgar Square when the rain began – a sudden, unEnglish monsoon, over-running the drains and flooding along the gutters as if London's subterranean rivers were erupting, one of those violent summer rains that make it seem the whole grey, non-porous city must drown. They were drenched within a minute and took shelter in an airline salesroom's doorway. Sian and Alida had occupied the recess before them. The women were tipsier than Neil and Adam, a condition and opportunity that they clocked straight away, their decom-missioned chat-up instincts still whirring.

'We're having a party,' Sian said, after the sizings-up and jokes about swimming for it. 'You should come.'

'Who else is going?' Adam said. The downpour felt like a carnival.

'Just us,' Sian said. She cocked her hips and pinched his lapel. The rainwater was trickling into the doorway.

'Come,' Alida said to Neil, casting down her eyes so as to turn them up again. Twenty-seven, Neil estimated. Twenty-eight. Knee-high suede boots, tight jeans, leopard-print accessories. Grown-up women: drunk, a long way from home and looking unfussily for a good time.

It was odd, in a way, that the two of them had never been through this rite together, not like this. The backing up and egging on and keeping pace. Adam glanced across at Neil – questions and permission and joint amazement that this could still be happening to them, in their mid-thirties, with their kids and careers and the rest, that they might be allowing it to. Neil nodded.

'What sort of party is it?' Adam said. The rain had slicked and darkened his hair.

'Well, Henry, it's this sort,' Sian said, pushing onto her tiptoes to kiss him. As their lips met – just the lips, briefly – Adam's eyes found Neil's again.

Neil and Alida kissed, too, politely, understanding that they were supposed to. Her lips were cold like a mermaid's, the back of her coat where he gripped her was wet and warm at once. He kept his eyes open and saw the scalp beneath her hair, the brown roots that betrayed the blond. The water penetrating their hide-out looked like urine. When she diffidently introduced her tongue he pulled away.

The rain eased off and the four of them walked up the Strand and into the Aldwych, notionally to find a taxi to the women's digs near Euston. A bus splashed gutter water over Neil's legs, and outside the cocoon of the doorway and without the transfiguration of the rain, he could see that this was impossible. A swivel of his eyes and a nod from Adam and they absconded, diving into an unlicensed cab that pulled up serendipitously at the kerb.

That was the night Neil's grievance over California lifted, or seemed to. To begin with he hadn't been certain that it would. The first time they had seen each other after Adam told him, a year earlier, had been strange, strangerish, as if they were beginning their relationship again. Jess and Claire were there, and that had helped, since they couldn't talk about California in front of them and, though the women didn't much like each other and rarely pretended to, their niceties filled the air time. The next time had been at a kiddie-friendly party at the Taylers'. Neil was in the kitchen, watching Adam's father show the children, other people's children, how to strike the piñata that was strung up in the living room. Adam came in for a glass of water. As he turned the tap, Neil said, 'To be honest, Ad, I'm not sure what I'm doing ... I mean, to tell me now, after – something like that – after ten years ...'

Adam had shot a nervous look towards Claire and rasped, 'You told me it was nothing.'

'That's all you care about, isn't it? Her not finding out.'

'Tell Grandpa my turn,' Harry said, taking Adam's hand and leaning forward to drag him away, like a miniature workman on a cable.

Adam left the tap running; Neil turned it off. Jeremy struck the piñata over-arm and viciously, as if he were playing tennis, and split it.

From the beginning Neil had wanted to forgive him: in the underpopulated scheme of his life, he hadn't seen what other choice he had. But he only truly managed to that night in the rain. The point was, Adam would have gone through with it. He would have gone to Euston with Sian and Alida if Neil had required him to; if that had been his price. The kiss in the doorway was enough, the new secret and shared vulnerability that they needed. An equal secret, this time. Again the two of them against the world.

On the back seat of the taxi, steam rising from his rain-soaked trousers, agreeing never to mention this without either of them saying a word, their Balkan driver pining for Pristina, Neil's resentment seemed to wash away, as if it had only ever been an act. That was the end of her, he had hoped that night.

JESS was furious when he told her. Neil flew in from Baku, Jess from Buenos Aires, both of them retaining the rumpled vigour of the business-class traveller. They had sex immediately, out of habit as much as appetite, the sense that they ought to desire each other, the ghost of desire, as much as the thing itself. The lights were out as always, very little said, the distance Neil needed in his intimacy.

They showered. He shaved. They plugged in their BlackBerries, which rubbed alongside each other on the kitchen counter like mating reptiles. Neil told her about Rose. She couldn't remain a secret, or a risk, or a threat. He would bring her into the open, neutralise her, on his own terms.

Neil told her about the girl, the tent and the uproar in the morning, the competition the night before, how they had left her there, crying. 'I know I should have asked her,' he said. 'I know I should have told you about this before. I don't know, I'm sorry.'

Jess was furious, but not about Rose. Neil, the tent and Yosemite sounded quite humane, she considered, compared with, say, the concrete base of a war memorial, a winter night in Yorkshire, and a drunk, married man. Fifteen wasn't even that young, was her verdict. Little cow only got what she wanted, she was probably on a dare, who's to say she was a virgin, anyway?

'It wasn't like that,' Neil said. 'She wasn't.' He pictured her blushing and blushing when Adam flirted with her beside the campfire. Afterwards, in the tent, she had put her T-shirt back on, and her knickers, and she had propped her head on his chest and babbled about movies and friends and what the friends thought of those movies.

Her father should have known better, Jess said. (*Don't stay up late, honey.*) Anyway it was more than a decade ago, she told him. It was nothing.

Adam had better not contact her.

'That's what I keep saying, I know.'

She was furious with him for having taken the trouble to keep it from her. Not for not telling her, exactly. Had she found out about Rose accidentally, pursuing some leading remark that Neil let slip, this scrape wouldn't have mattered, Jess said. There were bound to be unmentioned details from their prior lives, half-forgotten summer jobs and abandoned hobbies, dead friendships and tipsy clinches too trivial to have brought up, which came as tiny yet salutary reminders of each other's mystery. She understood that. As for her, Neil didn't know the half of it, she told him. (Those men on the pedalo and her friend.)

The offence lay not in the trifling facts, nor in their concealment, but in the importance Neil himself had ascribed to them: in the secrecy and the conspiracy. A secret between him and Adam.

'You fucking boys,' Jess said. She picked up a corkscrew from the kitchen counter, registered that she was pointing it at Neil, and put it down. 'I mean, I can just see you. Stewing. Should I tell her? When should I tell her? Oh, Adam, what do you think? When I never would have given a fuck.'

'It wasn't like that.'

'What else do you two keep to yourselves?'

'Nothing.'

'What is it, then? Card school? Hash cakes? Little boys?'

'Jess, don't.'

'Christ, Neil . . . You're nobody's fool and nobody's child. You're your own you, that's the point of you, can't you see that? That's why I . . . You're all there. Except when you're with him, and you become this sort of adolescent sidekick. Look at him, Neil, and look at you. Look where you both are.'

'I said don't.'

'It's like he's your fucking father or something.'

'No,' Neil said. 'Not any more.'

Actually it had bolstered Neil, Adam's confession; it had tipped the scales in his favour. The yeoman and master routine was winding up. These days he saw Adam's faults, but had come to regard the annoyances (that thing he did with his jaw) as a part of his appeal. Fellowship in weakness was one of friendship's consolations.

'Or your mother.'

'What's my mother got to do with it?'

'Oh Neil,' Jess said. She picked up a knife and slashed open a packet of mozzarella, as if an aggressive pretence of normalcy might save them. The cloudy suspension ran over her hands. 'You're done for.'

The two of them had gone up to Yorkshire for the funeral of Jess's mother at the end of the previous year. A dozen mourners, plus a vicar who hadn't known the dead woman, in a church so cold that no one had removed their coats. No music, because neither Jess nor her mother had chosen any. On a shelf in her mother's bedroom closet, in a shoebox, Jess found: a yellowed local newspaper cutting about a rugby match in the twenties, in which her mother's father had played wing three-quarter; a photo of her parents on their wedding day, her mother in a satin dress, her father wearing a baggy suit, a gallon of Brylcreem and the smile of a man who had something to look forward to (though what did Jess know about that – what did she really know?); a letter from another man, not her father, written a year after her parents were married and a year before Jess was born, which said nothing in particular, and at the same time, between the lines, something very particular (*Ever yours, Ted*); a very small brown envelope containing a lock of Jess's baby hair (she hadn't realised how fair she had been); a letter Jess had sent home from university during what, judging from the date, must have been the middle of her first term, which genuinely said nothing in particular, between the lines or on them, and which she had no recollection of writing; a retirement card from her mother's colleagues at the primary school where, after she was widowed, she had worked as a dinner lady, as much for the company as for the money. More than the loss itself – which, truth be told, as Jess liked it to be, was sudden but less than devastating – what stung her, she said, was the sense of what her mother's life had been. And the unspoken question that this observation prompted, about what her own life would add up to.

Mothers.

'What do you—'

'It's only ever half of you, Neil. As if it's a part-time job or something. It's not only Adam, it's like a bit of you's missing.'

'What are you talking about?'

Jess laid the knife on the chopping board and looked down at the sliced mozzarella. He could still be surprised by how short she was without heels.

She sighed, then looked up at him. 'Is this it, then?' She had stopped her automated cooking, but for a moment Neil thought she was talking about their dinner. He glanced at the hob. 'I mean, for us, you twat.'

'Is what, what? What, Jess?'

He came round to her side of the counter, cornering her. Her face, from where he was standing, jutted into an outsized photograph of serried candy that hung on the wall behind her. She had bought it at the Museum of Modern Art, on a trip to New York for a meeting about a new Arab soft drink. Damage limitation: shut this down, get out alive.

'Come off it, Neil.'

'Jess,' Neil began, torn between wanting to talk her down and take her on, compromising on a soft, almost passive disagreement that vaguely implied she was unstable, and might have been expressly designed to infuriate her. 'Come on. We've hardly ever talked about it.'

'I suppose Adam's brats are enough for you.'

True: them and Sam, who was almost his, Neil was coming to believe, as much his, in a way, as he was his father's. Neil never wanted or expected to have babies of his own. He didn't feel equipped or trained for them, as if he were an animal that had been abandoned too early to know the proper procedure.

'What the hell are you talking about?'

'Oh, grow up, Neil. Fucking grow up. You can't be fifteen for ever, or however old you were when she died. Did you really think we'd go on like this indefinitely? Fuck, fuck, weekend break, fuck, fuck, conversation, new TV. Sex and holidays and buying cool appliances together.'

'Let's discuss it, then. Please.' Crying doesn't make you right, he thought.

She pushed past Neil, leaning into him more than she strictly needed to when their shoulders collided, Neil yielding less than he might have done. She retreated to the bathroom and closed the door. Neil picked up the mozzarella packet, meaning to put it in the bin, but some of the amniotic fluid was still sloshing inside the plastic, and he spilled it over the black and white floor. He swore and kneeled to wipe up the mess with a tea towel.

Jess came back while he was crouching, walking at speed and purposefully, her heels crackling on the tiles. 'You've done it again,' she said, in a voice that sounded angrier for being quiet. Her knee seemed to jerk in the direction of his forehead, and he momentarily feared she would injure him. The hand that wasn't holding the tea towel reached to fend her off. 'Your hair,' she said. 'Your fucking hair.'

Neil's hand moved to the crown of his head, pausing to finger the mole on his neck as it passed upwards.

'In the sink. Your fucking stubble. How many times?'

She slammed the front door on her way out. Neil stood up.

He hadn't told her that Adam had known about Rose. He lied to her about Adam's lie.

'ARE you getting divorced?'

Neil tickled Sam under his armpits.

'Stop it,' Sam said, kicking out. Neil moved out of range of the flailing legs. 'Stop it, Neil,' Sam repeated.

He fell, muddying his knees on the furrowed ground beneath the zip wire; he tried to brush his trousers with his hands, dirtied his palms, and rubbed them on his backside. He wiped his nose with a grimy index finger.

'Are you?' Sam asked again, not letting him off. Usually Jess came on their outings, but, since their quarrel three days before, she had been working to rule. She was businesslike, efficient in the discharge of her cohabitee's duties (tumble dryer, message from Brian, milk), but remote. She didn't feel for Sam what Neil did, she wasn't even close. She couldn't face the acting.

'We're not married,' Neil said. 'So we can't get divorced.'

'You know what I mean,' Sam said, impatient with the grown-up quibbling.

At eleven his face was leaner and his hair darker than they had once been. Physically he could still have passed for nine, but there was something worldly in his grey-green eyes and the shadows around them, a precocious intuition that life was not on his side, as you might expect in a child who spent too much time with his taciturn and immobile grandfather, and had seen his father wet himself. 'Fallen off the wagon,' Brian had whispered, though the last time Neil had seen Dan, his clammy skin and dull eyes, he worried that drink might not be the half of it. Dan had quit his plumbing course after a month.

'I don't know,' Neil said. 'Jess and me, we haven't decided. Don't think so.'

'Do you, you know, love her and all that?'

'To be honest, Sammy, I don't know.'

The following month, on the day of the bombs, the day people spoke to strangers and called their relatives – ranking them as they dialled, the instant, city-wide census of emotional priorities – Neil phoned Adam before he called Jess. He was furious with Adam but he called him first.

'Huh,' Sam said, racing away across the playground, his proto-adult interests supplanted by puerile ones, the twin identities overlapping and ironising each other. Beyond the playground fence and the scarred park trees, two giant yellow cranes supervised north-west London, ominously arrogant, the Triffids of the boom.

Sam climbed the frame and suspended himself from the monkey bars by the backs of his muddied knees. 'No hands! I can!' He began to cross the bars, his arms showily dangling.

Brian raised a palm from his thigh and indicated the danger with a wave, the weak swish of a superannuated pontiff. 'Careful,' he said. 'Tell him.'

'He's fine,' Neil said. 'Leave him.'

Halfway across Sam's foot hit a bar instead of rising over it; he tried again, was blocked again by the bar. He reached up with his arms but his stomach muscles wouldn't support him. Gravity took its chance, and for a moment Sam's free leg cycled in the air, the concrete awaited, and Neil thought the worst was happening, was truly and actually happening, in nauseating slow motion and on his watch.

Who's sorry now? His mother's voice rushed back to him, its crackly timbre as she crooned the old song she would launch into when he had improvidently ignored her advice.

Sam's errant leg regained the bar, and with the extra purchase he managed to swing his arms up. He dropped feet-first and harmlessly into a perfect landing.

The all-or-nothing moment passed, and it turned out to have been nothing. Neil glanced at Brian but he hadn't stirred (head on walking stick, face in grimace). He had experienced the same, transfixed powerlessness in California, when those strangers surrounded him, the police en route, Neil sensing that his life was taking a drastic turn but unable to correct it. He had thought of his mother then, too, wanting her to be there, a craving he hadn't felt for years, at the same time pleased that she could never know.

Sam was fine. Still, Neil felt as if some internal organ of his own had been bruised. His breathing was laboured. The child's balls hadn't dropped, for Christ's sake. He hadn't done anything yet. Travel, friendships. Sex.

Fifteen. Did you know that, you asshole?

'If you get divorced,' Sam said, 'can I come and live with you?'

'I don't think so, Sammy. It wouldn't be allowed.'

No harm done. Almost certainly no harm done.

'Who says?'

'You'd be too far away from your school.'

'I could go to a different school.'

Practicality had been a mistaken argument. Neil looked at Sam and saw that he was joking, though in fact the thought had crossed his mind: some sort of guardianship, he wasn't sure of the small print, he would have to find a lawyer.

She was fine. Almost certainly, she was fine.

Sam's weekends in Harrow had become long and frequent enough for his teacher to have written a series of escalating warnings to Dan, and perhaps, Neil feared, preliminary letters to social services. If he had his way, these getaways would end: he thought Brian should sell the house and move into something smaller. He could use the difference to help pay the saintly Filipinos who cared for him on an increasingly full-time basis, an entourage that, for the moment, Neil was quietly subsidising. He had driven up to discuss this plan, but Brian wouldn't consider

194

it. His father wanted to die in that house, Neil could see, die there with his dead wife on the mantelpiece, and he seemed stoically indifferent as to when this consummation came to pass.

Neil had changed tack – Fuck it, I'll give it a whirl – and told him that the house had been a fine place to grow up. That his had been a happy childhood, until the cancer. That he was grateful. His heart raced as he said those things. Brian said, 'I think I might have left the deeds in the safe.' The safe in the shop, he meant, which was someone else's shop now, an 'American' nail bar, Neil thought.

Sam wanted fish and chips. 'Or Chinese, if you fancy it. But, you know, fish and chips, if we can.'

'You two can,' Brian said.

'*X-Factor* in an hour,' Sam said.

The moment on the climbing frame could have gone another way, as every moment could. The damage might have been real. If it were, and even if it were inflicted by someone else, or by nobody, and you were only a bystander, but all the same you let it happen, what would that mean? Neil's mind returned to their first meeting with Farid. 'Everybody wants to think that, don't they? That they love their family as much as they can.' That was what Neil had said, more or less, though Christ knew he had been bluffing.

Her sob had sounded ventriloquised, as if it came from another, older person or a different species. The Charlie Brown T-shirt.

'God almighty,' Brian said, 'they sound like cats being strangled, the idiots on that programme. Why does everyone want to make bloody idiots of themselves these days?'

Jess didn't get it. Neither, for twelve years, had Neil. He had dodged and downplayed their behaviour, and lied to himself, and later, when Adam confessed, fixed on what the cost might have been for him. Adam alone had got it, and in the end, with his pitiless Googling, he had made Neil understand, he and Sam between them. Neil saw California anew that afternoon, saw it in the round, including the pain that would have followed later.

The guilt ebbed his way, towing his anger back. Only now, Neil thought in the playground, did he begin to appreciate what Adam had made him do.

And your mother!

'Right,' Neil said to Sam. 'Let's go. Help your granddad.'

2007

NEIL squeezed the key fob, his recessed headlights blinked at him, and he walked around the corner to Adam's road. These days he tended to park out of sight when he visited the Taylers, whether or not there was space nearby. Too much, somehow, for his car (a two-seater BMW, silvery grey, his choice, this time) to be visible through Adam's window, squatting extravagantly in the street like a visiting potentate's carriage. Likewise it would be uncouth to insist that Adam come to his new flat in Bayswater (Neil's place, all his, not rented and not shared, almost no mortgage). He meant this deficit of hospitality as a kindness, as he hoped his friend could see. Admittedly a kindness that might look like coldness, and in truth could gratify Neil as either. Though in point of fact he was hardly ever in his flat himself, between his meetings with clients in New York and Monaco, Abu Dhabi and Geneva, his client dinners in the stratum of London restaurants where only the host's menu lists the prices, and his weekend summonses to clients' mansions and estates. There was rarely anything in the fridge for him, or anyone else, to consume, besides half-drunk bottles of wine, fungal milk and Sam's pizza leftovers.

'Excuse me,' Neil said.

A woman was obstructing Adam's gateway; from where Neil stood she was framed by the white pointing that arced around the suburban front door. Elderly, grey-white hair in a bun, wearing an off-beige mackintosh even though the evening was warm. She was texting, leaning backwards to compensate for her long-sightedness, one bony, fastidious finger poking the keypad in regular, intrepid jabs.

'Not at all, dear,' she said, pressing her back to the gatepost as he passed.

The woman looked up at the building as if she were casing it. Neil considered challenging her until he remembered the *For Sale* board that was affixed to the fence. He skipped up the steps and rang the bell.

Claire's meet-and-greet smile flattened when she saw him. She peered around his shoulder as if she were expecting someone else.

'Come in,' she said, a few seconds slower than she should have. ''Fraid he's not back yet. Something about illegal immigrants, the usual.' Compensating, she added, 'Drink? Don't think he'll be long.'

They had known each other for twelve years, but Neil couldn't say that he and Claire were friends. Colleagues, in a way: mutually tolerant and intermittently cooperative, but dimly rivalrous and not entirely trusting. From the beginning he had wanted to like her, for convenience's sake, and he had tried to like her, but at the same time there had always been a tempting, grubbily competitive satisfaction to be had in not liking her. They had rarely been alone together, awkward intervals when Adam fetched a drink or scolded or consoled a child, and never for very long.

'Kids not here?'

'With my mum. There's a fairground on the common. I'm showing the flat today – can't really do it when they're rampaging.' She gave a jokeless, strained laugh.

Neil thought about making his excuses. A client's pet charity was throwing a reception in Park Lane, clean water for India, he ought really to be there, making a donation on Rutland's behalf, pretending to socialise while discreetly foisting his business cards on the high-rolling do-gooders. He was missing it only because he had already postponed this evening twice: dinner for Adam's birthday, the only birthday, besides Sam's, that Neil reliably remembered and marked. His treat; he would be permitted that minor generosity, at least. He had been looking forward to the largesse.

The doorbell sounded before he managed to decide. Neil was closest; he pivoted and opened the door. The texting old woman bustled through it and past him. He closed the door behind her. That had been his first chance to leave, he saw afterwards.

'I thought it must be you,' the woman said. 'Patricia.' She extended a hand and Neil shook it. 'Is this it? Of course it is, what am I saying? And this is your wife?' Claire tried to correct her but Patricia wouldn't be diverted. 'The estate agent couldn't make it, his message said to come anyway, I hope you don't mind. Start at the top?'

She helped herself to the stairs.

'Viewing,' Claire stage-whispered to Neil. 'Sorry.'

She turned and followed. Neil weighed his options. If he

left now, or stayed where he was, Patricia might be offended. He went upstairs to join them.

'Children's bedroom?' Patricia asked. 'How old are they?'

'Six and four,' Claire said.

'And such a pretty garden. Not yours, though. Never mind.'

Adam and Claire were selling up, cashing out. They couldn't muster the surpluses that London had demanded, not the steeplechaser stamina nor the virtuoso chutzpah nor the money. London was spitting them out, north or east, to Essex or Cambridgeshire or Buckinghamshire, somewhere in the commuter belt, they hadn't quite decided.

'Nice clean bath,' Patricia said. 'I insist on a clean bath. Do these open?' She pushed feebly at a sash window; it was paint-stuck and wouldn't give. 'They'll need to get out, you see.'

'Who?' Neil asked, heaving up the panel for her.

'Aesop. Aesop and Tallulah. They're quite safe if they have a ledge or a parapet.' She poked her head out of the window and peered down towards the front door and along the street. 'All those sleeping policemen, they're a plague. Still, nice light for the throne.'

Neil caught Claire's glance before they realised that eye contact would be calamitous. She tried to swallow her laughter, disguising it as a warbled question. 'Shall we see the other bedroom?'

'Don't,' she whispered to Neil. 'Please.'

Funny thing about the absurd: you could survive or ignore it on your own, but two made that impossible. Two made an audience, a confederacy, a secret.

'Now, dear, this is much more like it,' Patricia said. 'They can shimmy down that roof and do their business in the garden there. Neighbours won't mind, will they?'

'Don't think so,' Neil said, straightening his face. 'They're very reasonable.' Claire looked at the floor.

'What do you do, dear?'

'Wealth management. It's a kind of fin—'

'Yes, I thought so. He's something in the City, that's what I thought when I saw you outside. You'll be moving somewhere bigger, I expect.'

'Something like that,' Neil said.

'May I?' Patricia said, gesturing towards the wardrobes. 'Lovely. Lots of storage. Oodles. Will you have any more? If you don't mind my asking.'

'I don't think so,' Neil said. 'Actually she wants me to get the snip.'

Keep a straight face and we can keep it going.

Claire fixed her eyes on the dressing table.

'I wouldn't, if I were you. You might change your mind. People do. Kitchen?'

Neil tried to meet Claire's eyes again but she turned and hurried out. She had lost the weight that she put on with Ruby, Neil noticed. Her hair was still resplendent.

Patricia ran her texting finger along the kitchen counter and inspected it for dust. 'They'll need somewhere to sit down, of course,' she said.

'The cats?' Neil asked. Claire spread a palm across her face.

'Of course not. Not the cats. My grandchildren. I thought I explained. Yes, my son-in-law's in the money business like you, dear, he's away a lot – New York mostly, and lately these emergent markets, I'm not sure I'd put up with it if I were her, and between you, me and the gatepost I'm not certain I really trust him. Anyway I'm moving down to help a bit more. You know, after school, weekends.'

'How old are they?' Claire asked.

'Eight and ten, little bit older than yours. Nice children. Bit spoiled. Bit noisy sometimes.'

'Sorry to hear that,' Neil said.

'Oh, it's all right. The children are the main thing now, you see. We've sold the cottage – I have, I suppose. Now, this is lovely!' She moved into the living room. 'On the small side but lovely. Are these the original shutters?'

'Yes,' Claire said. 'South facing.'

Patricia had a large mole on her cheek that matched Neil's, he noticed, though hers was covered and advertised by a smudge of orange face powder.

'Yes, I can see them bouncing around in here. But it isn't much for the money, is it? And such a nice bath. Good luck to you both.' She ran a hand across her pale hair and smiled. 'Goodbye,' she said, letting herself out.

Claire leaned against the closed door, burying her face in the crook of her elbow. Neil sat on the stairs. She looked up and they let their eyes meet. They wanted to laugh but the hilarity had passed. Neil felt a flutter of guilt, less over the old woman than for the fact of the confederacy, the temporary partnership that was somehow misaligned.

'Drink?' Claire offered again. The smile that he had once considered superior seemed, this evening, ingenuously hospitable.

Neil glanced at his watch and hesitated. He could still make Park Lane if he hurried. But he was here now. Surely Adam couldn't be much later. 'I'm sure he won't be long,' Claire added.

'Go on then,' Neil said. 'Twisted my arm.' His second, best chance to leave, and he turned it down.

*

NEIL went through to the sitting room and scanned the bookshelves while she poured. Art books, history books, political memoirs, Adam's bid to maintain his student-age idea of his intellectual self. There were too few books on Neil's expansive shelves in Bayswater: some Rough Guides (Provence, Copenhagen, Istanbul, the last their intended, now aborted destination for that summer); some Ian Fleming novels; a few textbooks on finance and investment that Tony McGough had foisted on him. It was a caste affectation, Neil had always thought, this three-dimensional wallpaper, less a record of reading (he wondered how many of these books Adam had ever opened) than a signalling device or membership requirement for the upper-middle classes.

Claire came through from the kitchen bearing two full wine glasses and an open bottle of white. She set the tray on the coffee table. Neil took a glass and sat in the armchair, his arms resting perpendicularly in front of him.

'He saw your man,' Claire said. 'At the consultancy. Alan somebody?'

'He's not really my man,' Neil said. 'I just, you know, know one of the investors. I put a word in, that's all, really. Did they hit it off?'

'It went okay, I think. He hasn't heard anything yet, though. It would mean more money.'

'Fingers crossed. I'm sure he – what's that thing he says? – he spanked it.'

Adam's career reminded Neil of whichever medieval king it was in O-level history who won all his battles but lost every war. All his paper distinctions and mandarin respectability had left him naggingly unfulfilled and, he had managed to confide to Neil, unexpectedly impecunious. He had a chance, thanks to his friend, to escape the Home Office for

203

a private consultancy, where the work would be more varied and somewhat better paid. Money-wise, Adam was on his own, Neil knew. His parents' house had been sold during the divorce, and had anyway turned out to have been mortgaged to its fake-Tudor beams.

'It's funny, I think the fact that it came through you, it complicates it. Do you know what I mean? Crazy, really, you're his closest friend, the others have all ...'

'I know,' Neil said. 'I understand.' He was pleased to be able to dispense this favour to Adam.

'You boys,' Claire said.

By contrast Neil's had been the sort of mish-mash career that in another era would have connoted failure, but in his implied the perpetual, shark-like motion of success. He had quit Farid at the start of the previous year. Farid wanted the tenants of a retail development that he owned to overstate their rents in his paperwork, thus inflating the value of the building so he could borrow more against it. He deputised Neil to lean on them. Nothing to worry about, Farid assured him, the genuine rents would catch up with the fictitious ones soon. Up, up and away ... It was inducements, not threats or anything more sinister, which Neil was supposed to distribute. Farid's bankers, distracted as they were by his World Cup and Grand Prix tickets, were unlikely to spot the ruse. Neil had baulked. He walked out and into Rutland Partners, an investment fund for HNWIs: High Net Worth Individuals. Tony McGough was his new boss.

Claire asked, 'How are things with you?'

'Fine,' he said. 'Can't complain.'

Neil didn't know what he had meant by that dismal evasion. He should have said, I'm rich, Claire. Amazing, isn't it? I'm becoming rich. But she knew that already.

'Still travelling all the time?'

'Calms down a bit over the summer. Switzerland, maybe. And Cayman in September.'

Neil worked *client side*, peddling a discreetly asterisked vision of minimal risks, outwitted taxes and soaring returns, and sharing in the fat management fees that the HNWIs were reluctant but willing to pay for the dream of anti-gravitational prosperity. He had swung from the evanescing ether of Bimal's website to Farid's semi-solid buildings, then back to abstraction, this time in the guise of almost pure money. Money spawning money. The basics, he considered, had been constant since his peripatetic days in the pharmaceuticals trade, and his interminable summers and post-California stint in his father's shop. *Sell the customer what he wants to buy.*

'How is, you know, the market?' She gave another nervous laugh.

'Fine,' Neil said. 'You know, wolf from the door.'

They drank their wine, Claire taking tiny, feline but frequent sips. Neil looked at his watch.

'How's your father?' she asked.

'The same.' He made a quick slashing gesture with his left hand – flat palm, sharp rotation at the wrist – conveying both a dim estimation of Brian's life expectancy and a preference not to discuss it. Claire refilled their glasses.

'Sorry,' she said.

Her phone rang and she retreated to the kitchen to answer. Neil only half-deciphered the conversation: 'Why? ... Fuck's sake, Adam ... Okay.'

She stood in the aperture between the two rooms and said, 'He's late. I mean, he's even later. Christ. Doesn't know when he'll be back, minister on the warpath, apparently.' Neil began to stand. 'You're welcome to stay for another.'

Her cheeks had a sauvignon glow. Neil had never overcome his impression, formed instantaneously in the smoky pub where Adam had introduced them, that Claire looked down on him. His money, he had latterly suspected, had made looking down on him all the more urgent. *The market*: the way she said it, and still judged him, her and Adam both. Or perhaps he was being unfair. Her T-shirt had bunched and ridden up above the elastic of her velour trousers.

'Sure,' he said. 'Why not?'

They had never been friends, but neither could Neil say that he knew her, or had ever really seen her, unrefracted by her husband, separate from her assigned role.

Claire fetched the second bottle. Neil took a couple of quick, noiseless paces and sat on the sofa. Between it and the wall he noticed a graveyard of mangled toys – a digger missing a wheel, a doll minus an arm, cherished objects that devotion had not kept from violence.

Classical music wafted from the kitchen, intricate, fine-boned, a piano without accompaniment. Concerto? Minuet? The nomenclature escaped him. Claire returned with the bottle and a corkscrew and sat beside him on the sofa. She opened and poured. Bored, Neil thought. Bored and lonely. And tired. She curled her feet up and under her buttocks and balanced a glass on her knee.

'Do you miss her?' Claire said. 'If you don't mind my asking.'

'Not much, to be honest,' Neil said. 'Is that terrible? She feels – it's hard to explain it – she's like a film that ended, or a holiday. Or a job. It was supposed to end, I think.'

'I'm sorry.'

'Don't be. No reason.'

Even now he couldn't say for certain why Jess had gone.

Something to do with her age, a mid-thirties, stick-or-twist moment at which he had seen other women bolt, too; something to do with her mother's death, and also, she had intimated, something to do with *his* mother's death. She hadn't helped him to rank these motives. She had already done her grieving in her head, as you might for the victim of a long, terminal illness, so that, for Jess, the final, literal end was more a technicality than a crisis. She had no interest in his money.

For a moment Neil thought Claire was going to admit to never having liked her, that amateurish barbed condolence, but instead she said, 'She was sweet.'

Adam had come round with a bottle of whisky that evening but Neil had felt as much relief as anguish. They drank most of the whisky anyway. Even three or four doubles to the wind, Neil did not find his thumb poised to dial her number on his mobile. He slept better without her.

'Sweet's not the word I would have chosen.'

They both laughed, and Claire reached out and patted him on the shoulder. Neil glanced at the hand and across at her face; she withdrew the hand and smiled. Lonely and bored, Neil thought, and maybe also a harmless desire to feel desirable again. He remembered that moment in the pub when they first met, the ghost of flirtation he had glimpsed in the space between two blinks. He remembered how assiduous she had always been in laughing at his jokes. That had been fun, mean cruel fun, the interlude with the poor old lady.

They drank another glass of wine, sinking deeper into the sofa until they were almost horizontal. Claire began criticising Adam, gently, as an exasperated mother might, in low-key solidarity with Neil's break-up. There was something contagious about romantic discord, just as there could be in marriage and child-bearing, Neil believed, if you weren't careful. She said she wanted to shake Adam sometimes – of course he should take the consulting job if they wanted him, they really were very grateful. Sometimes Adam seemed so ... absent. He was wonderful with the children but they got the best of him. She sometimes felt that there was nothing left for her.

Did Neil know what she meant? He said he did, assenting to this tactful, joint demolition, her resentments of her husband rising up to meet his, all those years of Adam cutting the bread too thick, or whatever his domestic foibles were, a call-and-response ritual that, now, was less an inverted contest in intimacy than a mutual commiseration.

Neil could say to her, There is something else you should know about your husband, It was before you met him but I think you should know anyway ... Adam had been so adamant that she mustn't find out.

She rotated her body and the back of her head came to rest against his shoulder. He could smell her, the unmistakable whiff of posh-girl cosmetics, Chanel and high-end moisturiser. He could still distinguish the individual fragrances from his time in the business, the olfactory memories coming back to him like old song lyrics. He reached an arm around her to pat her on the far shoulder, and left it there, innocuously.

More than once, in the past two years, he had thought of telling Claire about Yosemite, anticipating the nice symmetry of the comeuppance. Yet now that the chance arrived, snitching seemed petty and obvious. Instead they talked about weekend plans, summer holidays, some stuff about the children. That had helped, Neil thought afterwards, the camouflage and double bluffs of their prattle. He spared her the details of the commodity prices, currencies and bonds that preoccupied much of his waking life.

His knuckles brushed against her exposed bicep. With their other hands, they drank.

The trouble with forgiveness was that it was hard to retract. Overtly, at least: not in his heart.

He asked about their house sale (top of the market, Neil reckoned, though it was a fool's game to try to call it). He moved his knuckles up and down her skin, very slowly, very slightly, a couple of inches at a time, the caress delicate enough for him to sense the microscopic down on her arm, and her tiny, involuntary jolts.

Still she didn't move. They drank; she gulped. The booze and the music and the moment had their own logic.

What the fuck was he doing?

When Neil thought of the randomness of it, all the reasons it could have been extinguished, not just the primordial grievance but neglect or drift or routine jealousy, his friendship with Adam was like a whim of evolution, a platypus or an anteater, so precious and unlikely. Even now, even these last few years, there was no one he trusted or needed so much. Neil trusted Adam more, in a way, because of his frankness over California. Among his living family, only Sam came close, Sam who was a different kind of relative, a friend, almost. This ought to be as taboo as incest. He began to blush.

At the same time, considered in a certain light, wasn't this what Adam wanted? To compete with Neil, and to incriminate him. What he had always wanted. In California Adam had ushered him into the wrong, urged, provoked and finally deceived him into it. In London he had assailed Neil with a remorse he hadn't recognised, needling allusions that he had privately interpreted as sabotage. Finally Neil had seen and suffered the shame that Adam had insisted on, and resented his friend anew, for both the insistence and, belatedly, for his part in the event.

She's up for it, mate. That was what Adam had said. *Stop making excuses.*

These past two years Neil had thought of her when he saw Sam. Sometimes he thought of her when he saw Adam with his daughter. Between the three of them – Neil, Adam and Rose – they had driven Jess away.

I knew she was younger.

Since Adam wanted Neil to be guilty, perhaps he should be. He could earn the guilt that had been foisted on him.

They babbled. Was Claire going back to work? Scarcely worth it – the costs of childcare. His mouth was dry; he drank. He curled his fingers inside her arm and around her ribcage. She sat up straight but didn't withdraw. With his other hand he put his empty glass on the arm of the sofa and fingered the mole on his neck.

He wanted a refill – there was still an inch of wine in the bottle – but he was reluctant to move. He was sober enough to know that he had drunk too much (he would have to leave his car and send someone out from the office). Her breasts were contoured against her sweater. His palms were damp; he felt the twitch of an erection, a warning-shot harbinger of his instincts.

Neil expected to regret this for ever; never mind for ever, he regretted it already. At the same time he felt wonderfully serene. Her head and her hair were warm against his shirt but the skin of her arm felt cold. An image came to his mind, from some ancient TV programme, of men in an exotic country (Brazil? Mexico?) stunt-diving from a cliff into the fearfully shallow water a long way below, their arms poised and cruciform as they tilted over the precipice. He felt as he imagined those divers must have felt: exhilarated, imperilled, yet tranquil in the inevitability of the fall.

'Claire,' he said. 'Claire.' He spoke so softly that she leaned still further into his chest to hear him.

He twirled a ringlet of her hair around a finger of his drinking hand. He could feel her breath against his neck. He had so wanted to match Adam, so admired his sophisticated charm, and envied it. He still did, despite everything that had happened since, what other people might construe as his success or Adam's failure. And these things that his friend had now, Claire and the children, a life Neil had so persuaded himself he couldn't emulate that he had resolved not even to want it.

He half-expected her to move or to stop him, but she didn't.

How much? That much?

She must be drunk, too. Drunk enough. A woman like her, who for much of Neil's life wouldn't have given him a second glance. If he had misread her, he might never see Adam again. He might never see him again if he hadn't. And yet the weight of her against him, her scent, her warmth, were so perfect. His senses were at once blurred and sharpened by the wine, intense but somehow indistinguishable from each other. So natural, so inevitable. It seemed to Neil that he had always wanted this, even if he hadn't known, a newly discovered pedigree for his desire that let the faithlessness feel less ignoble.

Claire let her hand rest on his leg. Neil caught his breath. He heard the blood drumming in his ears. In the kitchen the pianist was dallying in the upper scales, sentimental and manipulative. *I want it to be you*, Rose had said. During the night, in the tent, he had seen her features twitch and frown, the hieroglyphs of a dream, her lips synching the words or protests that her dream self must have been saying.

He tightened his grip on her ribs. He turned his face towards hers. This would be only fair.

It was the wine, maybe, or the nerves, but his timing was out. He leaned over too far, too fast, and kissed only her hair; several twisty strands clung to his lips when he withdrew.

That might have been all anyway, the spell broken for both of them, but Neil would never know for certain. The front door opened. She snatched her hand from his leg.

Neil stood up, checking that his trousers were respectable. Harry marched through the living room to the kitchen and opened the fridge. He turned off the music, scraping a stool across the parquet to the counter to eat whatever it was he had extracted.

'Hello, Uncle Neil,' he called out, in the ironic tone that kids seemed obliged to affect. He had reached the age when they could no longer count on a smile, their size, the sheer audacity and miracle of their diminutive yet capable bodies, to win the approbation and indulgence of adults. Harry had realised that, from now on, he would have to earn them, and he evidently wasn't pleased.

'Me too,' Ruby yelled as she trailed after her brother. She changed her mind and jumped onto the sofa, thrusting an illuminated, hand-held windmill into Claire's face. 'Hello, darling,' Claire said, hugging her daughter more tightly than their temporary separation called for.

Claire's mother came in with the children's kit. She was

thinner and greyer than Neil remembered her from the novelty cummerbund days. Her spectacles dangled on a long, professorial cord. She glanced from him to the bottle to her daughter.

'Hi,' Neil said, striding towards her and taking her free hand between his. 'Neil.'

'Yes,' she said. 'I remember.'

'Good to see you again.'

'Yes.' She turned to Claire.

'I was about to leave,' Neil said. 'Adam's not here.'

'Okay,' she said.

Neil called out goodbyes to the children, and to Claire, without looking at her. 'Me too,' he heard Ruby say to somebody.

He plucked his jacket from the banister and swam for the door, slamming it behind him more violently than he intended. He abandoned his car and swayed towards the station to find a taxi.

When he was almost home he took out his CrackBerry. He wasn't sure he would have Claire's number – he had no recollection of ever calling her directly – but there it was. He could sense the boozy ripeness of his breath in the cocoon of the cab. An early-onset hangover gripped the back of his head, competing for attention with his instant remorse. The car bucked and jerked in the traffic; the driver was telling a story to someone on his speakerphone: '. . . and he's only gone and got himself a man bag, the dickhead. I said, what you got that for? He said, it's for holidays. You dickhead, I said . . . '

Neil opened a window. *No harm done*, he thumb-typed. *Let's forget it.* He hesitated for a moment and then pressed *Send*.

I've bailed, he wrote to Adam. *Next week, maybe? Happy birthday*

As he was paying through the window of the taxi, his pocket beeped. He gave the driver a twenty, told him to keep the change, and read her message: *Forget what?xx*

NOT just undocumented immigrants working illegally. That would hardly be news to anyone in London who had renovated a home in the last few years or cash-in-handed a cleaning lady. Nor merely illegal immigrants working as security guards. Illegal immigrants working as security guards in the Home Office. And Parliament. And, very likely, Number 10 and MI6. It would be funny if ... okay, it *was* funny, but you could only laugh in the right company, Adam was streetwise enough to know that. One of the Downing Street enforcers had been in, demanding to know what could be done, when and how much it would cost (the prospect of front-page ignominy always conjured money from the ether). Everyone knew that two or three heads would have to be stuck on pikes in Whitehall. There were dark mutterings about a stash of discarded paperwork that had been discovered in a Croydon housekeeping cupboard.

Croydon: the eternal scapegoat, the illegal immigrants of the Home Office. Thank God for Croydon.

His would almost certainly not be among the impaled heads, Adam reflected as he walked home from the Tube. He was too lowly an official to be a useful sacrifice. All the same, it seemed providential that Neil had put him in touch with that consultancy. If that oleaginous interviewer wanted him, perhaps he should find a way to accept his friend's charity. He and Neil sometimes did a sort of skit when they saw each other, a pastiche of their former selves – Adam telling

214

most of the jokes, Neil residually gauche, or acting it, for history's sake, or for Adam's. This was one of the reasons Adam needed him: Neil carried a trace memory or reflection of Adam at the height of his possibilities, his maximal plumage, fresh from university, thoughtless of failure, absolutely ignorant of what awaited him. An image of him at his happiest and his freest, as well as at his most ... regrettable. Underneath, Adam knew, the power had already swung away from him, following the money, rather as, in old age, it ebbs to the spouse who stays healthier for longer, a basic animal hierarchy.

That was already their dispensation, whether or not he took this nepotistic job. He already owed Neil. In any case, Adam wasn't changing the world at the department. He wasn't changing anything. He wasn't even a 7.

Adam turned into his street and mounted the steps to the maisonette. He heard the familiar front-door serenade of play and conflict, sibling love and rivalry too entwined to be distinguished. He found Ruby perched on the kitchen table in her nightie; Harry was performing little standing leaps in his pyjamas, his upstretched hand reaching for the phone she was dangling above him.

'Careful,' Adam said; then, shouting, 'Claire!' It was much too late for this.

'Coming,' she called down.

'Get down from there! Clezz!'

'No,' Ruby said, squatting defensively in the corner. 'Naughty Daddy!' She flipped and clicked between the gadget's applications, with a native dexterity that made Adam feel both proud and old.

'Give it to me.'

'Mine,' Ruby said. She drew the prize into her torso.

'Give it to Daddy,' Harry said, confiscation representing, to him, a respectable draw.

'It's bedtime, lollipop,' Adam said. 'Where's Mummy?'

'I know how to spell *shit*,' Harry said.

'Me too,' Ruby said.

'Give it to me,' Adam repeated. He yanked the phone from his daughter's grasp with more force than she was expecting. After the shock, she began to wail.

'*Suh*,' Harry said, counting off the phonetic letters with his fingers.

Adam glanced at the miniature screen. The roulette of Ruby's clicks had landed on Claire's inbox. A message from Adam himself; one from Claire's mother; Adam again; the mother of one of Harry's friends; Neil; Adam.

'*Huh*,' Harry said, extending another elfin finger.

Adam placed the phone on the kitchen counter. Ruby was crying. He hated upsetting her, even when her behaviour and his self-respect obliged him to. He hated anyone upsetting her, but it was worse when he was responsible.

'I want a new daddy,' she said. 'I do.' She wriggled out of his embrace.

'Ruby-loo,' he said. 'Come back here.'

Why Neil? He and Adam had been in touch directly to cancel. Neil and Claire never texted each other, so far as Adam knew. He picked up the phone again and opened the message with a hasty, unthinking depression of his forefinger.

No harm done. Let's forget it

'*ii*,' Harry said.

'I'll ask Father Christmas for him,' Ruby said.

Forget it ... In theory, Adam could choose to attend to his daughter, rebuke his son, his wife would appear, the vertiginous moment would pass. In practice, only one course of action was available. He fumbled his way to Claire's outbox. Her reply was the last message she had sent.

Forget what?xx

Forget what? And those xx, so harmless when she sprayed them over saccharine messages to her friends, so incriminating in this one.

'*Tuh*,' Harry said. He grinned.

'Dadda?' Ruby said. She had stopped crying.

Adam helped her down from the table. The children bickered away and up the stairs.

His first sensation was a light-headed, instant nostalgia for the prelapsarian era that had just ended, the era of automatic trust that Adam felt he was only now appreciating, as a nobleman might recognise his privileges only after they are expropriated. A moment later he was dizzy with grubby surmises, hypothetical scenarios, a frantic scan of his memory for clues or tells. He gently laid the phone down again and looked at the floor. He ground his jaw.

His mother had known about his father's affairs, or so she had told Harriet. She knew, and she hadn't minded, at least not enough to divorce him. She had left him for a different reason. She was bored, she told Harriet. Just bored.

This was his biggest failing and worst mistake, Adam reflected in the kitchen: the wrongful imputation of harmlessness. Will from television, pole-climbers in the Home Office. His father. Neil. He was hopeless at spotting where the harm was coming from.

Neil?

People could live with these things, if they chose to.

Claire's cheeks were flushed when she came in. He thought he saw her glance at the phone. She told him about the viewings and asked about the office, and the minister, but he only grunted at her until the children were comprehensively in bed.

He turned on the satellite news. More about the missing girl and her broken parents; in Parliament, the new prime minister, the latest face of the age of war, lamented that week's glorious dead. Nothing, yet, about the illegal immigrants. They would sniff it out tomorrow, someone would leak it to damage someone else.

She sat next to him on the sofa. He could smell the booze on her, and something else, a lozenge or toothpaste that she had used to disguise it.

'How long did he stay?' Adam asked her. His voice came out blank and deadpan. 'Neil.'

'Not long. Till you said you weren't going to make it.'

He turned off the television. She carried on staring at the charcoal rectangle as if the picture were still there.

'Was he still here when the kids got back?'

'I can't ... Yes, maybe he was.' She would have lied if she were sure she could get away with it, Adam thought.

'What happened?'

'What?'

'With Neil.'

'Nothing,' she said. She put a hand on his arm. He saw her swallowing anxiously. This was it, Adam thought. This might be it for them.

'So what is there to forget?'

'What?'

'What did Neil want you to forget?'

She pulled away and leaned into the opposite arm rest. 'What are you talking about?'

'What have you already forgotten? Claire.'

Her eyes widened. The urgent ratiocination was legible in

218

the microspasms of her cheek muscles and the darts of her pupils. She braced a foot against the floor, as if she were preparing to flee. *Didn't I delete it?*, he thought he saw her think. *I meant to delete it. Fuck!* Next, he interpreted, she was considering a counterattack: *What are you doing, looking at my phone? What the fuck do you think you're doing?* He almost felt sorry for her, so little time to come up with something, and she was bound to be exhausted, she always was. In the end he guessed she was contemplating an outright lie. *You've got the wrong end of the stick, Adam, you always do. He meant no harm to his car, he reversed into the lamppost.* Or, *No harm done to his suit, after Harry jumped on him with muddy feet.*

She must have rejected that option. Too undignified.

'Nothing happened, Adam,' she finally said. Her hand crept along the apron of the sofa. 'We had a drink, a couple of drinks. You were late.' She paused but he didn't interject. 'This funny old lady came to look at the flat. She was going on about her cats, and the loo, and ...'

'What's she got to do with it?'

'She thought Neil and me were married. It's too hard to explain, Ad. We were trying not to laugh, and it felt like we were ... a team. You know how that is, don't you? I don't think it would have happened without the old lady.'

'What wouldn't have happened?'

'Nothing. We were laughing, it was a bit ... I don't know, flirty. That's all. You were late.'

'Don't.'

'We were sitting here, waiting for you, and ... honestly, Adam, it was nothing.'

Everything was always nothing, Adam thought. He looked down at the patch of fabric between his legs. This is where they had been.

'What *nearly* happened, then? Claire. What did you want to happen?'

'Nothing, I've told you.' He could see her deciding how honest to be. 'He put his arm around my shoulder. We ... sort of snuggled. That's all.'

'You don't even like Neil.'

'I don't,' she said. 'You're right.'

'No harm done,' he said.

'That's right. Adam?'

He stood, left the room, climbed the stairs to their bedroom and closed the door. The linen appeared to be unruffled. He sat on the edge of the mattress, elbows on knees, his face in his palms.

Adam wasn't sure what he was supposed to do. The situation wasn't like any other he had experienced. It was an escalatingly adult moment, akin to the first time someone in the hospital had asked, 'Who's the father?', and he had looked around, like a screwball comedian, before understanding it was him. Or the first time he had slapped four passports down at airport immigration and felt a decade older in an instant. Yes, you, this is happening to you. It wasn't even very like itself, at least not the straightforward version of the scenario that was familiar from TV.

He believed his wife that nothing had happened, at least in the technical, secretional sense. A cuddle. A cuddle plus, maybe. He had always trusted her in that way, squeamish as he had occasionally felt about her sexual history. Truth be told, he had rarely thought about her in that way, not since the children. In any case, how much anger did he deserve? He hadn't sat on their own sofa with Heidi, back in those cosy days before her promotion when she had been his proxy office spouse. But several times he had looked tipsily

220

into her eyes in a way that he intended to seem meaning-ful. In St James's Park one summer he brushed a fluff of pollen from her hair, and she stiffened and looked up at him as if he might kiss her. Once they held hands in the back of a taxi, gazing away from each other and out of their opposite windows in bittersweet silence.

He had never told Claire about any of that. He hadn't told her about those women on the Strand (another nothing, a genuine nothing). He hadn't felt any inclination or obligation to tell Claire. These things happened in a marriage, didn't they? They were part of a marriage. Fidelity, Adam consid-ered, was like the speed restriction on motorways. The official limit had a built-in margin that you were tacitly per-mitted to exploit, so long as you went no further. He thought of how, the last time they flew out of Heathrow, he had dou-bletaked one of the unobtainable Asian sales girls in Duty Free, how Claire had seen him and let it go.

She said they hadn't, and he believed her. But even if Claire hadn't broken the rules, Neil had. Marriage had a margin, but friendship had tighter parameters.

This was a punishment, Adam sensed. For what he knew about Neil – for what he had on Neil – and for what they had done together. What Adam had done. *It was what you wanted, wasn't it? You started it.* That was what Neil had said on the morning after, long before he knew the whole story.

I hope you find out how this feels.

Adam pounced down the stairs and went back into the living room for his car keys.

'What are you doing?'

He could hear the fear in her voice.

'Adam?'

He found the keys. It was a warm dry night, not yet dark. He left his jacket behind.

'Adam, where are you going?'

He slammed the door behind him.

ADAM had turned the key in the ignition before he realised that he didn't know Neil's address. His seatbelt was pulled halfway across his torso, his father's standard driving posture for several years after belts became mandatory (his mind went back to his father, even now, with an irksome canine loyalty). He had a pain in his back (sedentary work, carrying the kids, the same overconfidence regarding his chassis as he had always harboured about his weight). The sensation ran across his shoulder to his neck, then to the middle of his spine, but hurt differently in different places: sharp and neural in his neck, duller and achier lower down, as if the pain had matured or learned something along the way.

'Fuck,' Adam said, letting the seatbelt snap back.

He knew approximately where the building was. Neil lived in a red-brick mansion block in Bayswater, near a hotel, Adam recalled, with an elegant stairwell and an old-fashioned, sliding-grille lift. His was an internally plush but externally nondescript building, of a type Adam associated with foreign kleptocrats on the lam and their overindulged offspring or mistresses. Neil had only just moved in when Adam had visited; there was almost nothing in the flat besides an inherited bamboo bar and accompanying leather stools, screwed to the floor in the living room, fixtures that incited ribald speculation about the key parties the previous occupants might have hosted. Adam didn't like the place much (even discounting for his instant, envious calculation of how much his friend must have paid for it, he had been fairly certain that he didn't like it). High-ceilinged rooms, but boxy and over-regular, set off a faintly ominous corridor: the apartment felt more like a medical consulting suite than a residence, the kind of architecture that seemed designed to prevent anyone experiencing the place as home. But it was Neil's, and Jess had left him, and Adam had discharged friendship's duty of compassionate dishonesty, the kind lies you mixed with the dependable truths, and told him it was lovely.

He hadn't been there since. Neil had never asked him again, let alone invited Claire and the kids, a failure that Adam inwardly resented but never mentioned. He might be able to find the building, just. But third floor? Fourth? Sitting in the car, he had a bathetic vision of himself patrolling the pavement, waiting to accost Neil as he arrived or left, or hurrying through the doors when another visitor was buzzed in – like the fare-dodgers who sometimes squeezed through the ticket barriers with you on the Tube – then pacing the corridors and madly banging on strangers' doors. He could hardly ask Neil for the address: *Dear Neil, you are a cunt, please could I have your address so I can come round and throttle you?*

Two police officers, one of each sex, walked past his car, their hands clasped meditatively behind their backs, looking quaintly approachable, stab vests notwithstanding. Adam raised his buttocks from the seat to fish his phone from his trouser pocket. He would text:

Neil, Claire told me what happened today. I can't believe you would do that to me

Or: *You scumbag. You total scumbag*

Or: *Rape, Neil. It's called rape. Statutory rape, but still rape. You are a rapist*

Neither of them had ever applied that word aloud to what

happened in California, though it had often resounded in Adam's head when they were together, as, he expected, it had in Neil's – the legalistic modifier mitigating the noun to a greater or lesser extent according to his mood. A seventeen-year-old boy with a fifteen-year-old girl: that was more a technical than a moral offence, towards which the law and common sense were inclined to indulgence. But Neil's twenty-three to her fifteen were at the wrong end of the moral continuum. Neil had been a man. They both had.

So: *Rape, Neil.*

Or perhaps, he thought, just *Goodbye*

He navigated to Neil's number in his address book. *Dear Neil.*

Not *Dear.* Just *Neil.* Or *N.*

He abandoned his message. Texting would be uncivilised. Adolescent. He would call.

It occurred to Adam that he would be less encumbered in the passenger seat; he opened the door and walked around the bonnet to the other side of the car. A supermarket delivery van had pulled up outside a house along the street, blocking the road while its driver unloaded, hazard lights flashing in the dusk. From the other direction he heard the wail of an ambulance. Two men jogged past his car, the squatter of the two straining to keep up.

Do it. His hand shook, the phone quaking in his palm as he aimed his thumb at the keys. The connection was slow – Neil might be out of range, or out of juice – but then the number was ringing. This wasn't what he had expected. He had intended something dramatic, yes, and distressing, but less sudden, something he would have more time to think about and rehearse.

He grew stronger as he neared the safety of voicemail.

'You've reached Neil' – something gratingly American in that formulation, as if modernity required a transatlantic accent – 'please ...'

Adam hung up. Voicemail would be as undignified as texting. *Hi Neil, this is Adam, you are a terrible bastard, don't bother to call back*

He caught himself untensing in relief. He dialled again. Neil answered on the third ring.

'Hello?'

That tone ... Neil would have seen on his screen that it was Adam – everyone was pre-announced these days, like guests at a courtly reception – and yet the disingenuous innocence, that nonchalance.

Adam opened his mouth to speak, but it was dry and nothing came out, as if the nightmares he periodically suffered of muteness at a viva exam, or some uncanny capital trial, were being realised. He could feel his heart thrashing in his chest. He could hear it.

'Hello? Ants?'

'Neil, I ... I need to talk to you.'

'Just a second.' The hand over the mouthpiece, Adam's last chance to reconsider or reformulate. 'Yup. Ads?'

'Where are you?'

'Charity thing at the Dorchester. You weren't there and ... It was free booze or channel-surfing, you know.'

'Haven't you had enough to drink?'

'What?'

'You had a few earlier, didn't you? With Claire.'

'Look, Adam, let's talk tomorrow, all right? I'm supposed to be schmoozing. Tony's here. I'll give you a call in the morning, okay?'

'I don't give a shit about your schmoozing. Or about Tony.

Fuck Tony. Christ. I want to know what the fuck you think you were doing with Claire.'

Better: he was entitled to this.

'Hang on,' Neil said. Again the muffle, other blurred, male conversations, once or twice a bump of the phone against Neil's leg – Neil presumably leaving whatever banqueting suite he was stuck in, understanding that this was serious.

'Okay. Ants. What were you saying?'

Here we go, Adam thought, the same shenanigans as with Claire: the stonewalling and lies that had to be got through, before the only-half-lies and reluctant confession. He felt like a detective, or a torturer. Onto the second prisoner, who can never be sure what his accomplice has admitted. How bored they must get of this routine.

'It's Adam. And Claire's already told me.'

'What has she told you?'

Adam resisted saying, *She's told me everything*. Instead he said, 'She told me about . . . the sofa.'

Silence. Odd to be sitting in his car with his phone pressed to his ear, neither speaking nor spoken to. Embarrassing, somehow.

'Christ, Ad, nothing happened. Ad? Nothing happened.'

'Adam.'

'Fine, Adam.'

'No harm done?'

Another silence. To his own ear Adam's voice sounded caustic and distorted, the timbre more synthetic than human. He waited for the apology.

Neil said, 'We were rehearsing. We're doing a skit for your birthday. *Casino Royale*. No, *Wedding Crashers*. We're doing a scene from *Wedding Crashers* and we were rehearsing. Artistic licence. Adam?'

Adam smiled. He liked the lie. He had always enjoyed their lies, all the way back to San Diego. *We're hairdressers. We're masseurs. He's a set-designer.* The two of them versus. This was a classy gambit, he gave Neil that. A lie about coming on to his wife that was also, in their private code, an expression of loyalty.

A fly buzzed against the window. Adam reached over, turned the key in the ignition, and opened the window to let it out.

'Adam?'

The nicknames and the nostalgic humour: they were like the practised advances an old lover might make when she tries to re-seduce you, ingratiating with their echoes of everything you and the lover once had together, and once were.

'Don't, Neil. This isn't ... just don't.'

'Look, it was just a silly moment, really. Three glasses of wine in a hurry. I'm sorry, okay?'

Damn right you're sorry.

Neil should have opened with that, Adam thought. He said, 'No, it isn't okay. I mean, what have I ... I've always been ... there for you, haven't I? Haven't I? I've always ... encouraged you. Haven't I? I've never ... I've never ... I can't understand how you could do this to me,' he lied.

'You've never what?'

'Nothing.'

'What, Adam? What have you never? Looked down on me because I hadn't heard of Dante, is that it? Judged me for my horrid money-grubbing job? Yeah,' Neil said, 'you've always been very charitable, milord, I'm ever so grateful.'

'Is that it, then? Is that why?'

'No,' Neil said. 'No. Fuck's sake.'

'What then?'

'Look . . . never mind.'

One of them had to say it: 'California?'

Adam heard Neil's exhalation, long and sad.

'You said that was nothing.'

'It isn't like that – it doesn't go in a straight line. You know why it happened, I'm sure you do. I don't even mean what her dad told you about her that night. It wasn't only that. Even apart from that it happened because of us. And then you couldn't drop it, could you? I mean, you had to keep bringing it up. Finding her again, going on about contacting her, all that bollocks about what he said to you in the morning. What did you want me to do, kill myself? Turn myself in?'

Rape, thought Adam. He said, 'Don't be ridiculous.'

'And then when you told me – to be honest, I wouldn't say you were sorry, not as sorry as you should have been.'

'Oh, for fuck's sake, Neil, I was insanely sorry – I was paralytic with it.'

'I mean, sorry for me. You were sorry for her and for yourself. Very sorry, sure. And for Ruby. Jesus. Did you ever think, how was I supposed to feel, all that guilt pouring out of you, when all the time I was the one who . . . '

'You already knew she was . . . You already knew that. You said it was nothing.'

'Yeah, well, I changed my mind. It isn't nothing, okay? You win. I regret it, Adam, okay? If I could undo it, I would. If there was anything I could do, I would.'

'But whenever I—'

'I said, I'm sorry about it. I'm fucking sorry, I'm ashamed. Understand?'

'Why didn't you tell me you felt like this?'

'I just . . . I couldn't, Adam. Why didn't you tell me?'

'What do you ... I was scared, Neil. All right? I was scared.'

They were quiet again. A man in sunglasses, jacket slung over his shoulder, walked past Adam's car, talking on his phone. Adam had composed messages to the girl, revising and perfecting them, but he hadn't sent one, at least, not yet.

'So that's it, is it?' he continued. 'That's why you've done this? All of a sudden you regret what happened fifteen years ago, and to make amends you try it on with Claire?'

'I didn't ... Look, you asked me and I'm trying to explain, that's all. It was mostly the booze, we got carried away.'

Rape, Adam thought. He said, 'Maybe we should have said goodbye at the airport. I've often wondered about that. That could have been the end of it.'

'Yeah,' Neil countered, 'well, I sometimes think, if that old man hadn't been at home, the guy with the car ... Or if you hadn't asked me that night on the beach ... We could have left it in San Diego, couldn't we? Nice little one-night stand. We would never have met her.'

Strangers were laughing in the background at Neil's end. The renunciations hung on the line between them.

'Look,' Neil finally went on, 'can we get together tomorrow to talk about this properly? After work?'

'Sorry to have distracted you.'

'No, I just mean it would be better to talk in person.'

'No,' Adam said. 'Not tomorrow.' And then he said, 'I don't think I ever want to see you again.'

Adam looked out through the windscreen. There ought to be witnesses or an audience for this. But there was only, on the opposite pavement, a woman in a burqa pushing a buggy. She's trying to get it to sleep, Adam thought reflexively.

'Don't be silly. Don't say that. Ad?'

Even to Adam the threat seemed safely theatrical, free, an ultimatum he would never be called upon to enact. More a rhetorical flourish than an irrevocable event. Somebody will say something, he thought. Somebody will do something to stop this.

'Goodbye, Neil,' his voice said.

'What? Ad—'

He heard Neil say something else as he lowered the phone from his ear, but the words were too quiet to decipher. He pressed the button and looked at the screen. The call's duration was *6:23*. He held the phone in both hands, expecting it to ring again. But it didn't.

He reopened his electronic address book and scrolled down to Neil. *Are you sure you want to delete this number?*

Was he sure? To purge Neil like this might be tantamount to killing him, in Adam's life anyway. To kill Neil would be a kind of self-mutilation or partial suicide. So much of his last decade and a half were stored in Neil, shameful times and halcyon. Without his friend as his repository and witness, part of Adam's past – part of him – would perish, too.

He pressed *Yes I want to delete Neil*. He felt a queer kind of lightness or liberation. I will never see Neil again, he thought. Neil is dying, even though he is still alive. He will be dead and alive at the same time.

Adam stepped out of the car, closed the door gently and locked it with his key.

NEIL took another glass of wine from a waistcoated attendant and drank half of it in one unprofessional gulp. He didn't believe this. Not that Claire had told Adam, nor that Adam was livid: he believed all that. They had been busted by his drunk-texting, but she might anyway have felt guilty enough to confess. Splashing his face in the bathroom in his cavernous flat, he had thought, You idiot, Neil. You cunt. You could have left – twice – easily. How could you even have thought about her that way, let alone ... He came out again to this deathly reception, networking and tax relief dressed up as benevolence, to avoid confronting his sinful self any further.

He didn't believe Adam's goodbye. They had a tacit but firm agreement, Neil thought, to be always in each other's lives; it was much too late for either of them to rescind it.

With his free hand Neil retrieved the BlackBerry from his inside pocket to phone back. He dialled, but aborted the call almost instantly – before it rang, and, he hoped, before his number had flashed up on Adam's screen. Better not to. Not today. One of them might say something worse. It was bad enough that he had counterattacked when he should have stuck to plain apology (*Damn right you're sorry*). And that absurd Hail Mary joke about *Wedding Crashers*. Better to email.

He rolled and clicked with his thumb until the email template appeared (scientists of the future, Neil had thought, biologists or whatever, would wonder at the dramatic leap in thumb musculature made by Western man in the early twenty-first century). *Dear Adam ... Dear Ads ... Adam ... Mate ... Ants ... Adam, I'm sorry ... Adam, I'm so sorry ...*

'Who are you hiding from?' Tony McGough called to him. 'There's gold in them thar hills.'

Tony put a heavy arm around Neil's shoulders and rotated him to face the convocation of suits, shape-shifting yet cohesive like penguins huddling against the cold, individuals sometimes peeling off and scuttling along the group's perimeter before burrowing back into the mass.

'One of the Kumars is here,' Tony said. 'And a Levene, I think, or a capo from their office, anyway. Go get 'em, kimosabe.'

'Just a second,' Neil said, extending a finger upwards from the hand that held the BlackBerry. 'Just give me a second.'

Tony was a workaholic. He and his two partners had left jobs in insurance and private equity to start their firm (none of them was called Rutland, they just thought the name sounded trust-worthy). They had gathered their clients – including Farid, which was how Neil came to know them – in a remorseless, marriage-destroying campaign of insinuation and sycophancy at events like this one.

Still, as City bosses went, Tony was relatively humane. You could see it in his giveaway eyes, tender and melancholy, out of place somehow in his flabby, particoloured face, itself perched on a rectangular bouncer's body.

'Okay,' Tony said, removing his arm. 'See you in a minute, hotshot.'

'Of course.'

Funny thing: growing up, Neil had always thought that whatever he managed to do or achieve, he would have to do and achieve on his own, not counting on favours or connections and never enjoying any. Yet he *had* been helped, by Bimal and Farid and now by Tony, each propelling him upwards through London postcodes and income-tax brackets, before passing him on to his next benefactor. (Neil hadn't expected a goodbye, but on his penultimate day in Hanover Square he turned round at his desk and Farid was standing there; he raised an arm and caressed Neil's cheek with his knuckles, up and down once, as if tracing the line of a scar.)

232

Neil crouched to put his glass on the carpet and turned towards the wall to type. *Adam, I'm sorry for what happened . . . I'm truly sorry for what nearly happened . . . It was my fault, not Claire's . . . I didn't mean what I said.*

Or: *I guess the dinner's off.*

Better not. Beware the perils of email, Neil urged himself: jokes that might be missed, brevity received as rudeness, possibly, in this case, an apology that would seem insufficiently contrite, or, conversely, to be admitting more than he intended to. All these new ways to communicate, digital guarantees against losing each other, which were mostly new opportunities for misunderstanding. Everyone was inescapable, these days, but in place of the old jeopardy you found yourself clutching at holograms.

Probably best just to write, *Adam, I'll call you tomorrow.* Or, *Let's talk tomorrow.* Although that might seem curt and non-consensual.

Neil accidentally kicked over the half-drunk wine glass at his feet. He turned back towards the suits and plucked another from a passing tray. Best of all, maybe, would be to say and write nothing for a few days. Let his friend cool off. Let him and Claire patch things up.

He blamed the old woman (Priscilla?), with her cats and her orange-powdered mole. If she hadn't barged in, he might have left. If: If Eric hadn't turned in early that night. If the man who owned the truck had been out. If the girl in the sarong (she was the blonde, wasn't she?) hadn't lingered in the hostel yard. Or if Adam hadn't. All these random collisions, pinballing molecules. In the end you couldn't say where anything started, which was the main action of your life and what the interference.

Neil sipped. He gulped.

In any case, was it really only he who ought to apologise? He was in the wrong, he acknowledged that. Doubly wrong: he shouldn't have said the things he did. But some of what he said had been accurate, and not just about Adam's deceit: his tone, the superciliousness that had grated from the beginning, right back to Las Vegas, the condescension that incited Neil in Yosemite, which he thought Adam had outgrown, but which in reality he had merely disguised. *I have always encouraged you ... I have never criticised you.*

Who the fuck did he think he was? Neil didn't owe Adam anything. Morally speaking, they were quits, he reckoned, taking into account what happened in California. Quits at the least. In any case, for years Adam had been a kind of succubus, taking out of Neil more than he put back. Neil could have managed everything he had done without Adam. He could manage the future without him, if he must or if he chose to.

So: *We're quits, Ants. Fuck you.*

Tony was coming towards him with the Levene brothers' man. Neil replaced the BlackBerry in his pocket, cocked his head back and sluiced the last of the wine down his throat. He stepped forward for the handshake. 'Jonny,' he said. 'Good to see you.'

Neil, Tony and the man clinked glasses. 'Bottoms up,' Neil heard himself say.

When it was too late, or seemed to be, he reflected that his mood that evening – wrigglingly defensive, angrily ashamed – had been a hypocritical luxury. He had luxuriated in his pique because he didn't think the estrangement was real. His confidence in the friendship obscured its demise. In the morning Neil sent a secretary from the office to collect his car.

*

234

ADAM slammed the front door again. He didn't care if he woke the kids; he didn't think Claire would reproach him. As he started up the stairs, his phone rang. He expected Neil, but it was Nick, doubtless wanting to impart some new, baroque twist in the illegal-immigrant debacle – less than a day old, but already feeling prehistoric – or some fresh demand for unobtainable statistics, the wrong, inconsequential part of Adam's life interrupting his private crisis.

He switched Nick off. He pounded up the stairs to the bedroom and turned on the light.

Claire was in bed but awake. Adam avoided her eyes and didn't speak. He rolled the chair to the wardrobe and stood on it to reach the upper cupboard, surfing the swivels as he opened the doors. Forgotten objects fell or were thrown out as he rummaged. Maternity clothes; worn-out but hoarded shoes; a map of Barcelona from a pre-parenthood weekend break, sentimentally retained as if it might help them chart a path back in time; a university graduation certificate; the box for a digital camera. Why had they never sifted this stuff?

'Adam?' Then, more stridently, 'Adam – what are you doing?'

He succeeded, finally, in extracting a red biscuit tin from the junk. He balanced the tin on the lip of the cupboard, prised open the lid. These were Adam's special, once-important things: the letter that had offered him his first big-time job in television, some billets-doux from Chloe, tied up in a pretentious snip of lace, some old photographs. He found what he was looking for. He replaced the box, jumped from the chair and made for the door, leaving the detritus of his raid scattered on the floor.

'Adam, what ...'

Back down the stairs, the late, mauve summer dusk

shading to grey outside the window, a view he had always enjoyed but would soon leave behind, past the contaminated sofa and into the kitchen. He turned the photo over.

Two young men, almost equally foreign to him now, their arms around each other, gesticulating for the camera. Two young men who, naturally, had no idea what the next decade and a half would do to them; who had little idea what the next thirty-six hours would do to them, or what they would do in them. Adam felt affectionate, protective, belatedly apprehensive. He wanted to break through time's thick, soundproofed glass, sit between them, behind the sign that said *Faithful Couple*, put an arm around each of them and tell them not to do it. But they wouldn't have known what he was talking about. They were happy. They were together.

He grasped the upper edge of the photo between his thumbs, preparing to rip. *I sometimes think . . .* After a minute he stood on another chair and tossed the picture into the dusty, dead-insect limbo on top of the kitchen cabinet.

2008–10

ANOTHER thud from above, a few seconds after the first – the percussion, Neil figured, of something falling, then turning over or overbalancing. There was a scuffle of feet and the scrape of an object too big to carry being dragged across the floorboards.

'Sam?' Neil called up. 'Sammy, you okay?'

No reply.

Neil came out of his parents' room and took hold of the stepladder; its antique metal rungs wobbled as he climbed. He tried to remember the last time he had been in his father's loft (the house and bedroom would always be Neil's parents', plural, but in his internal designation the loft was eternally and exclusively Brian's, his mother's closest approach to it, so far as he remembered, being to stand at the bottom of these steps and call down whomever was up there for lunch, peering up into the murk with an expression of adamant distrust). He trod carefully on the narrow steps, trying to weigh as little as possible. The madeleine aromas of

237

damp paper and mouldy rubber assailed and stopped him halfway through the hatch.

Sam was kneeling in the beige glow of a single, unshaded low-watt bulb, his shirt smeared with a rich, well-matured dust. He was appraising an old black-and-white television – deeper than it was wide, three knobs, only ever three channels – which, Neil remembered, had been retired to the loft from service in his parents' bedroom, but which before the purchase of their colour set had been the screen on which they watched the Cup Final in the lounge, he and Dan alternately fiddling with the aerial when the zigzagging interference got too much; the screen on which they watched the Grand National, Brian having closed the shop early and visited the bookies' three doors down, placing a single pre-selected one-pound wager per family member, the boys clutching the betting slips as if they were enchanted parchments.

'You can take it home if you want,' Neil said. 'Might still work. Take it, Sammy.'

'Nah,' Sam said, squinting at the alien bulk like an archaeologist at a sarcophagus. 'No room. Stacy wouldn't have it, would she? Look at it. Shame, though. All these old things. It's like your own museum. Yours and Dad's.'

'Take something else, then,' Neil told him. 'Take anything you want. House clearers are coming next week. Never know, might be worth something.'

Neil's turn to reckon his family's life in things had come. A couple of archaic wooden tennis rackets, pressed between rectangular frames; an antediluvian computer, unrecognisable as a computer to Sam, and now, almost, to Neil, over which he and Dan had fought, viciously, no quarter asked or given, for seventy-two hours after it arrived one Thatcher-era

Christmas, quickly forsaking its binary games for muddier diversions; a pair of binoculars in a scratched leather case; a deflated yellow dinghy, unused since it was launched on a frigid beach in Suffolk in the mid-eighties. In one corner were a pair of promising-looking trunks, which upon inspection contained only several decades' worth of accounts for Collins & Sons ... Sam didn't have much that was truly his, but there was nothing among this junk that he could want. For reasons he couldn't identify, Neil needed him to have something.

He watched Sam stoop to rifle a suitcase. The boy was only a couple of inches shorter than him, with an adolescent incongruity in his proportions (bulbous head, outsized feet) that suggested he hadn't yet topped out; a trio of creases at the hems of his trousers charted their and Sam's extensions like the rings of a tree trunk. When you looked at him from behind, or in silhouette, minus the pointillist skin and affected glower, he seemed much older.

In the end he took a yo-yo, though only, Neil knew, because he wanted to be kind. Sam creaked down the metal steps. Earlier, when Neil turned the light on, it had blinked into action as if from hibernation. This time – the last time – when he followed and flicked the switch, the bulb went off immediately.

The end. He closed the hatch.

In the bedroom, in the wardrobe, Neil found his father's clothes, and on the adjacent shelves his mother's clothes, more or less untouched, so far as he could see. He glanced over his shoulder to be sure Sam wasn't there, pressed his nose into the fabric and inhaled.

Moth balls.

Do you cry when you think about it?

In the kitchen, beneath the sink, he found six dusty bottles of water, relics of an emergency supply that Brian had laid in, muttering about trade unionists, when a waterworks strike seemed imminent at the fag-end of the seventies. He put a paperweight, two vases and a few photos into a plastic crate. He could hear Sam moving around in Dan's room, opening and closing the drawers, ransacking his father's childhood. Dan had already pillaged the cutlery, plus a watercolour of a French harbour that Brian once hinted might be valuable, though Neil doubted it. In his father's paperwork he discovered that the house had been remortgaged, five years before, around the time of Brian's first stroke, in what the cheque stubs suggested was an eleventh-hour bid to keep Dan out of the gutter. Once he might have been aggrieved at the favouritism, but now he smiled at the secret, gruff kindness. *Your brother knew from the beginning.*

The doorbell rang.

'Mr Hinds told me,' Bimal's father began. Neil tried to place Mr Hinds and failed. 'I saw your car, you see. You don't mind ... I ... He was a gentleman. That's all, that's what I ... That's all.'

Bimal's father was wearing a suit, possibly the same, trademark garment he wore during their childhood. The skin above the bridge of his glasses was flaking, Neil noticed, white flecks on brown. He gawped around Neil as if he might be invited in, or be able to glimpse the corpse. Irritation rose up Neil's throat – *busybody, ghoul, vulture* – but he suppressed it before it reached his lips. Behind his visitor, above the unchanged sequence of houses on the opposite side of the road, the sky was too blue, inconsiderately perfect.

'Thanks,' Neil said. 'Appreciate it. Really.'

He asked after Bimal.

'Yes, very well, very well, thank you,' his father said. 'California agrees with him, as you know. And the children, they are getting their American accents.'

Neil hadn't known that Bimal had moved to America. He nodded in assent but said nothing.

'He was very proud of you,' Bimal's father said at last. 'Very proud. Always showing me the stock prices in the paper, you see. All your comings and goings. Very proud indeed. But you know that.'

He held out a hand for Neil to shake, somehow bony and soft at once, like the carcass of a battery chicken, and after that it seemed too late to ask for details.

'A real gentleman,' he repeated. He turned and walked away, erect but slow, with a mechanical, arthritic gait. He seemed smaller than Neil remembered him.

Neil stood at the open front door. 'Come on,' he called up to Sam. 'Let's go. Let's get on with it.'

NEIL put the rattly crate into the boot of his car, along with the two urns. Sam sat in the front, playing with the windows and reclining his seat at its expensively glacial pace.

'Are you, like, 'kay?' Sam asked.

'Yeah,' Neil said. 'Course.'

He glanced over at Sam and saw that he was wiping his nose with his finger. At the end of every horizontal slash his hand circled up to wipe his eyes, too, finger for one eye, thumb around the other.

'You?'

'Course,' Sam said.

Neil switched on the radio. *Told y'all I was gonna bump like this.* Sam turned it off.

He drove up through Stanmore, past the location of the golf course on which he and Dan had played pitch-and-putt as boys, Neil surreptitiously kicking his ball a few metres towards the hole whenever Dan, mighty Dan, turned his back. The land where the course had been was now a live-the-dream housing complex that had evidently missed its time. There was an advert on the fence, facing the dual carriageway. One corner of the plastic sheet had become unstuck and blown across the lettering: *Still Six Units Remai*

You were supposed to feel radically alone when the second one went, Neil knew. Finally orphaned; ultimately adult. That was what everyone said. No one left to forgive your mistakes, no generational buffer between you and your own death. No longer loved in that particular, enfolding way.

That wasn't how Neil felt, as he and Sam drove over the edge of London, and he saw no point in pretending. He was no lonelier than he had been two weeks before; if anything he felt younger, lighter, childishly unburdened. You were supposed to feel a futile, belated regret for everything you hadn't asked, everything you had been too timid or inhibited to bring up. That was another thing people said. There were indeed facts and episodes Neil found he would like to clarify, but it was gossip, really, that he coveted, not heirloom wisdom or five-to-midnight honesty. Not *Do you love me?* Or *Are you scared?* But *How did you lose your virginity? Did you ever have an affair? Have you ever committed a crime?* Smashed bottles and *Don't shit on your own doorstep* and the phantom girlfriend in Maida Vale whom Brian had mentioned to Adam that afternoon in the nineties. Too late now.

Neil looked across at Sam. He was craning his head out of the window to catch the wind in his hair, as road-trippers did on television. They had the rest of the day together. Neil smiled.

He pulled off the dual carriageway into a narrow country lane. After a few minutes he parked beside a pond at the beginning of a village. Neil remembered the four of them coming to this place for picnics, although it was possible that they had only come once, one luminous recollection that his memory had amplified or wished into a habit. He retrieved the urns from the boot and strode towards a field where (he was almost sure) his mother had called *On your marks, get set* for fraternal races that Neil invariably lost.

'Come on,' he called back to Sam. 'Sammy, come on.'

Sam loitered by the car, respectfully fastening the upper buttons of his shirt. Of the two of them, Sam had lost more, Neil saw. More of the less that he had.

Neil climbed over a stile and marched up the ramblers' path at the side of the field. Glancing back he saw Sam attempt to vault the fence and fail. He turned around quickly so the boy wouldn't know he had been seen. The field wasn't as he expected and wanted it to be (cows and grass where Neil remembered wheat), and he realised, as he walked, that he didn't know what he was looking for or where he ought to stop. Sam had fallen behind; Neil paused to let him catch up, sitting on the trunk of an old tree.

Dan had made it to the crematorium but vanished immediately afterwards, not troubling with excuses or goodbyes or bittersweet reminiscences or even a drink, leaving Neil in sole charge of both Sam and the ashes that had recently been Brian. Neil's first instinct was surreptitiously to leave the urn behind, but one of the attendants had scampered after him, presuming the dereliction was an oversight, and he had been obliged to take it. Putting the thing in the bin felt like too much, even for Neil. Sam suggested the stretch of pavement outside the shop, which was after all the place Brian had spent more of his waking life than any other, a fourteen-year-old's crazy and possibly illegal scheme that Neil had fleetingly entertained as reasonable.

Then he thought of the picnic place. The memory of it seemed to belong to someone else, inherited by the almost-forty Neil from some ancestor self, a figure who resembled and related to him as Neanderthals did to modern humans in biology-textbook sketches of the ascent of man. His childhood was a story about a person he only distantly knew; at the same time it contained incidents he could recall with an almost shocking clarity. The odour of damp at the back of the armchair when he hid behind it to filch a fresh-minted one-pound coin from his mother's handbag, the leathery smell of her bag as he persuaded himself that she wouldn't notice, or, if she did, that she would blame Dan. His reasoning and remorse on that day seemed nearer to Neil, as he sat on the tree trunk, than did the motives for more recent wrongs.

Sam caught up, perched alongside him and panted. Neil put his hand on his nephew's shoulder. When he regained his breath Sam stood up and in front of Neil, fidgeting – digging his hands into his trouser pockets, taking them out, entwining his fingers behind his back, replacing them in his pockets – from which Neil inferred that Sam thought this was the moment. It might as well be.

He stood and unscrewed the lid of his father's urn, trying to think of something to say. In the end he settled on 'Goodbye, Brian', the valediction doubling as a petty revolt, since he had never called his father Brian while he was alive.

'Amen,' Sam said, and swallowed.

Neil rotated the lid. He meant to do it slowly, a picturesque hour-glass trickling, but he misjudged the angle and the consistency of the ash, and it landed in a clump at his feet. It seemed sacrilegious just to leave the stuff there – he had a premonition of a cow ambling over and lapping it up – so he and Sam found sticks and spread out the flakes until they resembled a burned-out campfire. Sam dug his stick into the ash and the ground below it to mark the spot. 'Goodbye, Brian,' he repeated.

Neil decided to keep hold of his mother until he thought of something more decorous to do with her. Walking back to the car he dredged or conjured up a picture of her sitting in an alcove of wheat in a summer skirt, her legs curled under her, her shoes kicked off. He might have distilled a picture of his father, but halfway back Sam found a chewed-up tennis ball, hemispherically bald where a dog had mauled it. He kicked the ball at Neil; Neil inexpertly returned it. They stained the knees of their trousers on the overlong grass at the verge of the field. Sam ran out of breath after a few minutes.

'You okay?' Neil asked him.

'Yeah,' Sam said. 'No problem.'

'Right. Come on.'

Neil drove them to a pub he knew further up the lane, now accoutred with a kiddies' playground and a conservatory that he didn't remember. He left his mother in the boot. He ordered a gin and tonic for himself and half a pint of lager shandy for his nephew.

'So how's Stacy, then?'

'A'righ, s'pose,' Sam said, drawling like an American television gangster, at least when he remembered to. He took a swig of shandy but didn't seem to like it. 'She's a'righ most of the time. She's there a lot, you know, with me. More than him.'

What sort of woman, Neil had asked himself when Sam first mentioned Stacy, would take on his brother in his twenty-first-century guise? Dan was no longer sinking, exactly – he had stretches of work, weeks or months at building sites or warehouses – but equally he seemed to have given up hope of rising: he subsisted in a hand-to-mouth state of precariously deferred crisis. Stacy was the answer. Whether she constituted a net benefit to Sam, or was simply an extra embarrassment, Neil wasn't sure.

'Didn't want to come up?'

'Don't think he asked her. Not speaking much at the moment. You know, one of those.' Sam raised his eyebrows, a worldly gesture on the craterous man-boy's brow.

'What about Basingstoke? School and everything.'

'A'righ.' Sam's leg was twitching. He wiped his nose. He swallowed nervously, though he hadn't taken a drink. 'It's true, what he said. The old man. The Indian bloke. I heard him from up the stairs. He was mad proud of you, your dad. Brian. Always on about you. He got me to show him your website, you know, on the computer. Your company or whatever. We went to that internet place on the high street.'

'When I wasn't there,' Neil said, like some touchy adolescent. 'Only when I wasn't there.'

'Yeah, but anyway. Still counts. And he was grateful, you know, the way you were always coming up here. He told me. He was thankful. Even if you and him, you never said much.'

'You only get one,' Neil said. 'Dad, I mean. Might as well do your bit.'

'Huh,' Sam grunted, as if to say, *Don't I know it?* What he actually said was, 'He loved you, innit.'

Neil took a slug of G&T. 'He was proud of you too, Sammy.'

'Yeah...'

'He was.'

'Right.'

He noticed a cut at the corner of Sam's mouth where he had attempted to shave for the occasion; between that, his grimy shirt and stained trousers, Sam might have stumbled out of a fire or a collapsed building. A few months before, during the death-watch in Harrow, Neil had broached the idea of his nephew moving in with him – casually, he intended, presenting it as an all-round win. It was a mistake, he saw afterwards, to specify that Dan could see his son whenever he liked, as if that were in doubt. Dan had growled at Sam to get his stuff together, shouted a goodbye at Brian, and manhandled the boy away. Three or four more years – as soon as Sam could be comprehensively detached from Dan, and from Stacy, if she were still around – and Neil would redeem him. Money and somewhere of his own to live and a job, even: he was the sort of man who could pull that off now.

They drove back into London. Neil bought potatoes and cooking oil and made them chips for dinner, cutting the potatoes very finely while Sam watched.

HE WASN'T lonely. Neil told himself he wasn't lonely. He had friends, or quasi-friends, functional friends, people with whom his life overlapped, people with whom he shared common interests, mostly in the utilitarian sense rather than the recreational one. He had gym friends, friends at work, though with them, Neil found, all the gamesmanship and rivalry that crept in under the back door of civilian friendships were there in the hallway from the start. Simulacra of friends. After he put Sam on his bus, the morning after the ashes, he had an urge to phone Adam. Not because he was traumatised or bereft: he just felt Adam should know, as if the act of telling him and Adam's witness were a missing part of the event.

Neil's feelings had hardened in the weeks after what, at first, he thought of as 'the argument'. Every ungenerous thought he had ever harboured about Adam, from San Diego to Ealing, was collated in his defence, exaggerated and repeated with no kinder reflections admitted:

Smug bastard. Patronising bastard. Jealous bastard.

Fauntleroy. Failure.

Accomplice. Liar. Pimp.

He forgot that a friend's faults were among his consolations – that some of Adam's faults were virtues. They became only faults, worse and worse. He forgot his own culpabilities.

The blindness lasted over a year, until a few months after Neil's father died. When, that autumn, the banks collapsed, gravity was reinvented, and it emerged that, contrary to long-held London belief, economics wasn't only something that happened in faraway countries – Latin American basket cases and rabid Asian tigers – Neil felt sure Adam would be glorying in the blow-up. The image of Adam vengefully celebrating his comeuppance hardened into a certainty in Neil's mind: *chancer, spiv,* wasn't that what Adam had always thought of him, those only-in-England terms of disparagement, the commercial equivalents of the other English classic, *Too clever by half*? It sometimes seemed to Neil that there were only two or three socially acceptable careers in his hypocritical country.

Fuck you, then.

What are you really going to do?

That was the final swell of his anger, and at the end of the same year, after eighteen months apart, the bitterness lifted, slowly then suddenly, like a migraine or a grief. Now Neil floundered when he tried to recapture the logic that, on Adam's sofa, had seemed to link his grievance with this redress. His reasoning became so vague and inarticulable that it was astonishing to him, almost funny, that he had lost his best friend, his only whole friend, for ever over this.

He should have known that night in California, Neil finally acknowledged to himself. He hadn't needed Adam to tell him. Not just her nerves, nor the way her knees knocked together as she dried herself by the lake. He should have known in the tent.

Neil was in a post-crisis strategy meeting with Tony and the other partners when it struck him that in fact he *had* known, had only been pretending not to, hadn't asked because he knew what the answer would be; that therefore, in a way, Adam had nothing to do with it, there had been nothing for Neil to revenge, and he must bear all the responsibility himself, both for Rose and for Claire. He blushed violently, not just blushing but sweating, suddenly and feverously as if he had food poisoning, his hands shaking like an alcoholic's when he tried to take a note. He excused himself and rushed to the gents, hoping that Tony and the others hadn't noticed his disarray, holding on to the edges of the sink and bowing his head so as not to look himself in his bloodshot eyes. By that evening his certainty had dissipated, and he was no longer sure what he had known or when.

When he first kissed her she had closed her eyes and puckered her lips as if she were in an old movie.

Who cared what Adam had or hadn't said that night? He felt ridiculous and ashamed. That Christmas he considered texting. The number was still listed among the contacts in Neil's phone, and now and then he would open Adam's details and look at the meaningless digits and the handsome thumbnail as he was scrolling his way to someone else, privately embarrassed by this indulgence, the SIM-card necromancy. *It was my fault, all of it, I'm sorry.* But he didn't text, or call.

He had texted Jess about Brian, telling himself that she would want to know. *Sorry 2 hear that*, she replied.

HE HADN'T got his comeuppance. 'It's like that golf joke,' Tony said to Neil early in the New Year.

'What golf—'

'Two golfers, they're on the fairway, they see a bear. One starts to run, the other says, what are you doing, you can't outrun a bear, and the first guy says, I don't have to, I only have to outrun *you*. We've just got to be less fucked than the other fuckers.'

Neil laughed, aloud and inauthentically.

'Don't share that one with the clients, kimosabe.'

Tony had swapped a slab of stocks for gold, Swiss francs and American bonds. There was a bond-rush and a gold-rush, and six months on they were miraculously in profit, coming out of the crash with their reputation enhanced in the garrulous HNWI family. In hard times, Neil saw, the rich were the best business to be in. The rich were always with

250

us, ever anxious to be relieved of the awful burden of their cash.

He was learning to be picky about who he ran money for. He could smell the psychotics who would sue if you missed their pie-in-the sky targets, and the foreign tycoons who would laugh, then have you escorted from the building, when you proffered your humble but kosher ten per cent return. He could spot the neurotics whose money could only be extracted gently, reassuringly – the right-place, right-time mega-salariat of the eighties and nineties, whose share options had turned into one-way golden tickets, and who were petrified of losing their barely dreamed of windfalls. On the other hand there were the risk junkies, proud of their own daring, a pride you had to flatter and nurture.

During the spring after the crash he went to Miami, a nine-hour flight for a fifteen-minute pitch, though by now Neil tended to know within thirty seconds how the conversation would end. Through the retracted security gates and into the antiseptically pristine home (always over-housekept, these palaces, the life scoured and disinfected out of them like covered-up murder scenes).

The client was at his desk. He didn't look up. Neil said, 'How do you feel about losing money?'

They wired the investment to Rutland half an hour later. In London they would think Neil had reeled him in with some patented, supernumerate spiel. It was simpler than that: *Sell the customer what he wants to buy.*

That evening he flew to New York, and in the morning had two meetings on the Upper East Side. In the afternoon he saw a woman he thought he knew, something about the shape of her head, her hair, the elastic rhythm of her stride. He tried to put her out of his mind. Later, on Park Avenue, he saw the same woman again, or thought he did, and although he knew the familiarity might be psychosomatic, he ran. *I am not the sort of man who runs after a woman in the street*, he wanted to tell the Americans he passed.

She was gone. She made him think of times in his childhood when he had needed to prove, in some insoluble dispute with Dan, that the tennis ball was in, really it was, or, later, that he had been the first of them to ask their father for Saturday morning off – occasions when he wanted urgently to appeal to some celestial umpire for a categorical ruling. *Just tell me!* Possibly she was fine, but there was no one to ask, and you had to live with that, Neil realised, never knowing what your own actions meant.

Two years after 'the argument', drinking alone at his bamboo bar, Neil thought about killing himself. Not out of despair or anguish; not for any particular reason at all, in fact, but rather because of the absence of a clinching reason to carry on living. He had changed his mind about suicide. It had come to seem less an arrogance than a practicality, an efficiency saving. Sure, his work had its consolations. It was fixed, unsurprising, and success and failure, blame and virtue, were reassuringly clear, the therapeutic superficiality limiting the scope of disappointment. But work wasn't a sufficient incentive, and nor was money. For some of the others, money was less a commodity than a war, which they would always be losing so long as someone at the fund on the other side of Piccadilly was getting more. Neil knew he had enough. He was PAYEd more in a month than his father had earned most years.

He could leave it all to Sam. He could leave something to Adam, too, though Adam might be offended. He would write an apology into his will.

*

INSTEAD of killing himself he became a partner. He took Sam to Paris for a weekend on the Eurostar. They went to a circus, a proper, old-fashioned circus that featured abused tigers and sequined show girls for the dads. Later in the summer Neil took Sam to Lake Garda, putting them up for a few days at a hotel recommended by Tony. They shared a room, Sam hunting for porn on the satellite channels and Neil scouring the grounds for a BlackBerry signal with roughly equal alacrity. Sam wanted to go to a nightclub, and he looked old enough to pass, but Neil put his foot down. He had some blotchy bruises on his forearms; Neil tried to examine them but Sam squirmed away. He kept his T-shirt on when he swam.

Neil met Roxanna at a recession-proof restaurant in Soho (pan-Oriental menu, sub-industrial decor, the lighting regimen tenebrous in some places and glaring in others, like a secret-police interrogation chamber with multiple stations). Tony and one of the other partners were there, several analysts and a few secretaries, plus assorted other-halves and hangers-on. They sat at an awkward long table, everyone arriving in the wrong order and wishing they were next to someone else, or wishing that they weren't there at all, the room anyway too loud to hear what the person opposite was saying, as in most London restaurants, the diners barking at each other in an escalating aural brawl.

She was sitting between Neil and his colleague Dominic, a thirty-ish, obviously handsome stock analyst, not as posh as he would like to be, perhaps, but working on it. At first Neil assumed the two of them were attached, but during the starters she shot him an unmistakable get-me-out-of-here look. She was Iranian (not, apparently, a bar to boozing). She organised conferences, she was a friend of one of the secretaries, Tiffany, he thought she said, who had brought her in lieu of a date. She had ebony hair, matching eyes and endearingly irregular teeth. Neil tried not to be distracted by the acquaintances in his peripheral vision.

By the time the *Look! No notepad!* waitress brought the ironic fortune cookies, Neil was tired and anyway doubtful of his chances. Roxanna's cookie advised her that, *To give, you must first receive.*

Neil cracked his cookie, looked down at the slip of paper and up at Roxanna. 'It says here,' he said, boredom and loneliness welling up as audacity, 'that tonight I'm going to have sex with a stranger.'

Her eyes widened, she fixed them on the napkin across her knees. For a moment Neil thought she was going to leave, or to slap him.

She said, 'Come with me for a cigarette?'

She didn't smoke. On the way to the exit she steered him into one of the trendily unisex washrooms, pinning him between the rectangular marble sink and the door as it closed behind them. Neil felt at once decadent, worldly, like a desperado in a war zone, and embarrassingly teenaged. He had grown accustomed to the idea that some women might find him attractive: his weight was stable, ditto his hairline, as if protracted negotiations between him and it had established an agreed frontier. Money's gloss invisibly burnished his pale skin. But *this* woman, here, hitching up her skirt in a toilet stall?

The circumstances didn't inhibit her as to volume. She pushed a knuckle into his anus as he thrusted.

Dominic smirked at Neil when they returned to the table. Tony pretended he hadn't seen them. It was only the second time in his life that he had been so reckless. There was suicidal indifference in the recklessness, and also something like the opposite, a roulette spin for a richer life.

Understanding that this beginning could drive them apart they never mentioned it. She emailed; they went out for dinner without colleagues or sex, at the restaurant or afterwards, as if Roxanna were an ancient goddess who might magically have her virginity restored. Her parents had fled Tehran for England during the revolution, she told him. They moved to America while she was at university, separating not long afterwards, but she had stayed in London. She was thirty-five: one careful owner, like him, Neil concluded from oblique references to her romantic past.

He went to Zurich, on to Singapore, and didn't see her for two weeks. The third time, at a restaurant in Notting Hill, she announced that she had something to tell him. That's it, Neil thought.

'Neil, I'm pregnant. I'm pregnant, Neil.' Once-in-a-lifetime news, but no other way than just to say it.

You used something, right?

I'll take care of it.

He managed not to ask either *Is it mine?* or *Are you going to keep it?*, a double feat of self-restraint for which he was afterwards grateful. Her grin suggested that the second question would in any case have been redundant. His stomach sank, but he sensed another part of him levitating, taking off.

You could have a kid out there, you know.

They agreed that they would wait before she moved in but they didn't. After all he was alone in that overwhelming apartment, with Sam for the odd weekend. She could always move out again, they told each other. For New Year's Eve they went to Bilbao, dancing to a street band in the alleys of the old town. The first time the doll-sized knee or elbow poked at him through her belly, Neil felt as if he could fly; her new anatomy became so familiar to him, swelled so incrementally, that it came to seem this bloated form was the end-point, her finished state, rather than a beginning. He turned forty shortly before the baby was due, feeling that a lot of his life was behind him, and that little of that life was his.

They called her Leila. Neil was fascinated by her skin tone, which was neither Roxanna's nor his but a golden hybrid of her own. He convinced himself that he could glimpse his mother in her brow and around her eyes. He tried to imagine his mother as a grandparent, but he knew the speculation was a lie, that he couldn't ever know how she would have been. They enlisted a night nurse, a Ukrainian named Olesya, whom Tony had recommended. Olesya was pretty, defeatedly overweight, discreetly religious (Orthodox crucifix, mumbled imprecations, homeland pain written into the creases on her forehead and at the corners of her mouth).

Roxanna was in bed. Leila was asleep on his chest, her four limbs bent under her like a frog's. Olesya lifted the weightless body off him and ushered Neil out of the flat, shooing him away with a wise smile and a broken-English instruction to 'Go your friends.'

To begin with he didn't quite admit where he was heading. He pretended to himself that he was only driving. It was a cold grey night with a starless London sky. He drove across town, to the back of the pub in Southwark where he had first met Claire, after that to the end of Westminster Bridge that abutted the bowling arcade and the still-spinning wheel. He drove along the Strand, looking for the doorway they had shared with those Australian girls, he couldn't remember their names, his and Adam's alternate secret, which hadn't been enough. On his homeward loop he trawled the road at the back of Paddington Station to find the café in which he and Adam had sat, sussing out where they stood, whether the other was real, at their first meeting in England. Adam had worn his ridiculous cap.

The locations didn't tally with Neil's memories. Thinking about the nineties, the images came back to him washed-out and grimy: brown food and miserabilist films, boxy cars and chewing gum on the pavement, the streets in the centre of town streamed in filth, the rubbish bins removed lest terrorists stash bombs in them. In Neil's mind the contrast between that time and neon now replayed Dorothy's transition from dowdy Kansas to Technicolor Munchkinland. Scanning the unfamiliar shopfronts, Neil reckoned that the café had become an oyster bar. The airline office was now a high-concept fast-fooderie, he thought.

So inconsiderate, these changes. How were you ever supposed to find your way back, recover your old you, when the city was so different, as different, almost, as you were? You needed your own private London, preserved in formaldehyde, an archipelago museum of your imperishable moments. Instead your places were bulldozed and replaced with someone else's memories.

I'm going crazy, Neil thought, as he sat in his car, half mounted on the pavement, being hooted by taxi drivers, stalking a bar that had once been a café in which, a long time before, he had talked with a man who used to be his friend. A friend he hadn't seen for three years.

'I'm going crazy,' he said out loud. 'Sorry,' he said to no one, and to Adam, and to Rose, and drove himself back to Bayswater.

*

THERE was the usual rigmarole of pretending he might go back to sleep without relieving himself. Perhaps if he lay on his other side, or curled up, like this ... Finally Adam levered himself out of bed, as quietly as he could, his senses muted as if he were underwater, eyes outraged at being called upon to open, and, when they did, reporting an unfamiliar room, doors and windows bafflingly transposed, so that for a moment he wondered whether he was dreaming. The croaking of frogs outside the window tipped him off. His brain cranked up, and he padded to the cork-floored bathroom between their room and the children's. The door snapped shut, too loudly. Adam swore, counterproductively, but no one seemed to wake.

He had a challenging nocturnal erection. Sighing, he throttled his penis with his right hand, gripped the towel rail with his left, preparing to double over, as if he were executing a dive with pike – a fraught manoeuvre, but the surest way, when he was engorged, to avoid spraying urine across the seat and onto the floor, which would result in either an icky clean-up now or, if he neglected that courtesy, a bollocking from Claire in the morning. He bent his dick through another ten degrees, the organ bucking and resisting, and swore again.

The latch clicked as the bathroom door reopened. Adam straightened up and turned round, still clutching the angry penis, the look on his face on the cusp between ecstasy and excruciation.

'Oh,' Claire said. 'Oh, Adam.'

He followed her gaze to his genitals. So far it hadn't caused him much trouble, this penis. Less than he might have expected. Less grief than Neil's had caused them.

'It isn't what you think,' Adam said, releasing his grip. 'Clezzy, really. It's ... I'm just trying to piss.'

Claire hesitated for a moment before acquiescing with a sleepy smile. She squeezed past him to the toilet, naked, yawning as she peed, wiping herself robotically. The trust that they had almost lost had come back to them.

'Well,' she said, standing up. 'We're awake now.'

She took hold of the penis with one hand, made a *shush* sign with the other, and led him silently back to bed.

Three years before, as open-mindedly as he could, Adam had considered the possibility that he found the thought of Claire and Neil arousing. Briefly he wondered whether he might be on the high road to a life of orgies in south London warehouses (like the ones that, so one of the secretaries told him on his second day in the office, Hardy liked to attend), where he would be locked in a cage to watch while strangers fucked his wife. That wasn't it, he soon decided; he was as vanilla in his lusts as in his other tastes. Her brush with Neil had been a jolt rather than a turn-on, more medical than erotic, mild electrotherapy administered to a struggling heart. Or perhaps it was simply a coincidence when, a few weeks later – weeks of him ruminating on car journeys, his jaw grinding ominously, Claire glancing at him in silence as Harry and Ruby garrotted each other in the back – their sex life came back to them, too, like a rediscovered hobby. That summer they were anyway emerging from the tunnel of the children's infancy: the phase of repurposed bodies and burgled privacy, of holidays that were marathons of arse-wiping and miscalculated discipline, their sexual punctuation being, if Adam were lucky, one perfunctory, grisly hand-job. The mutual neglect that began as a necessity and developed into a stand-off. They blinkingly began to see each other again.

Claire had crow's feet around her eyes and her flesh was –

not flabbier, but somehow more yielding than it once had been. Adam's fingers sunk into her rather than stopping at her surface. She was still a beautiful woman, more beautiful, to him, because of what he had seen her body do. That same summer, after a decade of ordering grown-up drinks, or drinking nothing, she reverted to the alcosyrups she had preferred when they met, ginger wine and pina coladas and fuck-it Malibu and pineapples. The time poverty of parenthood had made her more decisive and demanding – in restaurants, in negotiations with telephone salespeople, in bed, where she directed his hands briskly or deployed her own.

Adam had kept his hair and, more or less, his looks. The sagging jowls had reconsidered and tightened back, the skin of his face coming to seem stretched and weather-beaten. When he looked in the mirror he had begun to see his father peering back at him, like an actor through his make-up.

The revived desire that his wife stirred felt like its own kind of transgression. Adam was freshly grateful to the him who had met and kept hold of her, and the him who had forgiven her for that nothing.

Afterwards he spooned her, clasping both of her breasts in one of his palms. 'Love you,' he said.

'Go back to sleep,' Claire said.

The trust had come back, but he hadn't told her about Yosemite. That would always be just between them.

'UP YOU get,' Ruby said, hurdling onto their bed. 'Beach time, lazyboneses.'

'I already told her, it's the castle today,' Harry said from the doorway. 'The one with the tree house, you know. It's definitely my turn, she chose yesterday.'

'Me too,' Ruby said. 'But it's the beach first. Please, Daddy.'

Adam hesitated. 'Tell you what,' Claire ruled, her toenails digging into his calf beneath the bed covers, 'we'll go to the beach, but' – she raised her voice above their son's objection – 'we'll go to that place you like for dinner, where the man gave you the sparklers.'

'I suppose,' Harry said.

Adam drew his daughter to him. Ruby submitted, but passively, only half present in the embrace. Seven already: the years in which she needed to be as close to them as she could as often as she could, to be piggybacked and tickled and enfolded, her marsupial years, were drawing to an end. Adam felt a pang of unbereaved mourning.

They dressed and drove to the lake. The sand was greyish, the water was silty and cold, the rocks where the sand and water met encased in slimy, emerald weeds that were unpleasant and hazardous to walk on. With a seven-year-old's talent for suspending disbelief, Ruby was in her swimsuit, across the beach and into the water before her parents had slipped off their shoes. She buried her face as she frontcrawled, as her instructor had taught her.

'You haven't got any sun cream on!' Adam called after her.

'Daddy,' Ruby called back. 'Stop worrying.'

Adam splashed in. He threw Ruby into the air, never quite relinquishing control of the slippery limbs as her compact body rose and fell. 'Higher,' Ruby shrieked.

Harry joined them, shouting, 'Do it to me!' He and Adam raced, caressed underwater by shadowy tendrils, Ruby clinging to her father's throat. Adam stood her in the shallows and waded back to demonstrate his butterfly stroke, splashing around like a demented walrus to small locomotive but great comic effect – the move a straight lift from his father's summer playbook, which was itself, he had inferred, a daguerreotype of his father's father's, and so on and on, back and back, probably, to some exhibitionist Tudor moat swimmer, the parenting tactics encoded and passed on like eye colour or high blood pressure.

Playing in the water with his children, Adam's mind went back to their peace lunch at the Chelsea fish restaurant several months before, the last time he had seen his father. It wasn't the adult thing to do, he knew, it was gauche and unsophisticated, but he had mentioned his mother once, twice, how she was staying with her sister, how she worried about Harriet, in her squat with her punky German boyfriend, somewhere in east London.

Jeremy Tayler had pressed his fingers to his temples, eyes fixed on the menu, silent. 'Asparagus,' he finally said, looking up. 'Then sole *meunière*. No, *bonne femme*.'

Anger had welled up in Adam, for his mother and also for himself, a kind of buyer's remorse. All that happiness, that enervating, debilitating happiness, which had turned out to be a lie. That had been another kind of bereavement, for the life he thought they had all shared. Later Adam noticed his father appraise the waitress's arse, as she bent to sweep the tablecloth with an accessory like a cut-throat razor.

'Daddy?' Ruby said.

She was kneeling in the shallows, recycling the murky water that lapped into her mouth, accustomed to going about her business while the adult worked through his or her distraction, emails, text messages.

'Sorry,' Adam said. 'Don't drink it, sweetheart.'

He pictured his mother's pursed mouth as she applied the

sun cream to him and Harriet, her firm, methodical strokes, only now intuiting the contest of devotion and boredom, and the other, veiled resentments that must have engraved her concentrating frown. Harriet had submitted herself obediently, he recalled, but he had always wriggled away ungratefully, desperate to show their father a dive, or how long he could hold his breath.

Fathers.

'Again the buttercup,' Ruby said.

'All right,' Adam said. 'Just once.'

He splashed the children as he launched himself into his stroke; they splashed him back. In the end the three of them slipped back across the rocks. Claire distributed towels for the children to dry themselves.

Along the beach three old men were playing dominoes underneath a sun umbrella. A thin man and fat woman were holding hands. Snatches of music drifted over from the open-air café. Adam remembered reading an interview in the paper with some septuagenarian film director, a Spanish or Italian man, describing how, one morning in old age, lust had left him, and how light he felt without it, as if he had been tethered to a goat for sixty years and suddenly cut loose. Adam was beginning to feel like that, but about ambition rather than his libido. This wasn't quite the life he expected, but what right, really, did he ever have to his hopes? They made enough money, just about. You never knew, they told each other, the business Claire was starting might take off, stranger things, the usual. Claire, the children, the nineteenth-century history books that he read on the commuter train from High Wycombe, a train on which, almost every day, he got a seat.

*

HARDY was the secretaries' nickname for Alan, the shorter and fatter of his two bosses. Alan/Hardy had a Humpty Dumpty belly that he attempted to corset in a self-mortifying belt. He dyed his hair a rusty orange and signed his name with an overcompensating flourish, his insecurities so flagrant that they were hard to resent. Laurel (Craig) was taller, an inexpert shaver who wore ill-fitting clothes, as if he were dressed by a hard-up mother who was keeping him in hand-me-downs until he finished growing. He had an absent, scholarly air that, so the secretaries whispered, concealed an actuarial coldness when it came to cutting people loose. 'P45 you as soon as look at you,' one of them said.

Adam had been hired by Hardy and feared Laurel. As a team the two of them were like the improbable couples you sometimes saw at weddings, the type with no obvious compatibility or resemblance, who nevertheless synchronised perfectly on the dancefloor. They fit. Adam struggled to decipher where the power lay between them.

The private sector, a realm so denigrated and envied by his Civil Service colleagues, turned out to be essentially the same. The same needs, grudges and laziness, distributed in roughly the same proportions across the office, interacting according to what was probably a scientifically predictable algorithm. The same atavistic subtexts to every disagreement in meetings. Only the vocabulary was different. In consultancy you sought *alignment* before a meeting by *syndicating* your findings to your team. Faced with scepticism or incomprehension, you would *walk them through the deck*. You talked about *value* and *performance* and *delivery*, and, as often as possible, *strategy*. The key phrase, the trump phrase, the term that dominated their spreadsheets and appraisals and reveries, was *billable days*.

It was known in the office that one of the investors had sponsored Adam, and to begin with his colleagues had cold-shouldered him, as if he were part intern (unlikely to stay long enough to be worth schmoozing), part informer; he ate his lunch at his desk, pretending to be busy. He had thought to be respected for his decade of public service, to leap across to this new ladder halfway up, the higher rungs immediately in prospect. He was mistaken. Most of his peers had joined from mainstream consultancies, with the odd, exotic accountant sprinkled among them. The minority who, like Adam, had defected from the public sector, came from the big-ticket, contract-rich departments, health and local government and welfare. Adam had irrelevant expertise, unremunerative contacts.

'Going forward,' Hardy advised him, Adam struggling to repress the image of him leathered and strapped into the orgy cage, 'you'll need some expert leverage,' meaning research assistants who knew what they were doing.

They were certain to fire him, he warned Claire. It was only a matter of time. Even with the smaller mortgage, they would be screwed. He regretted his rash, greedy career switch. He dwelled on the cost of the children's sports camp. The shame.

'Don't worry,' she told him in their bed in High Wycombe, dawn breaking outside the dormer window. She applied for part-time jobs and took one as a receptionist in a doctor's surgery.

He worried.

He brought in a smallish contract to find savings at a private prison, and he proved to be a good picker-upper, adept at knowing precisely enough to seem plausible. Half the time, Adam quickly saw, it wasn't substantive expertise that the clients were buying. The arrangement reminded him of that song of a decade before, in which the lyrics deny the singer is the man his girlfriend has caught in flagrante. *It wasn't me* – who decided you should be fired. It was Adam Tayler. *It wasn't me* – who recommended that you be privatised. It was Mr Tayler.

His true expertise was in taking the blame.

It wasn't me.

It isn't what you think.

It was a misunderstanding.

Adam often worked alone, sleeping in deathly identikit hotels while he terrorised some unfortunate regional hospital or council. He would take a book to dinner, less to read than as a prop to ward off garrulous travellers – a precaution he adopted after an evening in Hartlepool with a packaging salesman, a man with the hairiest ears he had ever seen, who, when Adam's interest lagged, had pleaded, 'It's not just paper, it's corrugated cardboard too!' Occasionally he thought of Neil, driving round and round the M25, Neil before he flew out to America, with only the radio and his shampoo samples and his ruthless customers for company. He became a connoisseur of the spoiling techniques deployed by doctors and bureaucrats. Outright rudeness and noncooperation were easier to handle, he learned, than oily hypocrisy. 'Wonderful idea' and 'fascinating insight' generally translated, in Adam's experience, as 'You cunt' and 'I will crush you'.

He went back to the Home Office to pitch for a contract at Croydon. Chatting awkwardly to old comrades, he wasn't sure whether to think of them as victors or as inmates: whether, in careers as in a battle, the people who survived were the strongest and the bravest or, on the contrary, the most cowardly. Whether he had escaped or failed. He saw Heidi in the lift, but other people crowded around them. She blushed, fixedly watched the numbers ticking down to *G*, and strode off when the doors opened, with only a curt, eye-contact-less 'Bye'.

After a year he was summoned to Hardy's office, and when he arrived found Laurel in there too. He glanced rapidly between them, looking for the driving-examiner smile.

'This is perfectly normal—' Laurel said.

'This is absolutely routine,' Hardy cut in, Laurel switching on a Zen grin to smooth over the interruption. They explained that Adam's temporary contract would be rolled over for another year. The same thing happened the following year. In his more sanguine moments he would still glance up the ladder, at job titles with the prefix *Senior* or even *Director of*, but at others he peered downwards to the abyss, and was grateful to have his lowly rung to cling to.

THEY had lunch at the café by the lake, cold meats that the children wouldn't eat and Coke they weren't supposed to drink. Afterwards they played *babyfoot*, like a family in an advert, Adam's eyes meeting Claire's as they registered the idyllic tableau. *This is us*. He whispered to Harry to let Ruby win, as he wished he had let Harriet win, once or twice, at table tennis or Risk. His son tried to comply, for a goal or two, but in the end he couldn't manage the self-effacement.

After the game Harry announced that he wasn't tired and fell asleep in the shade. Claire sat on a lounger to brush Ruby's beautiful hair.

Adam put on his Crocs, and the sunglasses that were the marker of sexual self-respect among young parents, and absconded for a walk along the shore. He hummed to himself, then sang aloud: 'Well I'm runnin' down the road tryin' to loosen my load / I've got seven women on my mind.' His happiness anthem. Away from the road and the café the lakeshore became wilder, rockier, unkempt, bottles and plastic bags and a lone flip-flop nestling in the crevices. But further along the rock gave way to a flat, curated stretch of sand, possibly attached to a hotel, though Adam couldn't see one among the trees.

Two young boys were playing bat and ball. An elderly couple dozed under a parasol like effigies of themselves. A young woman in a white bikini, sunbathing alone on a towel, sat up to remove her top. She was a pretty brunette, painted toenails, firm, catwalk breasts. Nineteen, Adam estimated, or thereabouts. The fidgeting of her hands behind her back drew his eyes but he forced them away.

Adam watched as two men walked towards her, whispering. She was lying on her back, topless, and didn't see them approaching. One produced a camera from a pouch around his neck; the other arced around the girl, using that studiedly casual, faintly comic, half-jog, half-stride gait that some people employ if the lights change while they are crossing a road.

The second man stood next to the girl, grinning. The first man raised his camera.

'Hey,' Adam shouted. '*Non.*' He shooed them away with the back of his hands, as you might a wasp or a stray dog.

The girl sat up and saw the three of them. She tried to shield her breasts with a forearm as she rushed into a T-shirt, gathered her belongings and stalked up the beach towards the trees, one foot stumbling in the sand as she passed the second stranger. Adam wanted to shout after her that he was trying to help, but his schoolboy French deserted him, she was gone too quickly, tripping again on the root of a pine tree but keeping going, escaping, this time, into the shadows.

The two men drew together and conferred, hands cupped to their mouths like conspiring tennis partners. They were younger than him, with the pointlessly bulbous muscles of gym enthusiasts, the wirier of the two, the man with the camera, somehow the more concerning.

Adam stood his ground, bluffing, wondering whether he had been rash to intervene. The comatose pensioners and the bat-and-ball boys would be no help. He thought of the wasteful casualties of nightclub altercations and road rage incidents that he occasionally read about. He was grateful for his sunglasses, which masked the fear that must be glowing in his eyes. He held the wiry man's gaze.

They couldn't read him, or they were bluffing themselves. They scowled, the wiry one spat on the sand, and they walked slowly away in the other direction.

Adam exhaled. He looked towards the old people for acknowledgement or approbation but they hadn't stirred.

He turned to rejoin his family, scrambling back across the rocks, thinking of Ruby yelling 'Higher!', of she and Harry swimming back to Claire on the shore. He thought of the girl on the beach in Tenerife, struggling with her towel beneath the yellow parasols, he and the cameraman watching through the viewfinder. He thought of the girl by the lake in Yosemite, her head buried in the water as she swam, how she slicked back her hair and grinned. Two men were watching her, and one of them was him.

They were eating ice creams at the café when he got back. The wind had picked up; Claire was wearing a sarong.

She gestured that it was time to go, thumb pointing back over her shoulder towards the car park, as in an old disco move.

They packed up their things and made for the hire car. Adam drove them out through the forest and across the farmland beyond. They passed war memorials, a sacked castle, a place where, so Claire's guide book informed them, heretics had once been burned at the stake. They were safaris of pain, these holidays in gory old Europe. So much cleaned-up blood and forgotten loss.

Adam still wondered about her. Not every day, nor even each week, but she would reappear at intervals, reliably incessant, and he was almost glad, sometimes, when she did. The memory of her had become a proof of who he was, a continuity between his forty-year-old incarnation and his younger self. Or, rather, she was a memory of a memory, since Adam understood that, after this much time, a person could only be an idea, as perhaps she always had been. He thought of her father, too, sometimes. *You do your best*, Eric had lamented, *you think you're doing right*, and Adam saw that he, at least, had tried to.

Of course he wished it hadn't happened. He wished he had blown the whistle that night (*My girl. You believe it?*), that there had been no reason to excoriate him in the morning. Not speaking up was the most reprehensible action, or inaction, of his life. All the same, the obsession had eased. The whole episode was regrettable, horrible even, but also ancient and, like those medieval atrocities, almost impersonal, another Adam as well as a bygone Rose. He couldn't have known then what he understood now, about daughters and about permanence.

The guilt he still felt had a new focus. In the end, Adam

reminded himself as he drove from the lake to the restaurant, *It wasn't me*. It wasn't him who had taken the girl into the tent that night. That fact was a partial mitigation, but also, now that he finally came to accept it, a kind of reproach.

It wasn't Adam. It wasn't Rose. It was Neil.

MORE than once, in the months immediately after their quarrel, Adam had considered contacting Neil, to let him know he had been right after all: his text had been prescient, no harm had been done, not to Adam and Claire at any rate. His email would be impersonal, caustic. If Neil replied, Adam would delete the message without reading it.

When, a year later, abstruse catastrophe beckoned – when everything the experts guaranteed would never happen, bankruptcies and bail-outs and nationalisations, happened the next day; when Adam's securocrat acquaintances were whispering about plans to impose martial law if the cash machines ran dry – he thought of Neil anew. Dodgily spliced investments, runaway derivatives, Farid's ramshackle property deals: Neil was implicated in everything that had caused the debacle. Neil and his money.

Adam called up the Rutland Partners website, hoping to find that the firm had gone to the wall, or at least was somersaulting towards the brickwork, a fate that would be adumbrated in some apologetic, lawyerly holding statement. Instead he read a screed of gobbledegook about how the fund had diversified its assets to minimise downside risk. He's got away with it, Adam thought. He's got away with it again. When his job at the consultancy faltered he blamed Neil for instigating the move. Neil had never understood the public-service ethos, never even tried. Perhaps he had known that Adam would come unstuck.

But he couldn't keep it up, and before long he found himself regretting his anathemas. He had been the man with the luck, Adam knew. Neil wasn't one of those congenital banking types whom he had met at university and sometimes ran into now, the type who wore those City-boy felt-collared overcoats, who had been destined for riches since their perfunctory conception in some stockbroker-belt bedroom. Adam had the drive, too, or so it had seemed in the beginning. Neil had been powered by a kind of indifference, which the world had rewarded as some men covet aloof women. He had done it all himself.

Later Adam would look again at the Rutland Partners website, but for clues to Neil's progress rather than evidence of his downfall; now and again he would Google him. For the most part he was able to prevent himself searching for anyone else. He fought off the impulse to contact Rose until it almost abated.

Adam still thought of Neil as dead. But after a couple of years he was no longer the shameful dead, an executed traitor or bubonic corpse, but dead in the manner of a rash, lamented duellist. That was one of the dead's advantages, Adam saw: you could choose which version of them to remember, as an obituarist was free to choose a photo from his subject's youth. Neil dragging him out of the ocean in San Diego. Neil with Harry's green shit on his coat.

As for the Claire thing, their nothing: his sense of scale had changed. His world was smaller, what was closest to him mattered most, and who, and so, in a way, they were quits. Rose was a contest and an idea, but Neil was his friend, had already been his friend that night in Yosemite. It made no difference that they had only known each other a few weeks. That wasn't how you measured obligation. Adam already

272

owed Neil that night, and he had defaulted. Joining him in the encirclement at the tent the next morning had been a bluff, Adam acknowledged to himself: he had asserted his innocence by exposing himself to judgement, self-interest and loyalty jumbled up.

If Neil were to be resurrected – if he were to get in touch – Adam might consider forgiving him. They would have to discuss it, he and Claire. But he would definitely consider it. That is, if Neil would consider it, too.

He wouldn't, Adam was certain. They had left it too long. The job was his memento of Neil, a debt that at first had rankled but was now more poignant than galling. He wasn't even sure whether Neil knew he had accepted it.

THEY stopped for an early dinner. Claire was still wearing her sunglasses, but he could tell that she was watching him, checking the temperature of his thoughts, while the children threw a ball for a stranger's dog in the square. Adam smiled to indicate that he was with her. Against her half-hearted objections he bought them preposterous baseball caps with 3-D wild boars, the emblems of the region, lolling on the visors.

On the way home the four of them sang a round, Ruby struggling with her cues but laughing at herself with the rest of them, Adam watching her, almost surreptitiously, in the rearview mirror. These were their headline memories, Adam realised, the memories his children would one day share with lovers and spouses, the moments that would come back to them, arbitrarily, as adults, in a meeting or on a train, their equivalents of his boyhood's fishpond and ice-cream catastrophes. The weight of that struck him afresh as he drove them back.

In bed he told Claire about the topless girl by the lake. She said, 'My hero,' and kissed him on the shoulder.

There was a pond behind the cottage, so pretty that, on the afternoon they arrived, Claire said the view belonged in a film, but overrun with lascivious frogs. That night Adam feared their croaking would keep him awake, but his wife put her arm around him and he fell asleep.

2011

WITH his back to the kitchen Dan couldn't tell that Neil was watching him as he made the coffee. He was sitting at the bamboo bar, standing up, sitting down again, standing, scratching, apparently unsure how formal his visit was, how comfortable or uncomfortable he felt, to what extent he enjoyed the status of a brother and how far he came as a stranger.

As Neil approached with the tray Dan raised one buttock from his bar stool and let out a rolling fart. He looked around, saw Neil, and grinned, pretending the salutation had been intentional.

'Old time's sake,' he said. Neil forced a smile.

Their accents had diverged with their lives. Both started from a clipped north London classlessness, but Neil's voice had migrated moneywards, assimilating the rounded, self-indulgent vowels of his ritzier acquaintances. He was half-ashamed of his vocal suggestibility. Dan seemed to have more or less given up on consonants (''ol 'imes 'ake').

Neil put the tray on the bar and sat down.

'What hospital is he in?'

'Hampshire . . . You know, North Hampshire.'

'Listen, ask the doctor where's best for his . . . for what he's got. Actually, tell me his name, could you? I'll ask him, if that's okay.'

'All right, Neil, but . . . '

'I'll pay for it. Forget it, Dan. Don't worry about it. What else did he say? The doc.'

'He said – what was it again? – he said there was "grounds for optimism", that's what he called it, but that, you know, we had to be realistic.'

'What the fuck does that mean?'

'I don't know, Neil. I don't.'

Dan peered into his coffee but didn't drink any. His skin seemed jaundiced; his eyes were Bassett-hound ringed; his teeth were so discoloured as to be indistinguishable from the gums, so that earlier, when Neil was letting him in, he had doubletaked to confirm that they were there. But Dan was still good-looking, Neil thought, in a dissolute, half-ruined way. Better looking than Neil. He used his left arm sparingly, most of the time letting it hang by his side. Building accident, he had said, winking, at once disguising and intending to advertise some more rakish explanation, though Neil couldn't imagine what it might be.

When Dan told him, Neil had been furious beyond words. Probably his rage was unjust; the trouble was, Dan was the only sublunary party available for his blame. Except for Neil himself: Sam's bruises and the breathlessness and his squirming.

'Did he say – did the doctor say – if you had – if we had . . . '

'He says in the – what do you call it? – the chronic – right – the chronic period, it's hard to spot. Always is, he says, the symptoms are so, like, normal. Specially when it's so slow. All right?'

Dan's face reddened and his eyes popped, as if he were holding his breath, or straining to take a dump. After a few seconds his colour and features settled again. He opened his mouth to say something else but closed it without speaking. When it came down to it, Dan was Sam's father, and he loved the boy after his fashion. He had his anger, too.

'All right. Is Stacy with him?'

'You know Stacy,' Dan said.

Neil tried to smile an assent, although in fact he didn't know Stacy, had never met her, not counting one occasion on which he had waved at a woman whom he presumed was Stacy through the window of a car that he likewise (perhaps naively) assumed was Dan's, the time they had come to pick up Sam in London the previous year. Neil had no interest in knowing Stacy. He let it go. 'I'll call the doctor,' he said.

Dan picked up his cooling coffee and put it down again with a noisy clack. Neil wanted him to leave now. He glanced at his watch, then regretted it.

'This euro thing,' Dan said. 'It hurting you?'

Neil wasn't sure where to begin and didn't much want to. But he saw that Dan was trying. He had a momentary, compassionate intuition of how hard this must be for him, all of it.

'Depends,' he said. 'Depends which way you bet. It's been bad for some people but okay for us. The money's got to go somewhere, you just have to make sure you get there first.'

'Yeah,' Dan said. 'Right.' He looked down at the bar. 'This

antique, then?' He rapped his knuckles on the Formica surface.

The front door opened. Roxanna wheeled the buggy in, closing the door fastidiously, hoping Leila might sleep for another half an hour. Neil could hear her being quiet – the effortful, tiptoeing footfalls and delicate clinks as keys and bags were shed.

She saw Dan first, straight away looking behind her at the closed door as if assessing her flight chances. Then she saw Neil.

'Just gone off,' she stage-whispered.

'This her?' Dan said. 'This must be her.'

He sank off the stool and headed for the buggy. Neil experienced a stab of limbic horror at the prospect of Dan touching his child, his rough hands on her flawless skin, the contamination. One of his arms twitched in Dan's direction but he reined it back.

'She's just gone—'

'Let him,' Neil said, in a tone so unfamiliar that Roxanna acquiesced and stared, mouth half-open.

Dan unbuckled the girl using his better arm, wincing slightly as he lifted her out of the buggy with both. She was asleep when he nestled her head in the crook of his elbow but opened her eyes when he stroked her cheek. She peered up at his unfamiliar, ragged face, but didn't cry.

'Da-da,' she said.

Neil grimaced.

'Beautiful girl,' Dan said. 'Beautiful.'

'I should change her,' Roxanna said.

Dan began a high-pitched, whiny hum, lullaby with a hint of love song. It failed to cohere into a tune and trailed off after a dozen notes. 'Beautiful like her mum,' he added.

He offered Roxanna a yellow smile, a tiny, self-parodic flashback to flirty, alpha, mighty Dan. Dan slurping water from the tap. Dan letting Tezza hide in the closet (or perhaps it was the other way around, Neil was no longer certain). Roxanna looked at the floor.

'More,' said Leila.

'This is Roxanna,' Neil said. 'Dan.'

Neil wanted to be generous. He knew what a niece or nephew could mean: the salvaging of someone from the mess, an outlet for affections that bottomless grudges had stifled, a chance for atonement. More than that, he owed Dan, he finally understood, because Dan had known about their mother from the beginning, back when they were teenagers themselves. He had lived with the secret for months, Neil's own, personal human shield, and for all Neil knew everything that had happened to Dan since began with that.

He let his brother handle his child, let him jiggle her and arch his body above her, holding her hands as she took a few precarious, drunkard's steps. They talked about the possibility of bringing Sam to a hospital in London. No, neither of them had been back to Harrow, a Romanian family had taken the house, Neil said.

'Dad,' said Dan, 'before he died ... You probably worked this out, I know you sorted the lawyer and that, the will. He tried to help me ... I was having a rough patch, you remember, and – the house – he ... '

'Forget it, Danny,' Neil said. 'It's fine, forget it. Really.'

Dan traced snail trails and mouse runs on the inside of Leila's arms while Roxanna unloaded her shopping. After a few more minutes, Neil said to his brother, 'Give her to me now, Dan. Now.'

*

SAM gave a thumbs up when Neil passed him the iPad, and another when he made a puerile remark about the departed nurse's arse. Neil regretted the joke immediately: better not to encourage that. Before she left the nurse had put an oxygen mask on Sam's face, and after that he couldn't say anything, at least not intelligibly. After a few minutes he closed his eyes. The iPad slid from his hand.

Neil had seen this gear before, on Brian, after his stroke. The ominous tubes, like extruded plastic intestines; the multiple drips; the monitors that made him feel like a cameo turn in the pre-credit sequence of a hospital drama, the heaving chords and contextual sirens of the theme set to cut in at any moment. The whole get-up looked wrong on Sam, outsized and fancy-dress.

He couldn't make out whether the boy was asleep. Probably he was in and out. Talk: he should talk. 'Hope you're comfortable, Sammy. Food okay? Guess you haven't eaten much. Roxanna sends her love. Leila would send hers too, but she can't speak yet, unfortunately. So.'

The gossip and niceties ran out pretty quickly. Then what? Depressing to talk about the illness, absurd to ignore it.

'Doctors seem nice, Sam. They say you're doing well.' Or so Dan reported: apart from making sure he scrubbed up on his way in, none of the hospital people said much to Neil at all, even though he was footing the bills, since he wasn't the primary relative.

'Does anything hurt?' He thought he saw Sam grimace. 'We can get more painkillers if it hurts. Shall I get her back?'

That nurse (Greek, Neil thought, possibly Spanish) ought to do something about the pain. Where the hell was she? Or the flinch might just have been wind, Neil supposed, like the neonatal creases of Leila's lips that he had optimistically interpreted as smiles. Or Sam might be wholly asleep and dreaming – fighting off muggers, tonguing Lara Croft, failing to revise for his exams, flying down the stairs, whatever the fuck it was that teenagers dreamed about these days. He might be listening to Neil and agreeing, or listening and disagreeing. Or his twitches might be gestures of protest against the cosmic injustice that had landed on him.

'I've seen your father. He seems okay.' He waited for a flinch but none materialised. 'Between us we'll see to everything, Sammy. And Stacy, of course. Whoever the hell Stacy is. Don't worry about your exams, I'll find someone to take them for you. I could get someone to take care of Stacy too, if you like.'

No flinch; no smile. Ridiculous, in a way, to ramble on when it was unlikely that Sam was listening. But these hospital-ward monologues were a bit like cooing over your child in public. You didn't feel embarrassed, you just had to do it. You had to talk, partly because it was the only thing you could do, and partly because of the strange, irrational apprehension that if you didn't keep talking, that might be the end.

What else? Reminiscences: '... that time you came to stay with me and Jess, you ate that knickerbocker glory, remember? You puked in a plant in the restaurant foyer, all over it ... That waitress ... The time we went out to that old airfield, you remember, I let you drive the car – how old were you? – and I had to grab the wheel back ...'

Reminiscences might be ill-advised, Neil saw, contrasting as they did the whackily eventful past and uncertain future. He trailed off.

Once, as a teenager, Neil had witnessed two men beating up a third outside a Tube station, their shoes thudding dully into his midriff and skull. He had run over, a reflex rather than premeditated valour, but the men had done enough and ambled away. To his surprise the victim sat up, coughed, spat and walked off. Up close, even routine violence was the worst thing in the world.

Sam's illness was like violence. It wasn't *like* violence, it was violence. The worst thing in the world.

The news, maybe: '... kicking off in Libya and everywhere else down there ... They've tweeted the *News of the World* to death ... Kicking off in Greece. Portugal next, they reckon, or the Micks, maybe ...'

Again the euro crisis: Sam wouldn't give a toss about the bloody euro crisis. Neil didn't give a toss about it, either, come to that.

Leila had been ten days old when Sam came to meet her. For a second, while Neil was changing the baby's nappy, he caught Sam's face in a mirror: open mouth, crestfallen eyes, which he righted when he saw that he was being watched. He had come to stay with them only a few times since.

Neil hadn't done what he wanted to do for Sam. He felt remiss, and, worse, he felt irrationally implicated. *Here you go*, the American girl had said when she gave him her address that morning, as if he had asked for it, which he hadn't, or might use it, which he never did. Perhaps it would have been better if they had called the police, and Neil had taken his chances in – he groped for the prison's name – San Somewhere.

Hocus-pocus. Ridiculous.

What was left? Song lyrics: the last refuge of the bedside desperado. *You were working as a waitress in a cocktail bar, When I first met you ... In the jungle, the quiet jungle, the lion sleeps tonight ... Well I'm runnin' down the road tryin' to loosen my load.*

Sam flinched.

A flinch as in, *It's okay, I know you're trying*? Or, on the contrary, a *Knock it off, will you, for fuck's sake?* sort of flinch? Because, when you stopped to think about it, what was Neil really saying in all his talk? *You are ill . . . You are very very ill . . . You are ill and I am scared.* Nobody wanted to listen to that. Probably his chatter made only one of them feel better.

He shut up. He noticed a little crescent of zits above the corner of Sam's mouth, an adolescent affliction that seemed touchingly banal in the circumstances. When he was Sam's age, Neil had salacious, anarchistic thoughts about what he would do in this situation. Fuck hookers, punch policemen, egg the Queen. It wasn't like that at all.

The tempo of beeps from the monitors picked up; he looked around for a white coat but no one rushed in. Just as he was about to leave, Sam opened his eyes again and seemed to blink an acknowledgement. Neil felt the unwonted tears coming and fought them back. He reconsidered, tried to force them out, and felt something glide down his cheek.

YOU didn't get to choose when calamity struck. At a minimum, Neil caught himself thinking during the taxi ride from Harley Street, you should get a say in that. All this would be easier if it had come at a different time: easier in the practicalities, at least, if not the emotions. If the disease had held off until Leila was older. If it had developed before his split with Adam. That was a disreputable, egocentric thought, Neil realised; he was ashamed of it.

Sometimes, when he remembered Adam, he would feel a pain in the region of his liver, a sharp ache like the cramp he sometimes got if he drank too much coffee.

He let Roxanna know he was on the way. Theirs was a queer kind of closeness, he thought as he texted. He had seen her with her legs in the stirrups, wailing in her own shit and blood. He had licked her clitoris and tasted her breast milk (sweeter than he anticipated, with a hint of caramel). They were into the mature phase now, the time when the childishness started, struggling for dominion, picking fights, gaming each other, banking favours and concessions as he and Jess once had. Yet for all the proximity he hadn't yet assimilated basic Roxanna facts – the temperature at which she liked her bath, her allergies, her preferred orders in restaurant chains and coffee shops.

They were obscenely intimate strangers. On rare occasions when Neil's birth family came up in conversation she would ask polite but desultory questions, as if they were discussing characters from history. *Who shot Franz Ferdinand? Who was Henry VIII's third wife? What colour was Neil's mother's hair?* To her, his family was dead and buried, and she, Leila and Neil comprised a pristine new reality. She was kind about Sam, but she didn't see how, for Neil, he was the lone survivor, whom he had plucked for himself from the wreckage. She didn't know Adam, knew nothing of what had happened with Adam, neither what happened between Neil and Adam and Claire nor between Neil and Adam and Rose. Once, rummaging in the miscellaneous drawer in the kitchen, she had stumbled on the photo of the two of them beneath the Faithful Couple. 'An old friend,' Neil had told her, and they had both left it at that.

He would love her properly in the end, Neil thought, as he ducked out of the taxi at the corner of his street. He was almost there. He stepped out distractedly to cross the road;

284

a blue, by-the-hour bicycle swerved to avoid him (between the bikes and the susurrating electric cars, aural intuition no longer sufficed for London pedestrians). When he reached his building he raised his hand to punch in the entry code, but paused. He stood alone on the pavement for a few minutes before he went upstairs.

Roxanna was watching a box set, all charismatic psychopaths and impenetrable accents. When he bent to kiss her she ruffled his hair, asked if he was all right and was there anything she could do? Leila was in her cot, asleep. He ought to be anxious for her by association, but the two universes felt too disconnected – the unjust Sam universe and Leila's prelapsarian version – for Sam to be a warning for Leila or Leila a consolation for Sam.

He went into the under-used room they affectedly called the study. Outside, on the pavement, he had decided to go through Claire: a risk, obviously, since he couldn't be sure that she would cooperate, nor how Adam would respond to her mediation. Still, Claire might know whether Adam was amenable; whether the timing was bad; whether Neil had been forgiven, or could be. He didn't have an email address for her but the internet soon furnished one, from the contact page of what was evidently her new company: Claire@windinyourhair.com.

Good for you, Neil thought, with a small admixture of regret. One of them had been an entrepreneur after all.

He logged onto his email. He tried to keep it short (*Don't waste the customer's time*), deciding not to mention his father, or Leila and Roxanna, but to explain only about Sam. He wrote in a hurry and pressed *Send* before he had a chance to reconsider. No xxx below the sign-off this time:

Claire

To be honest I can still hardly believe that I'm writing this. I mean, not that I am writing to you now but what happened in the first place. I know its probably too late but I wanted to say again to you and Adam that I am sorry. Please tell Adam this if you think that would be appropriate.

I've tried too many times to figure out that evening and all I can think of is that somehow you end up with grudges against the people you care about most. You end up not being able to tell them apart, your failures and the witnesses to them, your friends and why you need them. Anyway I take all the blame on myself. All of it. Please tell Ad that. Tell him it was always my fault and I should have seen that earlier.

Obviously I don't know how things are with you and the kids although I would love to. I dont even know where youre living. I can see that you're in business now and I hope that it is prospering. I am getting in touch because I wanted Adam to know about something thats happened. I am sure that he remembers Sam, my nephew, I expect that you remember him too. He and Harry played together once or twice. Seventeen now, amazing.

The thing is that Sammy is ill. I mean very ill. He might be okay but we don't know yet. Ive always felt responsible for him and now I feel that more than ever. I don't know why exactly but I needed to tell Adam about it. I think he will understand.

Its a funny thing, isn't it, that you start off wanting nothing from each other and that is almost the whole point, the freedom that we had, and then you do want things and youre happy to give them, time and all the rest. And then you find there are some things that its too much to give or sometimes to take.

Please tell him that he doesn't have to do anything or answer this message if he doesnt want to. But I would love it if he did. Tell him I know we can't put everything right but we can still do this. Tell him I'm pleased the American man was at home that day.

Sending love to you all
Neil

She didn't reply. Not that day, nor the next, nor the day after that. Two days was a decade in this instantaneous age. You got twitchy if clients didn't respond within an hour, knowing that they, like you, were bound to their lesser lives by the beeps and permanent-emergency throbs of their supposedly liberating gadgets. After two days, Neil began to abandon hope.

THE apparition was joltingly surreal: two human faces frowning at the glass, thirteen floors and a couple of hundred feet up. It always took Adam a moment to remember the man-bucket, the cords and the sponges. Then the dilemma over whether to acknowledge them – with some tough-guy nod, blokeish cock of the head or ingratiating smile – a sharp example of the moral discomfort routinely inflicted by London, a place in which you were always rubbing up against less fortunate neighbours, importunate strangers. If he nodded or smiled at the men through the window, he and they would lock eyes in the shared knowledge that he was sitting in an ergonomic chair on the cushy side of the glass, while, a metre away and on the other, they were dangling from the roof. If he didn't, he would imply that they had no human claim on his attention.

The trying etiquette of inequality. The whole routine,

Adam knew, must be wearyingly familiar to the less equal. He went for a pursed smile and raised-eyebrow combination. One of the window-cleaners, the older of the two, gaunt and wearing a hoodie although it was a warm, clear morning, whispered something to the other; Adam thought he saw the younger man smirk as they heaved themselves out of view.

He shook his head at his own involutions. This would never be his city.

Laurel materialised beside his desk. 'Leisure Services?'

'Yup. Twenty minutes,' Adam said. 'Just need to spell-check it.'

'I need to syndicate,' Laurel said. 'Adam, I really do.'

Laurel's mis-shaven cheeks were marbled in a scraped yellow and pastel red. He was strangely gauche for a person of his seniority, Adam had noticed, for someone with a solid career at one of the 'Big Four' accountancy firms behind him. It was as if all the resources bestowed on him by evolution had gone into the substance of his work, the time-and-motion equations, leaving nothing over for social or cosmetic fripperies. In the past couple of years Laurel had grown slightly stooped, as if his height had become embarrassing to him; Adam found him intangibly camp – something in the stretch of his vowels and tight cross of his arms – though Laurel didn't seem to be aware of the effect. He had a wife, two or three kids, but in three and a half years Adam had never heard him speak of them.

'Twenty minutes max.'

'Clients this afternoon.'

'Twenty minutes.'

'Okay. See you at the meeting?' – a statement intoned as a question. Laurel smiled and loped away. He had the power, Adam had concluded, most of it, anyway, which was why he didn't mind when Hardy interrupted him. He had the long-haul confidence to be eclipsed.

Neither Alan/Hardy nor Craig/Laurel was his friend. The pair of them were yoked and segregated by an invisible barrier that everyone else could see, those two on the inside, the rest of the staff peripheral. They weren't his friends, but Adam trusted them. He trusted them when they implied that he was safe.

Since the new government came in, slashing and burning, public-sector consultants had been reviled. Not so much as bankers or journalists or the politicians themselves, but up there, in the league table of infamy, with estate agents or squeegee merchants. They were indolent and dispensable, a luxury of the incontinent boom. They were parasites. They were fucked.

The work had slowed, and Adam had worried again. They all worried. They were right to worry. He received a string of emails inviting him to leaving drinks for people he hadn't previously known existed. Sometimes the fall guy would follow up with his or her own valediction, rashly Replying All – some tragic, adrenalin-driven gush about how he would miss everyone and hoped they stayed in touch, or the snarky observation that she had enjoyed the job, *most of the time.* The various, equally pointless bearings of the tumbrel.

Yet Hardy had winkingly implied, one afternoon when they had shared a lift, that he was safe. He asked after Adam's family and Adam made a nervy crack about how expensive they were. Hardy mumbled something about a permanent contract just as the doors opened and they were released. Afterwards, when he was recounting the conversation to Claire, and he tried to conjure the precise phrases, the actual formulation, which had created the impression of security,

Adam couldn't grasp them. But he had been pretty sure that he was safe. He had his harness; he was strapped in.

He tried and failed to log on to the shared Leisure Services file. He felt the bile rising, in a way that only tailgaters and malfunctioning computers could induce. *Password incorrect*: he had distractedly input the one he used for his credit card and Amazon accounts. Bank accounts, shopping accounts, email accounts, newspaper subscriptions, multiple computers – Adam sometimes felt he had become the sum of his passwords, that his lazily disguised pet names, phone numbers and 'meaningful dates', the odd extra digit or letter affixed as required, were his new DNA, the double helix of the touch-screen age. If they got scrambled, you were lost.

Finally his fingers remembered the necessary sequence: *ruby*, followed by the six digits of her birthday (no space). He called up the document, ran the promised spell-check, passed an eye over the formatting. He emboldened the subheadings and introduced some bullet points in the executive summary ('... *service optimisation* ... *customer footfall* ... *DCMS strategy* ...'). He added his name to the unobtrusive middle of the list of authors.

He saved and closed the document and emailed it to Laurel, cc-ing Hardy. Outside his window the cords attached to the bucket were twitching, as if, somewhere below, condemned men were hanging and choking at the end of them.

HE HAD sworn off MySpace. He had vowed never to look her up again, had weakened once or twice and finally, the previous winter, when he was setting up a new computer, found that he had forgotten his log-in details. He had guessed and guessed, but on that occasion he couldn't remember them, which, for once, was more a riddance than a loss. The need to re-register had been enough to dissuade him, one of those tiny online impositions that had become demoralising obstacles, in this case turning the pursuit of Rose from casual hobby to blatant obsession. He had resisted Facebook and almost forsaken Googling, though he permitted himself Chaz and Archie. Also, every few months, Neil.

These days Adam could tolerate mentions of California, California was always everywhere, but Colorado still made him shiver. Once he switched off the television when a report about the poor little girl in Boulder came on; Claire had glanced across at him, but let it be. At the end of term, on prize day, as he watched Ruby climbing the stairs and crossing the stage, he thought of her striding across the campsite, alone in front of everybody.

Almost certainly, she was fine, Adam reminded himself at his desk, preparing himself for that evening. She might have her own children by now (he imagined Eric cradling them in his thick, hairy arms). Perhaps her life had been better than was her destiny before Yosemite, she being more studious or warier, less headlong in her rebellions, than she would otherwise have been. In which case, no harm had been done by either of them.

Adam would never know and nor, come to that, would Rose. He felt, that afternoon, as clear of her as he would ever be.

She might not be fine, of course.

In the conference room he took a chair set back from the table, against the wall. He rarely said anything in these meetings. He didn't think that he was supposed to say anything; he suspected he was only invited out of courtesy. He slotted his chin between his thumb and his forefinger, stroking his stubble, a pose he valued for its contemplative appearance, but more for the micro-pleasure of the stubble's rough, synthetic feel, its diurnal reliability.

Laurel came in with a photocopier-hot set of Leisure Services reports. He fanned and distributed the copies as Hardy arranged his jacket on the back of the chair at the head of the table. Laurel sat at his partner's right hand. He crossed his arms and smiled.

'Okay,' Hardy said. 'Let me walk you all through the deck.'

HE WAS safe but stuck. After the early prisons contract Adam had struggled to bring in further work, and when, after the election, the commissions became scarce, it made no sense to send him out to a hospital or council when other, more proficient associates were available. The bill of his billable days was shrivelling. To the colleagues who had begun to invite him for after-work drinks, or for lunchtime sandwiches by the river, thinking that he might be a permanent someone, he was again an uninvitable no one. He was leprous, precarious. He was dangling from a rooftop by a thread.

He was rescued. Hardy had noticed, and Laurel agreed, or said he agreed, that Adam had a valuable, marketable skill, namely his familiarity with the English language. They called him back to Hardy's office (he had installed a tub of moisturiser on the desk) and told him that, henceforth, his job would be to edit the product: to beautify the unreadable reports that outlined their scorched-earth or asset-stripping advice to clients, or at least to remove the most painful of the excrescences that crowded his colleagues' mogul-run prose. 'The Civil Service gift for story-telling,' Laurel called it, and smiled.

Adam became a ghostwriter. He was the consultants' wing man; he was the other guy.

At the beginning, at the television company, he had wanted and expected to be a star, a virtuoso, to awe his peers and astound his bosses. When he first joined the Civil Service, and he and the other fast-streamers gathered in their Whitehall pubs to gauge each other's progress, they would debate how much good they were doing in the world, in their hearts never countenancing their rhetorical doubts. Now, like some meek but well-coached hostage, Adam wanted only to be the grey man, inoffensive and set fair to be overlooked when the violence began.

After Leisure Services he went back to his desk. For want of a better way to seem occupied he scrolled through his spam filter. Did he want to chat with a Russian woman? Did he want to satisfy his wife tonight? Did he want to buy a replica Rolex?

A stray message from Harriet (he promoted her to *Approved Sender*). The subject was *Stefan walking!!!!* There was a video attachment: Stefan wasn't walking, he was hauling himself along the side of a coffee table. The video lurched and ended when the child banged his head on the table's edge. Harriet was happier in Munich. She had been happier since the truth about their father came out, once the shock wore off, at least: it took away his entitlement to judge. She had visited with Stefan a few months before, and over dinner she and Adam had sung their number from *Lady and the Tramp*. Harry and Ruby sat and watched, agape at this glimpse of their daddy's childhood.

He frowned at the screen in ersatz contemplation as Laurel passed his desk again. This time he wasn't looking at Adam, or didn't seem to be. Laurel crossed the floor to Hardy's office, opened the door without knocking and closed it quietly behind him.

The contracts had started to trickle in again. The government had discovered that you needed to spend money to save money: somebody had to work out whom to sack and whom to keep. 'Creative destruction,' Hardy called it. 'Friction costs,' according to Laurel. They still needed to say – more than ever, they had to be able to say – *It wasn't me*. Only trouble was, they were being screwed on price. In the end they would get what they paid for, Hardy was muttering.

They had rolled over Adam's contract for one more year. Between his salary and what Claire and Poppy had begun to pay themselves, they were okay. He eschewed his old ambitions and his universal rivalry, left them behind him like a naive summer romance. They could have dropped their struggle by now, he and Neil – though, on the other hand, the struggle had started at the very beginning, in California, in the hostel yard. So perhaps the struggle was the point.

He was strapped in. He was safe.

The bucket sailed past him, going down again, fast. The men had turned away, looking out towards the sky. This time Adam couldn't see their faces, but their hands, he noticed, were almost touching on the outer rail.

WIND chimes. Frosted glass in the beginning, delicately jagged rose-coloured shards and cobalt icicles, and later bamboo pipes and miniature Japanese bells. Claire and Poppy pinged their design sketches between High Wycombe and Colchester.

Manners and goodwill had kept them in touch since they overlapped in the gallery. They weren't close enough to count as friends, not really, but nor were they indifferent or ruthless enough to drop each other entirely: an email or two a year, later a couple of chaotic outings with their kids to London museums. As a student Poppy had designed jewellery; as the children careened around the Turbine Hall, Claire suggested that she scale up to ornaments. The wind chimes were manufactured in a workshop in Dorset and sold through garden centres, craft and furniture shops and the rudimentary website made for them by Poppy's husband (he was more than the single trait Adam had ascribed to him in their lazily competitive twenties).

You never knew, Claire and Adam said to each other. You never knew what might come of your past, who might shimmy out of it to catch up with you. They were hopeful of cracking the accessories list of one of the department stores. They were thinking about wind spinners and babies' mobiles.

BY LATE afternoon Adam couldn't concentrate. He left his computer on, a half-drunk cup of tea on his desk, his jacket draped tactically on the back of his chair. He ducked through the emergency exit and skipped down a flight of stairs, lest the bosses spot him waiting for the lift. The elevator doors opened several times on his way to the lobby, admitting other heliotropic skivers and early-doors drinkers. Adam enjoyed these fractional, five-second glimpses of alien floors, strange companies, unknown lives, currency traders and oil traders and the vendors of medical insurance. He had visions of the doors retracting one day to reveal an illicit poker game, or an elephant rearing on its hind legs, or a masked orgy.

Adam was early – much too early, no way he would be going home this early – but it was as if, having decided, he had to get on with it. Bizarre, having decided, to do anything further that afternoon. Adam wanted to ambush himself, too, to minimise his opportunities to change his mind.

He would have to cross the river to Embankment for the District Line. He strode along the passageway at the side of the Royal Festival Hall and up the steps to the pedestrian walkway. The wheel rose behind the railway bridge – toweringly close, but the base occluded – looking, from Adam's angle, as if it might spin free and crush him. A newsstand sold papers in a dozen languages. The tarpaulins of the restaurants stretched along the riverfront; the overpriced tourist boats glided on the grey water. A tide of money had washed across London since Adam worked at the television company a short hop along the Thames. The tide was going out but the city was still soaking in it.

Just below the bridge, on the small riparian beach (plastic plates and broken bricks and washed-up electrical wires among the pebbles), someone was shouting. He looked down to see a child, a girl – four or five, he estimated – standing alone at the water's edge. The shout came again, and a man ran from the bottom of the steps that led to the beach and snatched the girl up, reprimanding her lovingly.

Adam took out his BlackBerry and dialled as he made his way onto the bridge. Two rings and she picked up.

'No,' Claire said. 'Not on the mantelpiece ... Yes. Adam.'

'Just, hi, to say I won't be home for dinner.'

'Absolutely not ... What? It's our takeaway night. I thought we'd have Japanese.'

'Sorry, darling,' he said. 'Can't help it, you know.'

'That's it – both of you. I said, that's it ... Sorry. Adam.'

He had always been faintly afraid of this bridge, ever since he saw a news item about two posses of muggers who, late at night, had trapped their hopeless victim in the middle. But this evening it was beautiful, festive, the discreet power of the ministries on one side of the river, the carousel and prom-enaders on the other.

'Anything new today? Orders, I mean.'

'Three from the Cotswolds,' Claire said. 'Two from Brighton. One from Dartmoor. Oh and that man from Habitat called again.'

'That's great, Clezzy.'

'It's just an enquiry.'

'That's wonderful.'

'Harry wants you.'

Her palm over the receiver, then Harry's, muffling it differently, then his son's quick breath.

'How many did you score today?'

'Only two, but one was a header.'

'That's great, Harry. Wonderful.'

'A header!'

'Wonderful, Harry. What did Miss Franks say about—'

'Bye, Daddy.'

'Your mother called,' Claire said. 'She wants to come round with Godfrey. Sunday, she said.'

His mother was okay, too.

'Sorry,' Adam said.

'It's all right. I'll do fish pie.'

A beggar was squatting halfway across the bridge, disturbing the pedestrian flow. He was wrapped up much too warmly for the temperature in his coat and his blanket and his sleeping bag and, probably, everything else that he owned. Adam turned back towards the beach. The girl and the man were gone.

'She there?' he asked. 'Put her on.'

'Just a sec ... Ruu-beee ...'

The rustle of ear on phone.

'Go on then, lollipop.'

'The sloth bear is the only bear that carries its young on its back.'

'I like that one. That's a great one. Any others today?'

'When are you coming home?'

'Who's my favourite girl?'

'I know, Daddy.'

'Love you.'

'I know.'

'Is it Laurel?' Claire said.

'What?'

'Me too,' Ruby said in the background.

'Is it Leisure Services, then? Why you're late today.'

When Claire told him, Adam had got her to show him the email immediately. He had felt a constriction in his throat, and tears that would have needed only a little encouragement. He hadn't forewarned her that it would be tonight: he didn't want to jinx it.

'Office karaoke,' Adam said. 'Three-line whip, unfortunately. Thought I told you. Sorry, Clezz.'

Adam smiled at his lie. Fleetingly he had a vision of himself as one of those Japanese men you sometimes heard about, who get dressed in the morning, go out as if to work, and sit on a park bench all day, their calls forwarded to fake clearing-house secretaries.

'Don't overdo it,' she said. He heard their doorbell ring. 'Shopping's here.'

'Love you,' Adam said.

'No, you *won't* answer it . . .'

He descended into the claustrophobic, white-tiled maze of the station. On the platform he picked up an evening paper from a cubby-hole shop, like a child's model of a shop, and scanned the front page without taking in the words. Electric adverts in the underpasses, electric music in people's ears: boredom had become a dread threat that had perpetually to be resisted, as if all of life were an American basketball game, all its gaps and pauses filled with diversions and analgesics. Adam got off the train and emerged into the bonus evening sunshine.

PEOPLE who wanted him to help save the tiger. People who wanted him to save Darfur. A person urging him to take out a gym membership on a soon-to-expire special offer. A bearded man wearing boots without laces who wanted twenty pence for a cup of tea; a better-dressed, more ambitious woman who wanted a quid for her bus fare (*Inflation!*, Neil thought). People in suits and miniskirts and veils, lots of them talking on mobile phones, in English and Arabic and Russian and other languages that Neil couldn't identify, meandering and gesticulating and obliviously halting to the rhythm of their conversations. Shops that invited you to call home, fly home, change money from home and send it there, eat like you do at home, read newspapers from home, tan or cover up as you do at home. Walking down a London street had become a financial and moral obstacle course. You could feel virtuous, callous, conned and xenophobic in the space of a hundred metres.

Neil had left his taxi and its catastrophist driver (*Trafalgar Square: nightmare! The Olympics: meganightmare! West Ham United: what a nightmare!*) on Bayswater Road and walked up Queensway. He and the doorman outside the hotel nodded at each other, a consoling evening ritual that had somehow evolved between them, though they had never actually spoken. It was a hot, blue evening, the kind that, every now and then, lets London feel Mediterranean, or Californian. Neil took off his jacket and swung it over his shoulder. He cut off the main road and turned into his street.

He saw the legs first, emerging from the doorway onto the pavement: the ankle-booted feet and besuited calves; the inflection at the knees, a pair of hands resting on them; the downslope of the thighs, descending to an unseen waist in the recess. One of the legs jiggled nervily at the ankle. Shit: he was supposed to pick up some milk and ... something else.

He took out his phone to reread Roxanna's message. Milk and wet wipes. He would be coming out again later to meet Dan at the hospital. He would do the shopping then.

When he looked up from the screen, the torso in the doorway had leaned forward into view. Also, in profile, the head: dirty blond hair, the handsome face bisected by the tortoiseshell arm of the sunglasses, the visage familiar but receding into obscurity again as the body rotated back.

Neil froze. He crossed to the other side of the street for a squarer view. Another five paces and he would be sure.

He thought he might be hallucinating; that the figure in the doorway might be an urban mirage. He screwed his eyes closed, and when he opened them again the view was blocked by a stationary van. Instead of what he thought and hoped might be Adam (and, mixed in with the hope, feared, because of the momentousness and the delicacy), he found himself staring at a man with a crew cut and a cigarette behind his ear, who was incongruously mouthing the words to a love song on the radio. *I hate that I let you down ... I guess karma comes back around.*

Neil stood still until the van moved. The driver glanced at

him as he pulled away, and Neil half-expected a finger or an insult, but the man only smiled.

It was him.

The thought occurred to Neil that he could run off. Adam hadn't seen him; he was wearing his sunglasses but seemed to be looking down at his shoes. Neil chased the thought away. This apparition was what he had hoped for the previous week, though not with much faith, when he sent Claire his long-shot email.

Neil smiled – a freakish, Blairish sort of grin, it must have been – but Adam still hadn't looked up. Should he thank him? Make a joke, tell one of their lies, ask after Claire? Maybe he shouldn't mention Claire. She had evidently passed on his message, but he didn't know how things stood between them. Their kids: Adam might have another one by now, for all Neil knew. *He* had a child – he, Neil, was a father, a fact of which, astoundingly, Adam was still ignorant. He worried whether he should repeat his apology, or, on the contrary, should never mention that day and the sofa again.

They had been apart for four years. It was eighteen years since Yosemite. After she gave him her scrap of paper that morning Neil had said 'Thanks', as if she were a sales assistant handing him his change. That was all.

He had to pause in the middle of the road, perched on a white dividing dash like a shipwrecked sailor on flotsam, while high-spec four-by-fours eddied behind and in front of him. It was while he was crossing the second lane, when he was no more than ten metres from the doorway, that Adam looked up and saw him.

ADAM had stood for the first half-hour. Standing was better for his back, and it had seemed to him more fitting to be

301

upright when or if Neil arrived. To be eye to eye (or nearly). When he came to look for it he had found the building easily. There was a row of them, richly anonymous Edwardian mansion blocks, red-brick with white detailing, bay-windowed, blinds drawn, all of them called Something Court. But only this one had black-and-white chequered tiling in the entrance, and filigreed ironwork around the ground-floor windows, both of which Adam recognised. For a few minutes he patrolled the pavement outside, in a little circuit that took him twenty metres past the door in both directions. Then he worried there was a chance, a small chance, that Neil's entry or exit might coincide with one of his turns, like a POW blindsiding a guard in an old war film. He squatted on the marble step, trying to smile harmlessly at residents who left or arrived, exactly as he had imagined he might do on that night four years before, now with the opposite purpose.

Harry had nudged him into it that morning. The children overheard them discussing Neil's email over breakfast; Harry remembered him, and asked, and they explained what had happened in drastically periphrastic terms. An argument; adults had them too; very sad.

Harry had shrugged and said, 'I get it, you defriended him.' Adam had realised that he hadn't, and wouldn't, even if he never saw Neil again, despite what they had done to each other and together. That wasn't how he was wired.

He knew he had to come in person. No more desiccated electronic messages, nor the eerie semi-presence of the phone, both of which conveyed only words and left out half of what mattered. No more screens or handsets or intermediaries. He would open with Sam. Anything else would be bad manners. Everything else would wait.

Adam doubted the location first. He was confident that he had the correct building, but realised, belatedly, that he had no idea whether Neil still lived there. By now he might have moved to Kensington, or Primrose Hill, or New York, or Zug. Or he might be visiting one of his plutocratic clients on a yacht or at their schloss. Or he might indeed be living here, and in London this evening, but be preoccupied with some trans-time zone arbitrage gambit or wining-and-dining marathon. Adam might end up waiting there all night.

He wouldn't wait all night. He would give it till seven-thirty, seven forty-five at the outside, then head for Marylebone Station and home. Neil had another hour, Adam decided. An hour or that was it.

Only after the practical questions did his mind reach the emotional risks and pitfalls. He walked himself through it. Assume he was in the right place; Neil came; they spoke, perhaps embraced; Neil invited him in; they were both sorry and glad. But equally it could go a frostier way, all unprocessed bitterness and hoarded recrimination, or, worse (a possibility Adam nauseously considered only too late), it might be sullen, awkward, nothing to say and silently obvious that there could be no going back, therefore no way they could go on, and at the end they would trade a few terminal niceties, like schoolmates who bump into each other in the street and are obliged to pretend that they were once close. They would say goodbye and never see each other again, which might afterwards be more painful, less meaningful and memorable, than if he hadn't come at all.

Adam remembered a family pet, an old half-blind spaniel named Ajax, whom his mother had resolved to put down but kept alive, for a few extra days, until Adam came home from boarding school at Easter. He was fourteen or fifteen, keen to affect a macho indifference but not feeling it. Ajax had been Adam's dog, mainly, before he went away, and on the ride from the station he envisaged a heartrending, slobbery farewell. But when he came into the house and went to the basket, called the dog's name and patted him, inhaling the faecal aroma of canine decay, Ajax hadn't known him.

That could happen. That could easily happen.

Adam looked out into the parade of legs that were scissoring past him. Trousered legs, naked legs, bow, obese and arthritic legs. It was a child's perspective, the world below the waist, and he felt like a child, out of his depth and alone, boredom and excitement alternating as at a zoo or a funfair. Two or three times he thought the legs were Neil's – long and lean, the shape of the knee cap and fibula visible in the stride – and he looked up, and they weren't. Strangers.

With half an hour to go, primitive superstition advised him to stop looking, to focus on the floor instead, or else, like Father Christmas, Neil would never come. He remembered the sunglasses in his pocket and put them on, for luck.

His ankle continued to jiggle but his mind strayed. The spelling primers he was meant to order; the broadband prices he had undertaken to compare; the appointments with the dentist he was supposed to book: the multiplying duties of online fatherhood. A pair of brogues and plausible legs intruded into the upper periphery of his vision, standing in the road in front of him. He raised his eyes, more wearily than in hope, and it was Neil.

ADAM didn't manage to get up in time. The traffic parted and Neil was eight, then five metres away. By the time he remembered what he had intended to say, Neil was hovering in front of him, his crotch at Adam's eye level. He opened his mouth to deliver his lines – *I'm so sorry about Sam, Neil, we're both so sorry* – but closed it again before anything came out.

Neil looked down at the top of Adam's head: the swirl of his hair was still thick, still lush, now with a weft of grey amid the gold. He took in the companionable body on which, alarmingly yet consolingly, he could read his own ageing. The familiar, irrelevant shell of his friend. The notion entered his head that if he lifted a knee sharply, he would break Adam's nose. He shooed the renegade thought away.

He was about to speak – *Thank you, Adam. I'm sorry, I'm really sorry* – when the door of his building opened and an old woman edged through it. Neil recognised her: fourth floor, Russian. 'Evening,' he said, so nervous of swallowing his voice that it sounded too loud, almost deranged. The *babushka* pushed between them and left them alone.

Neil sat on the step. His eyes met Adam's sunglasses as he manoeuvred himself into position, but once he was down they both looked outwards at the street again, as if the two of them were waiting for someone else to join them.

They both knew it had to be Adam.

'Hello, Neil,' he said.

'Evening, Ants. I'm sorry.'

'So am I.'

Neil slowly raised his right arm and levered it around Adam, as you might tentatively put an arm around a teenage girlfriend, until his hand rested on his friend's shoulder.

Adam took off his sunglasses.

To buy any of our books and to find out
more about Abacus and Little, Brown, our authors
and titles, as well as events and book clubs,
visit our website

www.littlebrown.co.uk

and follow us on Twitter

@AbacusBooks
@LittleBrownUK

To order any Abacus titles p & p free in the UK,
please contact our mail order supplier on:

+ 44 (0)1832 737525

Customers not based in the UK should contact
the same number for appropriate postage
and packing costs.